BUMP AND RUN

RUN

a Wade Durham novel

by

Richard Helms

BLACK ARCH BOOKS

BLACK ARCH BOOKS
an imprint of
Barbadoes Hall Communications
ISBN: 979-8-9900412-2-6

For Elaine

The Muse I sleep with...

ACT ONE

CHOCTAW '77

ONE

Lester Corby had enjoyed better days, but not many.

For once, impatience didn't get the better of him, and his bacon didn't scorch in the pan and his eggs were as light and fluffy as an empty promise. When he stepped outside his door, he found a crisp new ten-dollar bill plastered to his stoop by the breeze. He pocketed the money and whistled a happy tune as he walked a half mile to the school where he maintained the boiler and tended to any other mechanical malfunctions as they arose.

Nothing broke all day, miraculously, leaving Lester the opportunity to check off every item on his daily maintenance roster for the first time in weeks. Finished by two o'clock, he spent the rest of the school day changing the bags in the outside trash cans, because it afforded him the opportunity to watch the kids playing during recess at the elementary school across the street. He liked their joy and enthusiasm, and sometimes he envied their naiveté. They still had the luxury of idealism and the delusion of security. Life hadn't kicked the turds out of them yet. Sometimes, if he worked at it, he could recall the feeling.

If Sarah hadn't sunk roots a mile into the Choctaw bedrock, Lester might have left years ago.

No point, now.

He'd had enough of the world. His bachelor years as a fiery young itinerant tent preacher, traveling the blue highways with his Green Book at his side, had sucked the wanderlust right out of him.

He still believed, but his faith was a private thing now, something his younger self would never recognize. After nearly seven full decades watching humans commit the most indecent atrocities against their fellows for no discernible reason other than blatant greed or hatred, and perceiving no evidence of divine intervention at all, his deity had shrunk enough to convince Lester the men of his acquaintance truly were wrought in God's image, warts and all. The revelation made God much less awesome, but infinitely more approachable.

Lester now regarded his deity as an occasional comforting sidekick, like Jiminy Cricket, rather than the hoary, thundering, vengeful Old Testament fire-breather he'd summoned in his youth under a sagging canvas tent to roil the sweating masses into a froth that would inspire them to flap their funeral home fans like hummingbird wings and dig extra deep into their pocketbooks when the hat was passed.

When his past haunted him in the blue-black hours of the night, Lester frequently imagined his memories were salvaged from another man's life.

Sarah was gone. Nothing he could do about it. He was too old to find anyone similar enough to her that he wouldn't spend every waking hour comparing them, so he lived alone. A year after she passed, he found himself adrift, sitting on his porch, anticipating day after day of tedium and loneliness, waiting impatiently for the white wings of death to flutter behind him as well.

A week later, he applied for an open maintenance position at the school. He didn't need the money. He needed the life.

The kids went home at three, but his day ended at six. He locked the maintenance room door behind him and noted a single car in the parking lot. Principal Masters was working late, as usual. She had a couple of young teens at home. Lester wondered who was taking care of them.

In mid-September, in most of North Carolina, the sun was still bright at six-fifteen in the evening, but the foothills and mountains surrounding the tiny Choctaw Valley had cast deep shadows across the entire town, and—as it frequently did—a strange temperature inversion generated thick clouds of mist that rolled over the slopes and blanketed the valley in a dense, damp fog. At the peak of Choctaw Knob, north of town, it was probably still a bright, crisp early evening. In the valley, twilight and shadows and fog had already triggered streetlamps to light automatically along the main town streets.

Lester Corby even found the fog delightful. It had been that sort of day.

He stopped at the Choctaw Grille for a beer and a bite. The bartender, Cullen Frasier, had a Bud draft on the mahogany bar top before Lester settled onto his stool. On the black and white television mounted above the bar, a man in an expensive suit he didn't own and hair that also wasn't his stood in front of a weather map. He drew lines and circles and letters all over the board with a dry erase marker, and earnestly explained in tedious detail why it might or might not rain the next day.

"How's your day?" Frasier asked.

"Remarkable," Lester said. He heard the rasp and husky wetness that had insidiously crept into his voice over the last years. He sounded weak and old. It was the thing he hated most about surviving for so long. "Thank you for asking. I have had an unexpectedly pleasant day. You ever have one of those? A day when, for no particular reason, everything goes your way?"

"Ever' day since my wife run off," Frasier said. "They'd be even better if she hadn't taken the dog."

Lester gave him a high-five, and smiled as he sipped his beer.

Lester said, "Once in a while, for no apparent reason, the good lord blesses you with a day like today to remind you he's thinkin' about you."

"Church is on the next street over. Here we pray to St. Pauli Girl," Frasier said. "But I don't begrudge you your excellent day. I figure if anyone deserves one, you do."

The TV news switched to sports, leading with film from the previous evening's Atlanta Braves game.

"Think we'll ever get a major league pro team here in North Carolina?" Frasier asked without taking his eyes off the screen. "Baseball, football, basketball? Anything? Something I can bet on?"

"Beats me," Lester said. "I been in Carolina since I was a pup, and far as I can tell, if it ain't wrasslin' or stock car racin', nobody around here is interested. Went to a Double-A game in Charlotte last year when I was visiting my daughter. Saturday night and the stands were a quarter full. Biggest city in the state. How are they gonna support a major league franchise?"

"But they do love the wrasslin' and racin'." Frasier saw Lester's glass was drained to the backwash. "Lemme top off your excellent

4

day with another on the house while Sammy's burnin' your burger back there. What do you say?"

"I thank you kindly, but only one more," Lester said. "It's a school night."

———

School night or not, Lester allowed himself to be talked into three more. No matter, he reasoned. He wasn't driving, his house was only seven blocks away, and nobody was waiting for him except his cat. If necessary, he could crawl home.

He drained the last glass shortly after nine, and thanked Frasier for the company. He stepped out into the thick fog and shivered, even though the temperature was still in the high sixties. Most of the shops on the Choctaw main drag were shuttered for the night. Every ten or fifteen seconds, a car would roll along Main Street, twin cones of headlights penetrating the fog, and it would disappear into the murk. The gas station was still open, the sign outside proclaiming new lower prices in fluorescent letters blossoming in the mist.

Lester had never imagined he'd see gas for a dollar a gallon before the greedy guys in the sandy countries pitched a hissy a couple of years earlier. After the panic, prices were back under a dollar, but still double what they had been before the embargo. Lester didn't drive much anymore. Gas prices were more a hypothetical inconvenience for him.

Since his retirement and Sarah's passing, he'd discovered most of the world's problems flew way over his head. He'd been passionate about politics and economics and especially civil rights in his youth. Somewhere along the way, the world outside Choctaw had muted itself, or perhaps he had selectively cut it off. His life had become insular, and his circle of friends had shrunk over the years. It made life simpler.

A song from the 1940s he had danced to many times with Sarah manifested inside his head, and he hummed along as he shambled over the sidewalk and turned off the main drag onto the street where he lived.

Ahead, circulating blue lights cut through the fog. Lester was curious, but not particularly worried, to see a Ford police cruiser sitting in his driveway. Two officers, one young and one older, both white, leaned against the car, their arms folded. The younger one slapped at the sleeve of the older cop and pointed as Lester rounded the corner. They pushed off the cruiser and held their arms at their sides. Their right hands rested on their holsters, which would have concerned Lester two or three pints earlier in the evening.

Twenty years earlier, when he was younger and more civically engaged, Lester would have known their names. Most people in Choctaw knew most other people in Choctaw. People came and went, though, and Lester—who spent most of his time either at work or at home or at the Choctaw Grille—recognized fewer of them each year.

The older cop stepped forward to meet Lester. The younger one held back, close to the cruiser. Lester was confused, but still not worried. He hadn't broken any laws.

"Officer?" he said as the cop approached. He read the name on the man's tunic. *Sanderson.*

"Sir," Sanderson said. "Can you tell me your name?"

"Lester Corby."

"Mr. Corby, we'd like you to come with us."

"Where?" Lester said.

"Sir, have you been drinking?" Sanderson asked.

"I was at the Grille. I had a burger and a few beers. Was walking home to go to bed. What's going on?"

"What time did you arrive at the Grille, Mr. Corby?"

Even through an ethanol fog, Lester recognized Sanderson's tone. He'd been rousted all across the Jim Crow south in his youth, and he knew the situation had turned serious. Lester took a closer look at the officer. He rubbed his eyes and shook his head to clear it.

"Something's happened," he said. "Is it one of my kids?"

"Please answer my question," Sanderson said. "What time did you arrive at the Grille?"

Lester tried to remember. He'd left the school later than usual, because the gym towels took longer to dry. It was a ten-minute walk to the Grille.

"Maybe…six-thirty. Perhaps slightly later. The news was still on the TV. Cullen Frasier and I talked about the weather and the sports while we watched. Why?"

Sanderson glanced back at the younger cop, who reflexively opened the rear door of the cruiser, and grasped Lester's arm. "I'm sorry, sir, but you need to come with us."

"Wait! Where are we going?"

"To the school, sir. I can't tell you more."

"Something's happened at the school?"

Sanderson had been patient, but now he pulled at Lester's arm insistently. Lester yanked it free.

"Hold on! Wait a minute." Cullen Frasier's generosity had scrambled all his circuits. He couldn't think straight. He pointed toward his front door. "I have a cat. He hasn't been fed yet. If this is going to take a while, I need to see he's tended to. Then we'll go to the school."

He took the first two front steps to his door and dug in his pocket for his keys.

Sanderson tried to grab Lester's shoulder again. "Sir, we can't let you—"

"It will only take a minute." Lester yanked the keys from his pocket. He carried his personal keys and all the keys for the school on the same ring. It was hefty and large and sometimes got stuck inside his pants pocket, as it did this time. When he finally yanked them clear, momentum carried his hand upward, the keys grasped firmly in his palm.

"Gun!" the younger cop shouted. Within a second, both he and Sanderson cleared their revolvers.

"No!" Lester said, waving the keys in front of him.

It was too late. The bullets were already in flight. Six in all, they slammed into Lester's chest. Designed to drop an assailant where he stood, the hollowpoints mushroomed and splintered, and they shredded and pulverized everything they hit. The keys flew from Lester's hand and jangled on the flagstone front porch. He fell back against the door, and slid to the ground, his eyes already dilated and fixed on a point no breathing man is permitted to witness.

TWO

The younger cop, Andy Frye, was three weeks out of the academy, on his first training assignment with veteran Marty Sanderson. Andy would never know it, but Sanderson had requested the rookie specifically after teaching his BLET classes at the community college in Burnsville. Saw promise in the kid. Now, as he watched Lester Corby slide down his front door, leaving an ochre smear on the paint, he regretted the decision.

Sanderson holstered his revolver and dashed to Lester Corby's side. Part of him was horrified, and a smaller part that shamed him admired Frye's tight grouping. Sanderson recognized how sick the thought was in an instant and he stuffed it deep inside.

"What…in…*fuck*…did you do?" he shouted.

Smoke still wafted from the barrel of Frye's Police Special. He hadn't holstered it. He stood, rock solid, the revolver still pointed and empty. "I…I saw a gun. He had a gun, Marty. I'd swear to it."

Sanderson lifted the key ring from the flagstone porch. "He had a bunch of keys, you moron. *Keys!*" He shook the key ring in the air.

Lights had gone on in houses along the street. Four houses away, a front door opened, and a woman stepped out on her front porch to see what was going on.

The adrenaline hit, and Frye shivered. "Oh, my God! Marty, is he…"

"Oh yeah," Sanderson said. "You took care of that, but good."

"Oh Jesus. Oh God. Oh hell. Oh fuck. Oh shit. I'm going to prison ain't I?" He dropped his revolver onto the lawn.

"Pick that up," Sanderson directed. "Nobody's going to prison." He lifted his pants leg and drew a palm-sized twenty-five caliber ACP he stowed in a holster around his ankle. "You have any idea how hard it is to locate a decent throwdown these days? I told you to get one weeks ago."

"What are you doing?" Frye asked.

"Saving your ass. You saw a gun? Okay. He had a gun." Sanderson wiped the little automatic with his handkerchief and placed it in Lester's right hand. He stuffed the keyring back inside Lester's pocket. "It's untraceable. Grabbed it off a kid who was caught speeding through town a few years back. He bought it off a street dealer. I ran the serial. No record. For all anyone knows, this geezer has owned it since Prohibition, before registration. You owe me a throwdown, kid."

Frye holstered his revolver and hovered over Sanderson. "This isn't right, Marty. We should tell someone."

"Who? Tell me who to call, and I'll call him. You stuck your dick in a blender, Andy. I'm unplugging it. You can thank me later. Go to the cruiser and call this in. Don't worry about sounding a little frantic. You just killed a guy."

"Okay," Frye said. "Okay. Got it."

"This ain't over, kid," Sanderson said as Frye turned toward the cruiser. "You better pray there's some connection between Lester here and the Masters killing."

————

Ted Wisniewski was the only police detective in Choctaw. He was also a fan of Monday Night Football. He would have preferred sitting in his La-Z-Boy recliner at home with a cold one, chuckling at the witty repartee between Howard Cosell and Dandy Don Meredith. Instead, he found himself in the high school principal's office, trying not to look too closely at the battered body of a woman he'd stood next to in the church choir for almost three years.

In life, Patti Masters was an attractive blonde woman in her middle forties. She wore large red square-framed eyeglasses, which now lay broken and twisted in the corner. Wisniewski had always been fascinated by her front teeth. One top incisor lapped slightly over its fellow to the right. Both teeth were now missing from the bashed-in mess of her lower face. Someone had worked her over in a fury.

The night custodian had discovered her about an hour earlier and called the police immediately. Not only was Wisniewski missing Monday Night Football, but he'd gotten the call on his rover as he was served a steaming plate of chicken parm at Tony's, the only Italian restaurant in Choctaw. The boxed leftovers were stinking up the inside of his unmarked car outside the school, which was fine. The farther away, the better. Wisniewski had lost his appetite and didn't anticipate it returning soon.

He was forty and had been divorced for seven years. The damn job. He didn't blame her, not a bit. Detectives are like doctors, on call twenty-four-seven. When they walk out the door, you never know when they're coming back.

He didn't begrudge her frustration. He'd caused it, after all. He did resent her hoovering up all their mutual friends in the process, though. After a year of awkwardly running into them at the grocery and drug stores, or at the dentist office, or in church, or about any-damn-where, Ted Wisniewski cast about for a job far away. A detective slot had recently opened in flyspeck Choctaw. The pay was shit, but the job came pre-sweetened with free use of an immaculate Craftsman-style bungalow with stone exterior walls, a deep covered front porch, a lovely garden out back, and yardwork done by town maintenance employees. Utilities included, so his overall standard of living had improved, slightly, even after paying alimony.

He'd liked Patti Masters, a Vietnam widow. He'd considered asking her out several times as he stood next to her at choir rehearsals. The moment had never seemed right, though, and now it would never happen at all. The fact he had imagined physical intimacy with the woman lying dead and degraded on her office floor made it even more difficult to examine her and the surrounding crime scene for clues.

A woman who lived across the street from the school saw the police cars in the parking lot and told the officers she was washing her dishes around six o'clock, or maybe slightly later, and noticed Masters' car still in the lot. She didn't make much of it at the time, as Masters' car was frequently the last to leave for the day. She also saw a lone black man walk away from the school and decided it might be important when the police arrived.

The assistant principal, a frail, sour-faced, balding man named Howard Kautz, told Wisniewski the school only had three black employees, and the one most likely to have still been around after six o'clock was Lester Corby.

"I can't imagine Lester would do something like this, though," Kautz said. "He's a retiree. Returned to work after his wife died. The most pleasant and agreeable man I know."

To cover all his bases, Wisniewski had called the uniformed cops over and asked them to find Lester Corby and bring him to the school for questioning, to rule him out as a suspect. The older one, Sanderson, took the address from Kautz and gestured for his rookie partner to follow him.

Wisniewski supervised the Coroner's Office techs as they zipped Patti Masters into a body bag for transport. The police chief, Elbert Tanney, strode grimly through the door. Tanney was a lifer in the bad guys business. He'd been a gun bull on the western prison command, a skip tracer for a bail bondsman in Asheville, and briefly a private investigator before he decided a regular paycheck and a desk job beat all hell out of chasing perps and getting shot at. He'd been the Choctaw chief for over a decade, and each year brought a new inch or two of belly lopped over the patent leather of his Sam Brown belt. All three chins wobbled as he spoke.

"Uh, Ted," he said, as quietly as possible. "We got us a situation. Those two boys you sent over to find this Corby fella?"

"Yes?"

"Seems they…you know…kinda killed him."

Wisniewski's head whipped around. "What?"

"They waited at his house. He resisted arrest, and according to Sanderson he pulled a gun."

"A gun?"

"A twenty-five. Popgun. Would barely hit the 'B's if you shot a phone book with it. But yeah. A gun. The kid, Frye, shot Corby."

"Shot him."

"Six times. Dead before he hit the ground."

Wisniewski walked away without a word and surveyed the room again. He closed his eyes, trying to imagine the place before it was trashed and Patti Masters was so viciously violated.

"Where was Corby before he arrived at home?" Wisniewski asked.

"He told Sanderson he was at the Choctaw Grille. Said he ate dinner there and had a few beers."

"What time did he arrive at the Grille?"

"Sanderson said six-thirty, maybe. No later than six-forty. I'll check it out with Cullen Frasier there. The bartender."

"Six-forty is uncomfortably tight, Chief," Wisniewski said. "Six-thirty is impossible. Whoever attacked…this victim got messy in the process. He'd have needed to clean before showing his face in public. His clothes will be spattered, and he'd have blood on his face and hands and any other exposed skin. He'd have it in his hair. Let's say the lady across the street is off by only ten minutes. If Lester Corby was the man she saw walk away from the school, and it was any later than six-fifteen, I can't see how he'd walk a half mile to his home *without* being seen by anyone along the way, ditch his bloody clothes, shower thoroughly, clean the blood out of the bathtub and anywhere else he transferred it, dress, and walk to the

Choctaw Grille all in less than a half hour. The timeline doesn't work."

"He could have killed her and showered here, in the gym, before he left."

"Possible," Wisniewski said. "When the crime scene guys finish here, I'll have them check the gym showers for traces of blood. I'm not feeling this one, though. Something's not right."

"How so?"

"The way Pat...the victim was beaten, the perpetrator should have bruising or abrasions on his knuckles. The autopsy on Corby will tell us if they're there. The person who committed this murder was angry. Nothing I've heard about Corby suggests any rage at all. All we have right now is opportunity, and even that's speculative. No motive. If Corby's hands are clean, we don't have means either. It's all circumstantial. For all I know, your rookie blew away the only witness who could lead us to the real killer."

"A little harsh. The kid's ripped to shreds over this."

"And it was hell on Lester Corby. Thanks for the heads-up. I suppose you'll handle the shooting investigation?"

"I hired the kid. I'm steering clear. We'll call in the SBI to do the shooting investigation. Sounds cut and dried, though."

"Why was he carrying a pistol?" Wisniewski asked, absently.

"What?"

"Why was Lester Corby carrying a pistol?"

"Why does anyone carry a pistol?" Chief Tanney asked.

"Exactly, Chief. Exactly."

———

Marsha Dumfries stepped out to her front porch seconds after Andy Frye pumped six hollow-points into Lester Corby's chest. She'd lived in Choctaw since she was a child and had seen her share of racist cop hijinks in a darker past, but she'd never seen a white policeman murder a black man before.

Sound carried on her street, even in the fog. She'd heard what the older cop and the young cop said to each other, and it amounted to only one possible conclusion.

Marsha Dumfries was a busybody. Everyone knew it. Nobody on Carlisle Street had been spared her attentions. She wasn't stingy with her observations, either. Besides being a snoop, she was a gossip. The ambulance hadn't arrived at Lester Corby's house before she was on the phone to her closest friend, Inez Wilkinson, who lived two streets over.

"Did you hear that noise?" Inez said. "Sounded like it was over your way. Fireworks?"

"You won't believe it," Marsha said. "I saw the whole thing. A policeman shot that nice Mr. Corby."

"Shot him!"

"Six times. I hear the ambulance now."

"I hear it, too. Why'd they shoot him?"

"I don't know, but I did know Lester Corby, and the man never lifted a finger against anyone. Sweetest man you ever met. I heard the cops who shot him talking. Something terrible happened at his house tonight."

Within minutes, telephones all over Choctaw's residential district jangled. People within a block of Lester Corby's house hiked around the corner to rubberneck. The newly arrived state patrolmen tried to establish a perimeter and keep people back. A kid from two houses away snapped pictures with his Brownie camera, the flash bouncing off Corby's house and creating bizarre shadows on the siding.

Nobody knew anything, except two white cops had shot a black man on his own front porch. Rumors rose and fell among the assembled crowd, which now numbered almost fifty people—a veritable mob in tiny Choctaw. Nobody believed Lester Corby had deserved to be blown into the afterlife, and the mood turned surly toward the cops who tried to control the scene.

A news truck from WLOS in Asheville parked at the curb. They had been in a neighboring town covering a school board meeting when they overheard the police radio in Choctaw call out an officer-involved shooting. Blood always bumps budget debates, so they packed their gear and headed over the mountain to scoop the other local media.

As soon as the television camera came out, everyone wanted to be a star. A dozen people in the crowd volunteered their personal accounts of the shooting, even though they had all been more than a block away when it happened, cloistered safely inside their houses. The exception was Marsha Dumfries, who held back and watched from the rear. As each of the volunteers spun a different hypothesis regarding how their poor neighbor had been shot, theories merged and intertwined. By the time the news crew turned off their lights and packed their gear, immense conspiracy theories had hatched among the more paranoid neighbors. Nothing but the deepest of corruption at the highest offices could explain the death of such a kind, peaceful man.

Marsha Dumfries had triggered a fission-like explosion in tiny Choctaw, North Carolina.

Sanderson and Frye walked into Chief Tanney's office and stood at salute.

"At ease," Tanney said, from behind his desk.

They relaxed and glanced around the room. In a chair against the far wall, Ted Wisniewski sat statue-like, his hands folded in his lap. He watched the two uniformed cops the way a cat watches a mousehole.

Someone knocked at the door.

Trent McCool walked in. McCool, the Town Council's attorney, was young for such an important post. Barely thirty, and only two years beyond the bar exam, he hadn't faced a great deal of competition, since the only other attorney within ten miles in any direction had probably clerked at the Socrates trial and coined the term *habeas corpus*. Word on the street had it McCool was a shoo-in for the district attorney's office in the next election. Movie-star handsome, and usually seen in expensive Italian suits, tonight McCool arrived in designer jeans, a Lacoste sport shirt, and Bass Weejuns. "Sorry I'm late. I was on a date with Babs Leakey. You know what that means."

"Yeah," Tanney said. "You're gettin' herpes."

"Worth every blister, I hear," McCool said. "This better be important. What do we have?"

Chief Tanney pulled an evidence bag from his desk drawer and laid it on his blotter. Inside was the palm-sized ACP automatic.

"Ted Wisniewski and I have been talking it over," Tanney said. "Which one of you wants to tell me where this pistol came from?"

"I swear I saw Corby pull a gun from his pocket, Chief," Frye said. "I'd swear to it on a stack of Bibles."

"Shut the fuck up, kid," Sanderson said. "You saw a wad of keys. The pistol's mine, Chief."

"Thank you for being honest about it," Tanney said.

"We'd have gotten there sooner or later, and I got plans for later. The kid panicked. Corby pulled a wad of keys out of his pocket. I mean, it was a horse-choker. In the dark, I s'pose it could have been mistaken for a weapon. I heard the kid yell *Gun*, and I cleared my weapon, but I saw the keys right away and never even touched my trigger. Andy here wasn't so observant. Please tell me Corby was involved in the murder at the high school, Chief, or I might use this popgun on myself."

"Sorry," Wisniewski said from the corner. "The timeline doesn't work in any way. The initial ME examination shows no abrasions or bruises on Corby's knuckles, and the first sweep of his home revealed no bloody clothes. Nothing in the school shower either. Corby wasn't the guy. So now I have two homicides on my plate."

"Enough of that shit," Tanney said. "We ain't using the word *homicide* here. Worst case, it's negligent manslaughter."

"Jesus," Andy Frye said. "I gotta sit." He wiped at the tear on his cheek. "All I ever wanted was to be a cop, Chief. This is a hell of a thing."

"I'm calling the SBI to handle the shooting investigation," Tanney said. "I got no other words for it, Andy. You made a tragic error in judgment. You screwed the pooch, and now you gotta raise the puppies. I'll try to work it so you keep your badge, but I ain't makin' any promises. Any way it ends, you're off the streets permanently. We'll put you in the evidence storage or something, if we can save your skin."

From his seat next to Wisniewski, Trent McCool said, "Let's throttle back a little and consider all our options."

Everyone turned his way.

"Options?" Tanney said.

"The ball's still in play. Someone out there killed Patti Masters, and we're ninety-nine and forty-four-one-hundredths percent certain it wasn't Corby. The real guy is still out there."

"Right," Tanney said.

"As long as you're still looking for him, he's going to ground. If someone else is taking heat for the murder, maybe he gets careless."

"What are you suggesting?" Wisniewski asked.

"Let the state boys handle the shooting investigation," McCool said. "In my experience, they'll take their time. Bench the kid for the duration. Let him ride a desk. You tell the world the shooting looks righteous, and it was related to the murder of Patti Masters, but everything is still settling out. The gun found on Lester Corby is under investigation. Ballistics and shit. I don't know. This is your thing. Drag it out. The thrust of the announcement is Lester Corby is still our prime suspect. Why else would he carry a pistol? Meanwhile, Ted continues his investigation, looking for the real killer. Until we find one, Lester's status as prime suspect shields Andy here from a manslaughter charge, 'cause all the plates are still spinning in the air. Worst case is he rides the pine until the real guy is caught."

"And if I never find the real killer?" Wisniewski asked.

"Eventually, the whole thing goes away. The public has a short memory. We live in dynamic times. The next shiny thing will wipe this entire affair out of their minds. If you never get the guy, it'll be another unsolved murder, and everyone will assume Corby killed Patti Masters even without charges or a trial. Memory is funky that way. With the passage of time, dumbass Andy here might even become the hero of this story, the courageous blue knight who brought to justice the vicious monster who killed the sweet local schoolmarm."

"That's the most disgusting and insulting thing I've ever heard," Wisniewski said. "I knew the victim. She was a lovely woman, and this scheme only demeans and degrades her further. You expect me to play along with this?"

"*I* do," Tanney said. "I'm still your boss. If I tell you to play along, you can play along or you can run along. Your choice." The telephone rang on Chief Tanney's desk. He answered it, grunted a couple of times, and said, "All right. Thanks."

He replaced the receiver and sighed. "Fuckin' Kevin Malory."

THREE

Kevin Malory stood among the legions of young college journalism students who had watched the ascendence of Woodward and Bernstein with a mixture of awe and inspiration. The Watergate scandal had made celebrities out of the media, and when Malory graduated from Chapel Hill, he entered the newspaper world with starry eyes and dreams of fame.

Along with thousands of other aspirants.

Malory found the pickings slim. The major state dailies had already snapped up the brightest students before they even graduated. Not being included informed Kevin Malory of his place in the pecking order. The best offer he found was a position as the editor of the *Choctaw Caller*, a weekly in the shadowy foothills of the Blue Ridge mountains, where the long-standing editor had been ordered to Arizona by his doctor.

Editor, in this case, included all the reporting duties as well as composition and circulation chores. A retired radio ad man two towns over put in ten hours a week selling ad space for a commission, so at least Malory didn't have to do that as well. Even in a town the size of Choctaw, putting out a weekly newspaper with a staff of one was a daunting task.

Fortunately, Kevin was charming and gregarious. He had recruited a cadre of busybodies around town, selected specifically for their dreams of writing steamy romance novels, to act as stringers. He encouraged them to write vignettes about any mild disturbance, positive or negative, in the daily monotony of life in Choctaw, and to drop them by his office on Main Street. He rewrote the truly newsworthy stories—his matronly stringers had evaded publishing success for good reason—and used them as filler. The big stories he wrote himself.

Marsha Dumfries had brought him a blockbuster.

While her neighbors burned the telephone lines in the gossip orgy she had instigated, Marsha found Kevin toiling away at his desk. Smoke rose in a column to the ceiling from a half-burned cigarette in the ashtray. A stained coffee cup obviously purloined from the Choctaw Grille sat on his desk, a film of artificial creamer coagulating on the cooling surface.

She told him everything the officers had said to each other after Lester Corby was shot to death on his front porch, and Kevin took copious notes.

"You're sure?" Kevin asked. "You were a hundred feet away. It was foggy."

"I could hear them talking," Marsha said. "My hearing is perfect. The young officer admitted he had killed Lester, and the older one planted a gun to make it look like Lester pulled it on them. The older cop said it plain as day. *I'm saving your ass.* I stand by it."

"Have you told anyone else about this?"

"Of course. I called Inez Wilkinson right away. Then I came directly to you."

"Why?"

"This is news, Kevin. Big news. A white policeman shot a black man in cold blood and is trying to cover it up."

"Why didn't you go to Chief Tanney?"

"Because I know him. He won't do anything unless public opinion forces him to do something. You print this story, and he'll do something."

"I need to verify it. Right now, all I have is your overheard conversation. This is gossip. I can't print what you've given me."

"But it's a start?" Marsha asked.

"It's a good start. Every bit as good as a bored security guard checking the wrong door at the Watergate."

She touched his shoulder. "I did well?"

He smelled her perfume. She'd gussied herself up before venturing out into the fog.

"You did well," he said. "I'm glad you brought this to me." He dashed out the cigarette in the ashtray. "I… may need to ask a few more questions, after I do some double-checking. Can I find you at your house later this evening?"

"Always," she said.

Kevin Malory didn't pay his stringers. They provided him with stories, though, because he rewarded them in other ways. They were all spinsters or divorcees or widows, lonely women still in their middle-aged prime who took great care of themselves and appreciated the attentions of an attractive younger man. There were a multitude of transactions associated with the stories that crossed his transom, almost none of them monetary. For his part, Kevin enjoyed the arrangement. Benjamin Franklin, he had long ago concluded, had not erred in his praise of older women.

Marsha Dumfries allowed her hand to linger on his shoulder for a moment, smiled, and said she needed to tend to some things at home, but he was welcome to stop by later if he had any more questions.

Kevin gave her a minute to change her mind and come charging back inside for a quickie. It wouldn't be the first time. Once satisfied she was gone for good, he dialed the number for the police. The receptionist put him through directly to Chief Tanney.

"You should know," he said. "One of my stringers overheard your cops talking after they shot Lester Corby tonight. I have her written statement, and it's a doozie. Don't say anything. I'm not digging for quotes right now. It's too late to do anything about it. She's already alerted the local gossip chain. By now half the town knows one of your guys tried to stash a throwdown gun on Corby. You need to get your story straight, because when I visit you tomorrow, I *will* ask for quotes."

————

The next issue of the *Choctaw Caller* wasn't scheduled until Friday. By then, the story would be colder than Marsha Dumfries' feet. Kevin Malory would be lucky if it kept until morning. After mulling over his options, he checked the Rolodex on his desk and dialed the state editor of the Associated Press office in Raleigh, one of his former classmates at Carolina.

"What's the haps, Kev?" Marvin Long asked.

"I have a story to submit, but I want the byline."

"No problemo, brother. The papers won't print the byline, though. They all credit the AP."

"Putting it in the resume bank, and of course I expect the usual compensation for the lead."

"You got it."

"Here's the story." Kevin had jotted notes based on all the information he'd gathered and read them to Long story-style.

"Hold on," Marvin said, stopping him near the end. "Need to feed some paper into the Selectric here. Gonna take the dictation myself."

"Don't put your goddamn name on the story," Kevin said. "This one's mine. Fuck with me and I'll switch to UPI."

"You'd hate them. They don't pay as well. Okay. Again. From the top."

———

The story went over the wire a half hour later. Within minutes, Chief Tanney's telephone rang for the first time of thousands over the next twenty-four hours. A reporter from the *Charlotte Observer* who seemed to have a *lot* of information about the shooting asked some difficult questions.

His back against the wall, Tanney verified there had been two deaths in Choctaw, and they might be related, but it was too early in the investigation to discuss details.

The *Observer* guy was no slouch. He called several random neighbors whose houses were close to Lester Corby's place. He learned enough from their accounts to be comfortable breaking a story about a double murder in Choctaw. It was still in time for the first edition.

Newspaper readers, radio listeners, and TV news viewers all over the state woke to the story.

———

Ted Wisniewski carried two folders into Elbert Tanney's office. Roger Gimball sat in one of the chairs in front of the chief's desk. Gimball was dressed in jeans and a flannel hunting shirt and wore a pair of hiking boots. He sported three days' growth of graying beard.

"Mr. Mayor," Wisniewski said.

"I drove back from my fishing trip at Lake James this morning," Gimball said. "Would have come last night, but the wife and I kind of tied one on at dinner. Wasn't fit to drive when I got the first call. Are those the autopsy reports?"

"Yes. The ME pulled an all-nighter. First the easy one. Lester Corby. Six bullet entry wounds, four exit wounds. All thirty-eight caliber, all from Andy Frye's service revolver. Shredded the pericardium, penetrated both the left ventricle and atrium of the heart and severed both the aorta and the superior vena cava. Nicked the pulmonary artery and pretty much destroyed the trachea. Any of the shots would have been fatal. No evidence whatsoever of other violence. No abnormal bruises or cuts or scrapes, and no abrasions or contusions on the hands. His home was clean. No bloody clothes, no blood in the bathroom or anywhere else, no nothing. Your boy blew away an innocent man, Chief."

"*Our* boy, Ted," Tanney reminded him. "We're all on the same team."

"What about Patti Masters?" Gimball asked.

"Somewhat more disturbing," Wisniewski said, opening the folder. "First, there was evidence of sexual activity in the report."

"She was raped?" Gimball asked.

27

"*Consensual* sexual activity," Wisniewski added. "Petechiae in her hard palate were consistent with normal—not forced—fellatio."

"What in hell is fellatio?" Tanney asked. "Some weird new hippie drug?"

"It's a blowjob, Chief," Gimball said. "Ask your wife for one. They're fun."

Wisniewski continued. "Anyway…it's hard to discern further because of the damage to the victim's dental and cranial structure, but the ME is pretty sure she gave someone a hummer shortly before she died. And that's not all. The fellatio was a prelude. She also had vaginal intercourse, probably two hours or so before she died."

"But not raped?" Gimball asked.

"No. The ME found evidence of semen, and he's typing it, but found no bruising or other soft tissue damage consistent with forced sex. Every indicator suggests she enjoyed a little afternoon delight before hopping the off-world express. Cause of death was blunt force trauma, a basal skull fracture that crushed the hindbrain, and a ruptured hyoid. Time of death appears to be around seven o'clock, give or take a half hour. I should note again that eliminates Lester Corby, because he was already at the Choctaw Grille when she died."

"Who was she fucking?" Gimball asked.

Wisniewski, who had harbored some romantic notions toward the deceased woman, winced. "We don't know, and probably won't know based solely on the semen evidence. It'll give us blood type, but that's about all, and ninety percent of the folks in Choctaw are probably the same type. The bad news is the killer didn't leave much behind in the way of physical evidence. Patti Masters was a nailbiter and didn't have a chance to scratch him or gouge at him."

"Unless the guy who killed her was the same one who pumped her a couple of hours before." Gimball observed.

"About that," Wisniewski said. "If she had sex around five o'clock, she had it at the school. Several witnesses have reported her car was still there when they left, and it was still parked in the lot after she was murdered."

"A teacher?" Tanney asked.

"Or a student," Wisniewski suggested.

"Jesus," Gimball said. "Don't make this even more tawdry than it already is."

"Has to be ruled out," Wisniewski said. "She wouldn't be the first principal to get involved with a student. Also, the degree of violence exhibited in the attack on her face is consistent with an assault by a teenager. Their self-control leaves a lot to be desired, and they tend to go overboard when they lose their restraint. I can imagine a scenario in which she tried to break it off with a student, he begged for one last roll in the hay, and later decided to make it her last time forever."

"So we're gonna check every high school boy's hands for bruises and scabs?" Tanney asked.

"If it comes to that," Wisniewski said.

"Town Council's meeting this evening. No public announcement," Gimball said. "School Board's gonna joint session with us. We need to appoint an interim principal at the high school and figure out a way to deal with the PR fallout from this murder and the killing of Lester Corby. I don't mind telling you; some of the council members aren't happy with the shooting."

"What's that mean?" Tanney asked.

"They're gonna want to hold someone accountable. You know how it goes, Elbert. It's never about who's responsible. It's always about who takes the heat. You might have to tender young Frye for the sacrifice."

"I'd rather not."

"Might come down to you or him," Gimball said.

"We'll burn that bridge when we get to it," Tanney said.

Chief Tanney's secretary knocked on the door and stuck her head inside the office.

"Chief? A man outside would like to talk with you."

"Some reporter?" Tanney asked.

"No," she said. "A preacher."

"This should be interesting," Gimball said.

"Show him in," Tanney said.

"I'm headed for the high school," Wisniewski said. "Gonna hang out and look at students' knuckles for a while, maybe ask some of the teachers if they knew anything about Patti Masters having an affair."

"Be discreet," Gimball told him. "We don't need a lot of rumors floating around. We're in enough hot water already."

Wisniewski exited without comment. A moment later, the secretary ushered in a sharply dressed black man. He was short and slight and young—no more than thirty—but there was a determination in his eyes only a fool would challenge. His most intriguing feature was a half-crown of scars circling the left side of his head, in the recognizable pattern of a motorcycle chain. As he entered the room, both Elbert Tanney and Roger Gimball stood to greet him.

"Reverend Bishop Angeloe Teeter," the secretary announced. They shook hands all around.

"You aren't local," Gimball said.

"No," Teeter asked. "I'm the resident pastor at the Garveyville AME Zion Temple in Morgan, in Bliss County."

"Kinda young for a bishop, aren't you?"

"I'm the same age Jesus was when he started his ministry," Teeter said.

"I know who you are," Tanney said. "The sheriff in Bliss County told me about you. You're the fella who organized all those protests when that colored girl drowned in Prosperity last year."

"The *former* sheriff," Teeter corrected. "That *colored girl* was named Sunday Free, and she didn't drown. She was drugged and gang-raped and fell into the pool when she passed out. She was murdered. But, because she wasn't white, nobody spoke for Sunday Free until I did."

"Seems you helped hustle a congressman off to prison as well," Tanney said.

"I was there the day he was arrested, but I was as surprised as anyone else. I won't say I was dissatisfied with the outcome. Justice was served."

"Uh-huh," Tanney said. "So I reckon I know why you're here today."

"I'd like to discuss the response to the shooting of Lester Corby."

"In what capacity?" Gimball asked.

"The capacity of a concerned citizen."

"I appreciate your interest and your concern," Gimball said. "And, of course, you are welcome in Choctaw. However, the situation regarding Lester Corby's shooting is…um, fluid. We're still gathering information, evaluating the medical reports, and of course there is the matter of the pistol found on Corby's front porch. We haven't determined its origin yet. It's so old, there may be no records of its manufacture or sale."

"I believe it is a small pistol, is it not?" Teeter asked.

"A twenty-five-caliber automatic. One-inch barrel. You can carry it in the palm of your hand," Tanney said.

"Or in a hidden holster strapped to your ankle?" Teeter asked.

Tanney's face reddened. "What are you suggesting?" he growled.

"I'm suggesting a rookie cop, in a moment of panic, shot an innocent black man on his own front porch and tried to cover his mistake by placing an untraceable pistol on his body. Is that plain enough for you?"

"How dare you, you—"

"Chief!" Gimball interrupted. "Take a walk."

"What?" Tanney asked, puzzled.

"Cool off. We're all under a lot of stress. Go grab a Coke."

Tanney's gaze volleyed back and forth between Teeter and Mayor Gimball. Finally, he shrugged his shoulders and walked out of the room without a word.

"As police chiefs go, you could do better," Teeter told Gimball.

"He's a good man under unimaginable stress. What do you want?" Gimball asked.

"A seat at the table."

"The table? What table?"

"The table the white man's been hogging for three hundred years. You got a black man lying on a slab at the morgue with six bullets in him that came from a white cop's gun."

"And right next to him is a middle-aged white woman who was brutally murdered in her office at the school. A witness saw a potential suspect walk away from the school around the time of the murder. She identified him as a black man. We had reason to suspect Lester Corby."

"But you didn't have reason to snuff out his life like an inconvenient candle," Teeter said, his voice even and paced.

"You forget the pistol."

"It was planted."

"You don't know that."

"Tell me I'm wrong."

"I asked before what you want," Gimball said.

"I checked on your town before I drove here, Mr. Mayor. You're white. You got a white chief of police. You got a white city attorney. You got two white cops in a tough situation. You got a white detective investigating the case. You got one dead brother, and a lot of people of color asking hard questions. You need someone on your side who can communicate with them."

"You."

"I'll do, until someone better comes along."

"And what's the alternative?"

"I'll talk to them anyway. You might not like what I have to say."

"Son, I already don't like what you're saying."

"Eighty-six that *son* crap," Teeter said. His voice snapped, but his eyes betrayed nothing at all. "We are not getting off to a good start here. I can be an asset to your investigation, and perhaps I can help you find a way out of this mess that leaves as many heads on as many shoulders as possible. You want me on your side."

"Because?"

"Because you absolutely don't want me on the *other* side."

"Kinda cocky for a kid, aren't you?"

"Ask former Congressman Rennie Poole. He gets one phone call a day at the federal penitentiary in Butner."

"You said you had nothing to do with that."

"I'm humble."

"The fuck you are. I see you, Mr. Teeter. You play the victim card nicely, and maybe you have the right to. We're not bad people here in Choctaw, but we are insular in our ways, and perhaps we lag behind the rest of the world some due to our isolation. What's happened is a genuine American tragedy, however it plays out. People are dead. We aren't used to that. Last person murdered in Choctaw died before World War One. We're all strangers in a strange land here."

"Nice speech. Very *Our Town*. Here's how I see this going, Mayor—"

"Call me Roger."

"Not in a million years, and you can call me *Reverend*. You know how every war ever fought ended?"

"How?"

"Around a table. Never much saw the point in all the killing and destruction. Why not talk from the get-go? I'm offering my services as your temporary liaison with the black community in Choctaw, and for that purpose alone. You tell me what you want them to know, and you can bet I won't shut up about what they want."

"Your analogy concerns me. It implies if we don't capitulate and include you in the investigation, you'll—what? Wage war on Choctaw?"

"A decade ago, a redneck nigger-knocker cop shot me in the leg and bashed out all four of my front teeth slamming my face into the rear deck of my brand-new car. I got these scars on my head from a motorcycle chain another shitkicker wrapped around it. That night, as I lay in the hospital, the people of Garveyville, the neighborhood where I lived, marched in the streets and stripped Morgan down to the studs. Never underestimate the wrath of people who will no longer tolerate being subjugated. Maybe I can help prevent such a consequence here."

"What's in it for you?"

"I plant seeds, Mayor," Teeter said. "Check with the City Council in Morgan. They consider me a bit of a nuisance. And they're right. I walked in here asking for a seat at your table, but my real goal is a seat at every table for every person of color in this country. Somewhere in this provincial Blue Ridge backwater is a young black person of vision and drive, who has a righteous fire burning in their belly. I'll locate that person, and when I leave, they'll remain behind to keep the good work going, and probably to be a pain in your ass. Consider me the Johnny Appleseed of racial justice."

"I think you're a lot smarter than you look," Gimball said.

"I'll take that as a compliment."

Gimball twiddled his thumbs for a few seconds as he considered his options. "What do you see as an acceptable outcome?"

"Justice for Lester Corby. His name is cleared and the man who shot him is held accountable."

"You'd toss a cop to the lions."

"I'd see to it a killer is brought to appropriate justice. Nobody pulled the trigger for him," Teeter said. His voice softened. "Maybe he's a kid who wasn't ready. Maybe he doesn't have a violent or bigoted bone in his body. Maybe he's a godly man with nothing but love in his heart for all humankind. None of that shit matters. He's a white man with a badge and a gun who slaughtered an unarmed black man on the steps of his own home. There are cops out there who *are* bigoted and racist. A lot of them. If he gets off, they are going to see this kid as some sort of role model. No black man in North Carolina will ever feel secure around a white cop again. You let this kid get off, and this state will burn, Mayor."

"You make a compelling argument."

"I will, of course, make it easy for you. This is probably a good time to tell you about the demonstration I've planned in front of Town Hall later this week."

"A demonstration?"

"No more than two or three hundred people. A lot of them will be local, but I have a network of civil rights activists across the state who'll also be here. I hope you can handle the parking."

"I don't get it," Gimball said.

"By then, we'll know for certain Lester Corby was completely innocent, and had nothing at all to do with the principal's murder. A man who should still be alive and kicking isn't, because a white cop drew down on him for pulling his keys from his pocket while black. That's the core story here. It's not only a killing; it may be a civil rights violation. The kid who shot Corby? He goes down in every version of this story. There is no happy ending for him. By the time my people come to Choctaw, you should have all the evidence you need to prove he acted in a malevolently negligent manner. Voluntary manslaughter at the very least."

"They'll rip him to pieces in prison."

"Segregated population. Cops only. A surprising number of guys stacking time used to wear badges. You can negotiate it at sentencing, and under the circumstances I believe the judge would be copacetic."

Gimball frowned again. "No violence at the demonstration." It wasn't a request.

"I am a follower of Doctor King," Teeter said. "Nonviolence is at the core of our practice and philosophy. My associates across the state are also committed to nonviolent social change."

"Well, good."

"We do make a great deal of noise, though. Enough for you to look like a hero by throwing oil on the waters and giving up the man who shot Lester Corby."

"You don't mean handing him over to *you?*"

"Do you see a white hood on my head? Lynchings are the Klan's solution. You talk behind the scenes with the District Attorney. The demonstration might be quelled by your announcement the DA is considering negligent manslaughter charges against the shooting officer."

"The SBI is investigating the shooting. They aren't even on scene yet. Won't be here until tomorrow."

"I said *considering.* My expectation, as a person now sitting at the table, is that he will be charged when the investigation—as I anticipate—demonstrates the shooting was not justified. And I *do* expect that conclusion. Am I making myself clear?"

"I believe you are. Nice little piece of political theater you're staging here."

"Not my first rodeo, Mayor. Someone's going down for killing Lester Corby. Better for everyone it's the guy who actually shot him."

Chief Tanney walked back into the office. He glanced at Angeloe Teeter. "Huh. You're still here."

"Not for long," Teeter said, standing to leave.

"What's the plan?" Tanney asked.

"You aren't gonna like it," Gimball told him.

FOUR

For the most part, moonshining in the Carolina hill country was a thing of the past. While conflicts between corn liquor distillers and revenue agents were part of the misty legend and lore of the Blue Ridge, the simple fact was booze was legal and cheap and readily available nearby. Going to all the trouble of building a still, cooking mash, watching it bubble and ooze as it fermented, and still only be halfway to a decent slug of potentially blinding radiator hooch seemed a little too much effort for the payoff.

That didn't mean illegal distilleries didn't exist anymore. Despite the gradual westward expansion of high-density cities and towns in the state, there were still pockets isolated by choice; enclaves where family trees resembled French braids, and reading and writing weren't considered fundamental skills. There were no newspapers and few books outside the family Bible, which sat in most homes as a largely neglected reverential shrine. They attended tiny churches with four or five pews, where men with pot bellies and stringy sweaty hair and tobacco juice stains on their lips and tar in their hearts bellowed them into compliance with an interpretation of holy scripture so tortuously convoluted that Jesus himself, if he sat in their number, would find it incomprehensible.

These were people who chose to live much in the way the original Scots Irish settlers did under land grants from the British governors before the American Revolution. They slept in rough-hewn cabins and ramshackle clapboard houses with teetering chimneys. Every yard had stretching racks on which deerskins and bear hides cured in the sun. An acre was cleared for planting communal vegetable crops, and another dedicated entirely to corn. Another, situated deep in the hardwood forest, was dedicated to raising an admirable stand of cannabis, which had supplanted homemade hooch as their cash crop.

These were people who came down from the hills five or six times a year to load their ancient wheezing pickup trucks with hundred-pound sacks of staples and bolts of cloth and boxes of supplies and disappeared again into the mist rolling off Choctaw Knob. Some could trace their own ancestries—through oral recitation—to settlers who had served as Regulators under the rule of King George when everything from Salisbury to the Tennessee border was a single county. Most of them, though, had no idea who their ancestors were beyond two generations, and many knew less than that.

Andy Frye had grown up in one of these communities. On the map, it was registered as empty unincorporated land, but the people who had lived there for almost three hundred years called it *The Ridge*. Nobody knew why, since there wasn't an actual ridge within a mile, and it didn't matter anyway, because the idea of incorporation would have seemed as foreign to the Ridge residents as paying taxes.

As they had quit cooking for distribution and profit, and with the IRS and ATF looking elsewhere for more interesting quarry,

The Ridge's white lightning operation was no longer secreted in a quiet spot in the woods. It had been moved indoors, inside its own small cabin conveniently placed on the edge of the settlement. Needing only to serve the requirements of fifty people or so, there was no longer a need for a huge fifty-five-gallon drum to cook the mash. The entire still was assembled, like Frankenstein's creature, from odds bits and bobbles including a repurposed beer keg, stainless steel refrigerator tubing, and a genuine propane burner—originally intended for frying turkeys—to replace the constantly tended woodfire. The still ran twenty-four hours a day, tended collectively by the community. While the volume produced was not prodigious, the quality was top shelf—for homebrew—and by the time the residents of The Ridge ran out of one batch, the next was ready for jugging. One imaginative wag had spent half a day torching the inside of a white oak barrel to charcoal over a campfire and had filled it with shine and set it aside, claiming in a few years he'd show those boys at Jack Daniels a thing or two.

Since The Ridge didn't exist, at least as any sort of administrative governmental entity, there was no electrical service or natural gas. No telephone lines extended to the compound. A single generator connected to a waterwheel on Rouge Creek supplied enough electricity through an alarmingly jury-rigged system of extension cords to power a communal refrigerator and freezer—for storing field-dressed game—and a single twelve inch black and white television used mostly for watching football and wrestling and stock car races. A communal well provided enough drinking and bathing and cooking water for the entire population. There was talk of installing a few septic tanks and bringing in flush toilets, but for the duration outhouses were still *de rigueur*. More than half the shanties sported a Confederate battle flag in a place of prominence, in the belief the Glorious South would inevitably rise again.

These were not people who had been set apart from civilization and trapped in time by some cataclysm, like Darwin's finches or Galapagos tortoises. They had broken off from society voluntarily. Some were former hippies who had joined the community to rediscover their communal roots. The vast majority represented families who had simply never elected to descend from the mountain and join the human parade in the flatlands. They distrusted outsiders, and particularly those who claimed to represent the government. Government men had never done them any favors. They were to be avoided at all costs.

Three days after the killings of Patti Masters and Lester Corby, Andy Frye sat with his uncle Verble Justice and several other men, clustered in low-slung beach chairs around a crackling campfire outside the still cabin. They were dressed in camouflage fatigues and their faces were still smudged with the greasepaint they'd applied before hunting that morning. It was crisp but not cold, and the men fortified themselves with a gallon jug of shine they passed from one to another.

"I'm tellin' you, they're gonna hang my balls on a fence over this," Andy said.

"Worst thing ever happened to you was getting taken to the flatlands," Justice said. "Seems you've faced one hurdle after another ever since."

Andy was inclined to agree. He hadn't lived at The Ridge for years. His mother had never adjusted to the place, and after his father died, she'd taken him away. One of the reasons he'd eventually returned to Choctaw was to be close to The Ridge. His mother, who still lived outside High Point, disapproved, but Andy was a grown man and allowed to make his own decisions in life.

"I overheard the chief talking to Mayor Gimball over the telephone. I couldn't hear both sides, but it was easy to figure out what Gimball was saying by the way Chief Tanney talked. This preacher from downstate is planning a demonstration day after tomorrow, and the mayor and the chief want to get out ahead of it. Those SBI guys raked me over the coals yesterday. It isn't gonna go well for me. I could tell."

"Head on up to the hunting cabin," Justice said. "Hell, the only people on earth who know where it is are sitting around this campfire. They can't put you in a cage if they can't find you."

"That won't solve anything. I can't hide in the woods forever."

"We've done all right for a couple hundred years," Ronnie Claymore said, on the other side of the fire. He slapped the chest of the man next to him, and they both snorted with laughter.

"The boy's right," Justice said. "World's shrinking so fast, sooner or later someone gonna try to put a Mac-Donald's on the hill where the hunting cabin stands. Seems to me the problem is this preacher fella. You say he's bringin' in a bunch of flatlanders to help with this demonstration?"

"That's what I heard," Andy said. "The preacher's printed flyers and he's passing them out all over town. The chief told Mayor Gimball he was worried there'd be all sorts of radicals coming in—socialists and communists and Black Panthers and who knows what?"

Verble Justice took a drag from the ceramic jug and passed it to Andy. Andy looked at it for a few seconds and passed it along.

"Damned commie hippies made us lose Vietnam," Justice said.

"Hey!" one of the boys said. "Watch that shit. I was a hippie."

"Present company excluded," Justice said. "But the fact is, these commies are ruining ever'thing they touch. I got no quarrel with a black man who knows his place and stays in it, but this preacher sounds like he needs to learn a little respect for tradition."

"If he didn't come to town," Andy said, "maybe all this shit would've blown over. Hell, even the city attorney said I might come out of this looking like a hero. Now they're fitting me for a prison jumper."

"One way or another, we ain't gonna let that happen," Justice said, his voice sluggish. "When your daddy died, I promised to step in if you ever needed help. Seems like this is one of those times."

"What are you saying?" Andy asked.

"We got your back, brother. Don't you worry."

FIVE

Ted Wisniewski had spent most of the last two days at the school, trying to fade into the shadows as he covertly examined every pair of hands he could—as inconspicuously as he could—for bruising and scabbing. So far, he had discovered nothing interesting.

He still favored the jilted lover hypothesis for the murder. In that scenario, Patti had boinked her paramour in her office after the school day. She probably gave him the kiss-off. Told him it was over, and hours later the lover returned to ensure he was the last man she'd ever boink. It was a cliché, but clichés existed for a reason. Given the sheer volume of homicides in the world, Ted Wisniewski marveled how few actual motives there were for them. Anger and revenge were right at the top of the list.

Another one—jealousy—he understood. He was ashamed he felt the smallest twinge of jealousy toward Patti Masters' lover. All of the church choir rehearsals were early on weekday evenings. He couldn't help wondering how many of those evenings he stood within inches of her only minutes after she left her lover, and whether she still throbbed a little from her rendezvous and carried his seed inside her. He wondered what might have happened had he been a more courageous or assertive suitor.

He forced those thoughts to the dark corners of his head and returned to his real job—finding Patti Masters' killer. It was the only thing he could do for her now.

Working on the assumption the principal's secretary was the only person truly wired into everything that happened on campus, he'd visited the school office to interview her.

Carole Baumgarner was about the same age as Patti Masters, in her mid-forties, but her face suggested she had been born old. Her hair was graying and wiry and frizzy, piled into a bun on top of her head, lighting bolts of jagged split ends casting in every direction. She had the recessed mouth and protruding chin and drooping nose of an elderly woman, and her pupils looked prematurely clouded behind the cat's-eye reading glasses she wore on a chain around her neck. Approaching her to talk about Patti Masters' sex life made Wisniewski uncomfortable, as she looked and acted like a woman who had never seen a grown man naked.

After the interview, Wisniewski admonished himself, once again, never to judge a book by its cover.

"I'm filling in blanks in the timeline," he lied, after introducing himself to her and showing her his badge. "What time did you leave work on the day Patti Masters was murdered?"

"Around four o'clock," she said.

"Was this your usual time to leave?"

"No. I usually work until five. Principal Masters sent me home early."

"Do you know why?"

She pressed an index finger to her cheek and gazed skyward for a second. "I suppose it was so she could knock off a little."

Wisniewski was momentarily confused. "I'm sorry. Do you mean take off early herself?"

"No. I mean she had planned a rendezvous in her office with her lover."

"I see. And do you know who that was?"

She smiled. "Dear me, no. I never caught them in the act, as you'd say."

"Then how do you know…"

"An employer depends a great deal on her secretary. You'd be amazed how dependent they become on that person. It becomes so easy, don't you know? *Call my dentist and cancel my appointment. Get the superintendent on the line. Please pick up my laundry at the cleaners. Please drop off my laundry at the cleaners.* Your wish is my command. It's like having a djinni at your disposal for eight hours a day. A few years in a relationship like that, and you notice when things change. You know how close Patti and I were? Our periods synchronized. You know who that happens with? Best friends and sisters."

"I…um…" Wisniewski said. No words came. He heard the resentment underlying Carole Baumgarner's words, and wondered whether she might have been jealous of Masters' lover herself.

"So how did I know?" She anticipated the next question before Wisniewski could formulate it. She tapped her nose. "Nothing else smells exactly like semen, don't you agree?"

"I'll take your word for it."

"I know. I don't look the type. Still waters and all. You might be shocked. You could be pleasantly surprised. Anyway, first thing each morning, I go into Patti's office, start the coffeemaker, and empty her trash can. She tended to work late, sometimes after the custodians were gone for the night, so her trash can was frequently full. Several times a week, I saw wadded tissues in the trash. The aroma was unmistakable. Got one of those sensitive noses. Sometimes, I could still detect the smell of sex, especially around her couch. I don't begrudge her, you understand. She was widowed young, and she was still in pretty good shape. A woman has needs. But I'm sure you know that." She eyed Wisniewski.

"Why carry on affairs in her office?" he asked.

"Where else? She had two teenagers at home. Maybe the guy was married."

"A hotel?"

She snorted. "In Choctaw? You aren't from around here, are you?"

She was right. Stupid question. "So, you left around four the afternoon she died?"

"Right at four."

"But on other occasions you discovered…um…evidence of sexual activity, you had stayed until five?"

"Most of them, yes," she said.

"When did you first notice…um…"

"Cum-stained tissues in the trash? Only a few weeks ago. School started the Tuesday after Labor Day. It was sometime that week."

"But not last year?"

"Not as I can recall. I could have missed it, but I'd say whoever her lover was, it began over the summer."

"Or they had somewhere else to go last spring," Wisniewski suggested.

"I'd imagine you have a difficult job," she said.

"She was sleeping with someone," Wisniewski told Chief Tanney. "It wasn't a one-night stand. They met regularly in the evening sometime between five and seven o'clock and had sex in her office. But the night she died, they might have met earlier, because she sent her secretary home an hour early, which puts the window for the sex from four to, say, seven o'clock. We know she died a half hour one side or the other from seven o'clock. I still say her lover is the killer. We find him, and we're ninety percent of the way to solving this case."

"Find him quickly," Tanney said. "I'm worried about this demonstration Saturday. The mayor tossed in with the preacher from Bliss County. They're gonna fling Andy Frye to the wolves."

"He did kill Lester Corby."

"I was a gun bull, Ted. I seen the inside of prisons. Even the segregated pop for cops is a meat grinder. Bad cops were bad men first. Andy isn't like them."

"It sucks for him."

"Kinda callous."

"It's his trip, Chief. Shit happens to good people every day, a lot of it self-inflicted. It's his turn. Yeah, he's a kid, and it sucks, but he pulled a trigger he can't unpull. He'll get the minimum sentence. Best thing he can do is keep his head down and pound it out."

Tanney sighed heavily and drummed his desktop with his fingers. "What really pisses me off is you're right. Kid's been in the brotherhood only three weeks. Hell of a career. But he's in it, and we support him, whatever he's done. He headed into the woodchipper, but that don't mean he has to do it alone."

"There but for the grace of God?" Wisniewski asked.

"I know how he's hurting," Tanney said. "I shot a guy on the work gang back in the day. He took off running when I was distracted. I shouted for him to stop, twice, and then I blew out his spine with a .308 from fifty yards, exactly the way we were ordered to do by the warden. He made it two or three steps with a hole in his chest the size of a softball before he tumbled into the dust. I didn't sleep for two weeks after. Sometimes the nightmares I still have about it keep me awake for hours. Andy Frye's fallin' through hell, and he's headed for a hard landing. His future's already written by the mayor and that preacher."

Trent McCool knocked on the door. He was dressed more formally than he had been the previous Monday, in a natty summer wool pinstriped suit with a crisp Pima cotton shirt and businesslike red and yellow tie. "Private party?" he asked.

"Not if you brought the booze," Wisniewski said.

"I bring only bad news. I couldn't get an injunction on the demonstration. The judge wouldn't issue it. Said it violated First Amendment rights protecting freedom of assembly."

"Who told you to get an injunction?" Tanney asked.

"The mayor."

"Thought he was tossing in with the preacher," Wisniewski said.

"He's playing both ends against the middle. Covering his ass. The mayor is a crafty man, in his way. Ambitious crafty men aren't usually concerned about the bodies they leave in their wake. He even told the preacher he was trying for the injunction, as if it was part of their staging for the martyrdom of Andy Frye. If you ask

50

me, he's satisfied either way it rolls from here, as long as he doesn't catch any of the shrapnel. Any luck finding the guy who killed Patti Masters?"

Wisniewski shook his head. "She was having sex with someone in her office, usually between five and seven o'clock in the evening, after everyone had gone home and before the night janitor arrived. This week, though, she sent her secretary home an hour early, and the postmortem suggests she had sex about two hours before she died, which puts it between four-thirty and five-thirty."

"Meaning?" Tanney asked.

"Meaning her lover is available regularly between five and seven, but for some reason had to meet her early on Monday. It's a break in the pattern. We can use it to narrow the field of suspects. People who work second shift, for instance, we can probably rule out."

"Maybe the guy's married," McCool suggested. "His wife expects him home by seven. He hustles to the school as soon as he gets off work at five, bumps uglies with Masters, and heads home for dinner and an evening with the missus watching *Eight Is Enough* and *Charlie's Angels*."

"So why did he come early on Monday?" Wisniewski asked.

"He was expected home earlier," Tanney said.

"Which means he had to get off work early," Wisniewski said. "When we finally narrow the list of suspects, a married man who left work early on Monday is going to be an attractive candidate."

"Wait," McCool said. "You have a problem with that scenario. If the guy had to get home early, he didn't have time to get back to the school in time to kill Masters. Finding her lover might not lead to her killer."

"We're still speculating," Wisniewski said. "Tossing out every possibility. I'm with the chief on this one. I'd like to solve it before the shit hits the fan on Saturday."

SIX

Cars started to arrive in Choctaw on Friday night. Most of the occupants were disappointed to learn the closest motel other than the Choctaw Arms, which was packed with journalists, was across the county line, seventeen miles away. Tiny Choctaw had never set its cap on becoming a tourist attraction, and was unprepared for the onslaught of news trucks, social warriors, and curious people who descended on the town with the expectation of a spectacle the next day when Reverend Bishop Angeloe Teeter's demonstration paraded through town to the Town Hall.

Chief Tanney and Trent McCool watched the cars filter in from the flatlands from a bench in front of the police department.

"Gonna have to send someone out in the street to direct traffic soon," Tanney grumbled.

"They'll leave as soon as they find out we don't have enough parking," McCool said.

"Gonna be shitshow tomorrow."

"Any word from Wisniewski?"

"Poor guy's yanking his hair out."

"I'm not surprised. If I was putting it to Patti Masters, I'd be keeping my head down. Whoever the guy is must have figured out by now he's a prime suspect."

A school bus painted in dayglo colors lumbered by. The windows were open, and the smell of weed rolled out of them as it went past the police station.

"S'pose I oughta do something about that," Tanney said.

"Dibs on whatever you confiscate," McCool said.

"Too damn much paperwork. Thinkin' about retiring, Trent."

"Me too."

"You're only thirty."

"I can still think about it. My goal is to get so fat I can punch out at fifty, buy a little villa in Italy, and tell the rest of the world to ram it. But if it happened next week, I wouldn't complain."

"Could be next week for me, easy. Got a nice pension, fully vested. Got a sweet cabin up in the hills. Got no reason to keep humpin' around this town with a badge and a gun like Marshal fuckin' Dillon. This Andy Frye situation might be the last straw. I hate to see the kid go to prison."

A Chevy van drove by, the speakers blaring 'Uncle John's Band.'

"Should hand in my papers right now," Tanney said. "Watching this clusterfuck tomorrow is going to be a lot more fun than wrangling it."

———

The men of The Ridge weren't about to let young Andy Frye go down without a fight. Verble Justice quickly assembled a cadre of backwoods moonshiners, seven in all, and they planned to drive into Choctaw on Saturday morning and disrupt the preacher's demonstration any way they could.

They gathered around the campfire at The Ridge on Friday night to prepare for the next day. As they passed the jug around the circle, Verble looked solemnly from face to face.

"I don't want nobody gettin' killed tomorrow," he said. "Not on neither side. But if we fall, we know we are falling in the cause of what's right. Young Andy truly believed he saw a gun. He was threatened, and for that he should go to prison?"

A round of slurred '*no*' echoed off the trees surrounding the compound.

"This rabble-rouser preacher from the flatlands has no business poking his nose into our affairs. If he hadn't come to town, none of this would be happening. And now, he's bringing hundreds of hippies and Black Panthers and commie insurrectionists and miscegenists and God-knows-what to Choctaw to force the police chief and the mayor to hand over Andy like a common thief. The boy lost his chance for a fair trial the day the preacher drove into town."

"Want me to kill him for you, Verble?" Davy Reynolds said.

"Dig the wax outa your ears, Davy. I don't want anybody killin' anybody. Jeezum Crow, boy, you got sawdust for brains?"

"Then what are we goin' there for?" Harley McTavish asked.

"Because them flatlanders are tryin' to drown out the truth with their wicked chants and their overwhelming numbers. We are goin' there to show 'em decent people still stand behind our law enforcement officers. Andy is innocent until proven guilty, and no jungle-bunny preacher is gonna change that."

He paused and surveyed the group. He'd known each of them for decades. Each one had joined in the minute he asked. They were hard men, who lived roughshod lives, but they were trustworthy—if a little hotheaded. He'd take any one of them by his side in a fight.

"We're goin' down there because someone has to take Andy's side and speak for his rights."

"We takin' guns?" Davy asked.

"You can bet some of the flatlanders are. But leave your guns in the car trunks," Verble said. "We're not there for a fight, but we won't back off if one breaks out."

————

Ted Wisniewski watched his alarm clock wind toward seven o'clock. Stress had always hit him in his guts, and he'd awakened at four-fifteen with wrenching cramps that made him leap from bed and run to the bathroom, barely in time. Two more episodes had prevented him from getting back to sleep.

The doctor called it *functional* disorder. Nothing medically wrong down there, and they'd dug around enough to know. Even so, every once in a while, his intestines decided to pitch a hissy that could leave him curled in a fetal position in bed, mewling for cathartic relief. Wisniewski avoided trigger foods like raw onions and caffeine when he could, but stress and anxiety would still bring on an attack, and he had rarely been as stressed and anxious as he had been since the murder of Patti Masters.

The clock ticked over to six-fifty-five.

He rolled the interviews over in his mind for the thirtieth or fortieth time. Whoever Patti Masters was seeing in her office, she'd kept it a big secret. Her teenagers, understandably, were devastated, having been orphaned, and they weren't much help in pinning down the identity of her lover. Wisniewski had been cagey with his questions, since they probably didn't know she was having an affair, and laying unexpected heavies on grieving kids could be a disaster. Instead, he'd couched his questions in terms of *special friends* and *confidantes*, hoping the kids might know the identity of their mom's lover without knowing he *was* her lover.

Nothing. They named a few close female friends, but when Wisniewski asked about men, they blanked. The empty and lost expressions on their faces when he told them how sorry he was about their mother, for the fourth time, would haunt him for years. In a different world, had he been bolder, they might have met under entirely different circumstances. As it was, excusing himself and abandoning them to their profound grief had left him exhausted and crampy.

Even the supposedly close friends Patti's kids named knew little about her personal life beyond her immediate family. One of them, Ginger McLeod, met him at a coffeehouse in town. They sat at an outside table. She was a real estate agent around forty, athletic and smirky. She said her real name was Margaret, but everyone called her Ginger as a child because of her strawberry blonde hair, which she had long since bleached pure blonde. Her voice was sultry and husky. From ten feet away, she was a stunner. From across the table, the years and mileage showed. She said she had suspected Patti might be seeing someone because of the way she acted, but the question had never come up, and Patti hadn't offered to disclose.

"What do you mean, the way she acted?" Wisniewski asked.

She took out a cigarette and lit it. She held out the pack, but Wisniewski waved it away.

"Patti acted like a woman who was getting laid a lot after a long time not getting laid," she said.

"Could you elaborate?"

"She looked lighter. Bouncier. Hard to describe. It's part of the girl genetic code," she said, and blew a cloud of smoke toward the sky. "We can probably subconsciously smell it when a close sister is getting some. I don't know. The same way our periods synchronize."

"That's the second time I've heard that this week."

"It's a thing. I saw a film in college. Some guy laid out a hundred metronomes, all running at different rhythms. Within a minute, they had all synched up. It's like that."

She sucked a quarter inch off the end of her cigarette and turned her head to blow smoke toward the street.

"Patti's husband died..."

"Nine years ago. 1968. Tet Offensive. It was brutal. I hear they buried his boot or something. All they could recover."

She shuddered and took another drag. She hadn't touched her coffee.

"You suspected she had taken a lover recently, but you have no idea who it might be?"

"I probably should have asked, but Patti held her cards close to the vest. She didn't disclose much. I was happy for her. Life seems brighter when you're getting some. Don't you agree?"

"Well, I'm divorced, so..."

"Join the club, Slick. Hell. Half the people I know are divorced or widowed."

"If you don't know the name of the man she was seeing before she died, are you aware of any other men she'd slept with since her husband died?"

"Why do you ask?"

"People come and go in our lives. Old romances are rekindled. Maybe she had renewed an old affair."

"Oh, sure. I get it. Yeah, she slept with other guys. There were exactly two, but it won't help you much."

"Why?"

"They aren't local, and she hasn't seen either of them for quite a while. Patti told me about them. Principals go to a lot of educational conferences. She met both of them there, one in Milwaukee and the other in Atlanta. Alcohol was involved, and maybe some other stuff, but Patti was a school principal, so she didn't tell us *everything*. The first guy, in Milwaukee, was Greg. He and Patty hit it off in the bar, and she figured why not? The second, Atlanta, was Ralph. All I know about him is he was hung like Secretariat."

"So, one-night stands?"

"Hell, no. Like I said, she went to a *lot* of conferences. Half the time, one or the other would be there. If they were at the same con, they'd shack up."

"Good thing both men never attended the same conference," Wisniewski said.

"Who said they didn't? Philadelphia. Now that was one wild weekend, I hear. Patti rode the devil's tricycle. *I* haven't even tried that. But that was, oh, two or three years ago. She went into a bit of a drought afterward."

"I stood next to Patti in the church choir for three years," he said. "Now I'm thinking I never knew her at all."

"Your loss, Slick. Maybe." She pulled another cigarette from the pack. Her seductive moves were transparent, but chain smoking was a dealbreaker for Wisniewski.

"Neither of these two men ever came to Choctaw, though?"

"Oh, hell no," she said as she lit the cigarette. "How would they explain it to their wives?"

"Patti was open about her affairs at the conferences with you? From what you say, she shared all the details."

"She told me a lot. Plenty. Enough to make me moist once or twice."

"But she didn't tell you anything about the man she was seeing in her office."

"No."

"Any idea why?" he asked.

"No more than conjecture. Either it was someone who couldn't afford people to know he was shanking her—"

"Or someone she couldn't allow people to know about, because she'd get in trouble."

Ginger McLeod blew another cloud of smoke into the street.

"No reason it can't be both, Slick," she said.

Those last comments had kept Ted Wisniewski awake for most of the night, along with his—in hindsight—hasty rejection of Ginger McLeod's blatant advances. Half the night he wondered whom among Choctaw's men couldn't allow an affair to be divulged. The other side of the equation was easier. Maybe it was the Disco Age, and for the most part the worst thing you could catch from sex could be cured with a shot of antibiotics, but modern feminism had yet to creep widely into the Blue Ridge, and some archaic expectations for women's behavior were still deeply engrained in this insular community, especially expectations for women who worked with children. It was one thing for Patti Masters to indulge her inebriated hedonist serial impulses a thousand miles from home at a conference, among people she would likely never meet again. In Choctaw, North Carolina, in the ebb tide of the 1970s, social expectations for unattached women were still strongly bound to the Eisenhower era.

Of course, that didn't stop men from pursuing women they perceived as willing and easy. In Choctaw, the double standard was alive and thriving. If Ginger McLeod was right, and both Patti and her paramour had too much to lose to disclose their tryst, exposure might lead to the man's great discomfort and disgrace, but it could result in Patti Masters' ruin.

That was a hook he could work with. Patty had much more to lose in Choctaw than her lover. What if she tried to break it off to protect her reputation, and the guy wouldn't leave her alone? Maybe she threatened to tell people about him to get him off her back, and he took it personally.

Six-fifty-nine.

Ted slapped at the alarm button before it could rudely remind him he'd wasted most of the night bouncing around inside his own head.

It was Saturday morning.

The demonstration would begin at three.

He sighed and dragged himself from bed for a cold shower and a bucket of coffee.

SEVEN

The demonstrators organized at the Choctaw bus station, the largest public space in town other than the Town Hall complex. It was six blocks from the bus station to Town Hall, and Angeloe Teeter planned to speak at both locations.

Between the assembled protestors and the news crews from all over the Piedmont and beyond, Teeter's estimate of two or three hundred demonstrators had swollen half again. Nearly five hundred souls crowded into the half-mile main drag, their cars parked for a mile along the shoulders of the highway on either side of town. A pair of broken-down hippie-painted school buses shuttled four dozen people at a time into town.

Some of the people gathered were seasoned. Their signs were garish and professionally printed, featuring hastily enlarged images of Lester Corby's church directory photo, and slogans like *Justice for Corby!* and *'End Police Brutality Against Colored People!'*. Others carried signs scrawled in Magic Marker on poster paper in the car on the way to the demonstration. A mid-fifties Chevy panel truck parked across the street from the bus station. The owner rigged huge concert amplifiers on his roof, and played protest songs by people like Janis Ian, Crosby Stills and Nash, and Bob Dylan. The music revved the crowd, some of whom gathered in huge group hugs and sang along.

Reverend Bishop Angeloe Teeter watched from the steps of the bus station, and he was pleased. The turnout had surpassed his expectations.

As the clock neared three, Teeter signaled for the guy in the panel truck to cut the music. Another amplifier had been placed on the bus station steps, along with a microphone on a stand. Teeter stepped to the microphone, surveyed the crowd once again, and smiled.

"Welcome, friends!" he shouted. The crowd erupted in cheers, and Teeter—who had mastered crowd manipulation years earlier—waited patiently for their cheers to ebb. "I am deeply gratified to see so many people here today!" More cheers. "Only five days ago, a peaceful, unassuming black man named Lester Corby was gunned down by a white Choctaw police officer on his own front porch!"

Boos and catcalls. Teeter let them vent and held his hands up for quiet.

"I do not wish to make this about race," he continued. "But, in the end, all racial turmoil comes down to one issue. Who has the power?"

"The Man!" someone shouted in the crowd.

"In the broadest sense, yes. The Man has the power. But who is The Man?"

"Whitey!"

"Please! We're trying to solve problems, not make them worse. The Man is anyone who has power but uses it for his own ends instead of the general welfare. The most powerful people in this world wear badges and carry guns. They can go anywhere and do anything they want unless some higher power reins them in. If you give a man a gun, sooner or later he will use it, the way Andy Frye used his gun on Lester Corby on Monday night. We are assembled here to send a message to the people who run Choctaw, and the government of North Carolina, and to all the peoples of the world. *This…will…not…stand!*"

The crowd joined the chant immediately, spurred on by a cadre of Teeter's closest supporters.

"This…Will…Not…Stand!" they chanted, over and over, as Teeter stood on the bus station steps and conducted them like they were a symphony orchestra. The chants repeated for almost ten minutes, reverberating off the brick walls of the town buildings. Finally, as the rally lost intensity, Teeter stoked the flames again.

"We march today, because after three hundred years, a black man in America is still not safe on his own property. We march today, because rather than openly admit their own officer made a tragic mistake, the Choctaw police still maintain Lester Corby was at fault for his own death. We march today, because someone must speak for Lester Corby. We march today, because *we* speak for Lester Corby. Who speaks for Lester Corby?"

He held out the microphone, and the crowd, as one, shouted *"We do!"*

"Who speaks for Lester Corby?"

"We do!"

After five or six rounds, the mob was charged again. Teeter instinctively knew it was time to move.

"Now we march!" he shouted into the microphone. "We will march straight to Town Hall, where we will demand justice for Lester Corby! March, soldiers! March!"

Teeter stepped to the street, and five hundred strong fell into step behind him as he turned in the direction of Town Hall.

———

"Okay," Trent McCool told Mayor Roger Gimball and Chief Tanney. "Everything is in place."

They sat in Roger Gimball's office in the Town Hall. As it was an early autumn afternoon, the windows were open, and the sounds of the rally at the bus station wafted in. The crowd chanted *"This Will Not Stand"* over and over.

"The District Attorney is on board. If the SBI investigation determines Andy Frye acted in an irresponsible manner, the DA will charge him with negligent homicide."

"Homicide?" Tanney said.

"Believe it or not, the penalty is more lenient than manslaughter. Negligent homicide is what you charge someone with if they accidentally fry someone in the pool with a hair dryer."

"What kind of penalty?" Tanney asked.

"A year, maybe. Time off for good behavior. He'll spend it in the segregated cop pop, away from the rest of the prisoners."

"He'd be done as a cop," Tanney said.

"He was done the minute he pulled the trigger," Gimball said. "We'd like it to be otherwise, but there was no way Andy Frye was ever going to wear a badge again, unless he's a night watchman or mall cop."

"It'll kill him," Tanney said.

"No it won't," McCool said. "It'll fuck him up a lot, but he's young. He'll recover."

Gimball scowled at McCool. "Were you born a dick, or did you acquire it along the way?"

"If you want, I can call Hiram Lane out of retirement to take my place today. I figure his oxygen tank will hold out long enough."

"Fuck it," Gimball said. "None of us looks good in this thing. How will it go?"

"In about ten minutes, Teeter and his mob will arrive at the Town Hall. He's going to make a nice rabble-rousing speech on the front steps and get the crowd good and riled. Then you and Chief Tanney walk out the front door and join him."

"They aren't going to throw shit, are they?" Gimball asked. "This is my best suit."

"No promises. Anyway, you're going to pacify the crowd by giving them exactly what they want."

"Andy Frye. On a platter." Tanney dug under his ribcage, as if he was massaging an ulcer.

"For them, it'll feel that way. You announce the investigation by the SBI is ongoing. Make them the bad guys if you want. Suggest the state boys are dragging their heels. Tell them the SBI will determine whether Andy was negligent, but you, as the proactive public servant you are, have unilaterally approached the county DA to discuss charges, and the DA has agreed to a potential charge of negligent homicide. You're the hero here. You're getting justice for Lester Corby."

"And if the SBI decides it was a righteous shoot?" Tanney asked.

"Then Andy Frye needs to move to Vegas and become a pro gambler," McCool said. "Nobody's that lucky."

"He's right," Gimball told Tanney. "One way or the other, Andy's going down."

Tanney said, "I'll type my resignation and have it on your desk first thing in the morning."

Gimball stared at the chief. "Are you serious?"

"I'm done, Roger," Tanney said. "Part of me wants to pack it in right this minute and go fishing, but I won't do that to you or to Choctaw, not with the mess outside. I'll ride this out with you today, but afterward, you need to look for a new police chief."

"You know how that'll look," McCool said.

"How?"

"Like you're taking the heat for Lester Corby's shooting. Like it was partly your fault."

"So?" Tanney said. "Nobody here is who they're pretending to be. Why should I be different?"

————

Ted Wisniewski stood in his third-floor office window at the police station next to Town Hall and watched the mob of protestors approach from the direction of the bus station. He was alternately groggy from lack of sleep and jagged out from caffeine which he knew would gnaw at his gut later, and he wasn't entirely certain he was perceiving the world correctly.

Movement on the other side of the Town Hall caught his attention. Three trucks had parked illegally in the loading zone in front of the hardware store. Nobody cared today, because cars were parked illegally all over town, and with Andy Frye and Ozzie Sanderson on suspension there was a shortage of officers to write tickets. The sheriff's deputies and highway patrol officers were disinclined to take up the town's slack, being primarily charged with controlling the protesters.

As the din of the crowd marching from the bus station reached Town Hall, the truck doors opened, and six men stepped out to the sidewalk. Wisniewski recognized the men from their bimonthly forays out of the hills for supplies. They were dressed in camo fatigues and wore military-style bush hats. They huddled together on the sidewalk for a few seconds, apparently discussing something, and a tall man among them pointed in the direction of the approaching crowd.

Folks from The Ridge had never caused trouble in Choctaw, mostly because they were so seldom there. Wisniewski had encountered his share of backwoodsmen and knew them to be—in general—bigoted, short-tempered, and impulsive. Some were more than a little crazy. Their general cantankerousness was one of the reasons they eschewed polite society and chose instead to live back in the trees.

These men were unpredictable and potentially dangerous, and the fact they had arrived in Choctaw on this of all days did not make him happy. He grabbed the phone and dialed the mayor's office.

"You still planning to go out there?" he asked when Gimball answered.

"Of course. Why?"

"I see a bunch of hillbillies out in the street, squatters from The Ridge. Getting a bad feeling. Put Chief Tanney on."

Gimball handed the receiver to Tanney.

"Yeah?"

"Did you tell me once Andy Frye lived at The Ridge when he was a kid?" Wisniewski asked.

"His mother took him away when he was nine or ten. Why?"

"There's a gaggle of Ridge squatters collected across the street, in front of the hardware. They look unhappy. I cannot imagine their presence today is a coincidence."

"I hear you. I'll call the Highway Patrol commandant and see if he can concentrate some more troopers in the center of town, in case these guys get jumpy."

"Ten-four. I'm gonna try to eavesdrop on them, see if I can figure out what they want."

"Be careful," Tanney said. "These guys don't like cops much."

"I'm in street clothes, and I'll keep my distance."

———

Verble Justice gathered his Ridge compatriots next to the middle truck. A station wagon with a stoved-in driver's door parked behind the trucks. A seventh man climbed out the side window and joined them.

"I got the guns in the back of the wagon," Buford Claggett said. "They're under a tarp if we need 'em."

"Only as a last resort," Justice said. "We're here to support Andy, not start a riot. We only shoot *back*. Got it?"

Buford nodded, but didn't tell Justice about the Colt Python he carried in a holster in the small of his back underneath the tail of his flannel work shirt.

Reverend Teeter's followers were only two blocks away now, marching slowly and chanting. They stood shoulder-to-shoulder, from one gutter to the other, choking Main Street as they made their way toward Town Hall.

"Damn," Davy Reynolds said. "That's a shit-ton of people, Verble."

"I didn't expect there'd be so many," Justice said. "Buford, keep the wagon tailgate unlocked if you would."

"Already done,' Claggett said. "Jesus, Verble. You think we brought enough guns?"

———

Ted Wisniewski crossed Main Street in front of the police station, continued one street over, and returned to Main Street so he could approach the mountain men from behind. Easier to listen in that way.

By the time he reached them, the crowd had arrived in front of Town Hall. Reverend Teeter mounted the steps to a microphone stand, and he held up his hands to silence the chants. Within seconds, the mob grew quiet.

"I stand here, on this beautiful afternoon," he said, as his voice boomed over amplifiers and echoed off the storefronts of Main Street, "to remember a man of peace. I wish to tell you about a family man, a man whose entire life was built around his wife and children and his Lord. A man of the cloth in his youth, who traveled from pillar to post to share the Gospel and found his own salvation in a small town that embraced him and his family like prodigal children. This man was Lester Corby, who never harmed a fly in his entire seventy years, and who even came out of retirement to serve the children of Choctaw as a school maintenance engineer. Lester Corby was a rare man, my friends. Lester Corby was loved by everyone who knew him, which is why we are so deeply and profoundly shocked by his murder, so much so we have traveled from all over North Carolina and surrounding states to remember this man, and to demand the man who shot him in cold blood receive the consequences he deserves!"

The throng, after hours of building tension, burst into cheers and shouts for justice for Lester Corby.

"Make no mistake!" Teeter continued when at last his massive flock settled. "This is a tragedy for everyone involved. We harbor no anger or hatred toward the officer who needlessly took Lester Corby's life. By all accounts, he is a decent man who made a horrible decision in a moment of fear and confusion. But that does not absolve him of responsibility!"

"No!" someone in the multitude shouted. "Make him pay!"

The mob hooted and yelled their approval.

"Hold him *accountable,*" Teeter corrected. "We are people of the law, and the law will determine the fate of the man who killed Lester Corby. Our mission today is to remind the authorities in Choctaw that the law applies to *every* man, regardless of the color of his skin or the contents of his heart. All we ask is justice for Lester Corby!"

On cue, Teeter's shills in the crowd chanted *"Justice for Lester Corby!"* The convergence picked it up, and within seconds five hundred people strong chanted *"Justice for Lester Corby!"*

Teeter, knowing this was the moment, stepped back from the microphone and basked in his accomplishment. Behind him, the Town Hall doors opened. Mayor Roger Gimball and Police Chief Elbert Tanney stepped outside and descended the steps. Gimball shook hands with Teeter and stepped to the microphone.

"I'm Roger Gimball, mayor of Choctaw," he said. Immediately, about half the pack booed. Gimball patiently waited for them to quiet enough for him to be heard, and he said, "I'm here today to provide an update on the investigation into—"

Gimball never finished the sentence. From across the street, someone hurled a lighted M-80 firecracker toward the Town Hall steps. It exploded before it hit the ground, and people immediately in front of the steps recoiled in panic, fearing they were being fired on from above. Two more cherry bombs sailed in from the perimeter and fell inside the crowd, and in seconds people were screaming and running in every direction, trampling one another.

"Good God, boys, them Commies are tryin' to kill the mayor!" Verble Justice yelled. Four of the men dashed around to open the rear of the station wagon. Buford Claggett yanked the Colt Python from his holster and waded into the crowd, looking for anyone with a gun.

One of the protestors saw Claggett's revolver and shouted, "There's the shooter!"

Two other protestors pulled cheap revolvers from their jeans. Before Claggett could respond, one of them shot him twice. One bullet hit him high in the chest and missed most vital organs, but the other gut shot severed the abdominal aorta and killed him in seconds.

Screaming people ran in both directions from Town Hall, pushing each other out of the way. Somewhere down the street, a storefront window shattered as a protestor threw a trash can through it. Chief Tanney grabbed Mayor Gimball and Reverend Teeter by the jacket sleeves and dragged them up the steps to safety, Teeter protesting all the way. As soon as they were inside Town Hall and the outer doors were locked behind them, Tanney clutched at his chest and leaned back against the wall. Slowly, he lowered himself to the marble floor and sat, red-faced, staring blankly into space as he huffed and tried to draw air into his lungs.

Verble Justice and his men grabbed shotguns and semiautomatic rifles and pistols from the back of the station wagon. Ted Wisniewski took his own service weapon out and approached them.

"Choctaw Police!" he shouted in his best authoritative voice they had taught at the academy. "Return your weapons to the vehicle."

Gunshots barked from the crowd. People screamed and ran past in a panic, distracting him. One of the men from The Ridge snuck behind Wisniewski and slammed the butt of a Mossberg pump shotgun into his back, at the base of his neck. Wisniewski crumpled to the ground, still conscious but stunned and temporarily paralyzed.

Verble Justice saw Buford Claggett lying in the street, mortally wounded, and he wailed at the sky in fury.

"They done killed Buford!" he called to his partners. "Open season on Commies, boys!"

———

The Choctaw Shootout led the national news that evening. Television news crews from all over the state captured it, and by six o'clock film had been loaded to every station in the country.

Protestors and mountain men both believed the other side started the shooting, but in the end, they wound up shooting at each other. As hundreds of protestors and curious Choctaw residents fled in terror, a small cadre of armed demonstrators faced six seasoned hillbillies with shotguns, semi rifles, and handguns.

By the time the Highway Patrol troopers swept in and put an end to it, five demonstrators and Buford Claggett lay dead in the streets. Dozens more had been injured in the mad scramble away from Town Hall, some of them trampled by the mob. Verble Justice took a nine-millimeter round in the hip, and he never walked right again, but he survived, as did the other five backwoodsmen who were also shot.

You had to dig down several paragraphs in the newspaper accounts the next day to discover Choctaw Police Chief Elbert Tanney had died later in the evening in the hospital fifteen miles away after suffering a heart attack dragging Roger Gimball and Angeloe Teeter up the Town Hall steps to safety.

You had to drill down even further to discover Choctaw Police Detective Edward Wisniewski had suffered career-ending injuries in the shootout when he was struck with a shotgun butt that fractured a cervical vertebra and left him with tingling and numbness in his arms and hands that would never completely disappear, and he tended to call things by the wrong names now.

The mountain men did time, but not much. After their release they returned to The Ridge and their reclusive brethren who had not been incarcerated, and their lives continued much the way they had before the killing of Lester Corby.

Andy Frye served eight months in a segregated population at a minimum-security unit in the Sandhills. After his release he also vanished into the mountains surrounding Choctaw to join the people of The Ridge.

Ironically, reporters mistakenly interpreted the mad dash up the Town Hall steps as the mayor and Teeter rescuing a faltering and stricken Chief Tanney, instead of the opposite truth, which only enhanced Reverend Teeter's reputation and national fame. Mayor Gimball ran for Congress the next cycle and won, for the same reason.

With Elbert Tanney dead and Ted Wisniewski permanently incapacitated, the investigation into the murder of Patti Masters languished for a while, and with the passage of time it was forgotten altogether.

ACT TWO

THE BLADE

EIGHT

Forty-Five Years Later

Tim McCool watched the Hunter Moon rise like a giant spotlighted orange over the gorge separating the twin ridges of Choctaw Knob and Blind Top, north of Choctaw, North Carolina. State Senator Carl Royster shanked golf balls from the makeshift carpet tee he'd installed beyond the patio of his chalet cabin into the par three course he'd built in the valley. Between swings, Royster sang verses of Merle Travis's *Dark As The Dungeon* in a surprisingly impressive baritone voice.

> *It's Dark as the Dungeon*
> *And damp as the dew;*
> *Where danger is double,*
> *And pleasures are few...*

"…Goddamn. Sliced it again."

Darrell Tanney slouched on a chaise several feet away. His left hand rested on the neck of a twelve-year-old asthmatic one-balled bulldog named Waylon Jennings, who stared almost without reaction as Royster wildly swung his Big Bertha driver, launching balls in random trajectories all over the valley. Tanney's right hand cradled a glass of Pappy Van Winkle already obscenely diluted by melted ice. His eyes were slit shut, and he didn't give a damn where the balls landed as long as they didn't fall on him.

"Can't figure out what I'm doing wrong," Royster said. "Whaddaya think, Darrell?"

"You asking about golf, I can't help you, sir. Never swung nothing but a baseball bat and a truncheon in my whole life. If I was to hazard a guess, though, I'd say your balance is thrown all off kilter because of them five bourbons you drank at dinner. 'Course, nothing but a guess, like I said."

Tanney was a North Carolina state patrolman, assigned more or less permanently to special security detail for Royster. The assignment was made by Royster's cousin Thad, a superior court judge who, with good reason, believed the Senator needed closer supervision after a couple of DWIs and a near-disastrous encounter when he was caught pulling his pud while driving next to a school bus carrying a girls' high school softball team to the state finals in Raleigh.

Waylon Jennings wheezed, groaned, and rolled over, hoping Darrell Tanney would scratch his belly. If so, he was to be sorely disappointed, as Tanney snored softly after placing the glass on a table next to the chaise.

"So," Tim McCool said. "Are we gonna discuss this Winlock Savage situation, or what?"

"What's to discuss?" Royster said, as he centered another ball on the pad. "There is no fighting the guy who saved Choctaw's ass. Best thing is to lay still and think of England, son."

"Don't call me that. I have a dad."

"Yeah. Where is Trent anyway?"

"Fuckin' Aruba," McCool said. "Honeymoon with number five. I think she was born about the time I graduated junior high."

"Speaking of which, how's Babs?"

"Mom? She's fine. Wants nothing to do with Choctaw, but that's understandable. She has her Park Avenue paradise and an open account at Bergdorf's. She's happy."

"I should drop by next time I'm in Manhattan."

"The line to her apartment forms in the lobby. About Win Savage."

Royster swung and topped the ball, sending it skittering across the lawn and over the edge into the valley. "Shit. Whatever. These balls are drunk anyway."

He casually tossed the graphite club over his shoulder and shambled over to the bar.

"Here's how I see it," McCool said. "Ever since I-40 was moved thirty miles south, Choctaw's been doomed. We're way out of the way for anyone trying to get from one end of the state to the other. We're withering on the vine. Our…um…tragic history only made matters worse."

"Win Savage helped turn it around."

"Yeah, well, this new ski resort on Choctaw Knob could be our salvation. Give people a reason to come to Choctaw again."

"Be a lot cheaper to change the town's name," Royster said.

"If Win Savage gets his way, that might be our only option. Fuckin' elitist environmentalist tree-huggin' douche. Has more money than God and doesn't know how tough it is for all the rest of us scrambling for scraps at the base of Mount fuckin' Olympus."

"That's your mother in you," Royster said. "Babs was always a hothead. Your dad, now. If he'd been in charge of the Nixon White House, Haldeman, Ehrlichman, Mitchell, and Liddy would've gone over a cliff in a flaming van full of audiotapes. End of story. Trent McCool got shit done."

"And he did time for it in the end."

"Not much. And now he's seventy-six years old, partying in Aruba with a hard-bodied twenty-five-year-old who can suck a peach pit through a hypodermic needle. Don't tell me crime don't pay."

"There's nothin' on Choctaw Knob to protect anyway. Won't hurt a thing to carve a few ski runs out of it. But noooo…Everybody's All American has to butt in, says we're stripping the Knob of its natural splendor in worship of the almighty dollar."

"He's right," Royster said. "Don't forget that."

"Being right isn't putting Choctaw back on the map, and it's not putting any money in my pocket," McCool steamed.

"Why don't you kill him?" Royster said.

"Not funny."

"You can kill him or negotiate with him. He can't own everything. I'm sure there's something he wants."

Darrell Tanney roused, and his head swiveled around, leaving a pool of saliva on his shirt front. "We killin' someone?" he slurred.

"False alarm," Royster said. "You can go back to sleep."

"A'right," Tanney mumbled. Seconds later, he snored softly again.

"Sometimes I wish I was an evil person," McCool said.

"No time like the present to start," Royster said.

―――――

At that exact moment, Winlock Savage, the savior of Choctaw, was balls-deep inside Taylor Pettigrew, who straddled him on a chaise next to his pool and demonstrated the form that had won a bronze medal in women's gymnastics at the Olympics. She gazed into his hazel eyes as she bucked and ground against him, the intensity growing until she slammed her eyes shut, gripped his shoulders, tensed, and collapsed with a loud cry, gasping as she brought him off at the same time.

She fell against him, her bronze skin sweating and slick against him. Like most gymnasts, she was like a three-quarter-sized human, almost tiny in his arms. Her long acrylic nails raked gently at his chest, and her trademark shaved head nestled against his neck.

"Damn," she said. "I like the way you negotiate."

"Negotiating? This was only the icebreaker."

"Fuck you, Savage. Going for a dip."

She pulled away from him, walked naked around the pool to the one meter diving board, took a single bounce, and executed a perfect flip before entering the water with scarcely a ripple.

At sixty-three, Winlock Savage still displayed the recognizable physique that had carried him to a trivia-question Super Bowl win four decades earlier, and a long career as a sports broadcaster after his legs and arm went south. Strands of gray had invaded his chest hair, and the finely chiseled lines of his body had begun to blur slightly as nature and time had its way with him, but he still got a carbon steel diamond cutter without the help of any little blue pills. Taylor Pettigrew had assured him he was the hottest sexagenarian piece of meat she knew, and among the top five across all ages, which was nice to hear.

Taylor surfaced and swam gracefully to the edge.

"Coming in?"

His cellphone vibrated. He pointed toward it.

"In a minute," he said.

She swam toward an inflatable raft in the middle of the pool.

"Savage," he said, answering the phone. When he heard the voice on the other end, his forehead furrowed, and his face darkened. "Hold on."

He left Taylor in the pool and padded through the sliding door from the lanai into his room. He tossed on a robe and sat on the bed.

"I have a visitor. Wanted to get somewhere private. What is it?" He listened patiently, and said, "I can't help it. Of course, I'll try, but in the end it's entirely out of my hands."

The person on the other side raised their voice.

"Wait," he said. "I didn't say it couldn't be done. It's not up to me...Because it isn't. Other people make that decision...Sure...That's dangerous. If anyone found out..."

The person on the other end got wordy. Savage felt pressure build behind his eyes, and the tinnitus that had plagued him for forty years, ever since the vicious headbutt at Green Bay, grew in intensity.

"All right," he said, at last. The fatigue and resignation in his voice weighed heavy in the room. "I'll do what I can."

Whatever the other person said next bothered Savage intensely. He tossed the phone on the table when he walked back out to the lanai. Without a word, he ditched the robe, cannonballed into the pool, and nearly swamped Taylor, who was floating on the raft.

"Good news or bad news?" she asked as he surfaced and swam toward her.

"There's a difference?" he asked.

———

Fred Tinsley had been mayor of Choctaw for almost a decade and had already decided not to run for office at the next cycle. He wasn't particularly political, had never cared much for public policy, and found most meetings boring. He had only run in the first place because one of his most hated high school classmates had decided to run for the other party, and Fred knew the entire town would turn to shit if the other guy won.

Turned out nobody else liked the other guy, either, and Fred Tinsley won in a landslide, and won again at the next election. His third term nearly half over, he'd had enough.

Fred Tinsley was a quiet, reserved, fiscally conservative tax accountant. He liked schedules and numbers and frequent isolation. He'd have been a completely incompetent politician in any community where everybody didn't already know everybody else, because he hated meeting new people. His only saving grace in Choctaw was he did almost everybody's taxes—at least those who didn't foolishly do their own—and all of his customers wanted to stay on his good side, so they voted for him.

He was where he always was on a weekday, cocooned in his tax office on Main Street, hiding from every person he could. He found the classical station from Davidson on the radio and allowed a slightly crackling Sibelius to soothe him as he tackled yet another row of comforting numbers.

His telephone rang, disrupting his reverie, and he cursed—mildly—as he punched the connect button.

"What is it?" he asked Margaret McLeod, one of the Council members.

"We're being sued."

"What? Who?"

"The Council, among others. Tim McCool. You. Me."

"Over what?"

"The Choctaw Knob ski resort. Fucking Win Savage decided to take the town to court to stop it."

"Language, Margaret."

"Fuck that shit. I'm on a tight margin as it is. I don't need a court settlement hanging over my head. Neither do you. Why in hell doesn't Savage buy the damn Knob and keep it for himself, if he doesn't want it developed?"

"Why bother, if he can save the money by suing us out of developing it? If he wins, he'll probably ask for legal costs as well. This sounds like a delaying tactic, though. He knows the funding for the Choctaw Knob project is time-sensitive, and he has the resources to lay the town to legal siege until the clock runs out."

"What a bastard."

"I didn't even like him when he was a football player," Tinsley said.

"Try getting dumped by him in high school, right before Homecoming," Margaret said.

"Really? You never told me."

"Another story for another time. What do we do?"

"Normally, we'd get Tim McCool to litigate the case, but he's a defendant," he said.

"What about his dad?"

"Trent? Out of the country."

"On the lam?" she asked.

Tinsley chuckled. "No. Honeymoon, for another week or so. I can ask him. Took him twenty years to get his law license reinstated. Might as well put it to good use. He won't come cheap."

"Fuckin' Win Savage," Margaret said, and Fred Tinsley winced again. "I should have busted his fuckin' kneecap back in high school. He'd be running a fuckin' Dairy Queen now instead of being a pain in my ovaries. Sometimes I feel like Dolly Parton in *9 to 5*. We ought to round up a posse of cowpokes to kick the livin' shit out of him."

"That's not the answer."

"No. Now the only way to stop him is to kill him."

"Don't say that," Tinsley said. "I don't like talk about violence."

"Sorry," she said.

"On the other hand," Tinsley said. "Despite what he's done for Choctaw, I've about had it with Savage's incessant goody-two-shoes meddling. While I might not wish him ill, I believe I would read his obituary with great relish."

———

Gaby Reyes was furious. Win Savage had avoided her for weeks, and she was not going to stand for it.

With a two-day break in her recording schedule in Nashville, she boarded a plane to Asheville and drove directly to Choctaw to confront Savage and demand to know why he had ghosted her. She'd arranged for a limo at the airport, and with nothing to do in the backseat during the hour-long drive except stew and drink, she was ready to fight when the limo finally turned into the quarter-mile drive leading to Winlock Savage's house on Blind Top, overlooking the Choctaw Valley.

She banged on the door several times. Finally, it opened, and Gaby prepared to bull her way inside, only to find a bald bronze munchkin standing in her path.

"Aren't you Gaby Reyes?" Taylor Pettigrew asked. She wore a few strips of translucent yellow cloth that aspired to be a bikini someday. Her voice was high, but decidedly not giggly. "Wow. Want some blow?"

"What?" Reyes asked.

"Win's in the shower. I was doing a couple of lines. Want some?"

"Who are you?"

"Taylor!" She held out her hand. "I'm so excited to meet you! I love your music."

"Win's in the shower?" Reyes asked.

"Yeah. He'll be out in few minutes."

"Who are you again?"

Taylor smiled. "Oh, yeah. I work for Aries Sporting Goods. They sent me out to negotiate the terms of Win's endorsement contract renewal."

"Looks like he's taking you to the cleaners."

"We were relaxing. How do you know Win?"

"Excuse me," Reyes said as she pushed past Taylor into the house and walked directly back to Win's bedroom. She took one look at the tousled sheets on the bed and the scattered clothes on the floor, peeked in at Win in the shower, and flushed the toilet. Savage yelped as the water turned scalding.

"Bastard!" Reyes slammed the bathroom door. She stamped back into the living room, where Taylor stood holding her cell phone.

"Can I get a selfie?" she asked.

"You're shitting me, right?"

Taylor's eyes were glassy and dilated as she shook her head. "I don't think so."

"You don't know about me and Win?"

Taylor shook her head again. "What? You're together?"

"We *were*," Reyes said. "Run me out a couple lines of that shit, honey. You and I need to talk."

"We do?"

"Is this the way you negotiate?" Reyes asked. She hoovered the line Taylor cut for her and winced, snorted a couple of times, and pinched her nose. "Fuck Win. He always has the best shit. Yes. Win and I are together. Or we were until I walked in here and found *you*."

"Oh, we're not dating or anything," Taylor said.

"Just fucking, then?"

"It's cazh. If I had any idea you and he were together, I'd never have done it. He didn't say a word."

"Bullshit."

"For serious. I've had guys step out on me before. It sucks. If it helps, I'm sorry. Sounds like your beef is with Win."

Win walked into the room, wearing a pair of running shorts. His hair hung in wet ringlets around his face.

"Oh, shit," he said, when he saw Gaby and Taylor.

Gaby opened her purse and took out a small nickel-plated thirty-eight caliber pistol sporting a nacre handle. She pointed it at Win Savage's crotch.

"Um…hi, Babe," he said.

"Are we together or not?" she asked.

"I'll relax by the pool," Taylor said. "You guys have things to discuss."

When she was gone, Win sat on the sofa. Gaby Reyes' pistol followed him.

"It's complicated," he said.

"Uncomplicate it," she said.

"Okay, so it's not so complicated. You're never here. When we're under the same roof, it's great, but that happens less and less these days."

"I have obligations. I have tour dates and recording sessions and a thousand little bullshit PR appearances."

"Yes," he said.

"My career didn't end a decade ago the way yours did."

"You're being intentionally hurtful now," he said.

"I should shoot your balls off."

"I'd be grateful if you didn't," he said. "C'mon, Gaby. Admit it. You've been dissatisfied lately. Same as me."

The gun lowered a few inches. "Because I know you're sleeping around anytime I'm not in your line of sight. I came to find out what in hell is going on, and Tinkerbell out there proved me right."

"My attraction to you hasn't changed," he said. "Neither have my feelings for you. But, when you get right down to it, does monogamy work for either of us?"

"Those words just roll out of your mouth, don't they? How many times have you played this scene, Win? You make me want to kill you," she said. "You make me want to wipe you off the face of the Earth."

"I see three ways this ends," Savage said. "One, you shoot me, Taylor calls the cops, and you go to jail. Two, you *don't* shoot me, and we go on the way we have been—I'm all yours when we're together. Three, you admit we are not intended for happy-ever-after, you put the gun away, and the three of us open a bottle of wine and have a lovely evening together, and tomorrow we go our separate ways. I should say, I find you holding a gun on me sexy for some reason. Any idea why?"

She pulled the trigger. The little pistol popped and jerked, and a tuft of fiberfill blew out the back of Savage's leather sofa and swirled in the air before floating to the rug.

"Jesus!" Savage said. "I felt that go by. You have any idea how much this couch costs?"

"Fourth way this ends," Gaby said. "My father taught me to shoot a rifle and a pistol almost before I could walk. Five feet or a hundred fifty yards, it doesn't matter. I hit what I aim for. Enjoy your playtime with Thumbelina, Win. I have joined the legion of scorned women, and you have no idea what I'm capable of."

She walked out the front door and slammed it behind her.

"That was intense," Taylor said.

"I thought so, too, the first time," he said. "Never fall in love with a crazy person."

NINE

The best thing Willard 'Chuck' Hogan's father ever did was teach him how to smoke meat. His father's hobby had become Chuck's obsession and livelihood. While his father, a carpenter, had hoped his son might follow in his footsteps, Chuck had opted for a culinary program at the local community college.

The Chuckwagon Smokehouse was the best place for Western Carolina barbeque between Asheville and Charlotte. Barbeque wars had long since taken their place in the pantheon of Tar Heel quasi-religious feuds, alongside the Tobacco Road Rivalry between Duke and Carolina and the ongoing dispute regarding the outcome of The Recent Unpleasantness.

On a single drive from New Bern on the coast to Murphy on the Tennessee border, you could encounter separate and distinct barbeque cultures, from vinegar and pepper-only sauces mopped over whole hog carcasses that the east adored and the westerners considered an abomination, to the tomato-based dips and chopped pork shoulders from Lexington to points west, which everyone agreed had their place, as long as they didn't get pushy about it.

Chuck Hogan was an acknowledged master of the Western Rite of Carolina Barbeque, as he referred to it, a term he had lifted from the marquee outside a Masonic temple in Asheville. Whether it was pork shoulder, turkey breast, spareribs and baby backs, or even brisket—which almost nobody in North Carolina cared much about, but tourists from the southwest adored for some reason—Chuck smoked the best for miles around.

In the days when it appeared the four-lane running past Choctaw might eventually be converted into an interstate highway, Hogan had expanded his squat, whitewashed cinder block restaurant, and had installed a brand-new smokehouse in the rear. The smokehouse was made of stone reclaimed from several abandoned outbuildings on farms in the area, built on a poured concrete floor with a four-foot-wide, two-feet-deep pit intended for smoldering hickory logs and chuck charcoal and fruitwood chips. Massive beams set ten feet over the floor held long steel hooks on either side of the cinder trench, on which Chuck hung country hams for indirect smoking. Chicken wire racks along the outside walls held shoulders and half-carcasses. Chuckwagon Smokehouse Christmas hams were a tradition in hundreds of homes across the Blue Ridge, and he was sorely tasked each year to meet the ever-increasing demand.

Several years earlier, after reading an article in Popular Science Magazine, Chuck had undertaken to modernize his operation. He cleaned the pit of the accumulated ash and fats and installed a series of electric heaters that were controlled by a computer in Chuck's office to maintain a steady temperature of two-hundred-twenty-five degrees inside the smokehouse. Smoke was provided by a hickory pellet burner that piped the smoke in from outside the building, to prevent raising the temperature. Chuck would load the entire next day's supply of pork shoulders onto racks inside the smokehouse each night, fill the pellet hopper, set the temperature, and go home to sleep through the night as the shoulders slowly cooked. An alarm would alert him at home if the temperature inside the smokehouse ever dropped below two hundred degrees. With his fancy new high-tech smokehouse, Chuck had completely eliminated the need for a hired hand to monitor the smoking overnight, and Chuck's sleep had benefitted greatly from the innovation.

By almost any definition, meat had made Chuck Hogan a prosperous man.

Not surprisingly, Chuck Hogan had never married. He'd had his share of brief affairs, but no warm, red-blooded woman could ever give him the satisfaction of a perfectly smoked pork shoulder that fell apart the second you put a fork to it, which sometimes made Chuck Hogan wonder whether he might be slightly aberrant.

Curiously, when he woke on Saturday morning, he hadn't the slightest apprehension or misgiving at all. In fact, he felt pretty damned good, all things considered. The arthritis in his back and shoulders, brought on by decades of hoisting fifty-pound hunks of meat, was remarkably quiet. Saturday was traditionally the busiest day of the week at Chuck's, which meant he'd be depositing a fat moneybag at the bank later in the day. The prospect always brought a smile to his face.

The shoulders he'd stacked on the chicken-wire shelves would be nearly cooked through, the ligaments and gristle melted into collagen, ready to be pulled, sliced, and chopped for the day's customers. Same for the turkey breasts he'd stashed slightly farther back in the corners, to keep them from drying out.

The sky glowed pink over Choctaw Knob as he pulled into the gravel lot outside the Chuckwagon Smokehouse, the sun peeking over the eastern horizon. As he did each day, he glanced at the chimney over the smokehouse, and was gratified to see heat shimmers and wisps of charcoal smoke wafting from under the rain shield at the top of the chimney. He could smell the aroma of smoked pork in the air. It was the most amazing perfume he'd ever known.

He pulled out his keys to open the padlock that secured the thick oak smokehouse door, but stopped when he saw the lock was already open.

"Huh," he said. In the morning chill, his breath hung in front of his face, slowly dissipating as he tried to recall whether he'd fastened the lock the night before. Nothing looked disturbed. He cursed himself lightly for getting old and absent-minded, and he swung open the heavy door. Heat rolled out of the opening, condensing immediately into a fog that coated Chuck's glasses. He stepped inside to check the progress of the meat he'd stacked the night before. He wiped his glasses with his shirttail and put them back on.

Seconds later, he slammed the smokehouse door and, gasping, dashed to the restaurant. He dropped the keys twice before he managed to unlock the front door and dropped them again running for the telephone. He dialed nine-one-one and gasped for air as his vision dimmed from hyperventilating.

"Police! Ambulance!" he cried when a dispatcher answered. "The Chuckwagon Smokehouse, on the Choctaw Pike. Somebody done hung a human body on a hook in my smokehouse!"

TEN

Wade 'The Blade' Durham had planned this hit for almost two weeks.

Junior French Junior had it coming.

"Payback's a bitch," Wade whispered as he watched Junior Junior draw closer. Inch by inch, Wade approached Junior until they were only a foot or so apart. Junior had to know Wade was back there, and what was coming. If he did, he didn't show it. Junior didn't swerve left or right to avoid him, which suited Wade fine. He had rehearsed this moment a hundred times over the last weeks, as he lay in bed, wide awake at two in the morning, contemplating his revenge.

A bump-and-run was the only fitting retaliation for what Junior did to him two weeks earlier, and a bump-and-run was what Junior was going to get.

With ten laps to go, and two thousand dollars in winner's money on the line, every fan at Hickory Speedway in the Carolina foothills anticipated a reprise of the wreck between Junior and Durham two weeks earlier. Durham had been out front that time, and on the last lap Junior tagged his left rear bumper as they arced into Turn One, spinning him into the outside wall. Instead of hoisting the trophy and pocketing the prize money, Durham finished fifteenth, and towed home to complete a couple of thousand dollars' worth of repairs on his car.

In southern stock car racing, the full contact motorsport, what goes around comes around, and tonight the wheel was going to stop on Junior Junior's number.

Hickory Speedway, which touted itself as the birthplace of NASCAR legends, hosted a weekly series featuring the Super Late Model stock cars. With their chopped, offset, wide-track bodies, foot-wide tires, and fire-breathing small block Chevy engines, Super Late Models were throwbacks to the original *'run what ya brung'* days of bootleggers who carved a track out of the Carolina red clay to see whose revenooer-beating car was the hottest.

Calling them *stock cars* was a joke, since few parts had ever been seen on a car in a dealer's showroom. His Chevy rode so low, Wade Durham's butt sat less than four inches from the asphalt. When he stood next to the car, the roof came barely above his waist. Supers were scary, overpowered, bestial machines, and one of the hottest rides on earth you could take with clothes on.

It was the final race of the season at Hickory, and the championship had been decided in Roy Hudgins' favor two weeks earlier, when Junior Junior ended Durham's hopes with an unnecessary trip into the concrete wall.

Wade Durham had won two track championships in his career. Except for Junior, it would have been three. In the eyes of Durham's working-class fans in the stands, his honor was on the line. It was time to get even.

The crowd, maybe three hundred people in all, were diehards who had stayed through an atypical early-autumn thundershower and remained huddled in the stands as wreckers dragged sleds made of old racing tires to dry the track and the temperature dropped in the wake of the incoming northern blast heralded hours earlier. The curious first timers and the canoodling teenagers and casually interested spectators had long since gone home. The hardcore fans who remained were there for one reason—they remembered Junior's dump on Wade Durham two weeks earlier, and they were primed to watch The Blade settle the score.

The track announcer, Buckshot Travis, might have had a hand in their expectations, as he'd referred to the coming grudge match repeatedly the previous week and over the course of the evening leading to the marquee modified feature race. As the race progressed, and Durham worked his way through the field toward Junior Junior's bumper, Buckshot's voice ranged higher and higher, until, with two laps left, he sounded like a demented castrato.

"Here they come!" he shouted over the two dozen loudspeakers arrayed along the front stretch as the leaders roared under the flagstand. "Flat out and belly to the ground! Two laps to go! You know it's a-comin', folks! Keep your eye on Junior and The Blade!"

"Two to go," Tony Leach's voice sounded tinny in Durham's ear. Leach watched the race from the top of their hauler in the infield and coached him over the two-way radio.

The speedway was only a third of a mile long. Each lap took less than fourteen seconds. Half a minute left, as long as some yokel back in the field didn't crunch the wall and bring out a yellow flag to end the race. Durham hoped he hadn't shaved it too closely.

Less than six feet separated them now. Might as well be six miles. To make his bump-and-run, Durham had to be right on Junior's bumper. On the back stretch, he decided his last shot was a crossover move. He planted his front bumper directly behind Junior, but he let the car drift high in the third turn, toward the top of the second lane from the track apron.

"The Blade overcooked it!" Buckshot screeched. "He pushed up the track!"

Running high, Durham didn't scrub off as much speed as Junior did running the bottom lane. Durham lost five or six feet running the high line, but when both cars came off Turn Four, Durham was faster—much faster. He immediately dove to the inside to keep Junior from blocking him as they passed under the white flag, signifying the final lap.

"He snookered him!" Buckshot squealed in delight. "The Blade's pullin' the crossover! Now watch this, folks!"

Junior had two choices. He could accept his fate, give Durham the inside in Turn One, and hope to outrun him on the outside with another counter crossover move. His other option was to intimidate Durham and squeeze him down to the bottom of the track, in a last-ditch gambit to hold the bottom and the lead.

Junior Junior made the wrong choice. He went for the squeeze play.

Gotcha, you son of a bitch, Durham thought as Junior swerved his car to the inside in a bid to run him onto the apron. Instead, Durham tapped the brake and let Junior slide in less than an inch from his front bumper. Durham saw Junior glance at the rearview mirror.

"Watch *this*," he whispered, and rammed Junior's rear bumper as they braked for Turn One. He didn't intend to wreck him. He just hit him hard enough to push him two lanes up the track. Durham waved at Junior as he drove underneath in Turn Two with a classic bump-and-run and pulled ahead. Junior flipped him off and fell in line for second place at the flag.

————

A half hour later, after the winner interview and celebration at the flagstand on the front stretch, and after the bleachers had largely emptied, and after the lights everywhere except in the pits had been extinguished, and after he had showered and dressed in street clothes in the motorhome that hauled the race trailer, Wade 'The Blade' Durham and his crew chief Tony Leach sipped Budweiser longnecks and supervised the two community college kids Leach hired to do the grunt work as they secured the race car inside the trailer.

Despite his nickname, Durham wasn't tall and lanky. He was tall enough, to be sure, but wide in the shoulders and chest, and thick in the wrists. He wasn't a classically handsome man in the matinee idol sense, but most people found him attractive enough, with his light brown eyes and his square jaw. His hair, formerly jet black but now laced with threads of silver, was thick and wavy, and showed only the slightest hint of receding. If his genetic history held true, he'd already lost as much hair as he was going to.

Tony Leach, the auto mechanics department chair at the community college where he'd recruited the crew, stood no higher than Durham's shoulder. He pointed up pit road and said, "Uh-oh."

Junior French Junior and his father, a phlegmatic, porcine, beer-bellied man unsurprisingly named Junior French Senior were headed their way. The Frenches, *pere et fils*, did not look happy. Durham smiled and rested the other palm on the Glock in the holster on his hip.

"That was a chickenshit move, Blade!" Junior Junior shouted, pointing a finger in his direction.

"You should thank me," Durham said, "The alternative was stuffing you in the wall, the way you did to me two weeks ago, but I figured I'd be the bigger man and save you a few hundred bucks."

"So maybe you figure you ain't got all yours back?" Junior Senior said. "Mebbe you want to go a couple rounds with Junior here?"

"Why on earth would I want to do that?" Durham said. "I already have a speed bag at my gym. We're square, Junior. It all comes up even in the bottom of the ninth. Race is over. Season's over. We'll take it up next April."

Durham tossed his empty into the trash can next to the hauler and caught movement out of his right eye. Junior Junior had a tire iron in his hand and was raising it. Durham yanked his Glock from his service holster and pointed it at Junior Junior's heart. The tire iron clattered to the asphalt.

"You really want to raise a tire iron on an SBI agent, Junior? You know when I'm off duty?" He might as well have been asking the directions to the men's room. The Glock hung motionless in the air and didn't waver an inch from Junior Junior's ticker. "Never. I'm *never* off duty. I've carried a badge and a gun for twenty years, and I cannot recall a single instant during that time when I was off duty.

Raising a tire iron at me is assault on a law enforcement officer. Raising it against Tony makes it personal. You can stack a lot of prison time for one. The other, I settle personally. Scoot."

Junior Senior and Junior Junior didn't move. Senior gulped once. For a couple of seconds, Durham thought he'd carried it too far, and Senior might drop to the pavement with a coronary.

"Go!" Durham repeated. "Get out of here before I search your hauler for shatter. And don't think for a second I don't know you're muling. Lucky thing for you; the DEA and I are on the outs this week. Beat it."

The last part was unnecessary, because the notion of their hauler being searched had sent them scurrying.

"Damn, you're a badass," Leach said.

"It's all in the presentation," Durham said. "Got another beer?"

"Thought you were on duty."

"Sheesh," Durham said. "You believe everything you hear? Let's pick up the prize money and go grab us a steak."

———

The only place still open was a chain buffet on the Gaston Highway, but it was on the way to Charlotte anyway, and in Wade Durham's experience, the steaks there weren't bad at all. He and Tony finished loading their plates and sat at the table in time for his telephone to interrupt them. Durham glanced at the phone and sighed.

"I'm on vacation," he told Malik Mourning, the Special Agent in Charge at the SBI Southern Piedmont office in Harrisburg.

"Vacation's over," Malik said. His voice was permanently raspy and muddy, like a wet whisper. "Sorry, Blade. We pulled a hot one."

"C'mon," Durham said. "I have another week coming."

"You can take it after clearing this case."

"By the time I clear it, whatever it is, you'll pile on three more."

"Not this time. I'll owe you. Northwestern District's overwhelmed right now and can't spare a field investigator. They need our help, which means I need you. Take you five days, maybe, and you can go back to wrestling alligators or whatever it is you do for relaxation."

"I'm at dinner, and my steak is getting cold. Call you back in a half hour."

"Wait—"

Durham silenced his ringer and turned his attention to the steak.

"He's gonna shitcan you one of these days," Tony said.

Durham's phone rattled the tabletop.

"He can't afford to. Besides, he already knows I won't turn him down." He stuffed a slice of sirloin into his mouth and chewed contentedly. After swallowing, he said, "Damned if I can figure out how you make a sirloin this tender at this price. No, I'll work the case. And he'll owe me. Again. Somewhere down the road, I'll need his signature on a pricey expense voucher, and I'll remind him how I saved his bacon on whatever the hell it is he wants me to do."

"I bet I know what it is," Tony said, staring at his phone. "This just came over the news services."

"Lemme see." Durham took the phone and read the news bulletin. "Wow. Winlock Savage. This should be interesting." He handed the phone back to Tony and attacked his steak with renewed vigor.

Tony drove straight to the community college to unload the race car at the college auto shop, and Durham retrieved his pickup truck, a restored 1950s Chevy finished in candy apple red. Only after he was on the way home did he call Malik Mourning back. Durham could almost see the director fidgeting in his office chair, probably immaculately dressed even after midnight on a Saturday night. Mourning had a career many agents dream of, back when he was the state's most prominent SBI agent, but three bullets he'd taken on a major case involving the Klan had benched him from field work. That was good for Durham, because Mourning was also a hell of a supervisor. They respected each other. Usually.

"You dining at the White House?" Malik said. "How many courses was that dinner, anyway?"

"I had company. I'm home now. Winlock Savage, huh?"

"You heard about it?"

"Saw a bulletin on Tony Leach's phone. Break it down for me."

"You'll like this one. They smoked him."

"Who?"

"You're missing the operative word here. Somebody hung Winlock Savage on a smokehouse hook sometime last night, and they cooked him. Ever heard of The Chuckwagon in Choctaw? Barbeque place?"

"Ate there a few years back, passing through. Pretty good, as I recall."

"Chuck Hogan, the owner, was the first on the scene, early this morning. He found the padlock on the smokehouse door open, and he was positive he locked it before leaving the night before. He was smoking a few dozen shoulders and a bunch of turkey breasts for the Saturday traffic. The ME in Asheville is up against the wall on time of death, because, well—"

"Got it. Makes DNA a problem as well. Guess that's why it took you all day to call me. How'd they finally ID him?"

"Found his clothes in a pile behind the smokehouse. His wallet was in the pants pocket. His dentist provided the rest for positive ID. That was about three hours ago."

"Any prints on the wallet?"

"Just Savage's."

"Press picked it up quickly," Durham said.

"They do that. Got a call from Raleigh a few minutes before I called you. The top cop in Choctaw, Chief Navarro, is shorthanded, and worried they aren't prepared to handle a case like this. Says there hasn't been a murder in Choctaw in over forty years, and nobody's trained to work one."

"No detective?"

"Died last year. The pandemic. They're still searching for a replacement, and Navarro says none of the current officers are qualified. They need North Carolina's Greatest Sleuth on this one, and your number came up."

"Technically, my number is still on vacation."

"Technically, my pay grade gets to tell your pay grade what to do," Malik said.

"Whatever gets you through the night. I won a race at Hickory four hours ago, and I'm pooped. Gonna grab some rack time. I'll drive up to Choctaw tomorrow after breakfast. You say the chief's name is Navarro?"

"Two '*A*'s, two '*R*'s one '*O*'. I'll text the number to you. There's only one hotel in town. The Choctaw Arms. We have you booked here for the next week. If the investigation runs longer, let me know. We need progress and we need it yesterday. You think the governor is a hardass when high-profile cases aren't moving along? Wait until you deal with ESPN."

ELEVEN

Wade Durham drove through the Chuckwagon Smokehouse parking lot on the way into Choctaw. A sign on the door announced the barbeque spot was closed until further notice. He could see crime scene tape across the door to the smokehouse out back, but otherwise the place was eerily quiet, the parking lot deserted.

"A shame," he said, as he dropped the truck back into gear. "A chopped pork sandwich would go down good right now."

He parked in a metered space on Main Street right in front of the police department, didn't bother to drop a quarter in, and locked the truck.

He felt a buzz at the base of his neck. He'd learned many years earlier never to ignore it. Something about the human brain seemed to know when a person was being watched, even if they couldn't see the watcher. Without making a scene of it, Durham quickly scanned the surroundings.

Main Street in Choctaw ran alongside a Southern Railway line that bisected the town. The sidewalk across the street rose gradually to a hill on which the tracks ran. Every hundred feet or so, the town fathers had installed park benches for strollers to relax and enjoy the lovely autumn weather and the changing leaf colors. Durham wore RayBan aviator sunglasses, which allowed him to turn his head in one direction while searching the landscape in another. He found the source of the buzz, a burly man with dark hair and sunglasses of his own, sitting on one of the park benches trying to look as if he weren't staring directly at Durham. The man had a high and tight buzz cut, like a Marine, and wore jeans and a black unprinted sweatshirt. His face looked fixed in a permanent scowl. Durham memorized his features, in case being spied on became a regular thing.

The bizarre death of obscure has-been athlete and former sports announcer Winlock Savage—however wealthy he might have been—apparently barely moved the needle on the international news meter. A couple of news trucks were parked a block or two away, locked and silent. Otherwise, there was little sign of the fourth estate in Choctaw. Durham approved. His job was always easier when reporters didn't watch over his shoulder and question every move he made.

The interior of the police station was strangely empty. It looked like every small-town cop shop he'd ever visited. The walls needed a fresh coat of paint five years ago, and the desks were piled high with folders and other papers. The place had a locker room atmosphere. It smelled like mildew and sweat, with a faint overtone of pine disinfectant. The front desk was deserted.

"Anybody home?" he called.

From far back in the holding cells, a woman said, "Hold tight."

Durham held tight. Shortly, the woman appeared at the doorway to holding. She was average height, maybe five-five. Her dark auburn hair was pulled back and tied in a bun, but Durham could tell it would be full and lush and would fall past her shoulders if she let it down. Her skin was the color of cinnamon, and her eyes were milk chocolate brown. She had an attractive face and a pleasant smile.

"Chief Navarro?" he asked.

"Can I help you?" She glanced at his Glock warily and rested her hand on her holster.

He was surprised at her accent. Northeast, somewhere. Maybe Boston. Not a local. Durham pulled his badge wallet from his rear pocket and flashed the brass. "Wade Durham, SBI. I hear you're the one who needs help."

Until that moment, she had regarded Durham with mild suspicion. Now she did the full head-to-toe inspection.

"Don't look like an SBI agent," she said. "I'm used to the button-down, three-piece-suit, wingtip types. You look like you hopped off a full eight-second ride at the Low-Rent Rodeo."

"I'm slumming for the weekend. I wear my dress jeans and my rattlesnake boots during the week. Where is everyone?"

"Sunday. The pentecostalists are in church, and everyone else is out fishing. I only have two uniformed officers, and they're directing church traffic. Come on back."

She led him to an office at the end of the other hallway, away from the holding cells. The glass on the door was frosted. The lettering read *Chief.* No name.

Durham mentioned it to her.

"Turnover. I've been here a little over a year. Jury's out as to whether I'll be here this time next year. The previous two chiefs lasted about three years each, so I'm not confident. It's easier to not paint a name on the glass."

"Why's it so hard to keep people on the job?"

"Want coffee?" she asked.

"From a police station pot? No thanks. I swilled a quart of strychnine on the drive from Charlotte."

She smiled and poured herself a cup of sludgy black mess from the pot in her office. "Concentrates the caffeine. Only way to survive this job unless you're courting a meth habit. Charlotte? You aren't from the Northeast District?"

"They're shorthanded."

"A lot of that going around. Choctaw is dying, Agent Durham."

"Call me Wade."

"Heard they call you *The Blade*."

"My reputation precedes me, once again. *Wade's* fine."

"Well, Choctaw's dying, Wade. Ten years ago, we had a thousand residents. Less than half as many live here now. When the interstate planners decided to run thirty miles south a few decades back, people abandoned the blue highways. Nobody cares about the journey anymore. They want to get where they're going as quickly and painlessly as possible. Nobody stops to smell the roses, and they sure don't have time for Choctaw. We lose another fifty people or so to the flatlands or Asheville or Hendersonville each year. In ten years, this will be just another decrepit, crumbling Appalachian ghost town."

"Yeah. I read that already in the Chamber of Commerce brochure."

She smiled again. Durham liked her smile.

"A year or so ago, the Town Council blue-skied a plan to turn part of Choctaw Knob into a ski resort. We're high enough in the Blue Ridge to get plenty of snow but close enough to the Piedmont that people could make it a day trip. Would be a cinch to bulldoze a few runs into the hillsides and install a lift."

"They wanted to bolster the local economy with tourism dollars."

"That was the idea. Put Choctaw back on the map."

"What happened?"

"Winlock Savage happened. He's a local boy, you know."

"I'd heard," Durham said.

"Went to high school here. After all the bad press this place got way back in the seventies, he helped to rehabilitate the town's reputation by winning the Super Bowl."

"After which he immediately retired."

"He cashed in, pure and simple, and he'd tell you the same thing. Can't blame him. It's a lot easier to get rich talking about football than playing it, especially if you have a target on your back the way a quarterback does. Once you hoist the Lombardi Trophy, however bizarre the circumstances, you don't have much left to prove, and the injuries only heal slower with time. Most people know him as a TV guy now. A lot have forgotten he was once a superstar on the field, if only for a few hours."

"Winlock Savage was the fly in the ski resort ointment?"

"You could say. Got a real bug up his ass about preserving the Knob. Some of the Town Council members said he went Hollywood, seduced by all those liberal left coast snowflakes. The way they tell it, LaLa Land turned Savage into a tree-hugging weenie. Once he moved back here for good, he became the burr under the council's saddle. He filed a lawsuit against the town a few weeks back to stop the resort development."

"He's made a lot of enemies on the council."

"Now you're talking like a cop. I had the same suspicions. My working hypothesis is someone who wants the ski resort to take off scraped its biggest speed bump off the runway."

"It's a good first guess. Occam's Razor and all. You sound like you did some college."

"Did it all. Got my master's in criminal justice. N.C. State. Did my bachelor's at BC. Atlantic Coast Conference baby all the way, I suppose."

"Went to Chapel Hill myself, but I'll try not to hold it against you, long as you didn't go to Duke. Sounds like you have a good sense for what happened to Savage. Why do you need the SBI? You know your people around here better than I do."

"Don't have the time or the manpower. Malik Mourning tells me you're the best."

"And he will, as long as I have those incriminating pictures of him."

"Because I gotta tell you. First impressions? You come off as kind of a flake."

"Would you believe those were my first two partners' dying words? Any place to get a good lunch around here?"

In the distance, church bells pealed. Chief Navarro grabbed her hat. "Traffic's gonna be a bitch for the next hour, and we won't be able to get a seat in the diner until the church crowd's had its shot at the trough. Why don't I drive you to the smokehouse? Show you the crime scene. We can grab a bite and I can fill you in on all the players after everyone's home snoozing it off."

They left Durham's truck parked in front of the station and took Chief Navarro's cruiser out to the Choctaw Pike and The Chuckwagon barbeque joint.

"You have a first name?" Durham asked.

"Why?" she said, from behind her sunglasses.

"So I can call you something other than *Chief.* We're going to be working together for four or five days. Formalities make me chafe."

"A sensitive cop," she said. "You're strange in a variety of ways, Blade."

"Tell you what. You call me Wade, and I'll call you…whatever."

"I'm Roberta. Most people call me Bobbi. Here's The Chuckwagon. Ever eaten here?"

"Once a few years back. It was good, if you like Lexington style. I'm an Eastern guy myself."

She screwed up her face. "Everyone around here says the flatlanders are crazy."

She parked the car between the restaurant and the smokehouse and shut off the engine.

"Chuck was the first to arrive yesterday, around six in the morning," she said.

"Nobody was around all night to monitor the smoking?"

"Chuck's been doing this for forty years. Meat practically smokes itself around here now. It's all electric. He set the inside temp, locked the door—he says—and went home. When he showed yesterday morning, the padlock was open."

"He isn't completely certain he secured it?"

"Same deal. Do something a thousand times the same way, you assume you did it that way the one time you didn't. Maybe he remembers doing it because he believes he did it."

"Took a few psych courses at State as well, I see. You're probably right. Doesn't explain why, the one night he forgot, someone snuck in and dumped Win Savage. That would suggest conspiracy. I hate conspiracies."

Bobbi pulled the crime scene tape X'd over the smokehouse door. The lock had been placed in an evidence bag the day before, so the smokehouse was unsecured. Inside the smokehouse, the concrete block walls were coated with soot. The alkaline odor of wood ash tickled their sinuses. The beams supporting the roof had long since blackened in the smoke and constant heat. A one-inch-thick stainless-steel hook had been bolted into each ceiling beam on both sides of the pit, the hooks about six feet off the ground. One of the hooks toward the back of the smokehouse was missing.

"Chuck found Savage hanging there," Bobbi said, referring to the missing hook. "They took him to Asheville for the autopsy, because the coroner in the county seat's backed up. Took the hook as well. Left it in him until the ME could determine if it was the murder weapon. Chuck closed the restaurant and went home around eleven, night before last. By the time he found Savage the next morning, the body'd been hanging and smoking for several hours. I could give you the details, but it'll all be in the autopsy report, and it's kind of grisly."

"But they couldn't establish the time of death."

"He'd been cooking too long. We're trying to back-time his movements the day before he was found to narrow it down, but, like I said—"

"Stretched too thin. Don't apologize. I'm here to take up the slack."

He pulled out his telephone, selected the low-light cam, and shot several pictures. He started at the front left corner and shot from each corner and wall. He shot the ceiling, the pit, and each beam.

"Kinda thorough with the pictures," she said.

Before he could answer, someone said, "Chief Navarro?"

The door swung open, and Chuck Hogan stood in the sunlight streaming through the opening. Bobbi made the introductions.

"SBI, huh?" Hogan said. "That's fine with me. Sooner we get this settled, the sooner I can reopen. It's going to take a week to get the smokehouse cleaned out and running again. I'm takin' a real bath here."

"We'll release the smokehouse as soon as the autopsy's complete and Agent Durham clears it," Bobbi said.

"Go ahead and reopen," Durham said. "The crime scene guys picked it all clean. These pictures are all I need."

"You don't want to wait for the autopsy?" she asked.

"No need. Go ahead and release the place. Between you and me, I'd like to give this western style cue a second chance."

"You let me reopen and figure out who hung Savage in there, and you can eat free for life," Hogan said.

"I wish I could accept," Durham told him. "Can't stop you from giving me the family discount if I should scoot by, though. Why'd you drop in on us today?"

"Why?" Hogan asked.

"Curious. Place is closed. It's Sunday."

"What are you saying?"

"Nothing. Did someone tell you the chief and I were here?"

Hogan scratched at the day-old beard on his chin. "As a matter of fact. Got a phone call from Mrs. Hatchell over there." He pointed toward a clapboard house down the hill from the parking lot. "She said Chief Navarro was snooping around the smokehouse with some fella. Dropped by to see if you needed anything."

"How well do you know Mrs. Hatchell?" Durham asked.

"Well enough, I s'pose. We went to school together when she was Hazel McCourt. I was a pallbearer at her husband's funeral."

"Is Hazel Hatchell a nightowl?"

"I don't know what that means," Hogan said.

"Does she go to bed early in the evening or late at night?"

Hogan blushed. "I'm sure I'd have no idea, Agent Durham."

"Call me Wade."

"Well, I don't know what you're suggesting, *Wade,* but I'd have no way of knowing when Hazel goes to bed or gets up, and I'm not sure I like the insinuation."

"We got off on the wrong foot," Durham said. "I wasn't implying anything. If Hazel is the kind of snoop who'll call you because the chief is parked at your restaurant, maybe she heard or saw something useful the night Savage was dumped here." He addressed Bobbi. "Did you canvass the neighbors?"

She shrugged her shoulders.

"Got it," Durham said. "Short staffed. No biggie. We're on it now." He turned back to Hogan. "You left around eleven, correct?"

"Right."

"You're an expert on smoking meat, aren't you?"

"I reckon I'm the biggest expert between Lexington and Asheville."

"Did you get a good look at Winlock Savage yesterday?"

116

"Too good. I reckon I won't forget that sight anytime soon. I found him, after all. I was there when the police and the ambulance showed up."

"How far along do you figure he was when you found him?"

"What?" Bobbi asked.

"How far along? For what?" Hogan asked.

"You've smoke whole hogs," Durham said. "Been doing it for longer than I've worn a badge. I bet you can look at a hog on a rack and know exactly how much longer it will take to finish smoking. A man is about the size of a hog. How many hours do you figure Savage had left before he was fit for pulling?"

"Durham!" Bobbi said. "Have some decency. You're crossing a line."

"It's a fair question," Hogan said. "I know what he means. Yeah, Wade. I figure he had maybe six hours left."

"Implying he had been smoking since—?"

"Midnight. I figure he'd been on the hook for six hours."

"Midnight. How much do you weigh, Chuck?"

Hogan looked puzzled for a moment. "Maybe two-twenty."

"How much does the average whole hog weigh once it's dressed?"

"Maybe a hundred twenty. Maybe one-forty, tops."

"You can hang one yourself?" Durham asked.

"Twenty years ago, sure. Not anymore. Back can't stand it. I gotta get help now."

"Could you hoist two at the same time back in your prime?"

Hogan grinned. "No way, no how. I never had that much piss and vinegar. Pardon my French, Chief."

"Don't believe I could either," Durham said. "Win Savage was a retired NFL quarterback. He went about six-three and two-twenty in his prime. Probably added twenty pounds of suet since, sitting around in television studios. The hook was six feet off the ground. Someone had to lift that much dead weight high enough to spear him through the ribs on the hook, and if rigor hadn't set in, it was floppy dead weight. That's a three-foot lift, dead reckoning."

"It took at least two people," Bobbi said.

"At least," Durham said. "I'm betting on three. I need to have a word with Hazel Hatchell. Chuck, could you provide the introductions?"

TWELVE

Hazel Hatchell was a wheelchair-bound but otherwise robust woman in her sixties, who greeted Hogan, Bobbi, and Durham readily. She wore a flowered dress, and her hair and nails were immaculately finished.

"Just got home from church," she said. "Sure wish you were open today, Chuck. I would love a chopped plate."

"I have some in the fridge at the restaurant. I'll heat it up and make you a plate soon as we're finished here. Extra hushpuppies. I'll bring one for myself as well. Keep you company," Hogan said.

"I am truly blessed to have you as a friend," she said.

"And we'll reopen as soon as I can get the smokehouse cleaned thoroughly and decontaminated. Agent Durham here cleared the way. I figure we'll be back up to speed in a week."

Hogan introduced Wade Durham. Hazel already knew Bobbi Navarro. Durham sat in the chair next to the sofa, next to Hazel's wheelchair.

"Chuck tells me you called him when you saw Chief Navarro and me at the smokehouse."

"Why? Shouldn't I have? Did I blow a stakeout or something?"

Durham glanced at Bobbi, then back at Hazel. "No. Not at all. But we'll come back to that in a minute. I'm sure Mr. Hogan appreciates you keeping an eye on the place. I can tell you're a good neighbor. You know what happened up the hill, right?"

She shook her head sadly. "I do. Winlock Savage, poor man. That's why you're here, isn't it?"

"It is. Since you're so diligent and attentive, did you see or hear anything suspicious in the smokehouse parking lot night before last?"

Hazel smiled and pulled out her hearing aids. "If it was after eleven o'clock, I normally wouldn't hear a freight train full of marching bands derail in the living room. I go to bed at eleven, regular as clockwork, and I sleep like a baby. Living next to the Choctaw Pike, it's a blessing."

Durham turned to Hogan. "You locked the smokehouse door at eleven, right?"

"Pretty close to it," Hogan said.

"And you went to bed around eleven?" Durham asked Hazel.

"On the dot."

"And you're certain Savage had been smoking right at six hours when you found him?" Durham asked Hogan.

"Could be a half hour one side or the other, but not much more."

Durham said, "Savage was hung between eleven-thirty and half-past-midnight. Anyone we interview needs to have a rock-solid alibi for that hour or they're a suspect. This might be all we have, because I expect the ME won't be able to estimate the time of death. We'll need to do it through interviews and establishing Savage's movements over the last day of his life. Ms. Hatchell, I'd like to thank you. You've been a big help."

"I'm not finished," she said. "You know, I watch a lot of detective shows on television. I never imagined I'd be part of a real investigation."

"Is that why you worried you'd broken a stakeout?" Durham asked.

"Well," she said. "There was the car parked there the night that poor man was killed."

"What?" Hogan asked. "You didn't mention it."

"You didn't give me time. As I said, I *normally* sleep dead to the world after eleven. On that night, I was still awake."

"Why?" Durham asked.

"I received a telephone call from my niece. I'd called to wish her a happy birthday earlier in the day, but she was out. She returned the call around ten-thirty, and we talked for quite a while. Poor thing was mortified that she hadn't called earlier, so I didn't want to just hang up on her just because it was my bedtime. Anyway, I looked out the window after hanging up with her and saw a car up the hill at the Chuckwagon."

"Do you know what kind of car it was?" Durham asked.

"Oh, no," Hazel said. "I can't tell one car from another anymore. It's not like the old days, when you knew a Ford from a Plymouth. Now, they all look alike and half of them are from overseas."

"Do you recall the exact time?" Bobbi asked.

"Oh, no. I didn't look at the clock. I already knew it was late."

"Why didn't you call me, the way you did today?" Hogan asked.

"For all I knew, they had pulled off the Pike to snooze for an hour or so. They never got out of the car, at least for the thirty seconds or so I was watching, and after a while they must have driven away again, because it wasn't there when I woke by chance around three. I didn't think much of it at the time."

"Do you recall the color of the car?" Durham asked.

"It was dark. I don't think it was black, but it was dark."

"Maybe navy blue," Hogan suggested.

"The Choctaw police cruisers are navy blue and white," Durham said. "Is that why you thought it might be a police car, Ms. Hatchell?"

"I never made the connection," she said. "I suppose I'm not that great a detective after all."

Durham said, "I think you see and hear plenty." He addressed Bobbi Navarro. "Chief, I want to interview every neighbor on this street after lunch. Now that we have a timeline, maybe we can find someone who saw something else useful."

————

The Choctaw Grille was mostly empty by the time Chief Navarro and Wade walked through the door. Bobbi pointed toward an unused booth looking out on Main Street.

Durham glanced across the street. The burly observer from earlier still sat on the bench, staring at the diner. Durham noted it and turned his attention back to lunch. He and Bobbi sat across from one another.

Within seconds, a redheaded server in her thirties appeared next to the table. She was close to Bobbi's height, but about as white as a human gets, except for the freckles that ran across her cheeks and nose and disappeared underneath the lace collar of her waitress outfit. Her eyes were cornflower blue. She had a turned-up nose and full pink lips and a seemingly permanent mischievous smile.

"You're the SBI agent, aren't you?" she asked. Her accent was pure Virginia Tidewater.

"Wade Durham, Kylee Wampler," Bobbi said, doing the introductions. "Kylee owns the Choctaw Grille."

"Congratulations," Durham said. "What gave you the idea I'm an SBI agent?"

"Well, you're wearing a Glock 17 on a speed holster clipped to your belt, and I can see the outline of the open badge wallet you've slid into your left breast pocket. And you're a flatlander stranger hanging out with Bobbi here a day after the most famous dude Choctaw ever spawned was roasted on a spit. I made an inferential deduction."

"The hell with this," Durham said to Bobbi. "You don't need me. This town's up to its ass in detectives."

"Get you something to drink?" Kylee asked.

Bobbi ordered Dr Pepper. Durham asked for an Arnold Palmer with sweet tea.

"You know what you want for lunch, or are you gonna make me come back four or five times?" Kylee asked.

"What's good?" Durham asked.

"Can't go wrong with a burger and fries, darlin'."

They both decided to go with the recommendation. Kylee grinned again, almost giggled, and scurried away to put in the order and retrieve their drinks.

"Yeah, I remember the first time *I* did cocaine," Durham said, as he watched her.

"She's a little hyper," Bobbi said. "But she serves a mean burger. You'll see."

"Without making a point of it, check the bench across the street," he said. "You know that guy?"

A second later, she scowled. "Darrell Tanney."

"Is that significant?"

"Maybe. Best to just steer clear of him. State trooper, believe it or not. He's in tight with Senator Carl Royster. Part bodyguard, part babysitter. One hundred percent asshole."

Kylee arrived with their drinks and hustled back to the kitchen.

Durham sipped at his Arnold Palmer and nodded in approval. "This is good. Didn't realize how thirsty I was. The navy-blue car in the smokehouse parking lot bothers me."

"It wasn't one of ours. We don't have any unmarked cruisers."

"Might not mean anything. Could be teenagers looking for a private place to make out. They weren't there the night Savage was dumped."

"Correction," Bobbi said. "They weren't there when Hazel took out her hearing aids and went to bed. You said he was dumped between eleven-thirty and half-past-midnight. Maybe she was sound asleep when they arrived."

"Excellent point. I'll check with the neighbors as well."

"You said we'd be working together for four or five days. You're sure you'll solve it before next weekend?"

"My average time to close a case is one hundred twenty-two hours. A little less than five days. Yeah. We'll have them by then."

"Why?"

"Because we estimate it took three people to hoist Savage onto the hook. And they weren't weaklings. You know what kind of case scares me?"

"Which kind?" she asked.

"A lone wolf. Some guy working off a deranged personal agenda, living the big secret. The kind of guy whose neighbors describe him after the fact as quiet and reclusive. Those guys are a bitch and a half to catch. Sometimes you're forced to wait for them to get bold and careless and make a big mistake. In the meantime, more people die. Y'know what kind of case I love?"

"Shoot."

"One with multiple perps. Benjamin Franklin said two people can keep a secret if one of them is dead. Three people? You do the math. Sooner or later, one of them will get sloppy, or he'll rat out his buddies when he can't sleep at night because his conscience won't leave him alone, or he'll order one too many and spill the beans while trying to impress a woman, or maybe the perps get nervous thinking one of them is a rat and they go after one another and there's another murder to solve. Grabbing off a case with multiple perps is like Christmas in July."

"It's October."

"Even better. Christmas in July without sweating. Case like this? Sometimes I just cool my heels and eventually the killers practically turn themselves in."

"Well," she said. "They'd better turn themselves in soon, or Founder's Day is going to be a washout."

"Founders Day?"

"Next weekend. It's a big deal. Bands and fireworks and a barbeque contest."

"Which, I presume, Chuck Hogan wins every year?"

Kylee arrived with two plates. The burgers looked delicious. Durham sampled one of the fries.

"Double fried?" he said, his eyebrows raised. "Is this Paris?"

Kylee grinned and slapped his shoulder loudly enough to be heard across the room. "Oh, now you're just flirting."

She returned to the kitchen, and Durham squirted a little ketchup on his burger before folding the two halves together. "This is the part where you promised to fill me in on all the players in Choctaw," he said. He checked outside. Darrell Tanney still watched from his station. Durham looked away when he dug in one nostril with his pinky finger.

"The Choctaw Five," she said, and let it hang in the air while she took a larger bite than Durham would have expected. She chewed and relished the burger. "Missed breakfast. This damn Winlock Savage thing has me off my feed. Famished now, though. Okay, Choctaw is the farthest point from the county seat. We're sort of situated in our own little valley, so folks there tend to forget about us except at tax collection season."

They fell into a spontaneous rhythm, one chewing while the other talked.

"Because of our seclusion, the county—hell, the whole state— tends to ignore what goes on here," she continued. "That invests the Town Council with extraordinary power over a tiny group of people."

"Fiefdoms are to be avoided," Durham said.

"And how. The council runs everything, because they *own* damned near everything. The same five families have controlled this town since six days before baseball. The biggest players—because they have the most money—are Tim McCool and Mags McLeod."

"Mags?"

"Margaret, but she hates the name. It was her mother's name, and I hear there was some friction between them back in the day. Call her Margaret if you want to get under her skin. She answers to *Mags*. Her great-something-something grandfather was one of the founders of Choctaw, back when it was a land grant from Governor Tryon before the Revolution. Really old money."

"And McCool?"

"Not far behind. Lot of old Scots Irish genes floating around these hills, Durham. I'm not a local, and obviously I can't trace my heritage back to the bonny highlands, but stories pass from generation to generation in a small town. Legend has it OGs McLeod and McCool were business partners in Glasgow, but for some reason they got the boot and hightailed to the colonies with only the clothes on their backs and two big steamer trunks stuffed with other people's gold."

"They got rich the old-fashioned way," Durham said. "They stole it."

"It became a family tradition. Tim McCool's dad Trent ran this town for years. Was elected mayor in 1980, when Roger Gimball— the former mayor—was elected to the US House. Served until he went to prison on charges of—as I recall—ungodly corruption. Been out for about twenty years now. When Daddy went to prison, Tim stepped up and took his spot on the council, but he hasn't made a run for mayor. Yet."

"So, what's Tim's deal?"

"Besides being an obnoxious little silver spoon piece of shit, he's the guy who came up with the idea for the Choctaw Knob ski resort. It's his baby. He sold the council on the project, and they've sunk a ton of development money into it."

"Then Win Savage stepped in and screwed up the works," Durham said.

"When he filed a lawsuit against the Town Council, it must have spooked them something awful, because Trent McCool has come out of retirement to represent them."

"Bringing out the big guns."

"Next comes Oscar Tattersall. More old money, but not as old as Tim McCool and Mags McLeod. Goes by Ozzie or Oz, depending on how much money you owe him."

"People owe him a lot of money?"

"He's the primary retailer in town. Owns the grocery, the drug store, and the feed and seed. Oh, and the hardware. I read a story about the Alaska gold rush a while back. The only people who made out like bandits stayed back in Skagway and ran the miners' supply store. Same here. During the pandemic, a lot of people in Choctaw were stretched to the breaking point. Oz was a hero to a lot of them, extending credit when others wouldn't. Yeah. People owe him. Some people—the ones who were hit the hardest—owe him a *lot*."

"Is he a hardass about it?"

"Hell, no. He's a sweetheart. He collects, sure, but everyone knows if you hit him with a pathetic enough sob story, he'll give you an extension. People in this town love his ass."

Durham chewed on his burger as he thought about Oz Tattersall. "He must have a *lot* of old money, if he can afford to let debts dangle in the breeze out there."

"I wouldn't know," Bobbi said. "In fourth place is Garrett Kinnison. Likes to be called Garry. He's a flatlander Johnny-come-lately. His family didn't arrive until after the Civil War. Carpetbaggers. Bought the old mill and the logging company, back when those were a thing, and made a buttload of money. Five generations later, he's the primary real estate owner in Choctaw. If you don't own your home, you're renting from Garry Kinnison. You're staying at the Choctaw Arms?"

"Yep. Only room for rent for fifteen miles in every direction."

"You're staying under Garry's roof. He rakes in a shit-ton of passive income. Not sure what to make of him. He's kind of a cypher. Civil War reenactor, Ren Faire role player. Kind of a big nerd. Farms out all the maintenance on his properties, so he never lifts a finger. Guess he has a lot of time on his hands."

"That's four. Who's Number Five?"

"I saved the least for last. Fred Tinsley. The mayor. But not for long."

"Why?"

"Never wanted the job to begin with. About ten years ago, Trent McCool tried to run one of his flunkies for the mayor's office. He'd been reinstated with the state bar, but he couldn't run for mayor again because the town charter has a *No Shitbirds* clause, and he wasn't eligible. He ran a sock puppet to regain control over the council, and Fred Tinsley wasn't having any of it. He ran an opposition campaign and won. He's regretted it ever since."

"Why?"

"Not his groove, I suppose. He's an accountant. Has his own tax prep business on Main Street, three doors from here. Likes the quiet life. He's not a good politician. Lousy at pressing the flesh and kissing babies, but he's been an okay mayor, so people keep voting for him. He only kept running to keep the McCool contingent at bay. Most people around here would chew off their fingers before they'd pull the lever for another McCool for mayor."

"But they're okay voting for him for Choctaw City Council?"

"Not much choice. We use ranked order voting for the council seats. Every four years, five people run and five people are elected. Want to guess who draws the fewest votes each election?"

"Maybe Tim McCool wants to improve his PR a little with the ski resort."

"Sure he does. He wants to be the Second Savior of Choctaw by putting this place back in play, and maybe erase some of the bad feelings toward his family in the process."

"He's put a lot on the line with this project."

"You bet."

"And Winlock Savage threatened it. Becoming the second savior of this town might be difficult if Numero Uno is still hanging around."

"Tim McCool would be at the top of my hit parade for this murder, too, except for one thing," she said.

"Being?"

"He's a total weenie. If guts were money, he couldn't afford a box of Chiclets."

"But now Daddy's back in town," Durham noted.

Bobbi's face clouded. "Yeah. He is."

"Back to Mayor Tinsley. How's he invested in the ski resort project?"

"Nowhere near as heavily as the others, I hear. He likes more traditional, safe investments. Municipal bonds and shit. Of all the folks on the council, he had the least to lose if Savage found a way to stop the project. I'd be shocked if he had more than a hundred thousand invested."

"Suggesting the other four could take a bath?"

"I'm new here. Only been around for a year. I hear things in the hallways at Town Hall, though. Words like *millions* get tossed around a lot."

"*Millions* is a lot of motive for a murder," Durham said. "Right up there in the top two or three. So, you're a cop. From what I've seen, you're a decent one. Of the Choctaw Five, who do we look at first?"

"For serious?" Bobbi asked. "You think it might be someone on the Town Council?"

"Why not? They had a lot to lose. At the least, they're a place to begin."

She chewed over the question with a few fries. "I'd start with Tim McCool and Mags McLeod. And Tim's dad Trent while you're at it, since he's back in the picture. In fact, I'd start there. Tim's a bit of disappointment to his old man, but if I needed a body hidden, I'd go to Trent McCool first."

"Nice to know," Durham said, as Kylee Wampler reappeared at the table, almost blinking into existence at their side, like Tinkerbell.

"How's the food, kids?" she said, as she refilled Durham's glass from a pitcher. "Need another Dr Pepper, Chief?"

"I'm good," Bobbi said.

Durham said, "Thanks. Hey, Kylee, is it okay if I set up shop in your diner?"

"What?" Bobbi asked.

"Fine with me," Kylee said.

"What's this about?" Bobbi asked. "Aren't you going to work out of the police station?"

"I imagine I'll be there enough," Durham said. "Police stations make some people antsy, though. They aren't comfortable in a place where something they say might incriminate them. People are far more relaxed—and far less defensive—in an informal setting. Tell you the truth, sometimes I stake a spot in a back booth in some diner and half the town comes by to check me out. Most of the discussions are worthless, but occasionally you learn something important."

"We have a booth on the other side of the kitchen door," Kylee said, pointing at it. "Nobody likes to sit there anyway because of the noise and traffic."

"Perfect. And thanks again for the refill," Durham said. Kylee grabbed his glass and returned to the lunch counter.

"Any other eccentricities you want to lay on me before I'm blindsided again?" Bobbi said.

"Bunches." Durham took another bite of his burger. "But we'll cover them as they come up."

"You wouldn't be flirting a little with Kylee, would you?"

"She seems to think so." He glanced over at her, as she refilled his drink. "What's her story?"

"She's single, if that's what you want to know. Transplanted flatlander. Works eighteen hours a day in the diner. A real drudge."

"Been in town long?"

"Beats me. She was here when I arrived last year."

"Any connection to Savage?"

"He's eaten here once or twice. Everybody in town does sooner or later. Why? You think she's a suspect?"

He had lifted the last bite of his sandwich, but he placed it back on the plate.

"You know why you needed my help?"

"Sure. We're shorthanded. My detective died of COVID, we haven't replaced him, and I only have two patrolmen right now thanks to the damned pandemic and the cheapskate Town Council. And neither of my patrolmen are even remotely competent to be a detective."

"Those are excuses," he said. "I've learned more from you about this case over the last two hours than I could have picked up on my own in a day and a half. You're more than competent enough to be the detective."

"I already have a job, and it takes all my time. I guess I'm kind of a drudge as well."

"I know a guy in Bliss County. Good cop. A real pro, like you. Name's Wheeler. Got his ass shot to pieces a few years back by some doped-up juvenile delinquent. He had one foot in the ICU and the other in Hell for weeks. He's the chief of police in a two-cop shop, like you. He's also the detective there. In fact, that's his job title now. Chief Detective. And he does it without a spleen. If he can do it, you can do it. But you won't because now I'm here. You're too close to this town to recognize that, until they're cleared, *everyone's* a suspect."

Kylee arrived with his drink. She immediately sensed the tension at the table. She put the drink down and retreated to the kitchen.

"That includes *you*, Chief," Durham said. "So let's get you out of the way first, because I need your help to do my job. Where were you between eleven o'clock on Friday night and one on Saturday morning?"

She sucked on her straw and made him wait.

"In the interest of not keeping secrets, I should tell you. I know who you are," she said.

"I knew I wasted my time introducing myself. Who am I?"

"Number seventy-five. You drop-kicked Junior Junior on the final lap at Hickory last night and won the race."

"You were there?" he asked.

"There's a guy in Glen Alpine. It's not a thing, but once in a while we hook up because neither of us has anything else going on. One of those *'see you next month'* deals. It's more pathetic than erotic, but you take what you can get sometimes. We have a half-serious pact. If both of us are still single when we hit forty, we'll marry each other for the security and the tax advantages. He's my Mr. Right Now, someone to scratch an itch with once or twice a month. He's a race fan. Took me to Hickory a couple of weeks ago, when Junior dumped you. Called me late last night when he heard about the murder, and mentioned he watched you get payback. He nearly busted a nut when I told him you were assigned to the case."

"I'm not certain how to respond to that."

"It was better than phone sex. For him. What can I say? He's a fan. He's fun and all, but folks in this town don't need to know *all* my personal business, so I either go there for a quickie or he leaves here early. He was here on Friday night. He'll vouch for me. I sent him home when I got the call Saturday morning from Chuck Hogan about the body."

"Checked off the list," Durham said.

"I gotta get back to work," she said. "On top of everything else, it's payroll time. You're headed back to the smokehouse to interview the neighbors?"

"Soon as I finish this lovely Arnold Palmer and a slice of that apple pie under glass on the counter and check in at the hotel. I'll drop by tomorrow morning to bring you up to date."

"Good enough," she said. She dropped a couple of tens on the table and rose to leave.

"Hey," Durham said. "We cool?"

"Find out who killed Winlock Savage, Agent Durham. That's all that matters."

THIRTEEN

There was an epidemic of sleeping sickness—at least after eleven at night—among the people who lived downhill from Chuck Hogan's smokehouse. Durham spent the afternoon canvassing the street, mostly without success. The constant din of traffic on the Choctaw Pike had inured the locals to the sound of cars, so if they hadn't looked out the window toward the parking lot, none of them were likely to have seen the dark car described by Hazel Hatchell.

The people he interviewed had lived there for years. A few had inherited their homes from their parents. Most of them had retired, some before the turn of the century, and many experienced hearing and vision problems.

One person, Harold Daniels, recalled seeing the same car once, about a week before the murder, but he didn't remember seeing it again. That was the sum result of Durham's afternoon, and he was not happy about it when he parked his truck in front of the Choctaw Grille shortly after seven on Sunday evening. Across the street, on another bench, Darrell Tanney stared at him as he climbed from the truck and locked the door. Tired of the charade, Durham shot Tanney with his thumb and forefinger before entering the diner.

The place was only half full. The usual verbal jumble of a dozen conversations had melded into a single din. It surprised him a little when he walked in from the relative Sunday hush on the sidewalk. As soon as he stepped inside, the conversations stopped. Everyone turned to look at him curiously. He didn't know whether to say hello or make a break for safety.

Kylee Wampler appeared out of nowhere, as she frequently did, and placed her arm in his.

"'Bout time you showed!" she said. "Your office awaits!"

She led him toward the back of the diner to an empty booth. During the afternoon, she had located a couple of curtain rods and some baling wire and had rigged a pair of café curtains that allowed people to see him only if they were directly beside the table.

"For privacy," she said.

"I don't know what to say," Durham told her. "This is nice. Thanks."

She beamed, and Durham decided he liked her smile almost as much as Bobbi Navarro's. Choctaw was growing on him.

"Happy to oblige. Have a seat. Sunday night's the best night of the week at the Grille."

"I'm too tired to make decisions. What do you suggest?"

"You've already had the burger. I don't recommend two in one day. The plumbing in the Choctaw Arms is over a hundred years old. Besides, it's Sunday Family Night."

"I appear to be a family short," he said.

"No problem. The main rush is almost over. I'll keep you company. White or dark?"

"Beg pardon?"

"White or dark? Your chicken. We serve fried chicken on Sunday nights, with two sides and biscuits."

"Uh, dark's good," he said.

"I knew you'd be a dark fella. Mashed potatoes with gravy and green beans good for the sides?"

"I will defer to your expertise and authority," he said.

"Another Arnold Palmer with your dinner?"

"I don't suppose you have any Old Mecklenburg Copper in the place?"

"Hell, yeah! OMB Copper is popular around here. Have it on tap."

"Even better," he said.

"Be right back," she said. And she was gone, silently, as if she'd never been there. Durham made a note to ask how she did that. It was a neat trick. She reappeared shortly with two frosted mugs. She placed one of them in front of Durham and slid into the booth seat across from him.

The beer was dark amber, the color of a newly minted penny. Durham took a sip. A shard of wet ice fell from the mug to the tabletop.

"The day I've had," he said.

"Tell me all about it," she said. She knocked back several ounces of beer and leaned forward, her elbows on the table.

"Not worth relating. Let's say I know no more about who killed Savage now than I did when I last saw you."

"What a shame. Guess it means you have to stick around a while longer?"

He took a deeper draft from the mug and savored it. "You know I'm a detective, right?"

"You bet," she said.

"Which means I'm kind of sensitive to subtext."

"Well, I sure hope so, whatever that means." A bell rang behind the counter. "Another order up. Be right back." She took the mug with her.

She had only been gone for a minute or so when two men stood next to his booth. One of them was Darrell Tanney. Durham saw them coming and had them analyzed before they said a word. Tanney was the muscle. The little guy was ostensibly the brains. He strolled through the diner like the guest of honor in a coronation processional. He was in his mid-forties. He looked like slightly less than six feet of smug, self-satisfied ego.

Before he could say a word, Durham extended his hand. "Mr. McCool. How cordial of you to drop by."

Tim McCool was taken off guard, and his swagger collapsed. He looked confused. He was only up to introductions, and he had already lost control of the conversation. Being a political animal, he took Durham's hand in a practiced politician's grasp, tight enough to show he meant business, but loose enough that he wasn't bragging about it.

"Have we met, sir?" he asked.

"Never. SBI Special Agent Wade Durham, out of the Charlotte office. I'm here to take care of your homicide infestation."

"But you know who I am?"

"I made an educated guess. I'd offer you a seat, but I'm not sure there's room for everyone." He measured Tanney with his eyes. "Yeah. I'm pretty certain there isn't."

"Wait out front," McCool told Tanney.

"You sure?" Tanney asked.

"Wait. Out. Front." There was more peevishness than malice in his voice. Durham immediately recognized McCool might be the boss, but he was wary—perhaps even a little frightened—of his hulking partner.

"You don't look like an SBI agent," McCool said.

"Nicest thing anyone's said to me all day, and you're not the first to say it. How can I help you?"

"I heard you were setting up a desk in the Choctaw Grille. Got a call you were here for dinner."

Kylee Wampler manifested out of the ether with his dinner plates. She saw McCool and her expression went flat. She quietly and efficiently placed the dishes in front of Durham.

"Hi, Kylee," McCool said, smiling like a disco era lounge lizard.

"Hey, Shit-For-Brains. You eating or loitering?"

"How about a take-out?" McCool said, his face suddenly reddened. "Three orders, one dark two white. The usual sides."

"Brimstone and lost souls. With extra biscuits. Got it. Another Copper, Wade?"

"Maybe after I'm finished with Mr. McCool. Thanks, Kylee."

And she was gone.

"She jokes, but she has the hots for me," he told Durham.

"It shows. So Darrell Tanney called and told you I was here, and—"

"I see you're already getting the lay of the land in Choctaw."

"He's kind of hard to miss. I'm still working out the roster, but yeah."

"As a representative of the Town Council, I wanted to ask how the investigation is going."

"You brought muscle to ask about my case? I'm flattered." He bit into the chicken thigh. "Wow," he said after swallowing. "You're hiding a big secret, Mr. McCool."

McCool suddenly looked anxious "I am?"

"This chicken. It is to *die* for. Forget the ski resort. You could make a fortune franchising Ms. Wampler's fried chicken. Hey. Let's get this out of the way. Where were you Friday night, between eleven and one in the morning?"

"I don't like what you're suggesting."

"I'm not suggesting a thing. I'm eliminating you as a suspect. Don't sweat it. A lot of people in this town are gonna have to vouch for their whereabouts. This is just your turn."

He took another bite of the chicken and closed his eyes, allowing the flavors to dance on his tongue.

McCool interrupted his reverie. "I was at home. Alone."

"Make any phone calls? Order in Door Dash? Rent a movie off Pornhub?"

"No. I was working. Council stuff. Nobody called, and I made a sandwich. I guess that doesn't look so good."

"Well, it doesn't eliminate you, if that's what you mean. But there are other ways. I'm sure we'll establish your innocence in no time."

"My—"

"I thought Tanney was assigned to Senator Royster." Durham pointed toward the front window, through which Tanney could be seen standing on the sidewalk, staring at cars.

"You know Royster?"

"Only by reputation," Durham said. "I don't know when I've had mashed potatoes this creamy. I'm tellin' you, Tim, you have a genuine gold mine here. Good thing Kylee has the hots for you. So what's Tanney's deal? If he's assigned to Royster, why's he here with you?"

"Carl's up at his house on Blind Top. I was visiting. When we heard you were here, I told him I'd drop by, say hello, and bring back some grub for dinner."

"Shame you weren't at his place Friday night. That would have been convenient."

"Sure would, but I wasn't, and I won't lie about my whereabouts anyway. I know I didn't kill Win Savage, and that's good enough for me."

"There's a smoky flavor in these green beans I can't identify," Durham said. "Remind me to ask Kylee about it later. Okay, Mr. McCool, here's the deal. Right now, I have diddly-squat to report."

McCool relaxed. "I see—"

"Except, that is, that Winlock Savage was murdered sometime on Friday evening, but not at Chuck Hogan's smokehouse. I believe he was transported there after the murder by at least two but possibly three people, likely in the trunk of a dark-colored sedan. One of those three individuals either jimmied or had a key for the smokehouse lock, and sometime between eleven o'clock and one o'clock on Saturday morning they hung Savage from a hook in the rafters and let him roast low and slow for about six hours until he was discovered by Chuck Hogan. None of the neighbors saw anything except the sedan, and only two of them saw it. Other than that, I'm largely clueless, which is, I'm sad to say, a familiar condition. I have established motives already for at least five people in town to have committed the murder, and one of them is *you*. Therefore, it may be a good idea if you didn't hover over my shoulder, at least until I establish that you had nothing to do with any of the events I've described, and maybe leave your buddy Darrell at home next time you visit. It all looks a little intimidating and suspicious. We cool, McCool?"

Kylee popped into existence next to the table. For an instant, Durham thought he caught a wisp of smoke. She dropped a large paper bag on the tabletop.

"Your takeout," she told McCool. "I put it on your account, so no need to hang around."

As quickly as she appeared, she disappeared.

"She is just nuts about you," Durham said through a mouthful of mashed potatoes.

"Maybe I should have a word with Senator Royster about the way you've talked to me tonight."

"Why wake him from a drunken slumber?" Durham asked. "Have you tried the peach cobbler here? I had apple pie at lunch, and it was great, but I'm partial to peach. I don't know. It's hard to decide."

McCool tried to stare him down. Durham tried not to crack a smile.

"Nice to meet you, Agent Durham," McCool said. He grabbed the takeout bag and turned away. "Perhaps we'll cross paths again."

"Oh, we will. In fact, I was going to invite you to drop by the station tomorrow anyway, if you can find the time. I need your fingerprints on file."

"What?"

"Like I said. You're a suspect until you aren't, and your alibi kinda sucks. The medical examiner already found fingerprints on Savage's clothing and wallet. Just want to make sure yours don't match 'em. Eliminating you would be the high point of my day.

Thanks for dropping by. I look forward to hearing what my boss has to say after he speaks with your buddy the senator."

Without another word, Tim McCool stomped through the diner to the front door and out onto the sidewalk. He slapped Darrell Tanney's arm and pointed across the street. Tanney ran off, presumably to retrieve the car.

Durham jumped a little when Kylee appeared behind him and said, "Fuck all. Now I gotta fumigate again."

FOURTEEN

Kylee Wampler handed Durham a receipt with her telephone number scribbled in the margin. He held it up as he headed for the door.

"Subtle," he said.

She winked and turned back to serving a couple of guys at the bar. He made sure she saw him stuff the receipt in his shirt pocket.

The Choctaw Arms was erected shortly following the Civil War by local real estate magnate Garrett Kinnison's carpetbagging ancestors. Over the years, it had expanded in almost every compass direction. The original core of the hotel remained in Reconstruction trim, while the wings were decidedly more modern—*modern*, in this case, referring to the Great Depression.

Durham's room was spacious and comfortable, with plaster walls, a gleaming hardwood floor covered by an expensive Persian rug that looked almost as old as the hotel, two double beds, and a desk on which he set his laptop as soon as he unpacked his bag.

He recorded the notes from his interviews that afternoon and made a short list of objectives for the next day. At the top of the list was *Search Savage's House.*

He emailed the list to his address at the SBI and copied Malik Mourning to leave a paper trail in case something happened to him. It was the longest of long shots, but if he did get taken out, he wouldn't be the first SBI agent to die on the job. It was good policy to leave a record of his investigation in case some other agent had to take up the mantle.

Something about the way Bobbi had bristled in the diner still bothered him. Perhaps it didn't mean anything. He probably would have reacted the same if someone had asked his whereabouts out of the blue. He was also right about one thing—by questioning his suspicions about the council members, she demonstrated she was too close to see the big picture objectively. She could be a valuable asset, but first he had to be able to trust her. The deep dive he planned to conduct on all the prominent suspects would establish that one way or the other. The buzzing sensation in the back of his head reminded him that, if she found out he was running a background check on her, she'd blow a gasket.

Someone out there thought they had a damned good reason for scraping Savage off the game board. The ski resort scenario provided a whole list of possible suspects, but if Savage was screwing over his own hometown, who else might he be cheating? The Choctaw Town Council could be the least worrisome of Durham's potential suspects.

He took a shower, sprawled on the bed, and thought about the case for a while. He turned on the television and watched a blowout in progress on Sunday Night Football. At the half, the announcers hosted a brief tribute and retrospective of Win Savage's brief and improbable career before cutting to a series of beer and car commercials. He watched until he didn't care anymore, and he turned off the television and thought about the case some more.

He should have been exhausted. He didn't get to bed until almost two in the morning the night before, and the first day of an investigation was always the hardest—except for the last, sometimes, if people didn't cotton to the idea of being arrested. Sleep was the best thing for him, but he could tell it would be a while coming.

Maybe a walk would help. He dressed in fresh clothes and tossed on a Tar Heels hoodie, as the temperature had dropped from the seventies during the afternoon to the crisp end of the fifties after dark. He parked his Glock on his belt along with his badge, and he set out into the night to stroll himself to sleep.

Only a little before ten, the Choctaw sidewalks were empty. Fog had settled on the town, rolling over the tops of Choctaw Knob and Blind Top into the valley. The streetlights were surrounded by misty halos which refracted the light into almost psychedelic spectral patterns. The autumnal atmosphere of decay nipped at his sinuses as he walked. Living on the middle floors of a high-rise condo in Charlotte, Durham sometimes forgot the smell of a rural town at night. He was too accustomed to the hydrocarbon ambience of the city.

He thought about how towns died, and the throes Choctaw was experiencing, slogging the long painful road to oblivion. He thought about the benefits of a ski resort for a town like Choctaw weighed against the damage and destruction it would do to the environment on Choctaw Knob, and, in the end, debated without resolution whether Winlock Savage was truly on the side of the angels.

The central commercial district gave way to the residential end of Main Street. Streetlights came farther apart, and the right-of-way between the sidewalk and the road was wide and planted with walnut and red oak and sycamore trees with crowns that grew together into a comforting canopy over the asphalt. As in most of Choctaw, urban sprawl here was a foreign concept. The houses were well-kept, with manicured lawns slowly being smothered by falling leaves. They spanned several periods, none more recent than the New Deal. It was the kind of neighborhood most towns would refer to as their *historic district*. In Choctaw, it was just the neighborhood.

He was strolling by a particularly fetching stone Craftsman bungalow when someone called out from the deep, darkened, screened front porch.

"Well, hello stranger."

Durham recognized the voice. He stopped and tried to look inside the porch, but the screen obscured everything except an open flame, and a figure sitting in an oversized wicker porch chair with striped upholstery.

"Chief Navarro?" he said.

"Come on in. Got the firepit burning. Making s'mores," she said. Her voice was perceptibly slurred.

He opened the screened door and saw her more clearly. She wore a red Wolfpack sweatshirt and a pair of jeans with Uggs boots. She'd let her hair down, and it was as full and lush as he had imagined. She had a bucket of longnecks in ice next to her. A Home Depot propane firepit kept the seating area cozy.

He pointed to his blue Tar Heels hoodie. "This isn't going to get awkward?"

"Tobacco Road's half a state away," she said. "Pop a squat. Got bored with the football game. Decided this was a better way to spend the evening."

She handed him a bottle and a church key. He checked the brand.

"I approve," he said.

"I'm so relieved."

"Still pissed at me?"

She took a slug from the bottle.

"You were kind of brutally direct," she said. "What pisses me off is you're right."

She handed him a long skewer and pointed to the bag of marshmallows.

"S'mores and ale," he said. "Breakfast of champions."

"I am too close," she said. "Maybe I hesitate to point fingers at people who sign my paycheck."

"I have no such reservations, even with the people who sign *my* paychecks."

"Which is why you're right. And it's why I needed you here in the first place. So, I guess, yeah. We're cool."

He pierced a marshmallow and held it near the firepit to roast. "Nice to hear it. I was wondering why you invited me off the sidewalk."

"Maybe because you assumed right off that I was Chief Navarro. Ninety-nine cops out of a hundred would have asked me where to find him."

"It was an educated guess. You were either holding down the fort because you were the boss, or because you were the least dependable cop on the force. You didn't look incompetent, so I went with Door Number One."

"Well, I appreciated it. You're a lot to bite off in one chunk, you know."

"As I recall, that was the central theme of my last performance review."

"Why do they call you The Blade?" she asked.

"I used to tell people it was a racetrack name they gave me because of the way I sliced through traffic."

"But that wasn't true."

"Sometimes it's hard to separate the truth from the legend."

"So, what's the hot poop and straight skinny?"

"Are you certain you belong in this century?" he asked.

"Does anyone? Would you *choose* to live right now? Give."

"What do I get in return?" he said. "You're asking for some intimate details regarding my past."

"I could tell you how I lost it." The IPA had started to blow out her filters.

"Why would I want to know that?"

"It's kind of a funny story. This one time, at band camp..." She dodged the marshmallow he lobbed at her. "For serious. How'd you get the name?"

"It's silly. I was six months into plainclothes. This is before I upped with the SBI. I was local. My senior partner, lifer named Art Ormsby, and I collared this three-block cocaine king in one of the projects. He was the hottest shit between Twenty-Eighth Street and Dumar Avenue, which you can cover with a decent line drive. He liked to run his mouth, though, especially when television cameras were around. One of the local news crews caught him busting an impromptu rap after we cuffed him in which he referred to getting taken down by *Wade the Blade and Art the Fart, the whitest cops in town.*"

"It ran on the news?"

"At six and eleven. I hear it was on the morning news as well, but by then I was on the job and some wag had written *BLADE* on my locker with a Sharpie. It became my call sign."

"Hmm," she said. "Could be worse."

"It can always be worse."

"You could have been Art. How long did it take him to live with the name Art the Fart?"

"He didn't. About a month later he keeled over in line at the Krispy Kreme. Blew out an artery inside his skull."

"You're shitting me."

He shook his head. "Wish I was. I liked Art. On the other hand, there is no finer demise for a cop. Twenty years ago? Shit. Now *I'm* the lifer. Gimme another graham cracker."

"So, what's the deal with racing? Being a cop isn't dangerous enough?"

As he skewered a marshmallow, he said, "It's the only sport I'm good at. My father was a three-letter man at Carolina. He majored in sweat. Had a thirty-minute contract with the Yankees organization coming out of college and blew it. The details aren't important, but his baseball career was over before he set one foot outside the dugout. He made a play for football, but no dice, and he was about five inches too short for pro basketball."

"Muggsy and Spud did okay."

"Muggsy and Spud are super-powered aliens wearing human costumes. My dad finally had to admit he'd been a hero in his own backyard, but everywhere else he was an ordinary joe. That sad realization rode on his shoulders right up to the day he died."

"You didn't inherit the athletic genes?" she asked.

"None I can identify. I was only okay at baseball. I can hit all right, but I can't throw for shit. The first time I tried out for football I got clobbered and had a concussion for a week. Lost my taste for the game. Same thing when I tried boxing, which left me with this damned deviated septum that gives me hell when the air's dry. I tried golf, but I fell asleep on a bench around the fifth hole."

"So how did racing come along?"

"Like most things. Completely by accident. My first job in the cop biz was as a sheriff's deputy in the Sandhills. A lot of us moonlighted by doing security work in uniform. I was working the pits at a local track, maybe twenty years ago. Got to know the guys, and I helped out some when I was off duty. One night they needed a driver. My head fit the only helmet they had. Turned out I had a knack for it. I finished third, and they put my name over the driver's door permanently. Maybe it was all the strategic driving they taught us at the academy. I don't know. Didn't take long to start winning. The extra cash is nice, and it gives me something other than perps to think about."

"You like it?"

"I love it."

"Why didn't you do it for a living? I hear those guys make out pretty good."

He assembled a s'more, handed it to her, and skewered another marshmallow.

"I almost did," he said. "Talked it over with a couple of the big NASCAR guys, drivers you'd recognize immediately, but I'm no name-dropper. I wanted to know what the air was like in the rarified atmosphere of big-time stock car racing."

"I'm sure they thought it was a hoot," she said.

"On the contrary. One of them asked me— like you did— whether I liked what I was doing, racing the weekly short tracks."

"And you said?"

"I love it. Like I told you."

"And he said?"

"If I loved racing late models at the local level, I should keep doing exactly that. If I went professional, he said, it would be all I'd ever do, and I'd grow to hate it. Yeah, the money's awesome once you hit the big time, but you pay for it. Between car development, seat fittings, tire testing, practice, racing, personal appearances, autograph sessions, dinners courting sponsors, and plain working on the damn car, I'd never have any other life. My entire existence would revolve around racing. The guy who told me this has a couple of NASCAR championship rings and three ex-wives, so he'd know."

"So you stayed with the local bullrings."

"The best cop I ever knew used to say, *'If you're in the presence of someone who knows more than you, you should shut your trap and listen to them.'* This guy had been to the mountaintop, and the view was not what he anticipated. I took his advice. Haven't regretted it yet. Besides, the bullrings are fun, and we don't go fast enough to to get hurt bad. I don't heal as quickly as I used to."

They nibbled on s'mores and sipped at the IPA, enjoying the evening.

"Always this foggy around here?" he asked.

"Only in town. You're asking whether it was foggy Friday night. This stuff hardly ever settles near the Pike."

"But Savage wasn't killed at the smokehouse. He lived on Blind Top, didn't he?"

"Yeah. I'm taking you there tomorrow morning. My guys taped it off, and they drive by several times a day to make sure no looky-loos are trying to get in, but we didn't snoop around. Decided to wait for a real detective."

"Are we having this conversation again?"

"Deferring to your experience. If you see evidence he might have been killed there, we can get a crime scene crew in from Asheville in about an hour."

"I have some people in the Charlotte office doing research for me. In a day or so, I should know every snippet of the council's lives."

"Just tell me what I need to know to move your investigation along."

"Why?"

"I have to live with these people, Blade. Don't look at me like that. It's a wicked cool nickname. I have to look these people in the eye and shake their hands and sit next to them at town hall meetings. I don't need to know who they're fucking or who they're zooming. I know enough unsettling shit about these people already."

"Know anything about Darrell Tanney?"

She had the bottle halfway to her lips, but she put it back. "What about Tanney?"

"Tim McCool brought him into the Choctaw Grille tonight to intimidate me."

"McCool? Talk about burying the lede."

"I made Tanney sit on the bench outside."

"You...*made* him sit outside?"

"I mostly suggested he was immaterial to the conversation. Turns out I was right."

She slipped another marshmallow on the skewer, drained her ale, and reached for a freshie.

"He'll take you over the hurdles for that," she said. "Tanney has a mean streak a mile wide. Yeah. He's a state cop. His supervisors don't want him back in uniform anytime soon, though."

"He's assigned to Carl Royster."

"He's more like Royster's babysitter. He's mostly there to keep Royster from OD'ing and to separate him from the high school girls. Royster's brother is a judge or some kind of shit. Trent McCool, Tim's dad, arranged it with him."

"What's the connection between Royster and McCool?"

"McCool owned this town back in the day. He ran Royster for mayor. Fred Tinsley ran to keep him out of office. Trent pulled a lot of favors to get Royster in the State Senate in the next election cycle. Royster's represented this district ever since. Trent McCool owns his ass. Tinsley and Royster hate each other's guts for some reason. It's a frequent source of friction between Tinsley and Timmy during the Town Council meetings."

"So, ultimately, Darrell Tanney works for Trent McCool," Durham observed.

"It's a lot more complicated. Trent McCool is Darrell Tanney's second daddy. Tanney's father was police chief here in Choctaw about forty-five years ago. He became something of a hero when he dragged the mayor and some preacher from the flatlands into

Town Hall while demonstrators shot it out *High Noon*-style on Main Street."

"I'm not familiar with this story," Durham said.

"The Choctaw Shootout?"

"Before my time. I wasn't an infant forty-five years ago."

"There's a framed newspaper front page in the police station, to commemorate Chief Tanney. The shootout put Choctaw on the national news for almost a week. Tanney practically carried Mayor Gimball and the preacher up the Town Hall steps, and keeled over with a heart attack as soon as they were safe. Gimball and McCool saw to it Darrell was provided for, in gratitude. Mostly meant covering for all his fuckups and misdemeanors through high school and juco, which is as far as Darrell got before he signed on with the Highway Patrol. When Gimball headed to DC, Trent became Darrell's primary go-to whenever he needed to be bailed out of a jam as a trooper, which was more or less all the time. Assigning him to keep an eye on Royster appeased a multitude of devils."

"You know a lot for being here only a year."

"Like it or not, the police chief position is a political appointment. Helps to know all the players on the scorecard, and which toes to avoid."

He cracked open the ale. She held out the graham cracker box. He waved it away.

"After the burger and tonight's Sunday Family Special at the Grille, I'm stuffed. I only ate the first two s'mores to be polite."

"So you met Tim McCool."

"The fruit that fell far from the tree."

"Like Darrell, I hear Tim got away with a bunch of shit as a kid, probably because his dad covered for him while he was raping half the countryside to fill his coffers. Tim thinks he's the king's shit. His father has similar opinions."

"I've seen dozens of his type over the years," Durham said. "Daddy must cast a huge shadow. Timmy is a walking poster boy for inadequacy. He imagined dragging Trent's bulldog along tonight would intimidate me."

"What does that tell you?"

"He feels threatened. He reached out to me, preemptively, to control the narrative."

"Did he?"

"We'll find out tomorrow if he shows at the station to leave his fingerprints."

She nearly did a spit-take with the ale.

"You told him to come to the station?"

"That's where they keep the fingerprint machine. Told him I needed to eliminate him as a suspect, because we found fingerprints Savage's killers left behind."

"First I've heard of it. What fingerprints?"

"The ones I hope now live in Tim McCool's head. Maybe he'll spread the rumor around. Seeking me out and trying to put the muscle on me launched him right to the top of my Suspect Parade. If he walks in glowing with bonhomie and overflowing with public responsibility tomorrow, I'll know he has nothing to hide. If he blows me off, on the other hand—"

"You SBI pukes are wicked devious. Has anyone ever mentioned that?"

"Don't tar all of us with my brush. I may be exceptional. My bottle is empty, and I have a big day tomorrow, which means *you* have a big day. What time does your watch begin?"

"Has it ended? News to me. I usually trot in around eight."

"I'll grab breakfast at the Grille and meet you at the station then. The first item on my agenda tomorrow is to do a proper survey of Win Savage's house." He stood. "Thanks for the drinks and the s'mores. Nice place. I like the house."

"Comes with the job. One of the nicer perks. Now you know where it is, don't be a stranger."

FIFTEEN

Winlock Savage's house looked more like a movie star's digs in the Hollywood Hills than a quaint Blue Ridge mountain home. Built on a slope on Blind Top, it overlooked the Choctaw Valley and the town itself. Constructed mostly of concrete and glass, with an integrated pool off a deep shaded lanai, it jutted over the valley, providing fifty-mile views to the east.

"Good thing Savage was into preserving the environment," Durham noted as he and Bobbi Navarro stood in the entrance hall to Savage's egotistical monstrosity. His words echoed off the concrete walls. "I've seen artillery bunkers with more personality."

Even though they both wore nitrile gloves, he didn't touch anything. Instead, he surveyed the house room by room, walking through and carefully examining each detail. In each room, he took multiple pictures of the walls, floor, and ceiling.

"Um, about last night?" Bobbi asked.

"Yes?"

"That business about not being a stranger? Don't misinterpret that."

"I didn't."

"I mean, I had drunk my share of ale. Made my tongue loose."

"*In cervisia veritas*," he said. "But don't worry."

Savage's bed was unmade but showed no signs of violence except for the tousled and tangled sheets.

"Let's bag the sheets," he said. "I see stains."

"Ick," she said.

They circled their way back to the living room, which—compared to Durham's—was roughly the size of a soccer pitch. A free-standing fireplace open on two sides sat cold and empty.

"No television," Durham noted. "A former Super Bowl winner would want to watch a game once in a while." He pointed to the ceiling, at a slit about ten feet wide and two inches thick. "There it is. Projection screen." He found the projector port on the opposite wall. That drew his attention to the sofa.

Bobbi had moved to the lanai. The water in the pool was flat and mirrorlike.

"Come look at this," Durham said.

He led her back into the living room and pointed at the sofa. "Tell me what you see."

She stared at it for several seconds.

"I see a sofa I couldn't afford with a month's salary. What am I supposed to see?"

"Look around the room. What do you notice most?"

She did another sweep. "You got me, Blade. What am I looking for?"

"Winlock Savage was into order. This room is as symmetrical as a room gets. The two chairs facing the sofa are exactly the same distance away and placed at exactly the same angle. The sofa is perfectly centered to the drop-screen TV. The coffee table is perfectly centered to the sofa. Walk through the entire house. The guy was into symmetry and balance. It's an OCD thing, I reckon. A lot of athletes are perfectionists. Maybe it's some sort of weird *feng shui* strategy. I don't know. One thing I do know is these two pillows do not match."

He pointed to the oversized throw pillows on each end of the sofa.

"It's like wearing mismatched socks. I had a sense something was wrong in this room, and I finally figured out what it was."

"So?" she asked. "What does it mean?"

He pulled the pillow away from the right end of the sofa and showed her a hole in the leather upholstery.

"Is that…a bullet hole?" she asked.

"I had the exact same question," he said. "Help me move this sofa."

Together, they slid the sofa toward the fireplace and pulled up the rug underneath.

"Holy shit," Bobbi said. The hardwood floor underneath the rug was splintered. They found another hole near the bottom of the back upholstery.

Durham pointed to marks on the floor where the sofa had apparently sat for some time. They were almost a foot and a half nearer the fireplace than the sofa sat now. "Someone moved this sofa to cover what looks like a bullet hole in the floor and replaced the throw pillow. It's time to call your forensic buddies in Asheville. This looks like a crime scene."

While Bobbi made the call, Durham circulated through the house again, this time looking more deeply now that he believed some mischief had taken place.

"Savage's clothes were found behind the smokehouse, but not his cellphone?" he called out from the back of the house.

"That's right."

"Did you ping the cell yet?"

"Sorry. I'm new to this murder investigation shit. On it."

She made another call and was put on hold. The conversation that followed was brief. She waited another several minutes and thanked whoever was on the other end.

"It's in the house, somewhere. Must have the ringer off."

"Better to let the forensic guys locate it," he said. "We don't need to contaminate this scene any more than we already have. Let's wait for them in the car."

———

The lead forensic crime scene tech was a kid who looked like she should be taking a chemistry class in her local high school. As he watched her and her crew of two other techs process Savage's house, Durham decided she knew what she was doing.

"It's a bullet hole," she said, pointing toward the floor. "The slug splintered into shards when it hit the concrete pad under the hardwoods. We found tiny pieces of shrapnel in several places around the room, so ballistics isn't going to be much help. Nothing much left to compare. After examining the sofa and the splinters we did find, I don't believe the bullet hit anyone. There's no splatter anywhere, and the sofa doesn't react at all to luminol. Someone shot the sofa, but I don't think anybody died here, at least not from a GSW."

"I'd like a rush on the DNA with the sheets," he said. "And run every fingerprint you find through AFIS. I want to know who has been inside this house." He thanked her and returned to Bobbi Navarro, who sat in a chair on the lanai, which had been cleared first by the crew.

"No love on the bullet or blood residue," he told her. "The damage to the sofa suggests a thirty-eight, or perhaps a nine-millimeter. Beyond that, I'm afraid this looks like a dry hole."

Bobbi lifted the evidence bag containing Win Savage's cell phone. "Not entirely. One of the techs found it on the floor in the bedroom, lying between the bed and the wall."

"Is it locked?"

"Win Savage was worth millions of dollars, and we know someone had it in for him. Yeah. It's locked."

"Please tell me it isn't a facial recognition protocol. I don't think the phone will recognize him now."

"Worse. Fingerprint."

"Sign it over to me," he said. "I'll get the geek squad at the SBI office in Charlotte to work it over."

The lead tech walked through with the bed sheets bundled inside a large evidence bag. "We'll try to get this done ASAP, but you know how long a decent PCR takes, even if it's on top of the stack."

Durham wrote a number on the back of one of his cards and handed it to her. "Malik Mourning's number. He's the SAC in the Charlotte SBI office. Call him as soon as you hand the sheets over to the lab and let him discuss scheduling with them."

She took the card and headed for the forensics van.

"Damn," Bobbi said. "I've been a cop for ten years, and I have seen my share of bureaucratic stonewalls. They don't exist for you, do they?"

"Clout has its benefits," he said. "For instance, I'm supposed to be on vacation this week, but the governor had other plans. I need to scoot to Charlotte for a few hours as soon as we're done here. I want to establish Savage's schedule on the day he died, and this phone is the best way to do it. Our geeks can crack this thing. I want to be there when they do."

"ME's office in Asheville called while you were in the back. The autopsy's complete. She's writing the report now."

"Did she give you a cause of death?" he asked.

"She said it's complicated, and everything will be in the report."

"Wonderful. I can never catch the easy cases. I should be back in about six hours. Let's meet at the Grille and swap our results. I'll call when I'm on the way."

SIXTEEN

Bobbi was waiting for Durham at the back booth when he walked through the door of the Choctaw Grille. She had a report in a manila envelope sitting on the bench next to her.

"Malik Mourning was on the phone with the DNA lab when I walked in," Durham said as he sat. "I love watching someone with real juice toss their weight around."

He placed the cell phone, still in its clear labeled evidence bag, on the table in front of her.

"You cracked it?" she asked.

"Took the whiz kids about ten minutes. I'm glad they're on our side. If they had a criminal bone in their bodies, we'd all be in big trouble."

Kylee materialized next to the table. Durham was certain he heard the faintest *pop* when she did.

"Whatcha havin', kids?" she asked.

"Aren't you required to chew gum and blow a bubble when you say stuff like that?" Durham asked.

"I might have a few sticks in the back. Want to help me look for them?" She winked at him.

"Might want to see a doctor about that tic, sweetie," Bobbi said. "Diet Dr Pepper?"

"Good choice," Kylee said, the snark unmistakable. "For you. And how about you, McGruff?"

"Arnold Palmer with sweet tea. Thanks."

"You're welcome. I know exactly how you like it. Back in a sec."

"For Pete's sake," Bobbi said after Kylee vanished into the kitchen. "Just fuck her already. Get her off our backs."

"It's an attractive notion, but I don't think she'd sit still long enough. The autopsy."

She handed him the envelope. He read over the brief postmortem report. He didn't smile as he read it.

"Well," he said. "This is grisly."

"I had the same response."

"Subjecting a human body—especially one not yet properly butchered—to boiling temperatures inside a smoky enclosure apparently does great mischief to one's remains."

Bobbi said, "She found scar indicators of his documented surgeries, including an ACL and an appendectomy—the old kind, where they cut you open. Had it when he was a kid. The body also had healed fractures corresponding to Savage's medical records. It was Savage, even if you couldn't tell by looking at him."

"Kudos to your ME. Might as well do an autopsy on a country ham. What's her name?" He lifted the paper to check the last page for the signature.

"Naomi Patel."

He looked up from the paper. "Neni's in Asheville now? That explains it. She's the best."

"Is there anyone you don't know in this state?"

"Yeah. The guys who killed Win Savage. As we suspected, livor mortis indicates he was killed elsewhere and transported to the smokehouse. Lord only knows how she spotted it."

"But it doesn't indicate a COD," she said.

"A byproduct of being cooked. By the time Hogan found him, he'd pretty much rendered out, and was split like a sausage from sternum to crotch from internal pressure. He could have been killed a dozen different ways that couldn't be detected in this much postmortem damage. They might as well toss him into a jet engine and autopsy the spray. Maybe the tox screen will tell us something useful."

As if on cue, Kylee appeared next to their table with their drinks.

"Ready to order?" she asked. Durham noticed she never carried a pad or pen. His estimation of Kylee Wampler rose several points.

"I'll pass on the pulled pork. Like, forever," Bobbi said. "A burger's fine."

Durham said, "Flounder sandwich. Extra tartar. Rings instead of fries. Thanks."

And, barely stirring the air, she was gone again.

"Look behind me," Durham said.

"Okay," Bobbi said. "What?"

"Is there a door back there I can't see?"

"No."

"Right. Here's the thing. Yesterday, when Tim McCool laughably tried to brace me, Kylee entered the kitchen through that door." He pointed over her shoulder toward the swinging doors. "When he left, she was behind me. She said something and I nearly jumped out of my skin. How in hell did she get there?"

"Beats me," Bobbi said, impatiently. "Are we going to look at the phone or what?"

"Already did." He pulled an envelope from the inside pocket of his windbreaker. "Full report on Savage's travels for the forty-eight hours before he was located, the calls he made, and his recent emails—mostly junk. I brought back the phone because this is still your case. It belongs in your evidence locker. Besides, it gives me the chance to walk you through his movements. Shall I jump to the final course, or do you like a slow burn?"

"Please, after yesterday, spare me the cooking puns."

He opened the envelope. "I could show you on the phone, but this is easier. Working backward, Savage arrived at his house on Thursday afternoon. According to the location tracking, which was turned on, the phone didn't leave the house again until we found it. Savage, we already know, did. But we can place him at the house as late as eight-twenty-three on the night he died."

"Let me guess. He made a call."

"He did indeed. The geeks in Charlotte isolated a ping off the cell tower closest to his home, on Choctaw Knob, and we know the phone didn't travel anywhere after Thursday night, so Savage was alive and at his house at eight-twenty-three."

"And he was dead four hours later."

"More or less. Possibly less. Don't you want to know who he called?"

She pretended to be nonchalant, sipping at her Dr Pepper. "If you feel like telling me."

"Gabriella Reyes."

"So? Does that mean something? I don't know anyone in Choctaw by that name."

"Probably because she lives in Nashville."

Her eyes lit with recognition. "You mean…Gaby Reyes? The singer?"

"I hit Google, and five minutes later I had eight pix of Savage with Gaby Reyes on his arm. So, I called her."

"How'd you get through? I hear she's surrounded by layers of handlers and agents and shit."

He tapped at the telephone on the tabletop. "Called her personal number."

"Oh," she said. "Duh. So you talked to her?"

"Mostly, I listened to her scream when she saw a dead guy's name on her phone," he said.

Bobbi nearly snorted a mouthful of soda across the table. "Wait! You used Savage's phone?"

"No reason not to. We'd already imaged everything on it. Nothing to contaminate. Don't look at me like that. I wore gloves, and I logged the call in case there's any confusion later. Jeez. I figured she'd be more likely to answer a call from Winlock Savage than one slugged NCSBI."

"You are one devious son of a bitch," she said.

"I'd take a bow, but I'm already seated. Did Tim McCool come by the station to be printed today?"

"Haven't seen him since I got back from Savage's house."

Kylee arrived with their plates.

"Y'all enjoy," she said, and she addressed Bobbi directly. "I went light on the mayo, hon. You can thank me later."

And, without another word, she was gone again.

"I'd cultivate that relationship," Durham told her, as he spread tartar sauce on his fish and pushed the two halves of the sandwich together.

"You think there's a relationship?" she said.

"Not yet. But Kylee knows things. And she isn't intimidated by the McCools of the world. She could be a great asset."

She stared at him over the burger.

"Just sayin'" he said. "The waitresses and secretaries of the world are invisible, and they hear everything. We'll need an interview space at the station tomorrow. Gaby Reyes is coming to Choctaw."

"Why?"

"Because I said *please*. I told her I was determined to find his killer, and she couldn't agree to help fast enough."

"Help."

"She was in a semi-serious relationship with Winlock Savage. Pillow talk, Chief. Who knows what he told her? Oh, Gaby Reyes shot the sofa."

"What?"

"I told her about finding the bullet hole and the splintered hardwood floor. She told me she shot the sofa a few weeks ago. She arrived unannounced and found Savage *in flagrante delicto* with another woman. She overreacted."

"And she has an alibi for the murder?"

"She was onstage in Lawrence, Kansas at eleven o'clock on Friday night. Well, it was ten o'clock there, but you know what I mean. She didn't do it."

"Who was the other woman at Savage's house?" Bobbi asked.

"You remember the Summer Olympics in 2012?"

"Hell, no."

"Neither did I. I had to look it up. The other woman took the bronze medal in a couple of the gymnastics events. Taylor Pettigrew. After she aged out of gymnastics, she grabbed off a fifty-buck California law degree and traded on her brief celebrity. She's a mid-level account exec at one of the athletic shoe companies now. Savage had an endorsement contract that needed renewing. Seems Taylor had some unorthodox negotiating strategies."

"I remember her now," Bobbi said. "Vaguely. Cute little girl. The one with the shaved head. Couldn't have been seventeen at the time."

"She's all grown now. I called her on Zoom while I was in Charlotte. I hate interviewing people online."

"Why?"

"It's harder to make them sweat when they're three thousand miles away. Anyway, she was in San Francisco on business, and she didn't have a motive anyway, but she confirmed that Gaby Reyes shot the sofa and missed Savage entirely. Savage didn't talk about the lawsuit with her, or much about Choctaw at all. She did say he received a telephone call one night that set him off, but he didn't talk about it. I have a team of rookies tracking Savage's call log, but if the troubling call came from someone on the council, we'd never know. It would look like any business call."

Bobbi swallowed the first bite of her burger. "What's next?"

"Tomorrow, I knock on doors and annoy people."

———

Durham walked into the Choctaw Arms Hotel and shot at the desk clerk with his finger on the way to the stairwell. The evening promised to be a long one. He needed to read the reports the Charlotte research crew had generated on the list of possible suspects in the Savage case, as well as the deep dive on the shootout nearly five decades earlier. By the time he finally turned out the lights later that night, he expected to know a lot more than he did presently. He might even have a better idea who roasted Winlock Savage.

"Agent Durham?" someone said.

An older man sat in the lounge off the main lobby. He looked in his seventies, at least. The remaining fringe of hair encircling his otherwise bald head like a laurel had gone full silver. He was of slightly more than medium height, and athletically built. His eyes were clear and sharp. He was dressed as if he'd strolled off the eighteenth hole at Augusta. The resemblance to Tim McCool was coincidental enough that Durham guessed his identity immediately.

"Mr. McCool," he said.

"Join me for a drink?"

"Why not?" Durham said. They shook hands the way serious men do, and Durham sat at the table. Instantly, the bartender asked for his preference.

"What's he having?" Durham asked.

"A Manhattan, sir. Would the gentleman like one as well?"

"Good god, no. I was just curious. What do you have on tap?"

He ordered a beer, and the bartender scurried away.

"I'm working late tonight," Durham explained. "Don't need to cloud my mind with strong spirits. Met your son yesterday."

"I know. I wanted to talk to you."

"Congratulations on your recent wedding."

"Thank you," McCool said. "Have we met, Agent Durham?"

"Call me Wade. No, sir. I saw the resemblance to Tim, though, and I expected we'd meet sooner or later anyway. Now's as good a time as any. Not that I think you run your son's life or anything, but I asked him to drop by the station today to get his prints on file. He never showed. Looks suspicious. Again, not that I expect you to do anything about it."

"You're a clever man," McCool said.

"Linguistically nimble, perhaps. In most other ways, I'm a dunce."

"Putting me off guard with a self-effacing feint is a nice tactic. I've used it myself from time to time. I don't intend to do anything about my son, sir. He's free, white, and twenty-one twice over. He can do what he wants, and he alone bears the consequences, good or bad, for his actions. I mostly leave him to his own affairs."

"Yet you're representing him and the rest of the council in Winlock Savage's lawsuit to stop the Choctaw Knob ski resort."

"Which, I expect, will dematerialize any moment," McCool said. He swished the ice around in his glass. "Unless his attorneys are interested in working *pro bono*, of course."

"Gosh. There's so much motive there. Boggles my mind."

"Again, that is why I wanted to sit with you tonight. My son is perpetually stuck in his frat house period. I suspect he made a bad impression. I'm not here to apologize for him or even justify his behavior. He was rude. Bringing Tanney along was a bad idea. Perhaps you got the wrong impression of people in this town as a result."

"People are the same more or less everywhere," Durham said. "Some good, some bad, some ugly. I don't anticipate Choctaw will prove any different."

"May I ask? How is the investigation faring?"

"It's early, yet. I received a large cache of background research this evening. It'll keep me busy for several hours at least. You're in there."

McCool drained the last of his glass. Within seconds, a replacement appeared at his elbow.

"My limit. Two a night," McCool said. "I usually prefer to spread them out, but what the hell? I expected you to look into my history, given my relationship to the lawsuit. I anticipate you will find it an entertaining read."

"I hope so. Most of these reports are dull as dishwater. I don't mean to sound rude, because you've been nothing but civil, which I suspect was your intent anyway. I get it. We're keeping the gloves on for now. I'm cool with it. I'm always happier working with cooperative witnesses and suspects. Keeping it friendly right up to the point I slap on the cuffs is always more fun. Like an old *Columbo* episode. So, I'm sure you can tell me where you were on Friday night, say, between ten and two in the morning."

"I didn't expect to be interrogated."

"And yet, here we are. It'll save me a trip to visit you again later."

"Oh," McCool said, "I have no doubt we are destined to meet again. Perhaps frequently."

"Goody. A new friend. Your whereabouts, please?"

McCool sipped from his glass and paused to savor it. "I was in Charlotte, visiting friends with my wife. We had dinner at their house and stayed overnight as their guests. I can arrange for an affidavit if you'd like."

"Not necessary. Names and address are fine. I'll take it from there."

"Have a pen on you?"

Durham took the names of a former Charlotte mayor and her prominent banker husband. He knew their address, as he had attended several parties there.

Durham slipped his notepad back in his pocket. "Thanks. No offense. Part of the job. You were here during the shootout in 1977, weren't you?"

"What do you know about the shootout?"

"Next to nothing. Have a file on it waiting upstairs."

"I was there, yes," he said. "Terrible tragedy. On the other hand, it launched my political career, from which I profited tremendously. Oh, don't give me that look. I'm notorious, boy! Everyone knows what I did, and how I went to prison for it. Let me tell you, it was worth every minute of the five years I spent in Club Fed. Don't ever let them tell you crime doesn't pay. It pays extremely well."

"It's done okay by me, but of course I'm on the back end."

He sipped from the glass again.

"Of course, that was over and done years ago. On the straight and narrow nowadays. Got my law license back, and—as everyone knows—all my ill-gotten gains in the Caymans are still drawing interest. I can't touch it, you know. If I bring a cent back into the US, I go bye-bye again. So, it's there waiting for me to finally pull the ripcord, retire for good, and knock the dust of this snoopy country off my sandals. It's a romantic notion, and a guaranteed conversation-starter at a cocktail party. In the meantime, I discovered it's almost as easy to rake in cash legitimately. Go figure. As careers go, you gotta love the law." He raised his glass as a sort of toast.

"I only ask about the shootout because a couple of the people I'm looking at are linked to it."

"Me and Darrell Tanney," McCool said.

"And your son, tangentially, but he was born later. You and Tanney were here at the time. Anything you can tell me about Tanney's father?"

"I imagine most of it is in your reports. Elbert—Chief Tanney—was the hero of the shootout. Saved the mayor and that rabblerousing preacher who caused the whole thing. Died of a heart attack later that day. I was a young attorney, the only one in town, so I was also the town's attorney, but I was in my office when it all went tits-up. I can tell you something that isn't in those reports, though."

"I'm all ears."

"Elbert Tanney planned to turn in his badge the day after the shootout. This comes from the mayor at the time, Roger Gimball. Straight from his mouth. Tanney believed the mayor and I were planning to send one of the Choctaw cops down the river, sacrificing the kid to quell the riot growing outside in the street—right outside these doors, in fact. If he'd been a lesser man, he'd have quit on the spot, but he said he'd stay on the job until the disturbance was over, and he'd turn in his papers the next day. Then all hell broke loose."

McCool leaned forward and cupped his forehead in his hand, the way old men do when remembering a great failure—or when they were pretending to do so. "I don't like to recall the day, sir. Tanney was a good cop. Roger Gimball and I tried to do right by his son."

"Did the cop get sent away?" Durham asked.

"Oh, yes," McCool said. "He did indeed. It will all be in your report. It's been a long day, and I suddenly find myself fatigued. Age will do that, with the assistance of these lovely aperitifs. I wanted to meet you tonight, get the measure of you. I wanted to know what kind of man you are."

Durham didn't say anything. He sipped at the beer and waited.

The old man smiled.

"Now that I've met you," he said, finally, "I suspect someone is in deep trouble. Good evening, Agent Durham. I believe we should keep our relationship on a formal basis going forward, as I may find myself counseling some of my clients regarding their discussions with you. It was a pleasure."

They clasped hands again, and the old man sauntered out the door as fleetly and nimble as Gene Kelly in *Singin' In The Rain*.

"Fatigued, my ass." Durham said to nobody as McCool stepped onto the sidewalk. "And, yeah. Someone is in a heap of trouble."

SEVENTEEN

When Durham stepped outside the Choctaw Arms the next morning, still bleary-eyed from reading deep into the blue-black hours of the night, workers had erected tall ladders along the Main Street sidewalk. Strips of patriotic multicolored bunting hung from several streetlamps, to be strung together the length of the commercial district. A banner already hung over the street directly outside Town Hall. It read:

CHOCTAW FOUNDERS DAY CELEBRATION!!!
SATURDAY, OCTOBER 21ST!!!
FUN! GAMES! MUSIC! FIREWORKS!

"Oh, great," he mumbled. The last thing he needed interfering with his investigation was huge crowds of people and the inevitable confusion associated with a celebration this size. The next weekend was supposed to be the first Saturday night in two months he wouldn't be strapped inside a race car. He had looked forward to spending it on his boat on Lake Norman, or at the beach, or maybe lounging on his couch watching a Tar Heels football game, not investigating some stupid murder of a has-been football player in a dying backwater burg in the Blue Ridge.

"Good," he said to himself. He was irritated. He always worked better when he was irritated. After poring over comprehensive data dumps on Choctaw's finest, it was time to make people uncomfortable, and this damned celebration wasn't going to help.

Within seconds of taking his place in his booth office at the Choctaw Grille, Kylee Wampler strolled over from the counter.

"Mornin' Blade," she said.

"Oh, hell," he said. "Who tattled?"

"Your nickname? It's all over town."

"And are you feeling all right?"

"Sure, Sugar. Why?"

"I saw you coming this time."

"Oh, honey, I am way too proud to jump on a straight line that sweet. Breakfast? You slept in this morning. Most of the regular crowd's already off to work."

"Coffee first. I was reading research late into the night. There was a lot to digest."

She returned with two cups of coffee and sat across from him.

"Want some company?" she asked.

"Sure. The conversation will keep me awake until the caffeine kicks in. I don't want to keep you from your work, though."

"The breakfast rush is over. Place is dead until noon. I put in an order for the Farmer's Platter. It'll either jumpstart your heart or clog it shut. Works different on each person. Kind of like Russian roulette."

"What's in it?"

"It's sort of a full English breakfast, except it isn't. I substitute liver mush for black pudding, for instance."

"Yum." He sipped his coffee.

"And they'd run me out of town if I didn't include grits, so the white sausage has to go. And country ham instead of whatever stuff I ate in London."

"Back bacon," he said. "You've been to London?"

"You haven't?"

"Sure I have."

"Well, there you are." A bell dinged at the counter. "Back in sec."

Some two or three tenths of a second later, his plate sat in front of him. It arrived so quickly, he thought he'd briefly fallen asleep in his seat. The platter was huge and packed with food.

"Wow," he said. "Did you leave any for the starving kids in China?"

"I had Nikos make it shareable." She pinched a crispy strip of bacon and nibbled on it.

"You called Tim McCool *Shit-For-Brains*," he said. "To his face."

"I was in a good mood. I went easy on him."

"He sat there and took it. Barely flinched. It suggests you two are familiar."

"Shoot, Blade, I run the only diner in town. Everybody rolls through here sooner or later. After a few years, we're all one big bundle of bosom buddies. Small towns are like that. But, yeah. Shit-For-Brains and I have a history. A short one." She held her thumb and forefinger about an inch apart. She giggled. Her giggle wasn't annoying at all. "I don't care. I'm not a size queen or anything. That wasn't the problem."

"What was?"

She speared a grilled mushroom with her fork. "I couldn't trust the sneaky little bastard." She wiggled the fingers on her left hand. "No rings, no strings, right? I didn't care if he was boinking someone else. It wasn't a possessive thing. I just didn't appreciate hearing about it at my book club."

"I can imagine the discomfort."

"I mean, keep me in the loop. I'm a big girl. It's simple good manners. Don't misread what you saw the other night. I don't hate Timmy or anything. He's not a terrible person. Juvenile and thoughtless, maybe, and kind of selfish in bed, and he's kind of full of himself otherwise, but deep down he's okay, in small doses."

"I believe we've just written his epitaph," Durham said, and shoveled a forkful of the eggs into his mouth. "This is good. How long have you been in the food service business?"

"Five years, three months, seventeen days, and—" She glanced at the clock over the counter. "—four hours, twenty-six minutes. And I can't take credit for the food. Nikos came with the diner. I pay him three times what he'd get anywhere else, because I want to keep him happy. If he ever dies or jumps ship, I'll have to sell the place."

"Your accent tells me you're not local," he said.

"Moved here five years and change ago."

"When you entered the food service business."

"You *are* a detective, aren't you?"

"Why Choctaw?"

"I have a connection." She popped a seared cherry tomato into her mouth. "My mother was raised here, but she moved away when she was a teenager. She told me stories about the place. Decided to check it out after I won the lottery."

"Pardon?" he asked.

"The lottery. I won it."

"We're not speaking in euphemisms?"

"The real lottery. Cold hard cash, Sherlock. I bought a lottery ticket and hit everything but the Powerball. Copped a cool million, before taxes. A shit-ton of taxes. Second biggest check I've ever written."

"What's the largest?"

"You're sitting in it. But there was plenty left over to make a fresh start. I hit town the same day the diner came up for sale and I bought it in a moment of weakness. Figured it was kismet."

"How long after you bought the diner did you and Tim McCool—"

"Within a week or two. He has some kind of radar for fresh talent in town, like those pimps who hang out in Hollywood bus stations waiting for innocent kids from Peoria to hop off the Greyhound with dreams of stardom. So I hear."

"But you're not bitter," Durham said.

"At least I have that. You really like the food?"

He pointed to the rapidly emptying plate. "Hits the spot. How about the other council members?"

"Oh, I didn't sleep with any of them."

"Not what I meant," he said. "But duly noted."

"I know. I'm jerking off your chain."

"The term is—"

"I *know* what it is, Blade. Geez. Okay. Mags McLeod. A real cougar, I hear, but she's discreet about it. She was Prom Queen or something back in the day. Still fills a dress nicely, and she's shrewd. She's currently on husband number three. He keeps mostly to his *pied-a-terre* in Asheville, and I hear he has a divorce attorney on retainer. She's so proud of the McLeod heritage, she never took any of her husbands' names, which is about all she didn't take. Mags is like the irresistible cream puff that gives you the everlasting squirts."

"You said she's shrewd."

"She's smart, and she's tough. She doesn't mind making hard decisions."

"Would she kill someone?"

"I don't think she'd mind *telling* someone to kill someone. I don't know if she could pull the trigger herself. Might mess up her nails."

"How about Oscar Tattersall?"

"Oz? Santa Claus is a suspect?"

Durham smeared some jam on a perfectly browned slice of toast. "Everyone is a suspect until they aren't."

"Including me?"

"Sure. Can you account for your whereabouts the night of the murder?"

"We do karaoke here Friday nights until eleven. Nikos and I were cleaning until after one."

"I'll mark you and Nikos off the list."

"Might as well scratch Oz, too," she said. "Everybody loves him. He loves everybody. Hell, I even saw him bending an elbow in here with Win Savage a couple of times, and they looked friendly enough. A lot of people in Choctaw would have gone under during the pandemic if it hadn't been for Oz Tattersall."

"That's the second time someone's told me that. So he's a good guy?"

"He gets elected every four years without even campaigning. Yeah. He's a good guy. I can't imagine him hurting an ant, at least on purpose."

"How about Garry Kinnison?"

"He's Mags McLeod's sock puppet, and he's a little mental. He wouldn't know which hole to pee out of if she didn't tell him."

"Colorfully descriptive."

"They eat together here three or four times a week. That booth, away from the front window. She's always on his case and he always looks like a kid in school who didn't do his homework. He has one of the nicest houses in town, and he rents out half the others, but he'd be as content living in someone's basement. He's a rubber stamp for anything Mags wants passed at the council meetings."

"What's her hold over him?"

"He's weird and a little spineless. Doesn't get out much. I wouldn't testify to it, but I've heard through the grapevine she keeps him in line with the occasional advantageously timed mercy hummer."

"You said Mags would easily order a murder, if it suited her. Would Kinnison kill for her?"

She giggled again. "You plan to interview Garry Kinnison?"

"I do."

"Come back afterward and ask me that question again."

———

Durham carried two foam cups of coffee into the Choctaw Police Station. He walked directly back to Bobbi Navarro's office. The door was cracked, so he nudged it with his toe.

Bobbi sat at her desk, scribbling on a yellow legal pad.

"Mid-morning pick-me-up," Durham said, handing her the cup.

"From the Grille?"

"I just finished breakfast."

She glanced at the clock on her office wall and raised an eyebrow.

"I worked late into the night," he added. "Had to assimilate a lot of information. Have you ever tried the Farmer's Platter at the Grille?"

"The coronary you eat with a fork? I hear they stuff it down a gander's throat to make *foie gras*. Sure. I've eaten it."

"Tell me about Founders' Day."

"The workers outside? It's this Saturday. I've only been to one, last year."

"Is it a big deal?"

"How do you mean?" she asked.

"Is it just locals, or does it draw flatlanders, like the Woolly Worm Festival in Banner Elk?"

"Mostly locals. We might have a few people drive in from Asheville or Blowing Rock or Marion. As I recall, last year's Founders' Day drew around a thousand people total, including the locals. Some Appalachian craftspeople set up sales booths along Main Street. Most of the outsiders come for that and the bluegrass contest."

"The timing could be better," he said.

"I agree, especially because I'm in charge of security. I'm feeling uncomfortably stretchy this week. Got a call about a half hour ago.

Gaby Reyes' private jet arrives around one at Asheville. She has a limo reserved and should be in Choctaw by three this afternoon. She asked whether she could stay at Savage's house. I told her it was still sealed."

"Three o'clock gives me time to do my interviews. Can you get with Chuck Hogan today and obtain a list of all his employees over the last five years?"

"Sure. You think one of them might have a copy of the smokehouse padlock key?"

"Are you certain you need my help?"

"I never thought about a second key until you mentioned Hogan's employees. I'll get the list for you."

"Thanks. One more request. This might sound a little strange. Is there some way I could lay my hands on the murder book for the Patricia Masters case?"

She looked puzzled. "I never heard of it."

"Patricia Masters was the principal at Choctaw High School in 1977. She was murdered. It was the trigger for the Choctaw Shootout."

"I heard the shootout was part of the protest after a Choctaw cop killed a black man."

"The man's name was Lester Corby. He was a suspect in the Masters case. It's why the cops rousted him in the first place."

"1977. Those case files were never digitized. I'm sure they're somewhere in our records storage facility."

"How about the forensic evidence in the case? Masters' clothes and medical samples? Are they in storage too?"

"I can't say. To tell you the truth, I've never even been there," she said.

"Can you assign someone to retrieve the murder book and any physical evidence they might have stored?"

She leaned back in her chair, which creaked in protest. She sipped at the coffee.

"I might, if you were little less cryptic. Is this related to the Savage case?" she asked.

"I don't know," he said. "There are some common threads. What bothers me is nobody was ever charged in the Masters murder. It's still an open investigation." He stood to walk out the door.

"Durham," she said.

He turned back.

"I don't mind handling your scut work, because you're doing me a solid here. But I'm getting a little tired of taking direction without any real explanation, you know? I want you to keep me in the loop. I want to know why you're doing whatever you're doing. I'm not without skills of my own."

"You're right," he said. He closed the door and sat again, facing her. "Sometimes I get wrapped up in a case and forget I'm not the only cop on the beat. The McCools and Darrell Tanney are part of the Choctaw Shootout story, as well as the Savage murder. If those links exist, there may be others. Things have changed a lot in forty-five years. We have technology nobody dreamed of back then. At the very least, maybe we can get Masters a little justice while we're solving Savage's killing."

"Your suspects?"

"I've cleared you, Trent McCool, Kylee Wampler, Gaby Reyes, and Taylor Pettigrew. Tim McCool's alibi is pure shit, so—while I hate to admit it—it's probably true. True or not, it moves him down the list. He's no Fulbright candidate, but if he had something to hide, he'd figure out a way to cover himself with a lie. That leaves everybody else. I plan to meet with the other council members today. Maybe one of them will try to shine me on. I'll fill you in on each of the interviews as soon as I return, before we talk to Gaby Reyes. Deal?"

"Fair enough," she said.

EIGHTEEN

Durham called ahead to locate Oz Tattersall amongst his vast Choctaw mercantile empire. He was tending to the hardware store. Chief Navarro gave him directions, and Durham set out on foot.

As soon as he exited the station, he saw Tim McCool walking toward him on the sidewalk.

"How about this?" McCool said, greeting him, and pointing to the banners and bunting going up all along Main Street. "Going to be quite a festival this year."

"Don't take this the wrong way, but I hope I'm gone by then," Durham said.

"I understand completely, and to be perfectly honest, I have the same hope. No offense, but an ongoing murder investigation might put a damper on the crowds."

"Seems we're mutually inconvenient for each other," Durham said.

"I wouldn't go that far. I, uh, didn't make it by the station yesterday like you asked. I had some urgent town business. I'm sure you can understand, with Win Savage dead, we aren't sure what the status is with the lawsuit over Choctaw Knob. The council met in emergency session to discuss our next moves." He held up his hands and wiggled his fingers. "Don't worry, though, I'm on my way now to get printed."

"Thank you. I met your father last night."

McCool blinked a couple of times. "You did? How curious."

"Yes. It was. I recognized him immediately. You favor him."

"Funny. He's never mentioned it. Any progress?"

"Here's the way investigations work, Mr. McCool. They drag and drag, until suddenly they speed up. We're still dragging. Don't worry, though. I expect to see things accelerate soon. Thanks again for giving us your prints."

————

Like everything else in Choctaw, the hardware store was a throwback to a bygone era. The linoleum floors and garish fluorescent ceiling lights and cement block construction of modern big-block facilities were nowhere in sight. Instead, the floors were heart pine with valleys worn in the aisles by decades of shoppers' shoes, and incandescent lamps the size of basketballs suspended under patinaed stamped brass shades on spindly poles from the ceiling. The bins on each aisle were made of wood instead of stamped steel. There was no garden department or outdoor grilling section or even a household appliance floor. The Choctaw Hardware was dedicated to the serious business of purveying tools and nails and screws and doorknobs and any other raw materials needed to build any project. If it was built of steel and could fit in a toolbox, you'd find it there. If it didn't fit, they could sell you a larger toolbox.

In the back corner of the store was a small booth labeled *Locksmith*. On the other side of the floor was another booth labeled *Post Office*. The building was old—at least a hundred fifty years, judging by the bricks and the mortar and the wavy glass in the windows. The inside smelled ancient. Durham figured there might be tools on sale that were already in stock when his grandfather was a boy.

He heard a sound in the back, behind a pair of swinging double doors.

"Anyone home?" he called out.

"Hold your horses," a husky, wet voice called out from the back. "Be a minute. Don't steal nothin' before I can get there."

Presently, the doors parted, and Oscar Tattersall walked through. When Kylee had referred to Tattersall as Santa Claus, she hadn't been far wrong. He stood slightly over six feet tall and went nearly four sideways. He wore trousers held up with red and green suspenders, over a tartan print flannel shirt. His beard was full and white as a new-fallen snowdrift and his shock-white hair fell on either side of his head in thick waves. His glasses were metal-rimmed and round. You could lose a soccer ball in his eyebrows.

"Help you?" Tattersall asked with a huge, apparently genuine smile. He spied Durham's sidearm, and the badge clipped to his belt. "Hey, you must be the SBI agent fella. How ya doin'? Oz Tattersall. Talked to Tim McCool yesterday. He told me you'd drop by sooner or later. C'mon. Have a seat behind the counter here. Want a Coke?"

He extended a hand roughly the size of a Virginia ham. His grip was loose and mushy and damp. A battered red Coca-Cola refrigerator bin sat behind the counter, next to a café table with a checkers set on it. Tattersall grabbed two bottles and popped the caps on the opener at the side of the bin. He handed one to Durham. It was ice-cold. Rivulets of water dripped down the sides as he grasped it.

"Sorry I wasn't out here to greet you. My manager's in Asheville for the day, and his assistant's out with the flu. I'm covering for them both. Had to tend to some deliveries in the back. So, how can I help you?"

"First things first. Can you tell me your whereabouts Friday night, say between ten and two?"

"I was sound asleep. Went to bed a little after nine-thirty."

"Alone?" Durham asked.

"That is my tragedy," he said, gesturing at his considerable girth. "Had a girlfriend a few years back, but she left me. Said she couldn't cuddle up to a skinny man like me. Went off to find someone with some meat on his bones."

He waited a full three seconds before laughing, deep and rumbling like cement tumbling in a mixer, at his own joke.

"Hell," he said, "Some days you gotta laugh to keep from cryin'. No, I'm a skylark, Agent Durham. Early to bed and early to rise. Don't have much use for the dark half of the day."

"So, nobody can validate your story?"

He held out his hands. "Slap 'em on, Inspector. I have no alibi."

"Let's not put the cart before the horse. Would you mind if I look at your telephone?"

Tattersall pulled an iPhone from his pocket. "Only if you promise to ignore all the porn on it," he said, and slid it across the checkerboard. Durham held the phone gingerly, and Tattersall burst into laughter again. "Pullin' your leg!"

It took Durham thirty seconds to isolate Tattersall's location app. Presuming Tattersall kept his phone with him, he'd been in all night on Friday. It was always possible he'd gone out and left the phone behind, but—at least so far—Durham was inclined to believe him. That made two suspects with horrible alibis whom he still believed probably didn't kill Savage, at least in person. He slid the phone back to Tattersall.

"May I ask how much money you have tied up, personally, in the Choctaw Knob ski resort?" Durham asked.

"A little under two million dollars," he said, without hesitation. "One-point-one-nine-something, if I recall correctly."

"Is it in escrow or being used for development costs?"

"It's long gone, I'm afraid. In fact, Mayor Tinsley and I were discussing the issue yesterday. All of us on the development team will likely need to pony up some more capital soon."

"You expect the project to go forward?"

"I see no reason why it shouldn't," Tattersall said.

"Now that Winlock Savage is out of the picture?"

"Frankly, yes. I have nothing to hide, and there's nothing shady going on with the Choctaw Knob project. Win Savage opposed the ski resort on ideological and environmentalist grounds. He never suggested or intimated the development board—"

"Which is identical to the Town Council?" Durham noted.

"I won't deny it. All the council members own stock in the development corporation. We have other investors as well."

"From here in Choctaw?"

"Yes. And elsewhere. To be completely transparent, the council constitutes approximately ninety percent of the current investment in the project. Win Savage never accused any of us of any wrongdoing. We wanted the resort. He didn't. It was a simple conflict."

"A conflict in which one side stood to lose millions of dollars. Could you estimate how much the development board has invested already?" Durham asked.

"I'd say, perhaps, seven million dollars. And change."

"With more to be raised before the project could continue?"

"We always expected there would be a second round of investment required."

Durham looked around the hardware again. "I'm truly impressed with this store. Reminds me of a place around the corner from my grandfather's house, a long time ago. Chief Navarro tells me you own several stores in the area."

"Most of them," he said. "Not saying much. I'm the big fish in the small pond. I own the grocery and the drug store and the hardware, along with a couple of other smaller concerns—a laundromat and small vending machine business."

"Can't help noticing nobody's come in since I arrived."

"It's a slow time of the day. Most people are at work."

"Chief Navarro also estimates the population of Choctaw has dropped by half since the turn of the century. She says there might be no more than four or five hundred people here now, and the number's still falling."

"All the better reason to keep my stores running. It's a long drive to Asheville or Marion or Burnsville, a lot of it over twisting mountain roads. Many Choctaw citizens depend on my stores to survive. It is one of the great privileges of my life to serve this community."

"And they sure love you," Durham said. "Everyone I've talked to has said the same thing. During the pandemic, you held this town together by extending credit to anyone who needed it."

"I did. Are you implying something?"

"Not at all. I'm trying to get a feel for the town and its people, and the people do admire you. A couple of them have suggested you're the heart of Choctaw. I figured, to understand the town, I need to understand you."

"I see."

"However, now that you mention it," Durham continued. "Being the savior of Choctaw probably left you with a lot of large red numbers in your Accounts Receivable ledger."

"If you're suggesting I'm profiting from this debt, I can assure you I'm not. I haven't charged a penny of interest on it. Those people needed help. It would have been inhuman to gouge them in their hours of need, or even now, when they're just getting back on their feet."

"Please, forgive me," Durham said. "I didn't intend to accuse you. Not at all. Exactly the opposite, in fact. I think you took a bath during the pandemic, and for the noblest of motives. Fortunately, at least for the moment, you could afford it. However, if every person in town who owes you money today paid it back tomorrow, you'd still only be even, right?"

"Right."

"And with the local population dwindling, anyone can tell the growth curve for your retail domain is on a downward trajectory. I can look around this empty store and see it."

"I don't see your point."

"You invested almost two million dollars of your own money in the Choctaw Knob project at the same time you were—admirably—extending credit to your neighbors, much of which has not been repaid. The one path for you to pull this hardware store and your other businesses out of a potential death spiral requires the Choctaw Knob ski resort to go through. The resort is your lifeline, Oz. Without it, bankruptcy looms. Maybe not this year or the next, but without tourist money, sooner or later this dying town won't be able to support your businesses."

"Are you accusing me of something?" Tattersall asked, his smile as benign as ever. He seemed almost jovial. "Should I contact my attorney?"

"Trent McCool?"

"Is he a problem? It sounds as if you think the sole possible motive for killing Winlock Savage was financial. I don't think so. I knew the man. In some ways, we were friendly, at least when we weren't arguing about one damned thing or another."

"You argued?"

Tattersall laughed again. "You trying to trap me, Agent Durham?"

"Call me Wade."

"Like I said. Nothing to hide. Not a thing. I'm too boring to have secrets. Win and I argued about all sorts of things. Politics. Whether the Panthers will ever go all the way. Whether the sky was blue that day. You name it. The guy liked to argue. And, we got into it a couple of times over the ski resort. It's the only time I had the impression he didn't enjoy the argument. So, yeah, we argued, but it was almost always good-natured."

"Why don't you think he enjoyed arguing about the resort?" Durham asked.

"Damned if I know. I didn't live inside the man's head. Maybe he wasn't challenging the resort alone. Maybe someone was pulling his strings in the background. Beats me. I'm sorry he's dead. I truly am. I enjoyed our conversations, even the arguments. He was one of those guys who never met a stranger. He could work a room like a master pickpocket. Having him around always made a party livelier. I'll miss him. But I won't miss watching my two-million-dollar investment clog the toilet on the way to the septic tank."

"To be clear, you *did* benefit from his murder?"

For the first time, Tattersall looked irritated. "So did every damned investor in the Choctaw Knob resort. Sometimes the universe, through no effort of your own, deals a hand in your favor. Who can explain it? I see what you're doing, and why you're asking these questions, but I am not required to enjoy it."

"It's a good thing your telephone supports your story about Friday night," Durham said. "You seem like too nice a guy to arrest on suspicion."

"Shoot, if I'd known ahead of time, I'd have called in some hooker from Asheville for a visit on Friday night to prove I was at home. Your expression is a hoot. Sure. Look at me. Y'know what I hear all the time, behind my back? *'Everybody loves Oz Tattersall.'* Well, let me tell you, *Wade*, everybody in town might love Old Oz, but nobody in this town fucks him. That's for damn sure. So, once in a long while, I swipe right on an outcall ad for a fatty-fucker hottie with granddaddy issues. They always love crawling all over Santa, because I tip like a sumbitch. I don't mean to shock you. I figured you'd run across this little tidbit sooner or later. Why keep it a secret?"

"I appreciate your candor, and more power to you. I don't care about your private life unless it can bolster your alibi. You and Savage were familiar. Did he ever mention any other disputes he was wrapped in?"

"I don't understand the question," Tattersall said.

"Was he suing anyone else? Did he owe anyone a bunch of money? Was he fronting for some other group trying to stop the ski resort? Did anyone else profit from his murder? The list of questions goes on for a several pages."

"I wish I had answers for you, sir. I'm an open book. Ask anything you want about me. When it comes to Winlock Savage, though, I have no idea what made the man tick. I liked him, but I don't believe I ever truly knew him, and I for damn sure had no reason to kill him. I'm on the wrong end of my seventies and I got the diabetes and my cholesterol numbers are like pinball scores. Odds are I won't live long enough for my businesses to go bankrupt, and I got nobody to leave my estate to. Killing Winlock Savage would have been a waste of a good drinking buddy. I'm sorry my alibi is weak, but so is my motive. Drop by any time, Wade. You're an easy man to talk to."

NINETEEN

Durham located Margaret 'Mags' McLeod in her real estate office inside a small arcade of sole proprietorships on Main Street, seven doors from the Choctaw Arms.

A four-color poster on the window outside her office advertised homes for sale in the Choctaw Valley. The poster was browning at the edges, and he noticed some of the home pictures had snow on the ground. The real estate market in Choctaw had suffered during the pandemic, and from what Bobbi Navarro had told him, it didn't look likely to recover. The natural next question was obvious. If McLeod's real estate business was faltering, where was she coming up with the money to invest in Tim McCool's ski resort scheme?

"I'm independently wealthy," she explained when he asked. "Ian McCool and Persistence McLeod founded Choctaw a generation before the American Revolution. No doubt you've already heard the story about their ill-gotten booty from Scotland."

"People have referred to it, but I don't know the details."

"Nobody does, darling. That's what makes it so fuckin' romantic. I can't complain. Generational wealth is nothing to sniff at."

Mags McLeod was in her early sixties, which you'd only know if you checked her driver's license or her hands. She looked like an hourglass that worked out in the gym seven days a week. She'd employed the services of a high-priced and masterful plastic surgeon, who had managed to make her look young-ish without the waxen, frozen cast of a typical stretch job. Durham had no doubt the rejuvenation continued all the way to her ankles. She was blonde and statuesque and almost too-perfectly put together. Even after six decades, she was a damned attractive woman, and she knew it.

She had ushered Durham into her office, which had been elegantly remodeled perhaps a decade earlier, and looked it. She directed him toward a loveseat and took the chair diagonal to him, being sure to cross her legs, which were excellent.

"Hope you don't mind if I cuss," she said. She had a whiskey-and-tobacco voice and the accent of a Grand Ol' Opry diva. "It's among my many unfortunate vices. I read in a magazine article that compulsive profanity is an indicator of a highly fuckin' intelligent mind. What do you think?"

"I suppose it could also suggest Tourette's, but I'm no expert," Durham said. "You seem smart enough."

"I can account for my whereabouts on the night Win Savage was killed. I was in Asheville with my husband, entertaining a couple of friends at Cúrate. Trent McCool suggested you might ask."

"Thank you," he said. "I noticed as I drove into town that a lot of houses, especially those at the far end of Main Street, are dark."

"We lost a lot of fuckin' people in the pandemic," she said. "Some were good friends. A lot of the houses are still in probate. They'll come on the market eventually."

"If you don't mind me asking, who will buy them?"

She cocked her perfectly coiffed head. "Beg pardon?"

"Everyone I've spoken with has said Choctaw is dying. The population is drying up. Nobody is moving in from the flatlands. Who would buy the houses if they're listed?"

She spread her skirt flat over her thigh. "Once the fuckin' ski resort is finished, people will return to Choctaw. They'll buy the houses if only to turn them into fuckin' B&Bs."

"You're certain it will be finished?"

"Of course."

"Despite Winlock Savage's lawsuit?"

"Trent has assured us the lawsuit will be dropped shortly. Even so, I don't think Win had a fuckin' prayer of winning in this district."

"What if he had the resources to keep filing appeals? He could starve the Choctaw Knob investors of cash simply by running out the clock. He didn't need to win the cases. He merely had to outwait your finances. He could have held the ski resort under an unbreakable siege."

"You have an extremely strategic mind, Agent Durham."

"Call me Wade."

"Not *Blade*?"

"Some people call me that as well. How much have you invested personally in the ski resort project?"

"A little over one and half million," she said.

"And now Tim McCool wants each of the investors to open their purses again?"

"How did you know—" she stopped herself. "Well. That sounded fuckin' defensive. It doesn't matter, does it? Yes. In order to move to the next phase of the development, I'll—*we'll*—need to invest again."

"Would it be fair to say Choctaw will be ruined if the ski resort isn't constructed?"

"I refuse to be pessimistic about the future of this town."

"But facts are facts, aren't they, Ms. McLeod? Your entire financial future hinges on the completion of the Choctaw Knob project. Without it, all those pretty little houses at the far end of Main Street will crumble into decay, waiting for buyers who will never show. How long can your business sustain itself without houses to sell and people to buy them?"

"What are you suggesting?"

"Maybe you didn't kill Winlock Savage," he said. "In fact, I'm largely convinced you didn't, at least personally. With him dead, though, the impact of his lawsuit on the ski resort is largely eliminated. Even if it goes forward, all you and the other defendants have to do is find a friendly judge and win the case. Who's going to file an appeal? So, you didn't kill him, but you'll probably profit from his murder, which makes me curious."

"Understandable. Your job is to suspect everyone. And I can tell you're good at it." The seductive undertone was unmistakable.

"What I can't explain is why you visited Savage's house the night before he died," he said.

Her mask dropped. It was as if her Botox suddenly quit working altogether, and everything sagged momentarily as she processed this new revelation. Her face snapped back into perfect control.

"Say what?" she asked, as sweetly as the adrenaline permitted.

"My team in Charlotte traced Win Savage's telephone activity over the day or so before he died. We needed to establish his whereabouts. We also traced all the calls placed to and from his phone. You had four conversations with Savage between Wednesday morning and Thursday afternoon. Two were from his phone. Two were from yours. They were lengthy, ranging from eight to fourteen minutes. I asked my Charlotte whiz kids to trace the activity on your phone—"

"Wait!" she said. "You can do that?"

"We're the SBI. We answer only to the governor. Who's going to tell us we can't? I had probable cause, in any case, given the length of the conversations and their proximity to his murder. Getting a search warrant was easy. You weren't calling him for the time and temperature. The trace placed your telephone at Win Savage's home on Thursday. You arrived at six-thirty-seven. Your telephone remained at that address until ten-twenty-two. Almost four hours. So, like I said, the fact you will likely profit from Savage's murder makes me extremely curious, especially because I don't know what you were doing at his place for almost four hours the night before he died."

TWENTY

"That horndog!" Bobbi said. "Savage was boinking Gaby Reyes, this gymnast chick, *and* Mags McLeod?"

"Shocking, isn't it?" Durham said.

"Tell you the truth, I'm a little insulted. He never even gave me the time of day. Okay. Dish. I want all the sexy details."

"It's a long-smoldering flame. Mags and Savage were in the same class at Choctaw High. 1978. He was the BMOC—according to Mags, in almost every conceivable way—and she was a cheerleader and Homecoming Queen. They were the hot item heading into senior year. Then they broke up. She says he called things off without warning at the end of summer vacation. He took all that BDE to a championship season, went off and became rich and famous, and Mags stayed in Choctaw."

"And, late in life, Win Savage came home," Bobbi said.

"It took a while to rekindle the embers. Mags still resented Savage. She also married three men who looked a lot like him, but we'll let Freud sort that shit out. After he moved back to Choctaw, she gave him the cold shoulder until they were forced to work together on a committee for last year's Founders Day. He apologized for being an idiot back in high school."

"That's all it took?"

"Hardly, but it was a start. They've been meeting for about six months on the sly. Mags' current husband never leaves Asheville, and he stopped caring who she screws years ago, so nobody gives a rip. Savage kept it a secret, though."

"Good thing, considering his girlfriend's Annie Oakley inclinations."

"Exactly."

"Speaking of which, Gaby Reyes' jet landed on time. She should be here any minute." She leaned behind her desk and handed him a corrugated cardboard box.

"What's this?"

She turned the box around and showed him the label on the front. There was some alphanumeric filing gibberish, and underneath was the word *Masters*. A thin file rested on top of the box. Durham glanced through the file.

"This is it? The entire murder book?"

"I looked it over already," she said. "The detective on the case was Blue Crossed during the shootout. He went on permanent disability. Something about nerve damage. This is all he collected in the five days between the murder and the riot."

"So the case was left to molder?"

"That's about it, Blade. Choctaw lost its police chief and its only detective in the same half hour. The riot put this town on its ass for years. By the time we recovered, nobody remembered the Masters murder. Most people around here wanted to forget the entire decade."

"I wonder if the detective is still alive."

"I'll find out," she said. "Shouldn't take long."

He sifted through the contents of the box. "Masters' clothes, her personal possessions. Her pocketbook—damn, I sure wish they had cell phones in the seventies."

Bobbi was searching on her computer for information on Ted Wisniewski, the detective who had investigated the Masters murder in 1977. "Why's that?" she asked without looking up.

"There are two mysteries in the Masters case. Who killed her and who was she sleeping with? They could both be the same person, and again they might not."

"It matters," she said, absently.

"Sure does. Figuring out one might give us the other. Cell phones provide a personal history and can be tracked. In 1977, you could go almost anywhere without leaving a trail. Let's have these clothes tested, especially Masters' underwear. The original report suggested she had sex several hours before she was murdered. She should have residue in her underwear we can draw DNA from."

"Something else they couldn't do in 1977."

"Why I love cold cases so much. Perps can't protect themselves against technology that doesn't exist yet. If there's DNA in the underwear, we can sequence it and match it to the online databases. Maybe we get a direct match, maybe it's a first or second degree relative. In either case, we can extrapolate from there anyone who lived in Choctaw at the time. At worst, it narrows the field of suspects. At best, we get the guy's name right off the bat. Let's send these to your lab right away."

"You still think there's a connection between this murder forty-five years ago and the Savage killing?"

"It's more like a Spidey-sense thing. I feel like they're linked. I just don't know how."

"I found Ted Wisniewski," Bobbi said. "You gotta love the state retirement system. They keep excellent records. Wisniewski's been on state disability retirement and Social Security disability since the Choctaw Shootout. He lives in Burnsville. Says here he's eighty-six years old, so you better get a move on. He might not last the week."

"I'll talk to him tomorrow. I still need to interview Gaby Reyes and Garry Kinnison today and get these clothes to the lab."

"I'll handle the lab," she said. "My evidence locker guy is dying to see what the outside world looks like. I'll send him."

The civilian assistant who maintained the front desk, a wide-eyed recent college grad, appeared in Chief Navarro's doorway. "Um, Chief," she stammered. she whispered, "Gaby Reyes is in the outer office!"

"It isn't a state secret," Bobbi said. "We're expecting her."

"This is so *cool!*" the assistant said. "Do you think she'd let me get a selfie?"

"First things first," Bobbi said. "Please escort Ms. Reyes to the interview room and make sure she's comfortable. Offer her a drink or something. Don't treat her like a suspect. Agent Durham will meet with her in a few minutes."

"Oh boy!" the assistant said and scurried off.

"Can you record interviews?" Durham asked Bobbi.

"Fuck off," she said. "We made it to the twenty-first century in Choctaw like everyone else. We have cell phones and big screen televisions and electric cars and everything. Yeah. We record the interviews."

"Great."

"Schmuck."

"I'm sure you meant that in the nicest possible way."

"I'll hang out behind the glass, though," she said. "I catch stuff better if I see it live."

———

Gaby Reyes looked nothing like Durham had expected. She'd dressed for the trip in a red silk blouse and designer jeans and athletic shoes. Her hair, always teased to the ceiling in her promo pictures, was pulled flat to her scalp and tied in a tight ponytail at the crown of her head. Her makeup was minimal. It made her look vulnerable compared to the feral stage makeup the world saw in most of her photos. She looked like any young housewife in any upscale bourgeois neighborhood in any affluent city in the country.

What surprised him the most was her size. Celebrities frequently appeared taller in the media. Gaby Reyes had a huge stage presence that made her look eight feet tall from the cheap seats. In fact, she stood barely five feet and change in flats. It made her look even more vulnerable.

After introducing himself and commiserating with her on the death of her lover, Durham said, "Perhaps the best place for us to start is the night you shot the sofa in Mr. Savage's house."

"I'm embarrassed to talk about it now," she said. "I was crazy jealous because Win hadn't returned my calls for several days. I knew he was sleeping around on me. I could feel it. I took my private jet to Asheville and hired a limo to bring me here. When I arrived, I found him in the shower, and that little half-naked elf was prancing around the house like she lived there."

"What elf?" Durham asked.

"The gymnast, Taylor whatever. She was sweet enough, and I don't think Win told her he was with me, but I did not need to show up and find her with him. He tried to shine me on, like it was no big deal, so I shot his sofa."

She reached into her pocketbook and took out the nickel-plated thirty-eight with the mother-of-pearl handle she had fired at Savage's couch. Reflexively, Durham was out of his chair and had his pistol braced at her within half a second.

"Put the weapon on the table!" he ordered.

Inside the observation room, Bobbi watched the one-way glass vibrate a little at his impressive command voice. She jumped up and dashed into the hallway.

"What the hell?" Gaby said, frightened. "I figured you'd want to test it."

"Leave the weapon on the table and back away," Durham told her. "Slowly."

Bobbi flung open the interrogation room door. "Durham! What the hell?"

"Secure the weapon," he told her.

Bobbi took the pistol from the table. Durham gestured for Gaby to sit back down.

"*Never,*" Durham told her, holstering his pistol. "Never never never *ever* bring a loaded weapon into a police station. It's the fastest way I know to get shot."

By then, Gaby was in tears. Durham knew he had frightened her, but it went both ways. He asked Bobbi to take Gaby's pistol to the evidence safe, and he tried to calm her.

"I know officers who have been shot inside their own stations," he explained. "This is our fault. Someone should have searched you before you were brought to the interview room, or at least asked if you were carrying. I apologize for shouting. Cop instinct. Training took over."

"Scared the fuck out of me, man," she said. "I'm trying to help here."

"Yes," he said. "And we appreciate it. Just never pull a gun on a cop again, okay? We're kind of sensitive about it. Can we get you something to help you relax? A soda? Some crackers? A Xanax?"

"Got my own Xanax, thanks," she said. "In my purse. If *that's* okay. You aren't going to shoot me over a Xanax, are you?"

"Pop it if you need it. I'll have someone bring you some water." He glanced at the mirror, knowing Bobbi would follow up.

"Thank you." She fished in her bag. The civilian assistant appeared seconds later at the door with a bottle of water. She lingered for a few seconds to adore Gaby Reyes, but left at a warning glance from Durham.

"Okay," he said, after Gaby dashed down a tab of Xanax with some of the water. "Can we try this again, without guns? You shot the sofa because you found Savage with another woman, Taylor Pettigrew."

"Yes. But it wasn't because he slept with her. I mean, I had nothing against her. She was sweet about it, like I said. I only wanted Win to take me seriously. I knew him. He lied. A lot."

"About other women?"

"About everything. I figured him out a long time ago. Eighty percent of Winlock Savage was carefully cultivated image. I mean, c'mon. He's twenty-four and comes off the bench after the AFC Championship Game when his quarterback is sidelined with the flu, and he pulls off the biggest underdog Super Bowl win in football history. It was like Doug Flutie's Hail Mary pass. He went from benchwarmer to superhero in two weeks. His entire reputation was based on a single game."

"You're a football fan?" he asked.

"Sure. I like it fine. My PR firm has a VIP suite for Titans games, and I go when I'm not on the road. I paid attention to the game. Learned the basics. But I was with Savage for over two years, and it was almost all he talked about. I mean, I get it. It was his profession. Got kind of tiresome after a while, anyway, especially after I realized his entire personality is fake."

"Fake?"

"It's a put-on. *Was* a put-on. Jesus. I'm still not used to talking about him in the past tense."

"So who was Win Savage?" Durham asked.

"His entire life, Savage was a frat boy jock. He never grew out of it. Stunted development or whatever. Failure to launch. He was permanently nineteen years old. Everything came easy for him. Once he had that Super Bowl ring, he was inducted into the Kool Kids Klub. Everybody wanted to court him. He was on all the talk shows and in all the magazines. *People* named him one of the sexiest men of the decade. That is a shit-ton of pressure to live up to, especially if it hits you all at once. Believe me. I know."

"I imagine fame can be a burden," Durham said.

"It's a double-edged sword. You take the good with the bad. A guy like Win Savage lapped it all up with a spoon, at first, and he started to believe his own PR. He was cover-model handsome, and he had this easy-going baritone voice and aw-shucks Carolina drawl, and he didn't trip all over his tongue on-camera. He was a natural for sportscasting. He was a natural at any job that involved sitting in front of a teleprompter and having someone in your ear telling you what to say next. He was the world's sexiest sock puppet."

"Why'd he quit?"

"He got old. Younger, sexier, better-known quarterbacks retired, and the networks needed his booth space on Sundays for them. First, he lost Sunday Night Football. Then he was booted off Thursday Night Football. Within a year or so, he was exiled to Sunday afternoon Cleveland Browns games, and the handwriting was on the wall. His next stop would be the Canadian Football League. He could see the future, and he wasn't in it. He decided to pull the ripcord himself before he became a public embarrassment."

"That's when he moved back to Choctaw?" Durham asked.

"More or less. I met him at a party Dolly threw in Nashville a few years back. I was on the way up at the time. Had just released my third hit single, so I had dodged the one-hit-wonder bullet. People started inviting me to the cool parties."

"Did you and Savage hit it off right away?"

"Shit, no. He was a shallow, self-absorbed white boy jock. In my opinion, at first, he figured getting it on with a Latina checked off another box on his liberal white guilt list."

"But he grew on you."

"It took a while. His public mask was glued on solid. I banged him the first time mostly because one of my friends said he was

212

hung like a Clydesdale, and I was seriously deep into my white nose period and had all this nervous energy I had to get rid of. And I did. He was good in bed. Well-practiced and surprisingly generous for a jock. Afterward, he dropped the bullshit and became a lot more open and vulnerable. I liked that guy. Would have been nice to see more of him."

"The night you shot the sofa. Was it the last time you saw him before he died?"

"Yes. I'm on tour. Had a one-week break for rest and relaxation, and I decided to surprise him. Surprise, surprise, right? Things could have gone better. I've been on the road ever since. We're on another break now. Can I ask? Are there any funeral plans yet?"

"It's complicated. The autopsy is complete, but as the case is still under investigation, he hasn't been released to a mortuary. Savage's parents are both dead, and he had no siblings. The police are still looking for someone to claim the body."

"He didn't talk about family. He didn't like to talk about his past here at all. It seemed to be a sore subject for him."

"Did he ever mention a woman named Mags McLeod?"

"Sure. I know Mags. She came out to the house for Sunday brunch a few times. Win believed he was a master chef. He was okay. I mean, I never choked on anything he cooked or wanted to toss it in the trash. He could have had a decent career at Waffle House if the football and television thing hadn't panned out."

"When was the last time she visited him while you were there?"

"Couple of months or so ago. Before the tour."

"How did they seem together?" he asked.

"I don't understand the question."

"Did they seem affectionate? Hostile? Confrontational?"

"It was brunch," she said. "We drank mimosas and bloody marys and ate blueberry *pain perdu* and shot the shit about everything except business, and then Win put a football game on the big screen. They were fine. Mags told me she and Savage dated in high school. They'd known each other forever. They always seemed comfortable together."

"This might be difficult," Durham said. "I have learned that Mags McLeod and Win Savage started an affair about six months ago, and it continued until the night before he died."

She sat for a moment, staring into space. "That son of a bitch," she said, finally. She sounded more disappointed than furious.

"Did Savage talk to you at all about the lawsuit he filed against the Choctaw City Council and the ski resort project?" Durham asked.

"No," she said. "I knew he filed it after the tour began, and the only time I saw him afterward, we had more important matters to discuss."

"I find it interesting that he was sleeping with a woman he was also suing."

"You wouldn't if you knew him. Win was the master of compartmentalization. He was an opportunist, and kind of a horndog. He was proud in his middle sixties that his dick still rose on command. A great deal of his life was dictated by that one-eyed monster. I've seen Mags in the pool at Win's place. We all skinny-dipped together on shrooms one afternoon with a couple of Mags' friends. She's tight for a woman her age. Well-tended. If she came on to Win, he wouldn't turn her down, especially since they have a history. Hell, he probably made the first move. I know I sound bitter. To be honest, the last month of my relationship with Win was the worst of our entire time together, and it isn't improving now that he's dead."

"Did Mags ever talk to you about the ski resort?"

"She tried to sell me on investing early on," she said. "I didn't like the idea. I liked Win, a whole bunch, but I didn't see us staying together forever, and I sure didn't want to own a piece of a ski resort in his backyard when we eventually went our separate ways. Besides, I knew Win opposed it. Investing would have just been one more stressor on our relationship."

"Are you aware of any of Savage's business associates? Did he collaborate with anybody on the lawsuit against the city?"

"After he retired, Win was into gig employment. He did a lot of personal appearances at twenty grand a pop. Grocery store openings, Thanksgiving parades, that sort of thing. His agent in Los Angeles set everything up. His name's Arch Cisneros. You have Win's phone?"

"We do."

"I bet half the calls from LA are from Arch. I'm surprised he hasn't already reached out to you."

"Yes," Durham said. "It is surprising, isn't it?"

"You think he doesn't know yet?"

"I think I can find out. You said you were skinny-dipping with Savage and Mags and a couple of her friends. Do you remember their names?"

"I only saw them the one time. They were nice. The guy was kind of goofy on shrooms, but, you know, in a cute way. The woman was fun. People get weird around celebs sometimes, but she was totally cool. Wait. That's it."

"What?"

215

"The guy's name. Cool something."

"Tim McCool?" Durham asked.

"McCool for sure. I don't remember his first name," she said.

"Older or younger fellow?"

"Older than me. Younger than Win. About your age. Maybe in his forties."

"How about the woman? Do you remember her name?"

She stared into space for a few seconds. "No. I could pick her out of a lineup if I had to. I have a good memory for faces and…you know. Stuff. She was closer to my age. Maybe thirty-five. Redhead. A lot of freckles. I mean, a *lot*. Bubbly. I don't swing that way, but if I did, I'd probably be attracted to her. I liked her, in any case. She didn't care who I was. We could talk about shit like regular people. You'd be surprised how rare that is."

"When was this?" Durham asked.

"It was hot. It was after July Fourth, because we were in Nashville for the holiday, and I had final rehearsals for the tour right afterward. I visited during a break in rehearsals, so it must have been middle July. It was a Sunday. Win suggested we do shrooms. Everyone was cool with it. The water felt amazing."

"I can imagine," Durham said.

TWENTY-ONE

The civilian assistant got her selfie with Gaby Reyes before the singing star left the station. It was the high point of her year.

Within a half hour, Durham and Bobbi had Savage's agent, Arch Cisneros, on a video call using the computer in Bobbi's office. Cisneros was in his forties. His office overlooked a clogged freeway in the San Fernando Valley, with mountains in the distance. He wore a tailored pima cotton pinstripe shirt and a tie probably woven from silk spun only by virgin worms. His face was stretched tighter than the skins on a pair of bongos. His grin looked painted on, kind of like his tan. He wore tinted eyeglasses. His pure Brooklyn accent seemed alien on a fellow so obviously Californian. His hair plugs had grown out nicely.

After identifying themselves, Durham said, "Your name came up in an interview with a witness in the Winlock Savage murder today."

"Terrible tragedy," Cisneros said. "Win wasn't just a longtime client. He was a friend. Have you made any progress in your investigation?"

"It's a process," Durham said. "We're expanding the questioning to people he knew outside Choctaw. One of the people we spoke with told us you were responsible for setting Savage's schedule."

"I was, though it became more difficult each year after he retired. People aren't as impressed with aging sports stars as they once were. I did what I could for him, though. I probably booked twenty or thirty appearances a year for him. He drew maybe twenty thousand a pop, sometimes more. I took my cut off the top. It was peanuts, but the guy was a pal, and he needed the money. Between that and his endorsements, he wasn't going to starve, but he was always strapped."

"He was?" Bobbi asked. "A guy like Winlock Savage?"

"What can I say? The man had expensive tastes and made a lot of bad decisions. He quit playing ball before he could cash in on his Super Bowl win with a huge contract. Didn't want to fuck up his *real* moneymaker, that gorgeous puss of his. The television money was terrific as long as he was in prime time, and he made a buttload on endorsements back in the day—shaving cream, razors, deodorant, sports cars, manly shit like that. Did the creepy underwear ad in the eighties where you could almost count the scales on that anaconda of his. The Hollywood nookie he knocked off from that ad, let me tell you. In fact, better I don't. Respect for the dead, y'know."

"You're a real mensch," Durham said. "Save it for the memoir, right?"

Cisneros beamed. "Thank you! You get it. Gotta love southern hospitality. Anyway, once Savage was relegated to regional games, the endorsements dried up. His salary dropped each year as the number of games he covered and his Q rating both plummeted, but he didn't want to let go of the sweet life. He pissed away millions of dollars, trying to maintain his image. I don't know how much he had left in savings, but the work I sent his way brought in, maybe, half a million a year tops after taxes. I know the shoe endorsement is about a tenth of what it was twenty years ago, and Aries was renegotiating *that* when he died. That's why he sold his Malibu house and moved back to Choctaw. Back east, he could live the life to which he had become accustomed without checking his bank balance every five minutes. I saw pictures of his house there. Sweet. Place like that up in Beverly Glen overlooking the valley here would run ten, twelve million easy. I think he paid a million two for it. Might look into real estate there myself someday."

Durham asked, "Savage filed a lawsuit against a ski resort development here. Did he discuss it with you?"

"A couple of times. Not so much about the ski resort, but about the cost of the attorneys to file the suit. He wasn't certain he could afford it. He asked whether some of my more socially and environmentally active clients might want to jump in as joint plaintiffs. I told him my job was to make them money, not tell them how to spend it. He was cool with it. He was always cool with everything. Real easy client to please. I'm gonna miss him."

"He's been dead since Friday," Durham said. "The person who mentioned your name was surprised you hadn't reached out already."

"You wanna know the god's honest truth?" Cisneros said. "Savage was not one of my A list clients. Hadn't been for years. I kept finding him gigs because I liked the guy. In public he was Everybody's All American, but if you got him in private and tossed a drink or two down his throat, he became the terrified kid everybody watched on TV, running out onto the field to play his first minutes of the season in the biggest goddamn game of the year. Shit scared him. Poverty most of all, but when the cameras turned off, he was just a bewildered kid trying to figure out how he got where he was. I'm sorry he's dead, but I've been up to my ass in alligators working for my clients who bring in the real bucks. When they tell me the funeral date, I'll send flowers."

TWENTY-TWO

Durham and Bobbi sat in Durham's booth at the Choctaw Grille. She nursed a Dr Pepper. He drank sweet tea.

"We might as well say it," Bobbi said.

"Something's rotten in Choctaw," Durham said. "The stories don't add up."

Kylee was at the counter, wiping it down before the dinner rush. When Durham glanced at her, she winked.

"Lot of freckles," Bobbi said.

"Yeah."

"Are we gonna dance around that?"

"No. It's part of what doesn't add up. Kylee told me she had an affair with Tim McCool, but it was over years ago."

"Had to be before I arrived. I never heard about it."

"Yet, it sounds like she was cavorting in Savage's pool with Mags and Tim and Gaby only three months ago."

"It *was* before he filed the lawsuit," Bobbi said. "Maybe they were friendlier then."

"Doesn't explain why Mags was testing the memory foam with Savage last Thursday night, and why she didn't break it off when he sent his attorneys after her and the rest of the council. According to Mags, she hoped to sway him with sex, seduce him into dropping the lawsuit. From what his agent Cisneros and Gaby Reyes said, he was stuck in adolescence. susceptible to persuasion. She might have been on to something. I think it moves her down the list of suspects."

"How?"

"She already had a plan to get him out of the way of the resort. She was still working it within twenty-four hours of the time he died. And she was out of town at the time of the murder anyway."

"That covers Mags, but what about—" She surreptitiously pointed toward Kylee from behind her palm.

"There are several ways to lie," Durham said. "Maybe Kylee thought we were just shooting the shit when she told me about the affair with McCool. But she still lied. People lie because they have something to hide."

"I liked it better when we had two clearly defined sides in this story," she said.

"Yeah. It's hard to tell who's zoomin' who." He pulled out his cell phone and poked out an email. "I asked my guys in Charlotte for a deep dive on Kylee Wampler. And I need to take another look at Savage's financials. The money for his attorneys came from somewhere."

———

Garrett Kinnison lived in the largest house on Main Street, past the terminus of the business district. It had been built by his great great grandfather on his arrival during the early days of Reconstruction and reflected the plantation style so prominent in the period. The house was three stories tall, with a sweeping circular front porch with twin staircases to the immaculately manicured lawn, now mostly covered with scarlet and golden maple leaves. When Durham pushed the doorbell, Windsor chimes resonated from inside.

A speaker next to the door crackled. "Who is it?"

"SBI Special Agent Wade Durham. I'd like to speak with Garrett Kinnison."

Another crackle. "Hold on a minute."

It took two minutes. Durham waited patiently. Eventually, he heard the sound of deadbolt locks being thrown, and the door opened.

Garrett Kinnison stood barely five and a half feet tall and was built like Poppin' Fresh. He might have been forty, but he could have been younger. His mousy hair was limp and fine, and fell across his forehead so frequently he reflexively shoved it back every ten or fifteen seconds. He had a plain, moonlike face. His eyes were reddened, and Durham detected a hint of weed emanating from his clothes. He wore thick glasses that magnified his eyes to bug-like proportions.

"Are you really Wade Durham?" Kinnison asked. His voice was thin and wheezy and sounded like he was permanently on the verge of reaching for an inhaler.

Durham flashed his badge. "I'm the one who works for the SBI. I hear there are others."

"Wade The Blade?" Kinnison asked. "The real one?"

"You got me," Durham said. "Guilty as charged."

"Wow. Come in. Come in."

He held the door open, and ushered Durham inside and down the hall to a Victorian study that looked untouched since the days of the robber barons.

"Have a seat," Kinnison said. He pointed toward an overstuffed red velveteen sofa with delicately carved walnut arms. It looked as if it belonged in the lounge of a wild west bawdy house. Kinnison sat across from him in a similar wing chair. "Wade the Blade. I'm a fan, you know."

"I didn't."

"Oh, yes. From television. And online. I play games. A lot of games. Would you like to see my game room?"

"Maybe another time."

"Because I don't know whether you've heard, but your car is on the iRacing AI. I've raced against you there. Even beat you once."

"Congratulations," Durham said. "I'm a hard guy to beat."

"I figured you for a gamer," Kinnison said.

"Nope. Sorry. Too busy catching bad guys and driving real-life race cars."

Kinnison pouted. Durham tried to recall the last time he'd seen a grown man pout.

"You're lucky." Kinnison sounded disappointed. "You encounter adventure in real life. Some of us aren't athletically gifted. I suppose you're here to talk about Winlock Savage."

"I am."

"Because you're interviewing all the Town Council members in order of their suspiciousness."

"More or less."

I suppose I should be relieved," Kinnison said. "I'm way down the list. People talk, you know. I know what you're going to ask. On Friday night, I was entertaining a friend."

"Here?"

"Yes."

"Did this…uh, *friend* stay here all night?"

"Not *all* night. But long enough. We were downstairs, in the playroom. Playing."

"Video games," Durham said.

"Simulations. So much more than video games, Agent Durham. Video games are for kids with pockets full of quarters in mall arcades. We go for the deepest immersion possible."

"Good for you," Durham said.

"No need to patronize me," Kinnison said. "What do you want to know about Savage?"

"What was your relationship with him?"

"He was suing me. I didn't take it personally. He was suing everyone on the Choctaw Knob board. Beyond that, I never knew the man. He spoke at several council meetings, but we never interacted."

"Any reason, or just the way the cards fell?"

"We had little in common. What would we talk about? We are from different tribes."

"I like your house," Durham said.

"Thank you. It's been in the family since 1868. I've lived here all my life. Never felt the inclination to wed or spawn children. Not my thing. I'm the last Kinnison in Choctaw. I wonder what will become of the house after I'm gone. Not that I'll care. Just curious."

"The police chief tells me you own over half the houses in Choctaw."

"That's a reasonable estimate. I also own some commercial properties, but the houses are my primary source of income."

"Sounds challenging, managing all those properties."

"Not at all. I just own them. Someone else manages them. Company over in Asheville. I have discovered the Fountain of Eternal Profit, Agent Durham. My management company takes their percentage off the top of the rents, pays the property taxes and maintenance costs, and I pocket the rest. It's the closest thing there is to being a medieval earl. Fiefdoms are neat."

"Until all the serfs desert you," Durham observed. "Driving in, I couldn't help noticing all the *For Rent* signs in front of houses with lovely lawns and trimmed hedges. The signs look old."

"The pandemic hit us hard," Kinnison admitted.

"It must be expensive maintaining all those properties without occupants. I bet it cuts deeply into your passive income."

"And, as Mayor Tinsley will tell you, it's a wonderful tax deduction. Are you trying to make a point, Agent Durham?"

Durham noted the fawning was in the rearview. He had Kinnison on the defensive.

"Y'know the first part of a movie, where you're trying to figure out who everyone is, and how they relate to one another?" Durham asked. "We're in that phase of the investigation right now. I'm gathering information. Looking for patterns. Trying to figure out who's telling the truth and who isn't. I'm a lot more interested in the people who lie to me. But we're cool. You've been upfront with me the entire time. I appreciate it."

"You're welcome. You aren't what I expected. I was put off."

"My apologies. Could you tell me how much you've invested in the Choctaw Knob resort?"

"About two million. I planned to put in only a million, but Councilwoman McLeod convinced me to go bigger."

"How exactly did she do that?" Durham asked.

"Persuasively."

"I don't think she had to try hard. I have thorough researchers. You and Margaret McLeod voted the same way one hundred percent of the time on council business over the last six years since you took over your late father's seat."

"More insinuations?" Kinnison said.

"Sorry. I seem to be stumbling over my tongue today. I didn't mean to imply anything except that you and she appear to agree on most issues. I figured if you put two million into the ski resort, you were leaning that way already."

"Perhaps I was."

"Which suggests you believed the project is in the town's best interests."

"It is. We need to revive interest in this valley, and bring more people in. At the worst, if the ski slopes open, I can rent out the surplus houses as vacation homes."

"How bad is it?" Durham asked.

"What are you talking about?"

"How close are you to the edge, financially? Remember. I have thorough researchers."

"Stateside, I'm stable for another three years or so. I have some overseas accounts, but they're for emergencies only. If things don't turn around, I may sell some surplus homes as scrape-offs."

"The ski resort is your salvation," Durham said.

Kinnison looked defeated. "It's the town's salvation. Without it, we'll die. Choctaw won't exist in a decade as more than a wide place in the highway."

"Winlock Savage stood in the way of your salvation. Here's my problem, Mr. Kinnison. Everyone can vouch for their whereabouts the night Savage was murdered. Some alibis are better than others, but when you get right down to it, I don't think anyone on the council has the stones to hoist Savage onto a smokehouse hook and leave him to roast all night. Motive? You bet. Tons of motive. I simply don't think anyone on the council killed Savage."

"Well, that's a relief," Kinnison said.

"Doesn't mean you didn't arrange it, though," Durham said. "Tinsley and McCool approached you recently asking for a second phase of investments in the resort, didn't they?"

"You already know they did, apparently."

"Might be a good time for a complete accounting of how the first phase was spent. If the council didn't kill Savage, maybe they paid for it. Follow the money, like Woodward and Bernstein said."

"Who?" Kinnison asked.

———

Durham returned to his room in the Choctaw Arms and took a short nap to allow all the information he'd digested to consolidate in his brain. It was something he'd learned years earlier, and it seemed to work. Eventually, patterns would emerge that would mean something. Right now, he was still turning all the pieces of the jigsaw puzzle face-up.

After a forty-minute power nap, he attacked the laptop again and examined the financial sections for each of the players in the Savage murder, and he thought about the case for a while. By the time his stomach reminded him he hadn't eaten since breakfast, he had also concluded he still didn't know enough to determine one way or the other who killed Winlock Savage. Too many questions remained unanswered.

One of the big ones involved Kylee Wampler. He'd fired a quick email off to Malik Mourning's best researcher with a request for a deep dive on her, and expected the results any time.

Durham decided a decent interval had passed since his first Choctaw Grille burger. He planned to order another at dinner, reasoning life was short, and nobody would care in fifty years anyway. Darrell Tanney sat on the bench across from the Grille when Durham arrived, watching.

Instead of entering the diner, Durham crossed the street and sat next to Tanney on the bench. He draped his arm over the backrest and leaned in. Tanney barely acknowledged him.

"Might as well get this over with," Durham said. "You want to throw down right here in the street, or take it out back of the school gym?"

"What are you talking about?"

"I can see the future, and somewhere in it I get to show you what it feels like to max out your healthcare coverage. Today's as good a day as any."

"Yeah. Right." Tanney snorted.

"You might be the worst state trooper I've ever met," he said. "Your employee record reads like a felony jacket. Who on earth gave you a badge in the first place?"

"Yuck it up, buttwipe," Tanney said. "I don't answer to you."

"Let me give you my itinerary for the next several hours, so you can save this bench the embarrassment of being in contact with your fat ass. I'm gonna get some food, and then I plan to head back up to my room, where I'll probably stay until morning. That's when the big ball of fire comes up over the mountain, in case you're curious, which I'm certain you aren't."

"Think you're tough," Tanney grunted.

"Maybe someday we'll find out. Tell you the truth, I'm kind of looking forward to it. If I were you, I'd keep my nose real clean, Tanney. I love busting crooked cops. I'm really good at seeing they stack their time in gen pop, too. Doesn't that sound like fun?"

He didn't wait for an answer. Instead, he walked away, toward the diner.

Minutes later, Kylee delivered his burger and onion rings, and a fresh Arnold Palmer. She sat in the booth across from him.

"How's it going?" she asked.

"Fits and starts," he said. He squirted a dollop of ketchup on the burger and folded the two halves together. "Heard something interesting today."

"What?"

"You know Gaby Reyes?"

"Sure! Doesn't everyone?"

"She dropped by the station for an interview. You know she was in an affair with Win Savage?"

"I'd heard rumors."

Durham took a large bite of the burger. It was every bit as succulent and beefy as he recalled from the first one. "Damned fine burger," he said after swallowing. "Gaby described a pool party at

Savage's place back in July. The story involved hallucinogens and skinny-dipping. No judgment. It's just curious."

Kylee's face had flushed, but to her credit it hadn't turned completely scarlet. That was reserved for her ears. She looked around the dining room.

"Gaby remembered Mags McLeod and Tim McCool being there, along with a woman whose name she couldn't recall, but whom she described as redheaded and freckled. A *lot* of freckles, she said. Said this woman used a ton of sunscreen, because she never got outside in the daytime anymore and burned easily."

"Yes," Kylee said.

He took another large bite of the burger and let her wait for him to savor it. He wasn't about to waste a great burger.

"I found it curious," he repeated, after swallowing and taking a sip of the Arnold Palmer. He dredged an onion ring in a pool of ketchup on his plate. "You see, Kylee, people lie for a lot of reasons. Sometimes they lie because admitting the truth would be painful. Sometimes they lie to spare themselves embarrassment. I've known people who lied to protect other people, even when it put them in a jam instead. Some people lie to spare other people's feelings. Lying to a cop, though…" He shook his head and bit into the onion ring. "Perfect rings, by the way. My compliments to Nikos."

"This is the part where I'm supposed to say *I can explain*," she said.

"Only if you feel like it," he said. "No point in spoiling dinner."

"I was there," she said.

"I know."

"It wasn't what you're thinking. Yeah. I was there with Tim. I didn't know Mags was going to be there as well. Tim and I had been

231

there, maybe, ten minutes before she arrived. It wasn't a date or anything. I'd had enough of the damned diner and needed a day away. I was bitching about it late on karaoke night one Friday, and Tim was sitting at the bar. He asked if I wanted to play hooky that Sunday with brunch at Win Savage's house. Hell, yeah. Are you kidding? I mean, he was half-plastered when he asked, but he didn't try to back out later. Why would he? He's been trying to get back in my pants for years. We agreed it was just me and Shit-For-Brains driving there together, though. Not a date or anything. There was no *quid pro quo*. Nobody told me Mags was coming."

"Did Tim and Mags try to corral you into investing in the ski resort?"

She looked at him quizzically. "No," she said. "Nothing like that."

"I thought Tim might have had an ulterior motive for bringing you there."

"No," she said, shaking her head. "Sometimes, contrary to his basic nature, Tim can be an okay guy. I couldn't put up anything, anyway. I don't have anything to invest. After paying for the diner, I had enough left to fund a retirement account. My money's all tied up. I'm smart enough not to touch it for anything, no matter how sure it is. I'm not likely to win the lottery again."

"I'm having a difficult time imagining Tim McCool engaging in a purely altruistic gesture," he said.

"Well, it is what it is. We drove there, we had a lovely breakfast with mimosas, and we lounged around the pool talking until Win said he had some shrooms. Asked if anyone wanted to try some. The rest of the day is kind of a blur, but if I fucked someone, I'd remember it. Nobody fucked anybody, at least while we were there.

We got stoned and threw away our clothes and tripped out on floats in the pool. It was fun. Nothing sexual about it. The next day, I was back at work in the diner, wondering if it had been a dream. I have to say, the experience improved my mood and my outlook, at least until Savage was killed. Now it's all kind of a bummer again. Do you think it was the shrooms or the company? Because I know where I can get some shrooms. Maybe I shouldn't say that to a cop."

"Screw it. That's the DEA's business. We aren't talking to each other right now."

"Anyway, what I told you was the truth. I haven't slept with Shit-For-Brains in over three years. I didn't lie about him."

"You didn't tell me everything, either. What else are you holding back?"

His telephone vibrated. The report on Kylee was ready. He opened the file and read it.

"Well," he said, and he cleared his throat. "Huh. Okay. Didn't see that one coming."

"What?" she asked.

He placed the phone back in his pocket and took a long sip of the Arnold Palmer. "You're a bundle of surprises today. I'm bewildered, for instance, that you never mentioned you were Patricia Masters' granddaughter."

TWENTY-THREE

"Yeah?" she asked. "What about it?"

"I've reopened the investigation into her murder forty-five years ago."

"Why?"

"There are connections between her murder and the Winlock Savage case. I can't discuss them right now—"

"You mean Trent McCool and Darrell Tanney," she said.

"And now you. Please tell me you aren't here on some sort of family vendetta."

She laughed. "Yeah. Right. I've lived in Choctaw over five years, Blade. That would make me the laziest avenging angel in history. Try another theory."

"Why are you here, then?"

She cadged one of his onion rings and sopped it with ketchup. "I never knew Patti Masters. Strange. I never even thought of her as my grandmother, just as *Patti*. Yeah. She went by Patti. My mother told me. When Patti was killed, my mother and uncle were still teenagers. My mom was fourteen. They went into the foster system for a few months until a cousin of Patti's stepped in and offered to provide for them until they were eighteen. My mother's life was awful during those years, especially because nobody ever figured out who killed her mother. It's still traumatic for her."

"She's alive?"

"Hell, she's only sixty. It wasn't that long ago."

"I'd like to talk to her. Does she visit Choctaw often?"

"Fuck no. You couldn't bribe her to come here. The town gives her the creeps."

"Yet, you settled here."

"I had to go somewhere. My mother's stories about the town, at least before Patti was killed, made it sound quaint and colloquial. I was curious. Something about Choctaw sounded right. I decided it had never done anything bad to *me*. In fact, when you think about it, without the murder, I wouldn't even exist. Mom isn't thrilled I live here, but she doesn't resent me for it either. She stays in Virginia Beach and sends me nice letters every several weeks."

"Here's what interests me. The afternoon she was murdered, Patricia—"

She glanced at him over her drink.

"—*Patti* Masters had sex with a man, sometime between four o'clock and six o'clock, after school. Nobody ever identified her lover. Three possibilities: First, her lover was also her murderer. Second, her lover wasn't her murderer, but the murderer killed her because of the affair. Third, her lover and her murder are completely unrelated."

"With you so far," she said.

"We'll toss the third option, because it leaves us nowhere to go. Besides, I don't trust coincidences. Secret trysts and violence are highly correlated. The statistics favor the first and second options.

My working hypothesis is that identifying the lover will lead me to the killer."

"After forty-five years," she scoffed.

"I have the clothes she wore the day she was murdered, and we have DNA technology now. Tomorrow, I'll drive to Burnsville to interview the Choctaw detective who investigated the case back then. Has your mother ever discussed your grandmother's dating life?"

"Oh, yeah. Sure. Why didn't you ask earlier? Mom gave me a complete list of Grammy's lovers. Patti kept a little red book in her purse, where she listed each paramour with code words for what they liked to do and how good they were in bed. I have it upstairs in my apartment. Want to see it?"

"If only it were true."

"Tell me how many guys your grandmother boinked, Blade. I mean, besides your grandfather. Be sure to list their names as well. I'm sure your mom told you all about them."

"Okay, I get it," he said. "Would she be willing to discuss anything she knows with me?"

"Patti's a sore subject for Mom. Not only was she orphaned; she had to deal with the embarrassment and shame of knowing her mom was dipping the pickle with some student in her office after school."

"Wait," Durham said. "Why do you say that?"

"Because that's what she told me. She had a couple too many one night and got all maudlin and depressed. Talked about how her life went sideways the day her mother was murdered, but maybe being killed was better than being exposed for fucking a student. That's the only time I ever heard my mother use the word *fuck*. She was really angry about it. Kinda brain-burned the conversation into my memory."

Durham mulled it over, and said, "I need to talk to your mother. Can you arrange a video meeting? I don't have time to drive to the coast right now. This case is coming together, and I don't want it to chill."

"Yeah. Sure," she said. "For real? You think you can figure out who killed Patti almost half a century ago?"

"I'll know better after I talk to the detective tomorrow. But yeah. I have a good feeling about this one."

"And finding out who killed Patti might help you figure out who killed Savage?"

"Jury's still out, but I'm hopeful it will give me some direction. In any case, after almost fifty years, maybe it's time Patti received a little justice. Even if it isn't related to Savage, solving the Masters case would be gravy."

"I'll get my laptop," she said. "It's *Wheel of Fortune* time. Mom goes radio silent while it's on, but we can video call her as soon as Sajak gives away that car."

He started to thank her, but she was already gone. He allowed himself a moment of satisfaction as he finished the burger and rings. The case was falling together. He could sense it. He still couldn't see the endgame, but he knew it was around the corner over the next hill. He sniffed it, like the petrichor hanging in the air after a thunderstorm.

Darrell Tanney swung open the door and stood in the entrance for a moment, scanning the room. He spied Durham sitting in his booth and gestured to two men standing outside. The three of them headed his way.

Tanney and State Legislator Carl Royster, he already recognized. The third man was slight, with thinning hair and a suit two sizes too large for his frame. He wore a businessman's bifocal glasses, with dark frames and wire bottoms. A smear of ink on the side of his left hand suggested he was an accountant.

Tanney veered off and occupied a booth across the dining room. He glared at Durham as the other two men stopped next to Durham's table.

"Mr. Royster. Mayor Tinsley, I presume," Durham said, as he slid from his bench and stood to greet them. He extended his hand. "Special Agent Wade Durham, SBI. Please. Have a seat." He pointed to the bench across the booth.

"I'm sorry," Tinsley said. "Have we met?"

"Trent said he does that," Royster told him. "I suspect he knows it's annoying."

"Just trying to be neighborly," Durham said. "Please. Sit."

He returned to his bench. Mayor Tinsley and Royster sat across from him. They all took each other's measure for a few seconds.

"Want something to drink?" Durham asked. "Kylee had to grab her laptop upstairs. Hey, how about this weather, huh? Sure is nice to have autumn back."

"You've been bothering a lot of Choctaw's most prominent citizens," Tinsley said.

"I'm sorry. Was I not supposed to? Are they immune? I didn't read the memo."

Tinsley looked at Royster. Royster sneered.

"Trent told me he was a smartass," Royster said. "He mouthed off at Tim McCool the other night too." Royster turned back to

Durham. "I got off the phone with your supervisor in Charlotte a few minutes ago. Mr. McCool—"

"Which one?" Durham asked.

"Both of them have expressed concerns about your fitness to conduct this investigation."

"Guilty people frequently do."

"Are you making accusations against the McCools?" Tinsley demanded.

"Not yet. Maybe tomorrow. The next day perhaps. Maybe never. I go where the evidence leads me, gentlemen. And I'm unimpressed by weight being tossed around the room. It's among my few redeeming virtues."

"Maybe after you talk with your supervisor, you'll be a little more respectful," Royster said.

"Got a twenty on you?" Durham asked.

"What?" Royster asked.

He pulled a twenty-dollar bill from his pocket and placed it on the table between them.

"What's this about?" Royster said.

"Friendly wager. If you don't have a twenty, I'll settle for information given freely and without reservation."

He dialed Malik Mourning's direct office number at the SBI office in Charlotte. When Mourning answered, Durham placed the phone on loudspeaker and put his fingers to his lips to keep Royster and Tinsley silent.

"Hey, Malik!" Durham said. "Finishing dinner at the Choctaw Grille. I wanted to call and prostrate myself before you in sincere and abject supplication. *Mea culpa. Mea culpa. Mea maxima culpa.*"

"What the fuck are you talking about?" Mourning said. "Have you been drinking?"

"Not yet. Might drown my tears in a margarita or two later, though, after you fire me."

"Fire you?"

"Carl Royster said he ratted me out to you today for yanking the wrong people's chains here in Choctaw. I figured you were going to cashier me." He paused and added, "Again."

"Royster? That eighty-proof gasbag? Yeah, he complained. What about it?"

Royster reddened. Tinsley seemed to shrink a few inches, and he could ill spare them.

"So I have the green flag?"

"Go get 'em, Blade. Anytime some empty suit from Raleigh calls and tries to push my buttons, my instincts tell me you're on the right track. Oh, and Mr. Royster?"

Carl Royster snapped to attention. He cleared his throat a couple of times, and said, "Uh, yeah?"

"The Blade almost never uses his speaker unless he wants someone to hear the conversation. I'll repeat what I told you on the telephone. The State Bureau of Investigation is an independent law enforcement agency attached to the North Carolina Department of Public Safety, which answers only to the governor. I work for the executive branch. Unless you're tossing around subpoenas, I don't have to give anyone in the Legislature or the Senate the time of day. I don't even have to take their telephone calls. I trust Wade Durham to conduct the highest-quality investigation possible because I've seen him come through time and time again, and until I received your telephone call earlier today, Mr. Royster, I didn't even know who the fuck you were. Do you need anything I've said repeated, sir?"

Carl Royster looked near apoplectic. Darrell Tanney stood beside his own booth across the diner, looking for a signal to rush to his boss's aid. Durham turned the speaker off and raised the phone to his face as he slid the twenty back off the table.

"Thanks, boss. Needed to settle a bet. By the way, am I cleared to solve a half-century old cold case while I'm here?"

"It's your circus, Blade. Do what you have to. If you couldn't get it done, I wouldn't have sent you."

"Ten-four, boss. Gotta boogie."

He secured his phone and faced the two defeated politicians sitting on the other side of the booth.

"Now, gentlemen," he said. "Let's start with the basics. Mr. Mayor, where were you between the hours of ten o'clock on Friday night and two o'clock on Saturday morning?"

"Surely you don't suspect me?" Tinsley protested.

"Surely, I do, until I don't anymore. To be honest, among the council members, you're the least suspicious, because you had the least to lose or gain, but you're still on the list."

"I suppose you want to know my whereabouts as well?" Royster said.

"We'll get to that. Mr. Mayor?"

"I was at home with my wife. She will verify it."

"Yes. She will," Durham said. "We doublecheck at the SBI. Mr. Royster?"

"I was at home on Blind Top the entire evening."

"And I assume Darrell Tanney can verify your whereabouts."

"I suppose we're each other's alibis," Royster said.

"Well, if you can't trust a branded state trooper and a politician, who can you trust?" He glanced at Tanney and shot him with his thumb and forefinger. Tanney scowled.

"Are you invested in the Choctaw Knob ski resort?" Durham asked Royster.

"No."

"Not a penny?"

"It didn't seem appropriate. I'm uninvolved in the development. To do otherwise might imply a conflict of interest."

"You'd like to see it in operation, though?"

"Anyone who loves the Choctaw Valley should," Royster said. "A ski resort could be the shot in the arm this district needs to pull it out of an economic nosedive. People will only pay for two things, Agent Durham. Convenience and entertainment. When you get right to it, every penny you spend satisfies one or the other. A ski slope an hour closer to the big flatland cities than Asheville or Boone? Hell, yeah. Entertaining *and* convenient. It checks all the boxes."

"A real boon to everyone in the valley," Tinsley echoed.

"The needs of the many outweigh the needs of the few?" Durham suggested.

"Absolutely, in this case," Tinsley said.

"Or the needs of Winlock Savage?" Durham added. "See, gentlemen, everywhere I look, I find motive. A lot of people in this town stood to benefit from Savage's demise. Motive's not the problem. Opportunity, that's what's bugging me. But I'll figure it out, don't you worry. I always do." He looked back and forth at Tinsley and Royster. "Any questions?"

Tinsley coughed lightly. "Well, I suppose not. Carl?"

"I think we all understand one another," Royster said. "Intriguing conversation, Agent Durham."

"Call me Wade. Everyone does. Nice talk, fellas. Mr. Mayor, I may drop by your office tomorrow with a few more questions if it's okay with you."

"Um, okay," Tinsley said. His expression made it clear it wasn't okay with him at all.

"Great. One more thing, Mr. Royster. This is the second time someone has dragged your pet troglodyte Darrell Tanney into this restaurant to intimidate me, and I'm pretty fucking tired of seeing his fat ass on the bench across the street. No, don't say anything, because interfering with an SBI agent in the performance of his duties is a felony in this state, and I enjoyed my meal too much to throw down in the middle of Choctaw Grille or fill out a lot of paperwork this evening. I know you need Tanney to wipe your butt and hold your hair and wash your dick and everything, but keep him out of my sight. You have a problem with me? Come at me head-on and leave your muscle at home. The next time he bucks up at me, I'm going to show him what a week in intensive care feels like, and I don't give a fuck what kind of badge he wears. As my supervisor put it, is there anything I've said you need repeated? *Sir?*"

Royster was about to pop an artery, but he had the political savvy to know when he'd been pinned. "You've made your position abundantly clear," he said, trying to regain composure. "I will be particularly attentive next year when we work on the state budget for law enforcement. Perhaps the SBI could use special attention."

"Threaten all you want," Durham said. "I have my twenty in, and then some. I can punch out with a full pension anytime I like. I'm just in it for the yuks these days. Anything else you wanted to discuss? I mean, you came to me, right? I'm a little embarrassed, monopolizing the conversation. Pardon my manners. Let me make it up to you. Hey, have you tried the apple pie? I might order a slice. Join me. My treat."

Royster turned to Tanney. "We're done here," he said.

"No pie?" Durham asked. "Your loss. Y'all be careful going home, you hear?"

———

"Damn. One of those two shitbirds had a really sweaty ass. Now I gotta Febreze this cushion," Kylee said as she opened her laptop. "I'm beginning to understand your deductive process."

"My deductive process?"

"Yeah. You piss everybody off and when, in the fullness of time, someone tries to kill you, you arrest them."

"Simplistic, yet effective. Fortunately, it seldom comes to that."

She slid out of her side of the booth and sat next to him. He already sat at the far end of his bench, next to the wall. Even so, she pressed her thigh against his, and he could feel the curve of her breast against his ribcage as she leaned against him and typed on the keyboard. She had about a foot and a half of cushion between herself and the open end of the bench.

"Two objects cannot occupy the same space," he said. "They teach that first day of race car school."

"Relax," she said. "The camera has a narrow field of view. I need to sit close so Mom can see both of us. There's a race car school?"

"There's a school for everything, but most people learn on the job. Usually the hard way."

Presently, the videochat window opened and Kylee clicked on her mother's icon. The screen filled and Durham quickly caught his breath. The woman on the other end was a dead ringer for the live photos of Patti Masters in his files.

"I know," Kylee said. "It's creepy. I have no idea where my genes came from. She forgot to turn on her sound again."

Kylee scribbled on a napkin and held it to the screen. Her mother fiddled with her computer.

"Can you hear me now?" she asked.

"Loud and clear, Mama," Kylee said.

"Who's the handsome man next to you?"

Durham introduced himself and held his badge up to the camera. "Ms. Wampler, I hope this isn't a bad time to let you know, but I've reopened the investigation into your mother's murder."

"Oh," she said. "My goodness. I never expected to hear that. Call me Deborah, please. And your name is Wade?"

"They call him The Blade, Mama," Kylee chimed in. "'Cause he cuts through cases like butter."

"Not true," Durham said. "But I do believe I can help figure out who killed your mother, Deborah." He filled her in on the clothes he had sent to the DNA lab, and his planned interview with Ted Wisniewski the next day.

"I remember him, vaguely," she said. "He talked to me and Jamie—my brother—a couple of times after the murder. I was sorry to hear he was hurt in the shootout. He was nice to me at a terrible time. I'm glad to hear he's still alive."

"Deborah, I was talking to Kylee about the murder. She said you told her Patti Masters was—excuse my directness—having sex with a student at the time she died."

Deborah Wampler stared at the screen, her lips pursed. "I didn't intend her to repeat that," she said, finally.

"Ma'am, this is important," Durham said. "I don't want to dredge up awful memories, but you could help with this investigation. How did you know she was involved with a student?"

"I overheard it," she said. "I was in a bathroom stall in the gym, maybe a week or two before the murder. Got my…you know. My monthly. Several of the cheerleaders came in after practice. They had no idea I was there. They were in the showers, but I could hear what they said perfectly. They were talking about Mama. At first it was just the usual stuff. Kids talked about the principal all the time. I'd gotten used to it, even though sometimes they said the most awful things."

"What did they say this time?" Durham asked.

"One of them was complaining about being sent to Mama's office for mouthing off at Mr. Steinmetz, the history teacher. One of the others stood up for Mama. Then the first one said, *Maybe she should spend more time minding her own business and less time fucking her students.'* Those were her exact words. I'll never forget them."

"That must have been hard to hear," Durham said.

"I was shocked, but she repeated it. Said she knew for a fact Mama was shagging some student, but she didn't say who. The other girls didn't believe her, but she said she had proof. I'm sorry, but that's all there is. They didn't say anything more, and I stayed in the toilet stall until they'd dressed and left."

"So you don't know if it's true?" Durham asked.

"I know," she said. "I asked Mama about it, after dinner that night. Jamie was off playing basketball with some friends, so it was only Mama and me. I told her what I'd overheard in the shower. I thought it was important for her to know what students were saying, so she could put a stop to it. I expected her to be angry. I didn't expect her to cry. I knew right away the rumors were true."

"Did she tell you anything?"

"She didn't need to. I knew my mama, Agent Durham. I knew when she was angry, and when she was sad, and when she was ashamed. This was shame. She tried to talk, three times, but each time she shook her head and cried some more, and eventually she walked into her room and closed the door. We never talked about it again. A couple of weeks later, she was dead."

"Did you tell any of this to Detective Wisniewski?" Durham asked.

"I don't think so. I remember being so ashamed and scared and overwhelmed myself after the murder, and I had no idea what was going to happen to me. I was just a kid. I wasn't thinking straight. Then came the riot and the shootout, and next thing I knew I was in a foster home halfway across the state. I honestly don't know if I told him or not. The way I felt toward Mama at the time, though, makes me think I didn't."

"Why, Mom?" Kylee asked.

"Shame. Guilt. Fear. Mama was dead. Nothing was going to change that. I figured there was no point in muddying her reputation on top of it." Deborah wiped at shiny wet spots beneath her eyes. "Goodness. I didn't expect to spend my Tuesday evening this way."

"I'm sorry to have disturbed you," Durham said. "But your information may be exactly the break I need to find your mother's killer. I appreciate your help. I'll drop by the school tomorrow and find out who the cheerleaders were that year. If they're still alive, maybe one of them knows who this student was."

"I can save you the time," Deborah said. "I recognized their voices. The one who said she knew Mama was...sleeping with a student was Beth Rose Clarney. The one who stood up for Mama was Mags McLeod."

———

Mags McLeod was working late in her Main Street windowed office when Durham knocked on the door. She saw him through the glass, and for a second her face turned sour, but she covered it quickly with the sort of smile she saved for major whale clients—not that she'd seen many of those lately in Choctaw. She invited him in, and he asked her whether she remembered rumors of an affair between Patti Masters and a student.

"What does this have to do with Win Savage's murder?" Mags McLeod asked.

"Nothing," Durham said. "Or maybe something. Hard to say. It's a separate case I uncovered while investigating the Savage murder. A cold case. Really cold."

"I'd imagine so. It was forty-five fucking years ago. I can't imagine how I'd remember a rumor spread by teenagers that far back. There were so many, after all. Girls like to gossip."

"This was some incendiary gossip. Ms. Masters' daughter overheard it, and she's remembered it ever since. It's kind of a dark moment for her."

"I'm sorry to hear that. It's one thing to hear bad news about someone you barely know, but if it's one of your family members...Well, I can sympathize, but I'm sorry I can't help you. I truly have no recollection at all about the conversation."

"Perhaps you remember the other girl. Beth Rose Clarney?"

"Sure. Beth Rose is a darling. One of my closest friends from high school. She beat me out for Head Cheerleader, and I got her back by winning Homecoming Queen. We were competitive, but even so we loved one another."

"I'd appreciate her contact information, if you have it."

"I have it," she said. "And you're welcome to it. I don't think it will help you much, though."

———

The receptionist at Highlands Memory Care Center was impressed by Durham's badge, even if she was confused by his appearance. He still wore his jeans and plaid flannel shirt, and his snakeskin boots, but he'd added an olive-green corduroy jacket with leather elbow pads. He looked more like a slightly bewildered English professor than a government agent.

"It's late," she said. "Dinner finished only an hour ago, and they'll be taking the patients to their rooms to prepare for bed soon. If you can keep it brief..."

"I only have a couple of questions for her. Her last name's Sensabaugh now, right?"

"Yes. Please have a seat in the parlor. I'll have an attendant bring her to you. Five minutes, now. No more."

"I appreciate it."

"One more thing," she said. "Please don't be disappointed if she isn't communicative. She has up days and down days. She might be sharp as a tack, and she might be completely shut off. Late in the day can be the worst. Once it starts to get dark. They call it sundowner syndrome."

Beth Rose Clarney Sensabaugh was sixty-three but looked a hundred and ten. Dementia robs a person of everything, and it had been particularly greedy with her. Her flat gray hair was dry and frizzy. Her eyes were watery, her arms shriveled to sticks. She looked as if she were constantly trying to whisper some great secret she could only barely recall. She was confined to a wheelchair. The attendant assured Durham that Beth Rose could walk when she was inclined, but she was unsteady and prone to falls, so a wheelchair was safer.

Durham introduced himself. She nodded as if she understood.

"I'm a detective," he said. "I'm investigating a murder that took place forty-five years ago in Choctaw."

"Yes," she said. Each time she spoke, it was as if the words had to fight their way out of her mouth.

"Do you remember Patti Masters?"

"Yes," she said again.

"Do you remember Mags McLeod?"

"Yes."

"Do you recall telling Mags McLeod, forty-five years ago, that your high school principal, Patti Masters, was sleeping with a student?"

"Did you bring little Stevie with you?" she asked.

"I'm sorry?" Durham said. "Little Stevie?"

"I love it when you bring little Stevie," she said. "Children grow so quickly. One day they're tiny, and the next day they…" she blinked a couple of times, and looked at Durham as if meeting him for the first time. "Hello," she said. "My name is Beth Rose."

"Hello, Beth Rose," Durham said, after glancing at the attendant. "It's a pleasure to make your acquaintance. You're looking very nice today."

"Thank you," she said. She turned her head and looked out the window.

"I don't think she's going to be much help," the attendant said.

"No," Durham said. "Two steps forward and one back. Story of my life."

————

Back in his hotel room, Durham opened the laptop and summarized everything he had learned that day in bullet points. The last point he wrote was:

Seeing connections, but no patterns.

He spent five bucks of the governor's money on a beer from the minibar in his room. He put his feet up and watched television to clear his mind. Between the twenty-four-hour news channels, the home improvement stations, and reality garbage on the legacy networks, there wasn't much to watch. He wasn't ready to dive into the Patti Masters file—such as it was— yet. Instead, he set his phone alarm and stretched out on the bed for a half hour power nap.

As frequently happened, as his brain uncoiled and relaxed in his slumber, pieces that had previously seemed random and unrelated fell together, and he opened his eyes with a sudden gasp.

"A third player," he said to himself. "Someone we don't know about. We're looking in the wrong direction."

TWENTY-FOUR

Durham needed fresh air. He tossed on a hoodie, took the stairs to the Choctaw Arms lobby, and strode into the crisp mountain air.

The fog from Choctaw Knob had descended on the town again. Most of the businesses on Main Street were shuttered for the night. The Grille was open, with only a couple of booths occupied, but Durham walked straight by. He wasn't up for another minute of Kylee Wampler's perky Nancy Drew disposition, at least today.

He continued to the end of the business district, his head down and his pace vigorous. The sudden solution to his problem only presented an entire bushel basket of new problems. Adages about swamps and alligators came to mind.

"A third player," he said to himself, perhaps for the fifth time. "But who? Who else benefits by killing Win Savage?"

"Beats the hell out of me," Bobbi Navarro said behind him. "Preoccupied tonight? I've been behind you for half a block. If I had it in for you, you'd be dead now."

She fell into step with him. She'd changed into her civvie outfit—jeans and a Wolfpack hoodie and running shoes. She wore her gun and badge on her belt, punctuating the fact that—while she might dress down —she was never off the job. Her hair was loose again. It flowed over her shoulders like a milk chocolate fountain. Durham decided he liked it down.

"I'm working through a new angle. Trying to figure it out. Oh, Patti Masters was screwing one of her students. Why were you stalking me?"

"I wasn't stalking. Saw you walk past my front porch with your head a thousand miles away. Figured I'd tag along to make sure you didn't fall into any open manholes. But let's go back to that other thing."

"Kylee Wampler is Patti Masters' granddaughter."

"Clearly, we have a lot to catch up on," she said. She sounded annoyed. Durham didn't blame her.

"Yeah. It's been an interesting evening. Kylee admitted she was—well, you know that already. As we discussed it at dinner, she mentioned her mother told her Patti was knocking boots with one of her students. We facetimed Mom, who looks exactly like Patti Masters by the way, and she confirmed it."

"She said her mother was boinking a student."

"Yeah. And guess who she was eavesdropping on when she heard it. Mags McLeod."

"Another connection between the Masters case and the Savage murder."

"They keep stacking up," he said. "I braced Mags about it, but she didn't remember anything. She knew how to contact the woman who made the accusation, so I drove out to Highlands Memory Care Center to talk to her."

"And?"

"And, if I ever land in one of those places, just shoot me with the biggest gun you can find. Poor woman was completely gorped. She won't be any help. But we know something now we didn't know yesterday, and once the DNA results come back, we have a smaller field to. rule out. It had to be a male student at the high school in 1977. In a town the size of Choctaw, there can't be more than fifty or sixty of them. A lot of them are probably already dead, which also narrows the field, as long as her boy toy isn't among them. Identifying him brings us a step closer to finding her killer."

"That's fast work on a case this cold."

"Don't applaud yet. I've seen breaks like this lead nowhere. I summarized the Savage case tonight and decided to take a nap on it, and while I was asleep the answer came to me. *Third player.*"

"Third player?"

"So far, we've focused on the conflict between Savage and the Town Council over the Choctaw Knob ski resort development. It's a rich vein of motive, but I'm falling short on opportunity. Sure, they could have farmed it out. I bet Trent McCool knows how to hire a button man. But the way Savage was hung and roasted suggests more than a simple professional hit. Those guys don't like to make statements. It's in and out and draw as little attention as possible. This looks personal."

"And?"

"Maybe someone else was pissed off at Winlock Savage, enough to make an example of him. A player we don't know yet. They hung him in a smokehouse, like what?"

"A ham," she said.

"A pig," he said. "Maybe it's symbolic. Whoever killed him wanted Savage to be remembered as swine."

"Kind of a reach."

"Sure. But it raises three questions. First, who paid for Winlock Savage's attorneys in the lawsuit?"

"Good luck getting them to divulge that."

"Second, what did Savage promise them in return?"

"And the third?"

"How did he fail them? If his backers are also his killers, somewhere along the line their deal went sour. If I find out who they were and how everything went tits-up, I may know who killed him."

"You plan to visit to his attorneys?"

"Yeah. I'll get to that tomorrow after I finish interviewing Ted Wisniewski."

He was ten steps ahead of her, lost in his own head, before he realized she had frozen on the sidewalk.

"Durham?" she said, softly. "C'mere."

When he was by her side, she pointed across the street to a darkened house.

"Need a second set of eyes," she said. "That's the Culbertsons' house. They're in Maryland at a funeral this week. Asked me to keep an eye on the place."

"Okay."

"I think I glimpsed a light inside. Like a flashlight. Got your gun on you?"

Through the sheers on the front bay window, Durham saw a quick streak of light arc along a hallway wall before disappearing.

"Always. Want me to cover the rear?"

"Quicker than getting a cruiser here for backup, if you're cool with taking the assist." She slipped him a pair of handcuffs from her back pocket.

"Call it in anyway," he said. "Better to go in from a position of strength. Whichever way this rolls, we'll have someone here to help if we need it. Give me a sixty-count to get around the back of the house. You ring the front doorbell and get the fuck out of the way, in case it's some idiot who doesn't know bringing a gun to a burglary is an additional five years on his burglary sentence. Bet you ten bucks it's some kid, though."

"You're on. Sixty…fifty-nine…"

He followed the driveway of the house next door to the back fence, which he scaled in a few seconds. The back yard was overgrown, but by only a few days. Through the fog, he saw a glow in the glass of the back door. The light moved. Someone was inside. Durham braced himself next to the rear door and waited. He counted, and a second or two after he hit zero, the doorbell chimed inside the house, and he heard an insistent knock on the front door.

"Choctaw Police! Open up!" Bobbi shouted.

Durham heard pounding footsteps coming his way inside the house, exactly as he expected. The back door flung open, and a large figure dressed entirely in black plunged through the doorway at a dead run. Durham stuck out his foot and tripped him on the top step. The figure flew through the air and sprawled on the lawn, a huge burst of air expelling from his lungs. He lay on the ground, gasping for breath, as Durham straddled him and jerked his hands behind him to slap on the cuffs.

"In back! Suspect down!" he shouted. Seconds later, Bobbi appeared at his side.

"Roll him over," she said, and Durham grabbed the man and pushed him over onto his back. The man glared at Bobbi, more terrified than angry.

"Holy fucking shit," Bobbi said.

"Hi, Chief," Oz Tattersall said, dejected and ashamed.

Durham said, "Santa's not taking the chimney anymore."

TWENTY-FIVE

"The fuck, Oz?" Bobbi asked.

"I think I'd like my attorney now," Oz said.

The Choctaw officer on duty, a kid named Pete, pulled to the curb in his cruiser, the lights flashing. Bobbi had called him as soon as she saw Oz on the ground, and told him to kill the siren and lights. She had lived in Choctaw long enough to know there would be political repercussions to this bust. After she recited Miranda to Oz, she and Durham helped him to his feet, with some considerable difficulty, and hustled him into the back seat of the cruiser. Houses along that stretch of Main Street were largely vacant, but doors opened in the occupied homes, and people started to congregate on the sidewalk and their front porches to rubberneck.

"As a courtesy, I'm not chaining you to the D-ring," she told Oz. "Don't make me regret it. You can call your attorney when you get to the station." She told the officer to hustle. Seconds later, the car had disappeared around the next corner.

"So much for an early evening." Bobbi looked at her clothes. "I'll be damned if I'm interrogating one of the town fathers looking like a frat rat at a kegger. I need to change at my place. Meet you at the station. Any idea what this is about?"

"No, but I bet it's going to be entertaining," Durham said. He glanced at the house numbers next to the front door. "Holy cow. Talk about coincidences."

"What, Blade?"

"This was Lester Corby's house back in 1977. Andy Frye shot him right on this front porch. Another weird connection to the Patti Masters killing."

———

Oz Tattersall sat in the only Choctaw Police Department interrogation room, staring glumly at his reflection in the one-way glass. He'd been spared the indignity of being cuffed to the D-ring in the cruiser on the ride over, but protocol dictated he had to be chained to a ring in the tabletop during the arrest interview.

As soon as he was crabwalked into the station by the patrolman, Oz demanded to make his telephone call. Durham had walked in as Oz hung up the phone with Trent McCool.

Bobbi arrived ten minutes later, five minutes before McCool marched into the station indignantly demanding to see his client.

"You want to explain what's going on?" McCool said. "This is a town councilman you have shackled to a table."

"If I could explain it, I would," Bobbi said. "Agent Durham and I discovered him creeping Bud and Betty Culbertson's house, in the dark, with a flashlight. He needs to explain why he was there."

"I'm sure you can comprehend how serious this matter is," McCool said. "Oz Tattersall is one of the most respected leaders in the community. The optics of parading him into the police station in chains and subjecting him to a third-degree interrogation are degrading in the extreme."

"And I'm sure the jury will find that a compelling opening argument at his trial," Bobbi said. "No offense, Mr. McCool, but posturing isn't getting us anywhere. I'm conducting an interview with Mr. Tattersall in a few minutes, and you of course are welcome to tell him to clam up. The facts are obvious, though. He entered an unoccupied dwelling without the knowledge or permission of the owners. That's B&E in any district of the country. When we searched him, we found a tennis bracelet he couldn't get around his middle finger and a pair of diamond earrings that would look awful on him. Once Betty Culbertson identifies the items as hers, we'll add burglary and larceny to the list of charges. He's welcome to maintain his silence, but any way you look at it, Oz Tattersall has a lot to account for."

"Well," McCool said, "We won't force him to do it under duress. That's why we have courts. I wish to speak with my client."

"Of course. I anticipated you would. I've disconnected the camera and microphones in the interview room, and I've cleared the observation room."

The officer escorted McCool to the interrogation room. Durham and Bobbi watched him go. She'd thrown on a blouse and dark slacks, with a blue blazer, and she'd twisted and pinned her hair back into her usual businesslike bun. Durham randomly wondered how she got so much hair into such a compact knot.

"Look at this," Durham said, offering the clear evidence bag with the contents of Tattersall's pockets. The tennis bracelet sported rubies and emeralds. The earrings glittered in the overhead lights. A housekey on a keychain with a plastic fob rested between them. "It's a master key," he said.

"So, we know how he got into the house," she said.

"He's a locksmith," Durham said. "I saw it when I interviewed him at the hardware store. I'll bet he has master keys for every lock in town. Hell, he probably sold most of the house locks and deadbolts in the first place."

"What are you suggesting?" she asked. "Oz Tattersall is some kind of serial cat burglar?"

"Exactly what I'm suggesting. When I interviewed him, he came off at first as everybody's favorite grandpa. By the end of the conversation, he sounded like a lonely, involuntarily celibate, disgruntled old man. He resents the people who admire and respect him. Feels superior to them. It's kind of sad. It's one step from there to breaking into people's houses and stealing their stuff when they're not around."

"Wouldn't we have heard about a burglary spree in Choctaw by now?" she asked.

"Not if he only took one or two items each time he creeped a place. The items in this bag aren't wedding rings or heirlooms. This tennis bracelet was fashionable thirty years ago. The earrings are small and easily misplaced. He could have been stockpiling trunk loads of booty for decades one bauble at a time. In the absence of evidence of being burgled and ransacked, the vics probably assume the stolen items are lost or temporarily missing. With time, they're forgotten altogether."

"Why take the chance of getting popped on a felony beef for trinkets?" Bobbi asked.

"It's not about the stuff," Durham said. "Like a lot of predatory crimes, it's about power and control. Like a peeper or a serial rapist. The real thrill is in taking advantage of people when they're at their most vulnerable and least able to defend themselves. In a way, it's the other side of the coin of his philanthropy. Maybe he extended credit to all those people during the pandemic because it left them indebted to him. They owe their souls to the company store now. That's a powerful position."

Her phone beeped. Bobbi checked the email. "I sent pictures of the items we found in Oz's pockets to Betty Culbertson in Chesapeake. She ID'd them as hers. We have him on burglary and larceny. Let's interrupt the conversation in there, shall we? You watch from the observation room."

"You looking for Oz Tattersall's tells?" Durham asked.

"No. McCool's. He got here in an awful hurry, and he was sweating. He's not a beck and call kind of guy. Something's up." She knocked on the interrogation room door. "I'm turning the camera and microphones back on," she told them. "We need to talk."

Before McCool could object, she closed the door again and switched on the electronics. When she saw Durham was positioned in the darkness of the observation room, she took the evidence bag into the room with her.

"You should know," McCool said. "I've advised Oz not to answer questions."

"Good advice," Bobbi said. "Doesn't help me a bit, but if I were in his position, I'd snap my jaws shut like a snapping turtle and not open them again until it thunders. Of course, I'm not in his position."

"What position is that, Chief?" McCool asked.

"I'm booking Oscar Tattersall on suspicion of breaking and entering and first-degree burglary. We'll take the evidence to the DA tomorrow morning to file formal charges. I'm getting a warrant to search Oz's home and businesses for evidence of previous burglaries. The key he used to get into the Culbertsons' house could probably work in a dozen or more houses along Main Street. Maybe more. Oz didn't act like a fellow who was caught on his first B&E."

"I'd like to request you release Oz on his own recognizance," McCool said.

"And I admire your cheek for requesting it," she said. "Unfortunately, that's not how this works, and you know it. I can hold him for seventy-two hours on suspicion. Oz is checking in for the night at least. Agent Durham, at my direction, is requesting search warrants as we speak."

Durham didn't miss the cue. Inside the observation room, he grabbed his phone and checked his contacts list for friendly judges who didn't mind being awakened at midnight.

In the interrogation room, Bobbi said, "If the DA approves the charges tomorrow, Oz will be arraigned, probably, Friday morning."

McCool said, "Is that necessary, Bobbi?"

"Under the circumstances, Mr. McCool, I think you should call me Chief Navarro."

"Well, *Chief Navarro*." The name rolled off his tongue like castor oil. "I fail to see the purpose of holding Oz in a cell for even a single night."

"I do, and it's my decision. I don't need Oz out there potentially destroying evidence."

"Hey!" Oz said.

"Quiet," McCool said. "I'll talk. Chief, holding Oz Tattersall in a steel cage is untenable and outrageous. I intend to return with a writ of *habeas* to secure his release pending any formal charges or arraignment."

"I wouldn't consider standing in your way," Bobbi said. "In the interim, unless you require any further consultation, and unless Mr. Tattersall is willing to discuss the circumstances that led to his arrest tonight, I need to escort him to holding."

"I'm not talking about shit," Oz mumbled, looked decidedly unlike Santa.

"Nighty-night it is, then," Bobbi said. She left the room.

———

"Good luck getting that writ of *habeas*," Durham told her when she rejoined him in the observation room. "I've put the word out. Half the judges in the western district already know about Oz getting nabbed in the act tonight. I mentioned he's also a suspect in the Winlock Savage murder. Unless McCool has a judge in his back pocket, Oz isn't going anywhere before the arraignment."

"I thought Oz was eliminated as a suspect," she said.

"Never. In fact, he was the only council member who had no alibi for his whereabouts the night Savage died. The master key got me thinking. If he has a master for door locks, why not padlocks?"

"Not following." She stared at Oz and McCool huddled together whispering in the interrogation room. Oz looked frightened. McCool tried to calm him, but it wasn't working.

265

"Chuck Hogan was certain he locked his smokehouse before he went home the night Savage was murdered. Maybe he did. Maybe Oz has master keys for padlocks as well as door locks."

"Are you suggesting Oz might have been involved in Savage's murder?"

"Oz is old, but he's still a large guy, and he looks healthy enough. He put up a decent struggle when I cuffed him. We already know it took two or three people to carry Savage into the smokehouse and hoist him onto the hook. Oz and another guy his size might have been able to pull it off. For three people his size, it would be a cinch. Let's get those search warrants as soon as possible. We might be looking for evidence of more than burglary. Oz Tattersall might be a murderer."

———

Bobbi initiated the process of calling judges for search warrants. In most cases, she'd have been satisfied with telephonic warrants to search Oz's home and businesses, but Oz was a pillar of the community, and she wanted everything ironclad.

"The old saying, *'If you shoot at the king, you'd better not miss'* comes to mind," Durham said, as he watched her type the forms.

"Go grab some rack time," she told him, without looking away from the screen. "It'll take an hour or two to get these approved, *if* we get them approved, and after that it's going to be a long night. We'll hit Oz's house first. He's more likely to stash any stolen shit where he can control who comes and goes." She looked up for the first time. "Scoot, Blade. I don't need you right now, and I will sure as hell need you alert later."

"Ten-four," he said.

He was halfway back to the Choctaw Arms when someone called him from behind.

"Agent Durham!"

He turned around and found Trent McCool jogging toward him on the sidewalk. The older man fell into step with Durham. He was barely breathing hard.

"I, uh, apologize for the rude reception Choctaw has offered you," he said. "Based on your inquiries to this point, I cannot help but worry this latest development might reflect badly on my dear friend Oz Tattersall."

"Not at all," Durham said. "Tattersall is no more or less a suspect in the Winlock Savage murder than he was before we caught him burglarizing a house."

"Adroitly parsed," McCool said.

"Admirably phrased," Durham said. "I seldom encounter the word *'parsed'* in everyday conversation. And who am I kidding? Off the record and between men, this makes Oz look guilty as fuck. If I discover he owns a master key to the padlock on Chuck Hogan's smokehouse, I'm going to send him away for the rest of his life."

"You will, of course, appreciate my attempts to thwart your efforts," McCool said.

"Goes without saying. Let's change the subject. I've reopened the investigation into the Patti Masters murder in 1977."

"Curious. Why?"

"It intrigues me, and there are connections between it and the Savage murder."

"Including myself."

"Yes. We have new evidence. Masters might have been carrying on an affair with one of her students."

"Tawdry," McCool observed.

"This from a guy who recently married a woman who was a fetus when he blew out fifty candles."

"I am what I am, and I don't apologize for it. I thought better of Patti. We knew she was having an affair with someone, of course, from the evidence at the time. I never considered it might be a student."

"We've sent her clothes off to the DNA lab for analysis," Durham said.

"I'll be very interested in the results. That was a confusing and dark time in Choctaw history. I'm not proud of how it turned out. If we can find out who killed Patti Masters, maybe something good will come out of it."

"I'm interviewing Ted Wisniewski tomorrow."

"Say hello for me. I haven't seen Ted in twenty years. He drew a tough hand. I hear he landed on his feet, though. Formed a security company in Burnsville. Turned lemons into lemonade. Well, here's the hotel. Tell Chief Navarro I intend to spring Oz first thing in the morning."

TWENTY-SIX

The call from Bobbi Navarro came around three in the morning.

"Sleep in," she said. "Couldn't roust a judge interested in signing the order before morning."

"No?" he asked.

"It's a different world here compared to the flatlands," she explained. "There're only three judges within an hour's drive, and they all know Oz Tattersall. They're going to want more than some podunk Blue Ridge police chief's word over the telephone before they issue the warrant. I'm driving over to the Yancey County seat in Burnsville tomorrow morning to speak to the judge in person."

"Small world. I'm headed there to interview Ted Wisniewski about the Patti Masters investigation back in the seventies. We can ride together, and after I finish with Wisniewski and you get the warrant, we can go to town at Oz's house. How's he taking prison life?"

"Snoring like an asthmatic baby in Holding Two," she said.

"Tell him to get used to it. The B&E and burglary alone will put him away for fifteen years."

"In Oz's case, that's a life sentence."

"It might be worse if he was in on the Win Savage murder."

"Still speculation, Durham."

"Part of me hopes it stays that way. I like Oz. I'll hate to see him do serious time, but getting the needle would be so much worse."

"It'll never happen," she said. "Even if he's convicted of murder, he'll die of natural causes long before anyone pumps the drop-dead juice into his arm. But any way you call it, his free life is over. Back to sleep. See you at eight at the Grille. We'll grab a bite before we head to Burnsville."

———

Ted Wisniewski was bald and properly wrinkled for a man in his eighties. His face was slack, and his nose and earlobes had lengthened with time. His face was covered with liver spots and lesions, but he didn't wear glasses, and he could still see the numbers on a license plate a hundred feet away. He sat in an electric wheelchair on the front porch of his house in the shadow of the Appalachian ridge that rose behind the town like a frozen tsunami, ten or twelve streets back from the four-lane highway. He watched as Durham parked Bobbi's cruiser on the street and hiked two sets of stairs to the deep, covered porch.

"Agent Durham?" Wisniewski said.

"Mr. Wisniewski," Durham said, taking the man's hand. "That's a haul up here for someone on wheels."

"I have a ramp in the back, next to the garage. I haven't been up or down those steps in years. I can walk well enough when the spirit moves me, but it's uncomfortable after a while. Around the house, it's easier to roll. Please, have a seat."

It was still early on a razor-keen autumn morning in the mountains. The air was clean and biting, but far enough into the fifties that it wasn't necessary to cocoon indoors. Since Burnsville was at a higher altitude than Choctaw, Durham had planned ahead and wore a fleece lined SBI winter jacket. He was perfectly comfortable on the porch.

"So, you've reopened the Patti Masters case," Wisniewski said. "I'm happy to hear it. I knew her, you know."

"Did you?"

"We stood next to each other in the church choir for almost two years. Our elbows touched frequently. I was only recently divorced, and still young enough to get regular morning wood. I'm afraid I may have harbored some unchaste notions about the schoolmarm."

"Must have been a shock when she was murdered," Durham said.

"Rattled me proper, Agent Durham."

"Call me Wade."

"All right, Wade. Yeah. It was tough. And then we had the other killing right on top of her murder."

"Lester Corby."

"Right. Took me a second to remember his name. Strange. Yeah, that was a real tragedy. Corby never did anything to anybody. By reports, he was the nicest man you could ever hope to meet. He was in the wrong place at the wrong time with the wrong kid wearing a badge and carrying a gun. You know they tried to frame Corby, right?"

"No. It isn't in the files."

"Damn right it isn't. I didn't allow it. One cop's career was crushed because of the Corby shooting. Couldn't see the point in flushing another as well. The younger cop, Frye, lost his cool and killed Corby because he believed a keyring was a gun. The older of the pair, Sanderson, tried to drop a throwdown to make it look like Corby pulled on them. Chief Tanney and I saw through it in seconds. I'd already ruled Corby out as a suspect. I only wanted to talk to him as a witness and sent them out to pick him up. Such a fucking waste. Still keeps me awake some nights."

"Frye went to prison over it."

"Yeah. Negligent homicide. Did his full bump in segregated population."

"What happened to him afterward?"

"He had ties to The Ridge. Last I heard, he disappeared into the hills."

"The Ridge?" Durham asked.

"A community of squatters on Choctaw Knob. Bunch of square pegs. Think of themselves as the last great frontiersmen or some kind of shit. Mostly moonshiners, and apocalyptic survivalists, and ex-cons who can't handle city life, and some genuine nutjobs who are better off away from regular people anyway. Way the world rolls these days, they probably have their share of militant white supremacists as well, real Gravy Seals types. You won't find The Ridge on any maps. There's no government or tax collector or police force or even a zip code. These people party like it's 1799."

"And this kid who shot Corby—Frye—lives there now?"

"Damned if I know. Andy Frye was born on The Ridge. After he got out of prison, his uncle drove him up onto the Knob, and I never heard of him again. I figure he's still there, distilling mash or cooking meth or whatever that crowd's up to these days. Best to steer clear, though. Folks on The Ridge don't take kindly to government types, especially those who wear badges. I went there once looking for a runaway. I was happy to put the place in the rearview. Found myself looking around for squinty-eyed kids playing banjos, if you know what I mean."

"You were injured during the shootout, I hear."

"Yes. I have one of the Ridge boys to thank for that. I took a mighty whack from the rear with something heavy. Newspapers said it was a shotgun butt. Felt like a baseball bat. Fucked me up pretty good, neurologically speaking. Had to learn to walk all over again, and my hands and feet haven't stopped tingling for forty-something years. Took a long time to string two sentences together. Now you can't shut me up."

"How did the shootout begin?"

"I have no idea who shot first. I was already down for the count. Word had it someone lit off a string of firecrackers. Spooked someone with a gun, and we were off to the races. I never saw a thing, and then I was out cold for days, and barely aware of the next couple of months. I probably saw more than I recall, but it's all gone now. Worst part was, after I took the shot to the neck, my junk don't work so great anymore. I was forty. Had a couple of girlfriends since, but they didn't last. Only one reason makes sense. Sure isn't my sunny disposition."

He cackled a couple of times and coughed a few more.

"Sometimes, I wish they'd done me in," he said. "You wanted to talk about Patti Masters?"

"I want to know what wasn't in the murder book," Durham said. "What were you thinking, but hadn't documented yet? Your suspicions."

"Give me a minute," he said. "Gotta think it all through. Like I haven't turned it over in my head a hundred times over the last forty years. A thousand maybe. We established from the report by her assistant that Patti met her lover periodically in her office, between five and seven in the evening. We established the timeline through the typical forensic methods, but also because Patti's assistant went home at five, and the night custodian came in at seven, and neither of them ever saw her with the lover. The assistant—can't recall her name, but she was a pistol—told me Patti sent her home early on the day she was murdered. She left at four o'clock. Patti was dead by six-thirty, according to the autopsy. She met her lover, had sex with him, including a blowjob. For some reason, that part of the report stood out for me. Probably says more about me than her. So, if she met her lover at four and they had sex in her office, he probably didn't leave—if he left—until five or shortly after. Let's say it was five-thirty. Leaves a sixty-minute window for the killing."

"Presuming the lover isn't also the killer."

"Exactly. And that's where I was when the riot broke out. Afterward, I cashiered out on disability and Social Security. Moved here to put the memories out of my mind. I like Burnsville. It's what Choctaw might have become if it had been luckier. I opened a security firm here a few years later. Hired retired cops to be night watchmen and the like, to bring in a few bucks. Sold it twenty years ago. Been watching the seasons come and go from this porch ever since. I've read a whole fuckin' library of books, I'll tell you. Ain't shit worth watchin' on television anymore."

"Maybe I can provide another piece of the puzzle for you," Durham said. "I spoke with Patti Masters' daughter yesterday. She overheard some cheerleaders in the bathroom talking about her mother. They said she was sleeping with a student."

"I considered that. If she was, I don't believe the lover was her killer. I staked out the school for a couple of days after the murder. The way Patti was beaten, the killer had to have bruised and scraped knuckles. I looked at every set of hands in the school. Nobody looked like they'd recently caved in the principal's face. When it didn't pan out, I considered maybe she was getting it on with some married guy who had to be home earlier than usual that night. I kind of liked that angle. Gave him motive to kill her, if she became possessive and threatened to expose him, *Fatal Attraction* style. So, it was one of the students after all. That changes things."

"How?"

"The schedule. She'd been meeting her lover after five o'clock. On the day she was murdered, she backed it up to four. I've always assumed it was for the guy's convenience, because as far as anyone knew, she didn't have plans for the evening. Why would a student need to see her at four instead of five?"

"Family obligations?" Durham offered.

"Okay. Sure. Henry Aldrich needs to be home for an early dinner."

"You know what's scary?" Durham said. "I get that reference. Hey, what if it wasn't a family thing? What if the student had a school obligation? Some kind of extracurricular activity they had to attend at an hour earlier than usual."

"If I'd known this in 1977, I could have done something with it. Now, there's no way to know what the schedules were that day. Hey, want to hear something crazy?"

"This whole damn case is crazy."

"Get this. In 1977, if she *was* banging a student, Patti wasn't breaking any laws."

"Go on."

"I checked. The age of consent in North Carolina in 1977 was thirteen, and nothing on the books prevented a teacher from sleeping with a student who had attained the age of consent. I'm sure the school board would have taken a dim view, and she would have been gone the next day if they ever found out about it, but she wasn't breaking any laws. Go figure. She kept the affair a secret not because it was illegal, but because it was so tacky and damaging to her reputation. The more I hear about Patti, the less I think I knew her, however many hours we spent sharing each other's air in the choir loft. Turns out she was something of—what do you call them these days? —a cougar."

"What did you call them back then?"

"Damned if I can remember. Don't think I ever ran into one anyway, at least none who paid me any mind. So, we need to ID the lover."

"It'll be easier this time around. I sent Patti's clothes to the DNA lab. We should know something as early as tomorrow. Getting the genotype is one thing. Then comes a lot of cross-matching. I have a crew in Charlotte who can help."

"Jesus," Wisniewski said. "If we'd had this Tom Swift shit back in the seventies, I'd have caught every goddamn crook in North Carolina."

"It's a tool," Durham said. "Like any other. The real work still happens here." He tapped the side of his head. "Oh, Trent McCool sends his regards."

"McCool? He's still alive?"

"Just honeymooned in the Caribbean with his fifth wife."

"Further evidence against the existence of God," Wisniewski said. "A snake like McCool grabs off young nookie right and left, and I can barely walk to the bathroom five times a night. Cosmic justice is a bygone concept, my friend. I kicked karma to the curb a long time ago. Hey. The SBI didn't send you to Choctaw to work a forty-year-old cold case, did they?"

"No."

"Good. I was going to say, if they did, you must have really screwed the pooch."

"I'm working the Winlock Savage murder," Durham said.

"I am in the presence of celebrity, then."

"The Choctaw PD's short-staffed and asked for help. The Masters murder came up in the process, and it interested me."

"Well, bless you for it. I've thought about Patti a lot over the years. What it could have been like if I'd had a stouter spine and spoken sooner. I'd like to see her get some justice."

"Let's go over the murder book again, and figure out what's missing," Durham said.

————

Durham pulled the cruiser to the curb in front of the courthouse, where Bobbi waited holding a manila envelope.

"Please tell me those are search warrants," he said as she slid into the passenger seat.

"You know, officially, I should be driving," she said, handing him the envelope. He opened it and scanned the documents inside.

"Yeah, and I saw how you took those switchback mountain roads on the way here. A pro should drive us back."

"Don't do a bump and run on an eighteen-wheeler on the way. Tell you the truth, I can use a little downtime. You drive. I'll snooze."

They were halfway back to Choctaw when Durham said, "I've been thinking about the lawsuit."

"What about it?" she asked drowsily.

"Exactly my question. Why did Win Savage file the lawsuit in the first place?"

"He's a conservationist. He thought the ski resort would carve up the Knob and destroy the delicate ecosystem."

"Was he, though? Nothing in his history suggests rabid environmentalism. He was more like a playboy sybarite. From what I can gather, a wade through the ocean of his soul would scarcely get your feet wet. Now, suddenly, he's concerned about the effect a life-saving resort for his hometown might have on the ecosystem on Choctaw Knob? I'm not buying it."

"I see what you mean," she said, now fully awake.

"I'm all for saving the Earth, but what's so environmentally critical on Choctaw Knob that it needs protection? Are they hiding Sasquatch up there?"

"I don't have an answer."

"He was protecting *something*," Durham said. "I still think we should look for a third player. Maybe that player is on the Knob. Wisniewski told me about some sort of commune or enclave there."

"The Ridge, yeah," she said.

"You've been there?"

"Hell no. It's outside my jurisdiction, and to be honest, the Ridge squatters give me the creeps. They ride into town once a month or so, big old caravan of thirty-year-old four-wheel-drive trucks, stock up on supplies, and disappear back up the hill again. They don't associate with Choctaw folks."

"How have they been allowed to stay there all these years?"

"Beats me. Ever since the shootout, we leave them alone and they leave us alone. It's a tradition now. We don't patrol there, and they don't ask us for help. Guess nobody wants to rock the boat. If one of the Ridge boys causes a ruckus in town, I'll deal with them like everyone else. Long as they stay on the Knob and out of my hair, we're all copacetic. There are all sorts of unincorporated hillbilly shantytowns scattered across the Blue Ridge. Folks just settled and never left. Civilization hasn't crept up to them yet. As long as nobody makes a squawk about it, I figure live and let live."

"Somebody didn't feel that way about Win Savage."

"True enough."

Her telephone jangled.

"Pete," she said, referring to one of her two uniformed officers. "He's minding the station while I'm away." She answered the call. After a few seconds, she said, "I'm not surprised. Take your time processing him. Like, a lot of time. While you're doing that, send Earl to Oz's house and wrap the doors tight with crime scene tape. Do the same at his businesses. Shutter 'em and tell the employees to take nothing home but their personal possessions. I have warrants to search his home and stores. If anything critical goes missing, people are going down for obstruction. Make that clear. Got it? I'm about twenty minutes out. We're headed straight to Oz's house. Meet you there."

She pocketed the phone.

"Trent McCool sprung Oz?" Durham asked.

"He found a judge somewhere to sign a writ of *habeas*. I can't hold him pending the arraignment, but I can sure slow-walk his release while I toss his digs."

"Kind of bad ass," Durham said. "I like it. Okay. First, we search his premises. Then we hit the stores. I want to do the hardware first. That's where his locksmith operation is located. The B&E shit doesn't interest me, but the master key and his shitty alibi for the Savage murder do."

"You still believe Oz was in on the Savage deal?"

"He keeps proving impervious to exoneration, as we used to say back on the farm."

"I can't imagine him murdering someone," she said.

"Twenty-four hours ago, you couldn't imagine him burgling a house."

She didn't say anything else for several minutes. "I hear stories," she said, finally.

"Okay."

"Choctaw doesn't have the sort of drug problems the cities in the flatlands experience. I mean, yeah, we see our share of weed, and occasionally we run across someone with bottles of oxy or Vicodin they can't produce a scrip for. Had a brief issue with Ex in the high school last spring. It's probably still there, but the kids are much cleverer about hiding the traffic these days. We're raising a whole generation of skilled drug dealers here in the valley. Long as nobody ODs and croaks, I don't pursue it much. One thing we haven't seen much of though is meth, which is kind of weird for the Blue Ridge. The western part of the state is Shatter Central, but here in the Choctaw Valley we hardly see any of it."

"Count your blessings," Durham said.

"Well, here's the thing, and maybe it's part of that whole *live and let live* attitude I was talking about. Rumors have it folks on The Ridge are cooking meth now instead of moonshine."

"Wisniewski mentioned something along those lines. Said they were moonshiners back in the day but have probably moved on to meth. Better profit margin."

"And how. If they have labs on the Knob, why haven't they accessed a market in the valley, right in their back yard?"

Durham drove on for several miles before he said, "Maybe the meth labs are our Sasquatch."

"Come again?"

"Like we said earlier. I'm not swallowing the story of Winlock Savage as a crusading environmentalist willing to put his money where his mouth was with a lawsuit against the town. He was portrayed as protecting Choctaw Knob from desecration by bulldozers and earthmovers. What if he wasn't protecting the Knob itself at all? What if he was protecting something else *on* the Knob?"

"Meth labs?" she asked.

"According to his agent, Savage was living gig to gig, and the gigs were drying up. He was marginal on finances. Yet, he was able to hire high-powered environmental attorneys to battle the ski resort project. How'd he pay them? Where did the money come from?"

"You think Win Savage was working with meth cooks on Choctaw Knob, and he filed the lawsuit, using their money, to protect their operations from being disturbed?"

"Our third player," he said. "The path we haven't explored, yet."

"So why did they kill him?"

"Something went south, maybe in a hurry. Maybe Savage grew a conscience and decided to back away. Or maybe someone on the council found out what he was up to, and *they* killed him."

"Keeps pointing back to Oz, doesn't it?" she said.

He didn't answer. The rest of the drive to Choctaw was spent in silence.

ACT THREE

THE LAW ON
CHOCTAW KNOB

TWENTY-SEVEN

Oz Tattersall's stash of burglary loot wouldn't fill a treasure chest, but it was impressive, nonetheless.

Bobbi Navarro found it in Tattersall's basement workshop, inside a large, stamped steel toolbox. When she popped the flimsy lock with a screwdriver, she found dozens of pieces of jewelry, a few watches, and strands of pearls—several pounds of apparently purloined valuables. If Oz only stole one or two pieces each time he broke into a home, the haul in the toolbox must have represented thirty or forty burglaries.

"No way of knowing how long he's been at it," she told Durham as they carefully catalogued and bagged the pieces as evidence. "I'll be weeks tracking the owners of this shit. Half of them are probably dead or moved away."

"Even if he's sentenced concurrently, his life is over," Durham said. "We're looking at dozens of felony counts here. The judge might have gone light on him and given him the minimum with a single offense. Maybe he'd have seen the light of day again. Now, though…" He didn't bother finishing.

"He can still deal," she said. "If he was involved in the Savage murder, he can make all this go away by ratting on his buddies. I should be sweating him in the interrogation room right now."

"Gotta find him first. McCool didn't bring him back here, and he hasn't gone to any of his businesses," Durham said. "We've got him on the burglary. I'm going to look for master keys at the hardware."

"I'll call McCool and tell him to bring Oz back in. His *habeas* paper doesn't apply to new charges." She surveyed the stacks of jewelry on the table. "It looks like he kept all of it."

"Trophies," he said. "Like I said, it wasn't about money. Oz Tattersall is Bad Santa. He got off on the danger of breaking into the houses of folks who adored him. Everything he did, however couched it was in philanthropy, was about acquiring power and control over the people of Choctaw. Just another skeevy guy leading a secret life."

"The kind of guy who keeps folks like us in business," she said.

He left her to her sorting and cataloguing and stepped outside to walk to the hardware. His stomach rumbled. He'd skipped lunch because he and Bobbi had been in such a hurry to get to the search of Oz's house. He considered stopping by the Choctaw Grille for a bite but checked his phone and discovered it was almost four o'clock already. He could hold out for another couple of hours.

As he stashed the phone, he noticed Oz Tattersall's ancient, detached garage at the rear of his lot. It was the sort of place many people turned into offices or workshops or potting sheds. Curious, he strolled over and tried to peek through the clouded, dusty glass of the double swinging doors.

Seconds later, he dashed into the house. "Bobbi! Do you have a bolt cutter in the cruiser trunk?"

"Sure."

"Keys," he said, holding out his hand.

She handed him the keys and followed him to the cruiser, where he retrieved the heavy steel-jawed bolt cutter. He broke the padlock on the doors and swung them open.

"Midnight blue Hyundai Sonata sedan," he said, pointing to the car nestled inside the garage.

"The car Hazel Hatchell saw parked in front of Chuck Hogan's smokehouse."

"It matches the description." He walked around the car, taking great care not to touch it. "No tags. I'm liking Oz more and more for the Savage murder. Impound the car, trace the VIN, and have the forensic guys from Asheville go through it, especially the trunk."

She had her phone out. "Already on it."

"You should call McCool next, make him bring Oz in before we have to go hunting for him."

———

The younger patrol officer, Pete, waited in front of Oz Tattersall's hardware store when Durham arrived. Pete was young, dark-haired, and handsome in a 1950s singing idol way. You could tell by the way he walked he was damned proud to be a cop.

Durham headed straight for the locksmith booth in the back of the store. He gloved up and rifled through drawers. At first, he found nothing out of the ordinary except boxes of various-sized key blanks, still wrapped in wax paper and smelling of manufacturing oil. The top drawer contained several metal files and emery paper.

The locksmith booth might have been as old as the hardware, and the accumulated tools and boxes of key blanks and other materials made the search tedious. As he closed the final drawer, his back aching from bending over as he searched, Durham considered this might be a dry hole.

He stood, stretched his back, and took a deep breath. He was in familiar territory, the part of the case when the pieces start to fall together. He was on the right track. He knew it, deep inside. He only needed to be persistent.

He spied a lone toolbox sitting on the floor at the rear of the booth, and he remembered the toolbox Bobbi had found in Tattersall's basement.

"Why not?" he asked the still air in the store. He opened the box and found an enormous key ring, filled with keys. Each key had a strip of masking tape attached with an address written on it.

"Gotcha," Durham said. He bagged the keys and headed for the station.

————

"We need to find Oz now," Durham said, when he walked into Bobbi's office. He dropped the evidence bag containing the keyring onto her desk. "I was right. He's been hoarding keys for almost every house in town. But look at these." He showed her a separate ring with a dozen unlabeled keys. "Padlock master keys. Schlage,

MasterLock, Abus, American, Yale, Brinks, they're all here. Oz could open any padlock in town and never leave a trace."

"Including the one on Chuck Hogan's smokehouse," Bobbi said. "The crime scene guys from Asheville are on the way to impound the Hyundai in Oz's garage. I've put in a call to Trent McCool already. No answer. Tried to ping Oz's phone, but it's apparently turned off. I don't like the way this feels, Blade. You think Oz is in the wind?"

"He's guilty as fuck, at least on the burglaries," Durham said. "So, yeah. He might have decided to get the rabbit habit."

"I'll give McCool another half hour to call me back, and then I'm putting a BOLO out on Oz."

"Ping McCool's phone while you're at it. Maybe Oz is still with him."

Bobbi's desk phone rang. She answered, listened for a few seconds, and said, "We're on our way." She cradled the receiver and grabbed her jacket. "C'mon, Blade. Something we need to see."

————

They met Pete and the older uniformed cop, Earl, at the hardware store. Earl was middle-aged and black. He was a part-time assistant football coach at the high school and looked younger and fitter than the gray hair creeping in at his temples suggested.

"What is it?" Durham asked. "I was just here."

"I kept searching after you left," Pete said. "Earl here was working the drug store. I didn't see nothing suspicious on the main floor, so I checked the back storeroom. C'mon. I'll show you."

289

He led them through the swinging doors to the loading dock and storage at the rear of the building. Twenty sealed boxes labeled *Clover Hollow Honey* were stacked against a side wall.

"Honey?" Durham said. "Oz doesn't sell honey in the hardware. This isn't Mast General Store."

"I had the same thought," Pete said. "I checked the boxes and found one light. Over here." He'd placed the box on a table near the door to the showroom. The tape seal had been sliced open and the ears of the box hung wide. Pete reached inside with a gloved hand and held up a gallon-sized zippered plastic bag. Inside the bag were shards of what looked like translucent glass.

"Hello, Sasquatch," Durham said. "Good work, Officer. Looks like we can add meth distribution to Oz's rap sheet."

"We need to find out everything we can about this Clover Hollow Honey company," Bobbi said.

Durham grabbed for his phone. "Bet you ten bucks they're on Choctaw Knob."

"No takers," Bobbi said. "And screw waiting an hour. I'm putting out a BOLO on Oz right now. I need to contact the DEA."

"No," Durham said. "I am not turning this case over to the DEA."

"The hell, Durham?"

"I don't like the DEA. We're on the outs right now. Soon as you call those guys, you lose all control over the case."

"Durham, I have a legal obligation—"

"To report a bag of—what? Save yourself potential embarrassment. Get it tested first. Slow-walk the test the way you did Oz's release. By the time we know for sure this is shatter, we can have the whole case wrapped up. Then you can turn it over to DEA. We get the snag; they get the paperwork. Serves 'em right."

————

"Clover Hollow Honey is a self-proprietorship registered in McDowell County," Durham told Bobbi as he read off the report on his phone. "It's owned by Clarence and Flossie Purdy. Their address is listed as Route 3, Marion."

"Out in the sticks," Bobbi said.

"Not far enough, and nowhere near Choctaw Knob. Should have taken that bet. You follow up on the BOLO, ping McCool, and arrange testing for whatever's in the baggie."

"We know what it is, Blade."

"Better to be certain. The DEA hates people wasting their time. I'd run to Marion and check out Clarence and Flossie Purdy, but it's almost dark now, and I want to see their operation in the daytime. I'll visit them first thing in the morning."

"Where are you going now?" Bobbi asked.

"Gonna have a chat with the mayor," Durham said. "It's long overdue."

TWENTY-EIGHT

Mayor Fred Tinsley was at his desk in the Town Hall when Durham walked through his door.

"Agent Durham!" he said, standing. "I wasn't expecting you."

"I like it that way," Durham said. "It's been a busy day. Haven't had a lot of time for formalities."

"I know," Tinsley said. "I've already fielded several telephone calls from the media. I'm simply shocked about this news. I never would have suspected Oz for so much as an unpaid traffic ticket. Please, have a seat."

"You're the only member of the Town Council I haven't interviewed yet. We're in a bit of a lull while we wait for forensic evidence to come in, so I decided to get it out of the way."

"No problem. I'm at your disposal."

"I want to pick up where we left off the other evening in the Grille. You said you were with your wife all night last Friday, when Win Savage was murdered."

"I arrived home around seven. We ate shortly afterward, and we watched television until about eleven, when we went to bed. I slept until I received the telephone call about Savage the next morning."

"Who called you?"

"Chief Navarro. She'd been called out to the smokehouse by Chuck Hogan."

"When was the last time you spoke with Win Savage?" Durham asked.

"Oh, my. It's been a while. We weren't close at all. Face to face, we last spoke four or five months ago. I talked to him on the telephone a few weeks ago, regarding his objections to the ski resort."

"How did he sound?"

"Funny you should ask. He sounded strange. I wrote it off at the time to drugs or alcohol, because the man had a reputation, you know."

"I've heard."

"He might have been nervous. Anxious. There was an edge to his voice, almost as if someone were holding a gun to his head as he spoke. He sounded strange. Forced. Worried."

"Do you have any idea why we might have found almost four pounds of crystal meth in the back of Oz's hardware store?" Durham asked. He watched Tinsley closely for a reaction. Anything other than shock would be suspicious.

He got shock.

"I can't believe it," Tinsley said. "I've known Oz Tattersall for over forty years. There is no way he would be involved in something like that."

"But you're perfectly comfortable with the notion of him being a serial burglar."

"Never," Tinsley said. "Until yesterday. I see what you mean. If you'd accused him of theft before yesterday, I'd have been just as surprised. Next thing, you'll tell me he killed Winlock Savage."

Durham stared at him.

"No!" Tinsley protested. "Oz is the heart and soul of this community. We might be a ghost town already if it weren't for him. Now you're telling me he's a murderer?"

"We found a car matching the description of a sedan parked outside The Chuckwagon the night Savage was killed. It was in Oz's garage, behind a padlock. No tags. Ever seen him drive a midnight blue Hyundai?"

"No," Tinsley said. "Oz drives a pickup truck. I don't know which brand."

"It took at least two people to hoist Savage onto the hook in the smokehouse. Probably three. Oz is big enough to be one of them. Best guess is Savage was killed elsewhere and transported to the smokehouse to send a message. If the crime scene guys find any evidence of Savage in the Hyundai's trunk, Oz is looking at a date with a gurney."

Tinsley slumped in his seat. "That's the last straw. I'm done with this job. Let someone else deal with the headaches."

"I still think this has something to do with the lawsuit against you and the council over the ski resort. But something's screwy about that, and I can't figure it out."

"What?"

"How heavily are you invested in the resort?" Durham asked.

"A couple hundred thousand. Nowhere near as much as the others."

"Why not?"

"I'm about to retire," he said. "I've been fortunate over the years to build an extremely comfortable financial position for my golden years. Gambling a huge chunk of it on something as speculative as a ski resort—however profitable it may turn out to be—didn't seem an acceptable risk. Unlike the other council investors who were born into money, I had to earn mine. I did not savor the idea of earning it again. I could afford to lose a couple hundred thousand, so I joined in to do my part for Choctaw. If it was successful, I'd pad my retirement accounts. If not, I'll be fine anyway."

"You're an analytical man, I take it," Durham said.

"I've never considered it. I am objective, perhaps compulsively so. I deal with numbers, and on a good day the numbers balance. On a bad day, I have to figure out why they didn't. I suppose that requires some analytical skill. Why do you ask?"

"Making an observation. When you ran for the mayor's office, it was to prevent Carl Royster from taking the seat, wasn't it?"

"In part, yes."

"Why? What did Royster ever do to you?"

"I'm not sure I understand your question. What does Royster have to do with Oz or Win Savage?"

"As far as I know, nothing. Darrell Tanney, on the other hand, has connections to both this case and one I'm investigating from 1977."

"Patti Masters?" Tinsley asked.

"Yes. How'd you know?"

"It was a logical conclusion. Had to be her or Lester Corby, and Corby's killing was resolved decades ago. I was a senior at the high school at the time. Patti Masters was my principal, at least for a few weeks. They brought in Howard Kautz to take her place. I never liked Mr. Kautz. Nobody did."

"We're working on reliable evidence that Patti Masters was sleeping with one of her students," he said. "Wouldn't be you, would it?"

Tinsley blushed. "Me? Oh, no, Agent Durham. Oh, my. No. I was what you'd call a late bloomer. I was a lot more interested in my cello and Science Club in 1977."

"How many people who attended Choctaw High then still live around here? Did a lot of people stay?"

"Not many. Maybe thirty from our class. People either sink solid roots in Choctaw, or they float away like tumbleweeds."

"Can you give me your wife's telephone number?" Durham asked.

"Whatever for?"

"She's your alibi, remember? I need to confirm she was with you all night Friday."

"Ah! Yes. Of course." He wrote the number on a yellow sticky pad and handed the sheet to Durham.

"Back to Carl Royster," Durham said. "Why exactly did you not want him to be mayor?"

"He was Trent McCool's candidate," Tinsley said. "McCool nearly destroyed this town before he was sent to prison. Between his autocratic dictates and his graft and corruption, he nearly flew Choctaw into the ground. Royster was a student at the high school in 1977 too. He was senior class president, and he had political aspirations. Once Mayor Gimball left for Congress, and McCool took over the mayor's office, Royster became one of his assistants. McCool sponsored his education at Carolina—undergrad and law school—and after he passed the bar Royster came back to Choctaw and took over McCool's former position as town attorney.

Royster's more or less Trent McCool Junior. He's the son Tim never could be. If Royster endorses something, you can bet McCool told him to."

"And McCool is why Darrell Tanney is always at Royster's side?"

"Well, in the final analysis, Royster is why Tanney is always at his side. Roger Gimball and Trent McCool practically raised Darrell after his dad died. Darrell was only ten. Something in him broke when his father keeled over. He became wild. His mother couldn't control him. Roger and Trent stepped in and helped as best they could. Tanney wasn't smart enough for college, so McCool arranged for him to get on with the Highway Patrol. When Tanney nearly washed out with the troopers, McCool and Royster's brother arranged for him to be assigned to Royster. Both Tanney and Royster owe Trent McCool in a big way. Probably debts they can never repay."

"I bet McCool exploits the hell out of that debt," Durham said.

"I wouldn't know. There's not enough moral fiber between Royster and Tanney to weave a postage stamp. Between you and me and the gatepost, I think McCool likes them together because it's easier to keep an eye on both of them."

"Yet, you seemed chummy with Royster the other evening. With all the bad blood between you, I was surprised to see you together in my booth."

"Politics makes strange bedfellows. Can't recall who said that, but they must have had first-hand experience. Trent is representing the council members in Savage's lawsuit, including me. Whenever Trent McCool is around, Royster comes as part of the package. I must say I found the experience distasteful, but I don't disagree with what Royster said, at least this time. Choctaw needs this ski

297

resort. I don't know whether it will save the town or not, and I'm not willing to bet my entire retirement on it, but this town is on life support, and the ski resort might be our miracle cure."

Durham's phone buzzed. Bobbi Navarro.

"Durham," he said.

"Got a ping off Trent McCool's phone," Bobbi said. "He's at Tim's place on Blind Top."

"Got a number for Tim McCool?"

"Hold on. Sending it now. You need directions?"

Durham turned to Tinsley, "You know how to get to Tim McCool's home on Blind Top?"

"Sure," Tinsley said. "Been there several times."

Durham spoke back into the phone. "I'm with Mayor Tinsley. He'll fill me in."

"You need backup?"

"Let me find out if Oz is hanging around first. If he is, I'll ask him to turn himself in. If he refuses, we'll take it to the next level."

TWENTY-NINE

Durham had just turned off the Choctaw Pike at Blind Top when his phone buzzed. He sent it to the truck's hands-free Bluetooth. It was Bobbi Navarro.

"We traced the VIN on the car in Oz's garage. It's registered to Stanley Purdy."

"Any relation to Clarence and Flossie Purdy of Clover Hollow Honey?"

"You're sharp. I'll give you that. Yeah. He's their son. And get this. His driver's license says he's six-two and goes about two-thirty."

"Big enough to lift Savage onto that hook with Oz's help," Durham noted.

"I was thinking the same thing. The car's registered to their Marion address, though. So, if you interview them tomorrow, tread lightly. Junior could be lurking around, and he might be a killer."

———

Tim McCool's home on Blind Top, the mountain that bookended the Choctaw Valley with the Knob, looked ordinary and humble from the road, much like a slightly oversized suburban rambler in any town in North Carolina.

The façade was deceptive. McCool had built his home cantilevered over a steep slope on the side of the mountain. Most of the house tumbled down the back side, three floors in all, ending in a lanai and pool overlooking the scenic Choctaw Valley.

Durham parked his car in a circular lot in front of the house and rang the doorbell. Nobody answered, so he rang it again. Shortly, a light turned on in the stairwell, and the shadow of a person appeared on the wall. Durham decided McCool probably used the street level only in the direst of emergencies.

Darrell Tanney opened the door. A wave of ethanol fumes washed through the doorway as he spoke. "What?" he asked. He didn't bother sounding polite.

"Oh, you live here too?" Durham asked.

"You want something?"

"Trent McCool. I need to talk to him."

"Who says he's here?"

"Ma Bell. His phone pings here."

"Huh?"

"Take me to him or bring him here. I don't care which. And if Oz Tattersall is here, I need to talk to him as well."

"Hold on." Tanney shut the door.

He also threw the deadbolt, which was a bad sign. Durham waited patiently for about forty seconds and considered hiking around the house. Tanney opened the door again.

"Come with me," he said.

Durham took Tanney's measure as he followed him down the stairs to the main floor of the house. Tanney was large, maybe two inches taller than Durham, and he probably carried twenty or thirty more pounds. Fortunately, Durham mused, it was mostly suet. Tanney might have been ripped at some point in his life—Durham doubted it—but he had allowed himself to go soft playing Carl Royster's nanny, and dissipation had made him slow. Durham figured he could easily take Tanney in a fair fight, something he also figured Tanney had never heard of. In an unfair one, Durham estimated he could still probably hold his own.

The suburban ennui of the street level yielded to a stylish modern industrial middle floor, built on a wildly open concept covering perhaps two thousand square feet. This was the real house. The one seen from the street was a ruse to deter would-be sneak thieves. The area was delineated into zones by various carpets and furniture groupings. A hallway led off to the right, presumably to bedrooms and baths. One side of the room was dedicated to an opulent kitchen with a horribly expensive Viking range and oven, and a central island only slightly undersized for holding a state dinner.

The entire main section was a cry for attention from a man who seldom enjoyed any. In Durham's imagination, he saw Tim telling an architect to design a home that would blow his dad's nuts into the middle of next week, a way of saying, *I am good enough!* It was impressive and pathetic at the same time.

"Stairs," Tanney said, pointing to an eight-foot-wide open stairway that led to the lanai.

"Cool." Durham took the stairs, walked through a genuine automatic sliding glass door, and found Trent McCool, his son Tim, and Carl Royster lounging next to a fully stocked bar under the lanai ceiling. Two radiant heaters mounted to the walls warded off the October chill, making the open lanai downright cozy.

301

"Agent Durham," Tim said, standing as Durham reached the bottom of the stairs. He held out his hand, genuinely, and Durham took it. He'd already decided he liked the younger McCool, even if he was still a long way from trusting him.

"Excuse me for barging in," Durham said. "I'm looking for Oz Tattersall. Anybody seen him lately?" He directed the question to Trent McCool.

"He isn't here," Trent said. "You're welcome to search." He sounded four highballs into a five-glass evening. So much for the two-drink limit he had bragged about at the Choctaw Arms.

"Chief Navarro has been trying to call you. You aren't answering your phone."

"I didn't know I was obliged to. I do screen my calls, Agent Durham. I typically ignore those from the police. We have a history."

"You arranged for Oz's release from jail," Durham said. "Where did you take him?"

"To his truck," Trent said. "He wanted to drive to his house."

Durham shook his head. "By the time Oz left the police station, the house was already sealed, and we were there searching it. He never showed."

"His *other* house," Trent said. "His cabin on the Knob. You don't know about it?"

"No."

"Oz built it years ago," Trent said. "A little weekend getaway cabin. Maybe a thousand square feet. He figured you wouldn't allow him back inside his house in Choctaw. He wanted to go someplace quiet and plan what to do next."

"Address?" Durham asked.

"Sorry, don't know it. I'm sure you can look it up."

Durham turned to Tim.

"I don't know either, off the top of my head," Tim said. "I've been there so many times, I know exactly how to get there but I don't remember the number or street name. I have it upstairs, though."

"Please, get it."

Tim trotted up the stairs, and Durham took a seat facing Royster and the elder McCool.

"Oz is in big trouble," he said.

"I think I can get him the minimum," McCool said. "He might even get probation at his age, as a first offender."

"Not anymore," Durham said, shaking his head. "We found his burglary stash. We have him on dozens of counts now, including probable conspiracy to distribute meth. You don't look surprised. Anyway, I'm taking him back in, and there's no chance in hell you'll get a *habeas* writ out of a judge this time."

"Time will tell," Trent said.

"I forgot," Durham said. "Different rules for the rich, right?"

"Sometimes. When it matters. But, you are correct. The writ I obtained this morning doesn't cover the new offenses. If Oz were here, I'd turn him over to you. Sadly…" He shrugged his shoulders.

Tim handed a slip of paper to Durham, who shot a picture of it with his phone before stuffing it in his pocket.

"I'll take you at your word he isn't here," Durham told both McCools. "If I find out you lied, you're all going down for harboring a fugitive. And if I find out anybody here called Oz to warn him I'm coming, we'll toss obstruction on the pile. Any questions?"

Nobody had any questions. Durham turned toward the stairs. Tanney stood at the base, glaring at him. Durham stopped and addressed the others again.

"Anybody here know a guy named Stanley Purdy?" he asked.

Tim McCool looked blank. Trent McCool and Carl Royster glanced at each other, which told Durham everything he needed to know.

"Never heard of him," Trent McCool said.

Sure you haven't, Durham thought.

———

Oz Tattersall's house on Choctaw Knob had the semblance of a nineteenth century mountain log cabin, or at least as close as a mass-produced modular prefab could approximate. Durham had seen advertisements for cabins like it, with pre-notched beams trucked in ready to stack like Lincoln Logs on a concrete pad as a shell, leaving the inside finish to the tastes of the owner. Even the chinking between the logs was concrete rather than wattle and daub.

As soon as he left the McCool house on Blind Top, Durham telephoned Bobbi Navarro. They agreed she'd assemble Pete and Earl for backup and meet him at Oz's driveway.

Fog had settled in the valley by the time Durham arrived. He could look down on it from above, the lights of Choctaw shimmering through the mist, some of them blinking out altogether as it thickened. It rose as he watched, and within minutes it enveloped the small clearing halfway up the Knob where Oz had built his second home.

Headlights cut cones through the fog as two police cruisers wended up the hill toward the meadow. The cabin itself was built back in the trees. A gravel driveway snaked through the woods, slowly being buried under a blanket of multicolored fallen leaves.

"No chance of sneaking up on him in the cars," Bobbi said after climbing from her cruiser and surveying the scene.

"I can hike it," Durham said. "If he's there, I can call you and arrest him while you're on the way up the drive."

"By yourself? It's risky."

"He's seventy-something years old. I don't think he's gonna give me much of a fight."

"We'll go together," she said. "Pete and Earl will hang back and provide support if we need it." She grabbed two high-powered LED flashlights from the cruiser and handed one to Durham.

"I like your plan better," he said. "Let's go."

"Hold on." She reached inside the cruiser and handed Durham a radio and an earbud. "We need to stay in touch."

It took them five minutes to approach the house, walking in almost complete darkness and wrapped in fog along the gravel drive. As the cabin shimmered into vision through the mist, Bobbi stopped and grabbed Durham's sleeve. She pointed toward the left rear corner of the house. The tailgate of a light-colored pickup stuck out a foot or two. "Oz's truck."

"The cabin's dark, but there's smoke in the chimney. Maybe he left the fire going and went to bed," he whispered. "Only one way to find out. You want the front or the rear?"

"You took the rear last night. Front's all yours tonight."

"If he's in there, radio Pete and Earl before we try to take him," Durham whispered.

They split and crept toward opposite ends of the house. Something about it didn't feel right. The house was too dark, too quiet. Durham stopped at the truck and checked the hood. Cold. No way to know how long it had been parked there.

"Truck's cold," he said after keying the radio.

"Back door's locked. In position."

Durham gently placed his foot on the first pressure-treated wood step to the porch and waited for a creak or squeak to give him away. To his surprise, the step was solid and held his weight without protest. Within seconds, he was on the porch.

"Checking the front door," he whispered into the microphone. He was within a foot of the door when he saw it was ajar. "Abort," he told Bobbi.

"What's wrong?"

"Door's hanging open about an inch. I don't think we're the first visitors this evening. Regroup."

He met her at the side of the house.

"I was on a drug raid once," he whispered. "The guy knew we were coming, and he left the door cracked. It's like catnip for cops. Two of our guys went through and caught twelve-gauge shotgun loads in the chest. Their vests saved them, but they were sore for a month. I don't walk through open doors anymore without double-checking."

"Were you the first or the second guy through the door?" she asked.

"Third," he whispered. "Oz had to know we'd find out about the meth once we tossed his store. Maybe he just dozed off with the door cracked. Maybe he had time to call Purdy for backup. They're in there, or they aren't. If they're in there and they wanted to ambush us, all we had to do was open the door. Gonna take a peek through the window. Hang back and cover me."

"Ten-four."

He crept across the clover lawn to the side of the house, took a snapshot look through the window, and ducked quickly. Cautiously, he looked again, a little longer this time. He holstered his weapon and hiked back across the clover to Bobbi.

"We need an ambulance," he said. "Don't bother with the siren and lights. Oz is dead, inside the door. Looks like he took a couple of shotgun blasts."

THIRTY

"I am fucking starving," Durham said, as he and Bobbi sat in her cruiser watching the red and blue lights of the ambulance and the crime scene kids' van from Asheville flicker hauntingly off the trees surrounding Oz's Choctaw Knob cabin. The fog was thicker, and it refracted the headlights into strange concentric rainbows. The entire effect was psychedelic. It was giving Durham a headache. "I should have eaten something before I drove to McCool's place on Blind Top."

"Maybe Oz had something in the fridge," she said.

"What time does the Grille close?"

"Ten, except on Fridays, when it's karaoke night."

"Only eight-thirty now. They'll be working inside the cabin for another hour or so. Want to drive into town and grab a quick bite?"

"I already ate. I should keep an eye on the proceedings. Take your truck. I'll catch up with you when I'm done here."

"Roger that," he said, reaching for the door handle.

"Hey, Blade," she said. He stopped. "What in hell are we dealing with here?"

"The picture's still fuzzy," he said. "I thought it was Oz and Purdy. Now I'm not so certain. Only thing I know for certain is Oz was hip deep in whatever it is. He's our focal point now."

———

Durham scanned the menu at the Choctaw Grille. The diner was empty save for Durham, Kylee, and Nikos in the back. He was trying to decide between a Greek salad with gyro and the avocado club with fries when Kylee slid into the booth across from him and placed an Arnold Palmer on the table.

"Saw you coming," she said.

"Thanks. Which is better?" He pointed to the two items on the menu.

"Six of one, half a dozen of the other, as my dad used to say. Club's quicker, if that means anything. Hey, is it true? Oz Tattersall's been robbing houses for years?"

"No comment," Durham said. "Ongoing investigation. I'll have the club sandwich. Honey mustard instead of mayo."

"Extra fries?"

"Why not? It promises to be a long night. I can use the carbs."

She was back seconds later, after handing the order to Nikos. "So, you haven't called yet."

"The underlying assumption being that I was going to call at all."

"I hope so. Girl likes to think she still has it."

"Oh, I suspect you have a whole bunch of it. The second underlying assumption is that I'm here to get my rocks off. You might have some inaccurate romantic notions about police from watching too much television. Mostly, I'm here to solve three murders and get back to my well-deserved vacation as quickly as possible. There's a king mackerel fishing tournament in Myrtle Beach this weekend and a space on the pier waiting for me."

"*Three* murders?"

"Shit," Durham said. "Gotta get more sleep."

"C'mon, Blade. Spill it. I know about Savage and my grandmom. Who's the third?"

The front door flew open, and Mags McLeod lurched into the diner. She looked like she'd come from a million-dollar showing. She zeroed in on Durham and headed toward his booth at nearly a dead run.

"Is it true?" she asked, ignoring Kylee. "Is Oz dead?"

"Ho-ly *shit!*" Kylee squealed. "It's Oz?"

"Please," Durham said to Mags. "Sit. I'll explain as much as I can."

"Glass of white wine," Mags told Kylee. "Make it a generous fucking pour."

Mags took Kylee's place in the booth, but within seconds Kylee returned with two glasses of wine. "Sounds like we can both use one," she said. "Okay. Shoot."

"I can tell you only this. Yes. Oz Tattersall is dead."

"God*damn* it!" Mags said. "The fucking town's screwed now. There goes the ski resort. He was the second largest investor."

"Your overwhelmed grief is emotionally moving," Durham said.

"Fuck that shit," she said. "Oz and I tolerated one another. I saw through his act years ago. I knew he was some kind of dirty. What happened? How'd he die?"

Durham shook his head. "Still under investigation."

"That's it?" Mags asked. "That's all you can fucking tell me?"

"All there is, until the investigation uncovers more information. Maybe you can help out. Let's go back a couple of sentences. You said you always thought Oz was dirty. What did you suspect he was doing?"

"Fuck, I don't know. Embezzling, extortion, diddling little girls. Something. I knew he was skeevy from the start."

"Distributing meth?" Durham asked.

"Jump back!" Kylee said. "For real? Oz was a drug dealer?"

"You read between the lines a lot," Durham told her.

"I wouldn't put it past him," Mags said. "It wouldn't have been my first suspicion, though. Now that I think about it, if you own every fucking mercantile establishment in town, you could set up a surprisingly effective network for transporting all sorts of things. Is that what we're talking about?"

"I'm only tossing stuff out. Who were Oz's best friends?"

"He didn't have any," Mags said. "I mean, everyone liked him. A lot of people loved him. But I never saw him hanging out with anyone in particular."

"He ate here alone," Kylee said. "A lot. He always had a book. I figured he was one of those people who like to eat and read."

"When he didn't eat alone, who ate with him most frequently?"

"Nobody," Kylee said. "Sometimes he was here with one of his store managers, and once in a while he ate with Mayor Tinsley. A couple of times with Win Savage. Oh, and he was here a few times with Senator Royster and Darrell Tanney."

"How many times?"

"Not certain. Four. Maybe five over the last year. And a few times with Trent McCool. In fact, probably more with McCool than anyone, but still not a lot. He dined alone, maybe ninety percent of the time, reading. Kind of sad, now that he's dead. Does this have anything to do with Win Savage's murder?"

"Can't say," Durham said. "Not enough information. Anything I say would be speculation, and I don't work on speculation. I go where the evidence takes me."

"So where is the evidence pointing now?" Mags asked.

"Something shady on Choctaw Knob," Durham said. "Beyond that, I know as much as you. Did you ever talk to Savage about the ski resort project?"

"Once or twice," she said. "We had a rapport."

"Because you were sleeping together for the last six months."

"I've slept with several people in that time, and other than Win they are all breathing and healthy. We both had our share of partners. Until we found ourselves on opposite sides of the resort project, I thought we were rebuilding our friendship nicely, on new terms."

"What terms?"

"Well, no strings, to start with. I wanted to avoid a repeat of…is this important? It was almost half a century ago. Look, we were high school kids. We didn't know shit. We were nothin' but fuckin' hormones in sneakers. He cheated on me, and I caught him, and he broke up with me, and I hated his fuckin' guts for a long time until I decided it was stupid kid stuff. I moved on. When we hooked back up, I told him we should keep it casual. He was cool with it. Didn't even make a pass at me when we were skinny-dipping at his Sunday brunch, did he, Sweetie?" She poked at Kylee.

"For sure," Kylee said. "Nobody did anybody. It wasn't that kind of party, anyway. It was sensuous."

"*Sensual*, darling," Mags said.

312

"No, it's *sensuous*. I'm certain of it," Kylee said.

"Whatever," Durham said.

The bell at the counter dinged, and Kylee dashed to collect Durham's plate. She also brought back a plate of nachos, which she placed between her and Mags. "I like a good snack when I listen to a crime story," she explained.

"Great idea," Mags said, and she dug in. Between bites, she said, "I spend my life talking to people, Wade. I know a lie a mile away. I'm sure you do too. I have no reason to lie about Savage. We were an item, a thousand years ago, and then we weren't, and then we were again, casually and briefly. If I slept with him ten times in the last six months, I'd be surprised. We were friendly again until this whole Choctaw Knob lawsuit. Things chilled a little after we were served the subpoenas, because—c'mon—it's an adversarial process and the investors stood to lose a lot of money if he won, but we didn't hate each other. That's where things stood the day he died."

"After you banged him for a few hours the night before." Durham took a bite of the sandwich.

"Did you consider maybe that's why he died?" she said. "Because *I* have. I can't get the idea out of my mind."

"This is awesome," Kylee whispered.

"Go on," Durham said.

"What if I changed his mind? Maybe he decided to drop the lawsuit, and his partners didn't like the idea? Considering everything you learned about Oz over the last twenty-four hours, my modest reading of detective novels suggests he's a more fertile field to plow. Listen, I have to run. Once word about Oz breaks out, it's going to be hellacious around town. I need to get some rest and prepare for the chaos."

"Chaos?" Durham asked.

"Everyone in town owed Oz money," she said. "Some people owed him a lot. The people in this town buy their food at his grocery and their medications at his drugstore and the nearest hardware is half an hour away. Between wondering whether they still have to pay back their debts—and to whom? —and the panic over the possibility the stores will close, people are going to demand information. See, Wade, Oz's death is going to complicate my life and the lives of all the council members far more than it would have been worth to kill him."

"I never said he was killed," Durham said. "I only told you he was dead."

"Whatever. I can't believe anyone on the council was involved, in *any* way. As long as Oz was alive, Choctaw was on life support. Lord knows what will happen to us now. Thanks for letting me know, so I can prep."

She walked out, leaving Kylee in the booth with Durham. Kylee reached across the scarred tabletop and stroked his hand with her index finger.

"So. Not gonna happen, I guess?"

"No," he said. "Not why I'm here."

She fake pouted.

"I'm not the only guy around," Durham said. "Have you met Pete over at the police station?"

She poured the remains of Mags' wine glass into her own and her eyes twinkled as she said, "Pete's gay," she said. "You couldn't tell?"

"He does have a nice haircut."

"He also has a fella in Asheville. Derek. Sweet guy. Friendly. Surprisingly sloppy dresser. Anyone else you want to set me up with?"

"There's always Timmy."

"Ancient history."

"I kind of like him. If he were out of his daddy's shadow, he might be an okay guy."

"Get fucked by him sometime and tell me that again."

"We're not talking about sex here, are we?"

"Timmy's not the one. Hell, I should have hooked up with Oz, the richest man in town. Shame someone went and killed him."

"I never said anyone killed him. People keep assuming he was murdered."

"Well," she said, after taking a sip of the wine, "There *is* a lot of it going around lately."

THIRTY-ONE

Durham handed Bobbi a cup of coffee from the Grille back at Oz's Choctaw Knob cabin.

"Thanks," she said. "They hauled the body off a few minutes ago. Took five of them to hoist him onto the gurney. Your first impression was a good one. Twin twelve-gauge shotgun wounds to the chest, point blank, center mass. Probably dead before he hit the floor."

"Any shell casings?"

"Nope."

"So it's a double-barrel, or a pro who cleans up afterward."

"No reason it can't be both," she said.

"Don't complicate my life. Word's gonna get around quickly. Mags McLeod braced me at the Grille. Wanted to know if Oz was dead."

"You confirmed it?"

"She already knew. The question is who told her?"

"Did you ask?"

"I was tap dancing at the time, and I've had six hours of sleep in the last three days. I could have been sharper."

"No accusations. This week is wearing us all down to the hubs. We'll find out tomorrow. Oh, Earl called. They found another packing box full of ice on the loading dock at the grocery store. Almost four pounds. Want to know what the box was supposed to contain?"

"Doorknobs? I buy mine at the Piggly Wiggly all the time."

"Close. Carpentry nails."

"This is starting to make sense," Durham said.

"Great. Explain it to me."

"Let's say we're right about the meth labs at The Ridge. You've already said there's no meth problem in Choctaw to speak of, yet we've located almost six kilos in town today."

"Presumed meth," she said. "Has to be tested first."

"Yes. But we're making shit up right now, so let's say it's meth," he said.

"Gotcha."

"What better way to distribute it than mixing it with real merchandise?"

"But why deliver it to the wrong stores?"

"Maybe Oz didn't trust his employees. Maybe they weren't in on the game. A hardware employee might open a box of carpentry nails, but if the store doesn't stock honey and ten cases of honey show up—"

"The clerk would call Oz."

"And Oz would take care of the situation. He'd load all the boxes and take them to the right store. If one of them goes missing along the way, who's going to know? Especially if the shipping manifest shows the correct number of boxes when they arrive at the grocery."

"He was holding back the crystal," Bobbi said, "And he shipped it down the line to the next link in the distribution chain."

317

"That could explain why Choctaw doesn't have a meth problem. Oz had a good thing going, being debtor to half the town. If folks are spending money on crank, they aren't paying off their debts. Maybe he agreed to help mule the shit in return for leaving Choctaw off their delivery routes."

"I can see it. His civic devotion and his greed combined and motivated him to protect the town while he was lining his own pockets. It flushes."

"Stanley Purdy is involved, because his car was in Oz's garage, and his parents own Clover Valley Honey."

"We need to find Purdy," she said. "I still don't get the connection to Savage, though."

"Me neither, yet. I'm interviewing his parents in the morning. Okay," he said. "Let's walk this out."

She followed him to the front porch. He opened the door. Oz's outline was taped on the floor, surrounding a slowly congealing smear of blood. The outline's feet were only a foot and a half from the door.

"He opened the door, and someone blasted him. Boom. Boom. Both barrels," Durham said. "He fell straight back. The door has glass panels in it, so he could see the person on the porch."

"He knew the person who killed him," Bobbi said.

"Maybe he was expecting them."

"Someone involved in the distribution?" Bobbi asked. "Maybe they found out about his arrest for the burglaries. Oz became a liability, so one of his own people knocked on his door with a double-aught farewell bouquet. Oz sees the guy in the door glass. Guy smiles and waves. Old buddies. Here to offer some support.

Oz opens the door and gets smoked. Leak plugged. Problem solved."

"I couldn't have formulated it better on eight hours of sleep," he said. "So, let's act it out. I'm about Oz's height. The initial information from the ME is Oz was shot dead level straight on. You stand outside, behind the door, and hold an imaginary shotgun low enough so I can't see it through the glass."

She stepped out onto the porch. Durham closed the door. Bobbi waited outside. The door opened from right to left. Durham grabbed the knob with his left hand and pulled—

And faced Bobbi standing on the other side of the sturdy screen door. She raised an imaginary shotgun and aimed it at his chest.

"Problem," Durham said.

"No shit," she said. "How'd he shoot through the screen door?"

"He opened it first," Durham said. "Only way. So, this time, pull the screen door, hold it open with your leg, and we'll try it again."

He closed the door and heard the scrape of metal as she opened the screen door and held it fast with her knee. He opened the door with his left hand again, and she raised imaginary shotgun level and pretended to shoot him.

"No good," he said. "You gut-shot me. You aren't tall enough to have killed Oz."

"Didn't know I was a suspect."

"Someone your size, I meant. We're looking at someone as tall as Oz. Someone close to my height."

"Stan Purdy's six-three," she said.

"Yeah. He is. If we can connect Savage to Oz and Purdy, I think we have it figured out. Let's wrap up here, get the paperwork done, and turn in. Tomorrow may be a long day."

Clarence and Flossie Purdy looked as if they'd stepped out of a Grant Woods painting. He was tall and lanky, with a dour face and bald head save for silver fringe over his ears. She was short and plump, with blue-tinted hair. They appeared to be in their seventies, or perhaps they were over a hundred. It was hard to tell.

Their house sat on a hill off the highway, separated from it by a fenced pasture. Behind the house were dozens of beehives.

"Don't worry about them," Flossie advised Durham as they sat on the Purdys' front porch sipping iced tea. "Honeybees seldom sting unless they're threatened. They're peaceful creatures."

"How'd you get into the honey business?" Durham asked.

"We're old hippies," Clarence said. "Went to Woodstock and everything."

"For real?"

"Oh, yes. I have the tickets framed inside. I ran a record store in Asheville for years. Perfect place for us at the time. Asheville was where old hippies went to die. Got tired of the old nine-to-nine retail grind, though. When Flossie and I retired, there was already a big to-do about hive collapse disorder with bees. Lemme tell you, Agent Durham, if the bees die, we all die. The apiary out back is an attempt to do our bit to save the honeybees. Little bastards make a lot of honey, we discovered, more than we could use in a lifetime, so we started selling it at the local farmer's market. One thing led to another."

"How much do you sell each year?" Durham asked.

"More than we pull in with Social Security," Flossie said. "In fact, we make so much now we have to pay taxes on our government benefits. We're not tycoons, but we're comfortable."

"What role does Stanley play in your business?"

Flossie and Clarence glanced at one another.

Clarence said, "When you said you were with the SBI, I had a feeling it was about Stan. What's he done?"

"I don't know yet," Durham said. "I'm trying to find him to ask some questions. We found his car in the garage of a murder victim in Choctaw yesterday. The Hyundai Sonata."

"Murder? Is Stan a suspect?" Clarence asked.

"Right now, he's a person of interest. He might have information that will help us find the killer. At the very least, I want to know what his car was doing there."

"Who was murdered?" Flossie asked.

"A man named Oscar Tattersall."

Flossie gasped and covered her mouth with her handkerchief, which had appeared seemingly from nowhere. Clarence placed an arm around her shoulders.

"Stan works for Oz Tattersall," he said.

"What does he do?" Durham asked.

"Deliveries, mostly. He works part-time for us, sure, delivering cases of honey. Tell you the truth, we don't have wide enough distribution to need his help more than once or twice a month, so mostly he works for Tattersall. Sometimes he tends the hardware store. He does mostly whatever Oz needs—needed—doing. This is terrible news, Agent Durham. And Stan's Sonata was in Oz's garage?"

"Yes. The tags were missing. Have you heard from Stan lately?"

Flossie dabbed at the tears on her cheek. "Stan isn't our son," she said. "He's our grandson. We take some of the blame. We raised him, pretty much, from the time he was five."

Clarence said, "His mama was a tramp, but our son wasn't much better, so I guess they were a match. We have no idea where he is now. I reckon the fruit don't fall too far from the tree. Stan was a tall order from the time he came to live with us. The schools had a name for it, but he had difficulty learning. Got into a lot of trouble. Once he hit his growth spurt, he got big. Bigger'n you. Bigger'n most the kids at school, and he started bullying them."

"We did our best," Flossie said. "Hoped we'd get it right the second time around. Stan calmed down some after high school, and he's always come running any time we needed him, but there's a lot he doesn't talk about."

"He doesn't live here?" Durham asked.

"Oh, no," Clarence said. "Hasn't lived here for years."

"His car is still registered in McDowell County."

"I know. We get the license tag renewals on it ever' year and call him to come pick them up. We keep telling him he's gonna get stopped someday and pay a lot of money in fines for not transferring to his new county."

"And where's that?"

"He's lived up Choctaw way for several years now," Flossie said. "Some place he calls The Ridge. We've never been there, Agent Durham. Is it a nice neighborhood?"

"Choctaw Knob again," Bobbi said when Durham described the conversation with Clarence and Flossie Purdy. They sat in his booth at the Choctaw Grille, stoking up on lunch because the case was coming together, and there was no way to know when they'd eat again.

"The answer is on the mountain," he said. "We need to turn our attention there."

"Don't want to," Bobbi said. "I told you, Blade. The Knob gives me the creeps."

"Something bad's going on there."

"I know. I just don't have to like it. We can drive up after lunch if you like." Her telephone buzzed. "Zoom call from The ME's office in Asheville," she said before answering it. She put it on speaker and propped the phone on the napkin holder on the table.

The medical examiner was a petite, attractive woman named Naomi Patel, but everyone called her Neni.

"Oh," she said, when she saw them. "Hi, Blade."

"Hi, Neni."

The awkwardness between them might have escaped a blind and deaf person. Possibly.

Neni cleared her throat and said, "Um, I have the DNA results back from your case. I was able to isolate some dentin in an unerupted wisdom tooth that hadn't been roasted. We compared it to genetic samples from his home, and we can verify beyond doubt that Krispy Kritter is Savage."

"Didn't know there was any doubt," Durham said.

"In a case like this, where the body is—how can I put this delicately?—done to a turn, dental records are usually sufficient for identification. One wants to be absolutely certain, though. I have a COD now, by the way."

"What was it?" Bobbi asked.

"Stab wound. Penetrated the pericardium and the right ventricle of the heart and lacerated the inferior vena cava. When Savage's torso…um…split under internal pressure in the smokehouse, it separated along the entry wound. I only found the internal injuries on extremely close analysis. Again, the heart and arteries had already started to dissolve in the heat along with most of the connective tissues, so it took a while. Sorry for the delay."

"I'm amazed you found it at all," Durham said. "Great work."

"Um…thanks. There's more, though. I also have the DNA report on those clothes you sent in. The cold case."

"Patti Masters," Durham said.

"Her underwear did have residue inside them. This is where things get interesting. When the results came back, I thought for a moment the lab had made an error, or there was some cross-contamination."

"I don't understand," Durham said. "Is there a problem with the sample from Masters' underwear?"

"No. I double-checked. There's no doubt. The results are identical. Blade, the semen in Patricia Masters' underwear came from your corpse in the smokehouse."

They were interrupted by a crash next to the table. Kylee Wampler stood there, in a puddle of tea and lemonade and Dr Pepper and ice, the wait tray hanging at an angle in her hand, her mouth wide open.

"Holy shit!" she said. "My grandma fucked Winlock Savage?"

THIRTY-TWO

"When this case is over," Durham told Bobbi Navarro, "Kylee is going to need a vacation."

"And how," she said. "I'll go with her."

They had left the Choctaw Pike and were headed toward the Knob. The crime scene tape still blocked the entrance to Oz Tattersall's cabin as they passed by. Beyond, the road became a serpentine series of elevation changes and one-eighty switchbacks as it climbed toward the clouds and The Ridge.

"Still think I should drive," Durham said.

"I've seen you drive. You crash a lot."

"Only when Junior Junior rear-ends me."

"I'll be honest, Blade, I don't actually know where The Ridge is located. I've never been there."

"I asked around. From what I hear, there are markers."

"And once we find the place, what do we do? Waltz right in and knock on doors? Presuming they *have* doors? For all I know, they live in tipis up there."

"Don't get spooked."

"I want a clear plan of action is all I'm saying. I'm a little nervous about communing with meth-cooking hillbillies without backup."

"You have backup," he said. "I'm here."

A mile or so later, she said, "Kind of a shock, Kylee learning about her grandma and Savage."

"Kind of a shock for everyone. Another connection to his murder case. The one degree of separation kind of connection."

"You think Savage killed her?" Bobbi asked.

"It's possible. There's some blood spatter on her blouse that wasn't tested back then. No reason to. The killer did a number on Patti Masters. He attacked her with an agenda and a bad attitude. There was blood spatter all over the place, and DNA testing wasn't a thing. But to do the damage the killer did, he'd almost have to leave a little of his own blood behind. Maybe some of the blood on her blouse came from him. We'll know tomorrow."

"What's the deal between you and Dr. Patel?" Bobbi asked.

"Deal?"

"She wasn't exactly happy to see you on the phone."

"Long story. Short version, I learned a few years back not to mix business with pleasure."

"And you broke that rule with Patel?"

"I learned it with her."

"Ah. I see. That's why you haven't made a move on Kylee?" she asked. "Or me?"

"You and Kylee seem to think that's an expectation. Did some other SBI puke roll through back in the day and knock up half the town? It's not part of the job description, y'know. I'm here to find a killer, and I'm delaying the remainder of my vacation to do it. Priorities. Besides, you have Mr. Right Now in Glen Alpine."

"You remembered?" she said.

"Mind like a steel trap. What about it?"

"If we aren't cannibalized on The Ridge, we should talk. So, what if it turns out the blood on Patti Masters' blouse belongs to Win Savage?"

"We close our cold case. Murdered by her lover. Kind of a cliché, but sometimes it's fun to dance to the oldies. There, up ahead. See the sign?"

Someone had nailed a two-by-two-foot offcut of plywood to a towering pine trunk, mounted diagonally. On the plywood was a painted Celtic knot. Beyond the sign, a dirt road wound upward through the trees. Bobbi pulled the car to the side of the road.

"Doesn't say anything about The Ridge," she said.

"Only sign we've seen, and it's only another several hundred feet to the top, even if you have to drive five miles to get there on these switchbacks. Gate's wide open. Let's check it out."

"Hold on," she said. She exited the car and opened the trunk. Durham joined her behind the cruiser. She handed him a vest.

"It's Earl's. He's about your size. I keep vests for each of us in each cruiser. Also, you might want this." She handed him a Remington 870 riot gun.

"Are we taking on the entire Confederate Army?" he asked.

"Taking no chances. If I let these hillbillies kill you, who knows what kind of head case they'll send next?" She donned her own vest and secured it. "Forget what I said earlier. Nerves. Now I'm pumped. Let's roll."

Before she put the car in gear, she radioed her officers. Earl was on duty.

"Blade and I are paying The Ridge a visit," she said. "If we're not home for dinner, send the cavalry."

"Ten-four, Chief."

327

They drove through the open gate, and the road became rutted and dusty.

"Hope we don't need a four-by-four to get up this hill," Bobbi said.

"Stan Purdy can get up and down in a Hyundai. We'll be okay."

The tree canopy merged above their heads, forming a leafy tunnel that cut three quarters of the sunshine, leaving only a murky twilight for navigation. Bobbi's headlights helped.

"Ted Wisniewski said this place spooked him forty-five years ago," Durham said.

"It's spooking the shit out of me now," she said. They broke out of the tree tunnel into a shallow valley between two small hills. Directly ahead was a mound of discarded tires, almost thirty feet high and sixty feet in diameter.

"What the actual fuck?" Bobbi said, as she slammed on the brakes and skidded to a stop only feet from the tires.

She and Durham climbed from the car and walked around the huge pile.

"There," Durham said, pointing into the trees. "Another road."

"It's a rutted path of mud," Bobbi said. "Admit it. We took a wrong turn. The sign was some hunter bullshit."

The unmistakable metallic clank of a shotgun pump interrupted them. They whirled around, weapons raised, to find a man standing beside the tire mound, pointing a Mossberg at them. He was in his sixties, average height, with waist-long braided silver hair and a rapidly graying beard. He wore camouflaged hunting coveralls and a camo cap. He also wore a Kevlar vest. Durham could see more than a dozen shotgun shells stuffed into the loops of the bandolier that encircled the vest.

"You're trespassing," he said. "This is Shire land. Best you head on back the way you came."

"*Shire* land?" Durham asked.

Bobbi pointed to her badge. "Choctaw Chief of Police Roberta Navarro. Lower your weapon immediately or face arrest. If you do not comply, I will fire on you."

"Who's the other one?" the man asked.

"North Carolina SBI Special Agent Wade Durham," he said.

The man cocked his head.

"Wait," he said. "Wade the Blade?"

"Oh, fuck," Bobbi said. "Another one."

"The very same," Durham said. "Suppose we both lower our weapons, and I'll explain why we're here."

"I enjoy watching you race cars, Mr. Durham, but I do not give two shits about why you're here."

"I'm lowering my gun," Durham said. "Bobbi, you do the same."

"Like hell I will," Bobbi said.

"I believe the armed guys in the woods behind us are gonna insist," Durham said. "We're surrounded." He lowered the shotgun and held it with the barrel pointed toward the ground "We're here on official business regarding the murder of Oz Tattersall. We're looking for Stanley Purdy."

"You're in the wrong fuckin' place," the man said. "And it's a damn good thing, too. Tell her to lower her gun. I don't like the way she's looking at me."

"Bobbi, it's okay. Put away the weapon. These aren't the people we're looking for."

"How do you know?" Bobbi said.

"Trust me."

329

Bobbi wouldn't take her eyes away from the man with the shotgun. Slowly, she dropped her weapon. "You'd better be right," she said.

"Now," the man said. "Allow me to introduce myself. Andrew Frye, Shire Reeve."

"Shire *what?*" Bobbi asked.

He smiled and said, "Shire Reeve. I'm the law on Choctaw Knob."

THIRTY-THREE

"Now," Frye continued, "Let's go back a couple of sentences, before we all got to know one another. Oz Tattersall is dead?"

"Murdered last night, about a mile down the hill at his cabin." Durham pointed at Frye's weapon. "With a shotgun."

"Don't try to intimidate me, G-Man," Frye said.

"That's the FBI."

"Even the SBI knows you can't trace shotgun pellets. Hell, everyone on the Knob owns a shotgun. But now I'm interested. You said you were looking for Stan Purdy?"

"He worked for Oz, and his car was found locked in Oz's garage yesterday. I need to find him."

"Why?"

"This all has to do with the murder of Winlock Savage," Durham said.

Frye took one hand off his shotgun and scratched under his chin. The barrel of the weapon never wavered an inch. He made a quick hand gesture, and Durham heard crushing leaves as footsteps receded into the woods.

"I reckon we need to talk, after all," Frye said. "Leave your car. Won't be much use to you anyway."

"What's with Mount Firestone?" Durham said, pointing to the pile of discarded tires.

"Yesterday's delivery. We haven't cleared it yet. You'll see. Come with me. It's about a quarter mile hike, if you're up to it."

He pointed toward the path through the woods, and without another word he almost disappeared into the undergrowth. Durham looked at Bobbi. Bobbi looked at Durham. They both fell into step behind him. The towering trees closed in around them almost instantly, and seconds later they could no longer see the pile of tires or their cruiser.

"If the tires weren't there, you could drive straight to The Shire," Frye said over his shoulder. "The delivery drivers don't want to make the climb, though, so they pile 'em where you found 'em. We'll bring our cherry picker and a dump truck tomorrow and haul 'em up the hill. Some of the folks here want to go to Choctaw and check out the Founders Day fireworks this weekend, so we need the road clear."

"You called this place *The Shire*," Durham said. "This isn't The Ridge?"

"Ridge is a couple klicks that way," he said, pointing northeast. "I don't recommend going there."

"Why?" Bobbi asked.

"You ever see that movie from the 1950s, *The Time Machine*?"

"Once or twice," she said. "Kinda had a thing for Rod Taylor."

"He was a fine-looking man, to be sure. Australian. Did you know that? Anyway, life on the Knob is kind of like the split between the Morlocks and the Eloi. Folks on The Ridge stayed behind after The Schism. They're the Morlocks. The rest of us moved here and established The Shire. I reckon we're the Eloi."

"When was this?" Bobbi asked.

"Little over a quarter century ago."

"You're Andy Frye," Durham said. "You shot Lester Corby."

"Don't much like to talk about that," Frye said. "It was a long time ago, and it nearly ended my career as a lawman. Only thing I ever wanted."

"*Nearly* ended?" Bobbi asked. "You went to prison."

"And I got out, and my uncle brought me back to The Ridge to stay. No way a killer cop was gonna find any way to live in the flatlands. Once't I settled in here on the Knob and got my head back on straight, I discovered some stuff needed cleaning up. My uncle Verble Justice and I tried to instill order. He was the first Reeve of the Ridge."

"That's the second time you've called yourself a *reeve*. What is it?" Durham asked.

"Old English law," Bobbi said.

Frye stopped and turned around. "What do you know about it?" he asked.

She said, "In small feudal English villages before the Norman Conquest, the circuit judges might only hear cases once every several months. Some disputes needed to be addressed sooner. The local earl was empowered to make decisions in civil complaints, like small claims court today. His second in command, the reeve, enforced those decisions. Are you saying you've established a community on Choctaw Knob based on feudal common law?"

Frye stared at her for a few seconds, and said to Durham, "Smart woman. She's a keeper. Come on. A little farther." He turned and trudged on.

"For real?" Durham asked Bobbi as they followed him.

"Some people didn't sleep through history in college," she said.

"Well," Frye said, "You ain't far wrong. Uncle Verble and me, we tried to clean up The Ridge. There were some bad elements there. Still are. Some folks welcomed a little order and control. Others—well, there was some resistance. Some of the folks kept to themselves even among the community. Talkin' about folks with family trees wrapped around each other like mating snakes. Criminal types who might have found life hardy in buccaneer times. Alleged humans whose primordial ancestors descended from a diseased tree. Some of us wanted to live differently. Led to The Schism. We got tired of fighting. Uncle Verble was killed by a meth cooker. I put that right, and that's all I'm gonna say about that, but things got worse afterward. Those of us who couldn't abide living like troglodytes finally pulled up stakes and moved."

The trees parted, and they stepped into a sunny meadow and the last possible landscape Durham expected.

The meadow gradually sloped over the course of an acre or so from practically flat to almost vertical. On the flat end was a half-acre communal vegetable garden, now in the process of being plowed under for the winter crops. At the point where the slope rose steeply, several dozen solar panel arrays had been arranged to collect the sun's rays throughout the day. More surprisingly, above the solar arrays, the hillsides were festooned with glass—huge sheets of tempered plate glass set into the hillside at an angle leaning in at the top. It was only when he looked more closely that Durham saw the glass panels that stretched for almost seventy feet in some places were windows in houses carved into the earth.

"Welcome to The Shire," Frye said. "An autonomous self-sufficient collective, living almost completely off the grid."

"The houses…" Durham said.

"They're called earthships," Frye said. "A new way of building. Allows people to live in harmony with the earth."

"Earthships," Bobbi said. "New one on me."

"Come on," Frye said. "I'll show you. This is my place." He pointed to a set of steps that led up the hill to a stone landing.

The outer walls of the earthship not clad in glass were made of concrete, inlaid with the multicolored barrels of glass wine bottles that had been epoxied together so light penetrated the entire wall.

Frye opened the door. He didn't use a key. "We don't need keys and locks in The Shire," he said. "We don't have property, the way you regard it, so there's nothing to steal. If I have something and someone else needs it, they only have to ask. We share everything in The Shire. If anyone ever did steal, though, they'd be gone, and they wouldn't be allowed to return. It's the law. Come inside."

They stepped into a hallway lined by the inward-leaning glass windows. Behind the windows, basking in sterling autumn sunlight, was a verdant seventy-foot long indoor garden of ferns, vegetables, palm fronds, and small fruit trees.

"Hydroponic, in a coco coir medium. We irrigate it with gray water from the kitchen and sinks and the shower. The filtered runoff supplies our flush toilets and is recycled to the aquifer as black water in our septic system underneath the solar panels. The windows provide passive solar heating during the winter, and plenty of light for each of us to grow our own food indoors year-round. What we don't eat, we preserve with canning. We do a *lot* of canning."

The wall across from the windows was the same bottle-inlaid concrete as the entry foyer. Behind the wall was a large open room divided into activity areas by rugs and furniture and a few live-edge columns made from tree trunks, the bark still attached. A hand-built concrete and fieldstone fireplace against the back wall faced a sitting area constructed so expertly from local hardwood, it might have come from a High Point furniture store. A flat-screen television sat in once corner, dark and quiet. The walls were hand-laid concrete, rubbed smooth as porcelain and inlaid in places with Mexican tile. The entire room looked like wax melted into place.

"We've taken recycling to the next level," Frye said. "The tires are used to construct the walls of the earthships. First we excavate the basic interior shape from the hillside."

"You have a backhoe?" Durham asked.

"By hand," Frye said. "It's like a barn raising, except it takes a few weeks, a lot of shovels, and elbow grease. Each house in The Shire was built by the entire community."

"The tires," Durham said. "Rammed-earth construction."

Bobbi glanced at him.

"Saw it on YouTube. You can find anything on YouTube," Durham said.

"Exactly right," Frye said. "We have collection arrangements with landfills all over the western part of the state. Flatlanders suck at recycling. Half the shit they throw into their recycling bins finds its way to landfills anyway, because nobody processes it. We incorporate other people's trash into our construction. We arrange with bars and hotels and whatnot to take their empty wine bottles off their hands for free. Same for tire stores and car dealerships and landfills where tires wind up. Once every couple of months, we send a truck around to collect all the stuff. This week it was tires."

"I don't get it," Bobbi said. "How do you build a house out of tires?"

"Once we dig the basic interior shape out of the hillside with shovels, we line it with the tires and fill them with hard-packed dirt." He looked at Durham. "Also by hand. We use sledgehammers and concrete-filled PVC pipes. Layer by layer. Takes several weeks to do the outer shell of a decent sized earthship. Once the layers are high enough, we fill it all in with concrete."

"No need for air-conditioning," Durham said. "Between the insulation of the tires and building into the side of the hill, the temperature stays constant, doesn't it?"

"Mostly," he said. "We have air conditioning, though. We bury galvanized steel culvert pipes several feet below the surface in the hillside and funnel air through them from the other side. One of the fellows here knows a thing or two about fluid dynamics, and he installed venturis in the culvert to accelerate the air and cool it even more though expansion. Even on the hottest days of summer, air coming into the earthship through the pipe is a cool sixty degrees. It stays comfortable inside year-round. Completely natural and no air pollution."

"The solar panels supply your electricity."

"Each earthship has its own bank of batteries. They also power our artesian well pumps. We have running water and septic tanks and everything else we need to be self-sufficient in The Shire. Everyone grows their own veggies in the communal farm plot and here in their inside hydroponic gardens, and if anyone runs short everyone shares. The people in the house we're about to build with the tires down the road are talking about raising goats, so there will be protein and cheese and milk in addition to the deer and turkeys and other game we hunt and freeze each season. We have a C-band satellite dish hidden behind the hill to keep up with the outside world. You'd be surprised how much free shit you can still pull in on one of those, and to be perfectly honest, you folks have kind of fucked everything up. I've watched a bunch of your races on it, Agent Durham. Otherwise, we're off the grid. No internet, no telephones, no nothin'. Our earthship roofs are turf and grass over concrete. From the air, except for the solar panels, we're practically invisible. Far as the outside world knows, we don't exist."

"I counted ten earthships along the hillside," Durham said. "How many people live here?"

"Twenty-seven, and four on the way. Word's getting out about The Shire. I don't know if it's a good thing. We've chosen to live simply here. Everyone has everything they need. We have enough. Not many people can say that with a straight face. I don't know whether an influx of idealistic Johnny-come-latelies is going to make things better or worse. But that's not why I allowed you here. We need to talk."

"About Stan Purdy?" Durham asked.

"About The Ridge. Don't go there. If you go to The Ridge, you might not come back."

"Explain," Bobbi said.

"They won't recognize your authority. There's only one authority on Choctaw Knob, and you're talkin' to him."

"Technically, this is county land. The sheriff is the local authority," Bobbi said.

"Ain't seen a deputy around these parts in twenty years," Frye said. "I'm the law on the Knob."

"You said that before. What does it mean?" Durham said.

"There's almost no crime in The Shire," he said. "Everybody knows the penalty for breaking the law. There's only one. Banishment, with no option for appeal. We base our society on one simple philosophy. You don't eat me, and I won't eat you. It's the ultimate social contract. If you wouldn't want it done to you, don't do it to someone else. Violate the law, and you forfeit the privilege of living in The Shire. Permanently."

"The Golden Rule," Durham said. "You're a utopian society."

"More like a communal libertarian experiment," Frye said. "It's a Garden of Eden. We work together, but we also all have special jobs. My job is to keep out the vermin and maintain peace with The Ridge."

"How do you do that?" Bobbi asked.

"I was born at The Ridge. I lived there for the first ten years of my life. My uncle Verble was a leader in The Ridge community. Half the people still there are one sort of cousin or another. When they won't listen to other people, sometimes they'll listen to me."

"You've built a hell of a community here," Durham said. "Aren't you afraid the state might come along and toss you off? You are squatters, after all."

"We agree," Frye said. "We're squatters. You know North Carolina law, Agent Durham?"

"Some of it."

"A year in prison left me a lot of time to read the law. If you live on unincorporated state land for twenty years without interruption, you can lay claim to it as yours. I've been on the Knob over forty years. I've been on this spot for a quarter century. Anybody makes a stink? I'll file my squatter's claim to the entire Shire. Hell, I built the first earthship here and ever' one since. Open and shut case."

"Why haven't you done that already?" Bobbi asked.

"And pay taxes? Screw that. Government hasn't provided The Shire with shit. Can't see a good reason to pay 'em for the privilege of being ignored."

"Doesn't change our problem," Durham said. "Chief Navarro and I still need to talk to Stan Purdy. His grandparents told me he lives at The Ridge. We were headed there when we met you."

"Can't let you go there," Frye said.

"Don't know how you can stop me."

"Never fuck with a man who's stacked time, Agent Durham."

"Okay, boys," Bobbi said. "Testosterone's getting a little thick in here. Mr. Frye, you were a Choctaw police officer once."

"For about three weeks," Frye said, not taking his eyes off Durham.

"Then act like one. We get it. The folks at The Ridge are bad-asses, and they don't respect badges. Can you confirm Stan Purdy is there?"

"I know he lives there. That's all. Can't say he's there right this moment."

"Could you recognize him?"

"Of course. He's real friendly with one of my cousins. This is about the meth, isn't it?"

"We think so," Durham said. "Is Purdy involved?"

"Ever'one there's involved. It's the primary reason for The Schism. When Barley Ferguson killed my uncle Verble, it nearly sparked off a war at The Ridge. Several people died before it was settled, and that's all you'll ever hear me say about that. I don't reckon The Shire would exist today if it weren't for the meth at The Ridge."

"This is kind of complicated," Durham said. "We believe Winlock Savage was involved with the meth cooks at The Ridge. You know about the plans for a ski resort on Choctaw Knob?"

"Sure."

"We think Savage sued to stop the resort in order to protect the meth operation at The Ridge. Oz Tattersall was involved in distribution. I don't know whether Oz or Savage knew the other was working with The Ridge. Stan Purdy worked for Tattersall in the distribution process, but he might also be involved in Savage's murder. You heard how Savage died?"

"I heard he was found in a smokehouse, yeah."

"We believe Savage ran afoul of Oz and Purdy, and they killed him."

"You are so wrong, it's almost funny," Frye said, chuckling. "You got the whole thing bass ackwards, Blade."

"How so?"

"Win Savage wasn't hooked up with the meth cookers over at The Ridge. That lawsuit he filed? He was protecting The Shire."

"What?" Bobbi said.

"Savage happened on The Shire about a year ago, just taking a hike on the Knob. Total accident. We gave him the same welcome we did you, at first, until he identified himself. He had a beard then, so we didn't recognize him right off. Once we did, we offered him our true hospitality. He stayed here in my earthship for a week, learning how we live. He decided we had a good thing going here. When he learned the folks down in Choctaw planned to carve up the Knob for ski slopes, he tried to stop it, to protect us from outside contamination."

341

"That does change things," Durham said. "It fills in a lot of gaps. But it doesn't change the most important fact. Oz is dead, and Purdy is missing. Everything points to The Ridge. You're absolutely certain they're cooking over there?"

"They have four separate labs scattered around the settlement. One's in a school bus. The others are in old moonshine still houses."

"Draw me a map?"

"I can do better than that. I can show you, if you can ride a four-wheeler."

THIRTY-FOUR

"The hell with that, Durham!" Bobbi protested. "We just met this guy. You aren't traipsing off into the wilderness with him on a hunch."

Durham pulled on a set of camo coveralls he'd borrowed from another resident of The Shire. "He knows how to get there, and if everything goes south maybe he can talk us out of it. Nobody there knows me anyway. For all they know, I'm a noob at The Shire out hunting for dinner with Frye." He slapped his chest. "If that doesn't work, there's Earl's body armor."

"It's a hell of a risk. At least let me call for backup."

"Sure," Durham said. "Be my guest."

She stepped outside but returned within a minute.

"There's no cell reception here, and the hills on either side of this meadow are blocking my radio."

"Tough deal. I'm not going into The Ridge itself if I can help it. This is recon, getting a feel for the place. Once I know the route, and whether Purdy is holed up there, we can decide how to go in."

"I'm hiking back to the cruiser," she said. "I had reception there."

"Good idea," Frye said. "Keep the radio on. If I need help, Blade'll call you. You should have radio reception point to point on the Knob, even if you can't reach Choctaw."

Durham said, "If I'm not back or you haven't heard from me in three hours, call DEA and request a raid on The Ridge."

"*Now* you're okay with the DEA?"

"Not at all. But I'm perfectly fine with them rescuing my ass."

———

The Shire maintained a fleet of all-terrain four-wheelers for traversing the mountain trails while hunting. Frye and Durham took two of them into the woods, with Frye leading the way. The path narrowed to little more than the tread widths of their machines in places, with the forest floor carpeted with fallen leaves and pine needles and ancient hardwood tree trunks snicking against their padded elbows.

Both Frye and Durham carried their shotguns. Durham had his Glock holstered on the belt of his coveralls, next to the radio he hoped he wouldn't have to use to summon help.

Like a mountain goat on a sheer escarpment, Frye navigated the twists and turns of the forest path nimbly, almost by memory, as Durham, using every bit of his racing skills, struggled to keep up. He didn't care for bikes or hand throttles and handbrakes in general, and it took him a few minutes to stop instinctively flinching his foot each time he had to jab the brakes to skid around a tight corner.

He could tell Frye was leading him higher on the Knob. The air cooled and became drier as they thrashed through the undergrowth, a constant fall of multicolored autumn leaves whipping at their faces. Presently, he turned uphill again and about a half mile later he held up his hand as he slowed. Durham pulled in behind him as Frye stopped.

"We walk from here," Frye said. "They've already heard the four-wheelers, but as long as we don't get closer, they won't be suspicious."

He took off on an even narrower path that rose a short hill and dropped into a ravine they covered in ten minutes, taking time to carefully hurdle fallen tree trunks that might be a haven for snakes or bears or even wildcats.

Frye stopped and turned around. "We're hunters, get it? People at The Ridge like their privacy. They don't like strangers lurking around their settlement. If they see us, I can explain we're hunting turkeys and you're with me. They'll probably buy it."

"Probably?"

"Eighty percent certain," he said. "From here on, we act like hunters, not lawmen. Follow me."

The trail slowly disintegrated over the next hundred yards or so, until it vanished altogether, and Frye led him along some invisible pathway only he saw, across a forest bed of decaying and mulched leaves. He pulled a turkey call from his jacket pocket and warbled it a few times.

"Plausible deniability," he said, and put the call away.

"You'd make a pretty good undercover cop," Durham said.

"I know. Okay, top of this hill. See the boulder? From there, you can look down on The Ridge. We'll hike there and set up a turkey blind."

Durham followed him along the side of the hill. When they reached the boulder, Frye pulled a folded camouflage tarpaulin from his backpack. They spread it across the ground cover and some bushes and huddled underneath it. Frye handed Durham a pair of binoculars.

"That way," he said, pointing southwest. The settlement sat about two hundred yards away.

The Ridge was squalid compared to The Shire, and clearly had existed much longer. Some of the log cabins might have stood on their sites for two centuries and could have benefitted from some maintenance. Newer structures more closely resembled ramshackle shanties, constructed of various scavenged materials and redesigned multiple times over the generations. Several single-wide mobile homes were scattered randomly around the clearing. Three of the buildings were made of concrete cinderblocks and looked newer than the rest of the huts.

"The concrete block buildings are the cook houses," Frye said, whittling a stick with his pocketknife and not looking at the village. "Back in the day, we distilled moonshine there. We never fought over moonshine. It was the meth what drove a wedge into the heart of the The Ridge."

Even though it was still afternoon, someone had built a fire in a pit so old the quartz stones lining it were blackened on their faces. Several men huddled in folding hunting chairs around the fire. One of them smoked something in a pipe and passed it to the next person on the right. Frye took a peek in their direction.

"Purdy's not in the circle," he said, returning to his whittling. "But that's only a few of the guys. Must be fifteen in all living at

The Ridge now. A shame. We numbered over a hundred in our heyday."

"You did a lot better at The Shire."

"Don't forget. Some of those men are my kin. Brother against brother ain't no way to live."

"You know what I think?" Durham said.

"What?"

"The Shire chose the right reeve. Can we get closer?"

"Those are mountain men, Blade. You develop different senses living back in the trees. We're lucky they haven't sniffed us out yet."

"Hey. We're turkey hunting, right? They're your cousins, right?"

"Tell me you're in way over your head without saying it out loud," Frye said. "Do not evaluate people of The Ridge by your traditional measures. They do not appreciate uninvited visitors, kin or not. They're kinda feral that way. There's Purdy." He pointed to a new figure who had stepped out of one of the meth cookhouses.

Durham watched him through the binoculars. Stan Purdy was husky and solid, over six feet tall, and had long dark hair that fell across his ears, and an enviable neck beard. He wore a tee shirt that revealed the kind of arms and pecs you get after a few million reps at the gym.

"I bet he could lift Savage onto the hook himself," Durham said.

"Yup. He's a big boy."

"He looks slow, though."

"He's a little musclebound. But he's strong."

Durham watched for a minute or so, but nothing interesting happened.

"How often do you visit The Ridge?" Durham asked.

"More than I care to. Why?"

347

"If you strolled in, would they take it personally?"

"If *you* strolled in, they might. Me, I don't think so."

Stan Purdy had taken a seat in one of the camp chairs around the fire. He stared at the flames as if they held the secret to existence.

"You can say no," Durham said. "No judgment. But I need a pair of ears around the fire. I want to know if anyone there knows something about Oz's murder, especially Purdy."

"You want me to spy on my kin?"

"I want you to be the law on Choctaw Knob. Maybe you were happy to turn a blind eye to the meth trade here as long as it didn't affect The Shire, but now people are dying. Like I said, you can say no, but if you don't do something, who will? My only other option is to call a DEA raid on this site, and I have a major beef with those guys lately. We can limit the collateral damage by focusing on Purdy. If we can cut him from the herd, maybe we can find out why both Oz Tattersall and Win Savage died without carpet bombing your cousins."

Frye gazed at the people sitting around the fire. "I can't find a decent enough argument to disagree with you. The plan is sound. I'm not a snitch, though."

"You're investigating a murder," Durham said. "You're one of the good guys."

"All I ever wanted to be," he said.

Durham took another quick peek through the binoculars. When he put them down, Frye had disappeared.

Durham heard the turkey call echo through the trees over the next five minutes. He watched the men sitting around the campfire through the binoculars. They were planted in place, content to enjoy the waning afternoon. A couple looked around the second time Frye used the call but apparently couldn't be bothered to investigate.

Finally, Frye hiked out of the trees, his shotgun hanging casually on his arm, pointed toward the ground. Three of the men around the fire stood immediately and took defensive postures but relaxed almost as quickly when they saw who it was. One of them waved him over and pointed toward the low-slung chair next to Purdy, who barely looked away from the fire when Frye sat. Frye appeared to tell a story about a turkey he'd been tracking in the woods, demonstrating the constantly increasing size with comically exaggerated hand gestures. The men around the fire laughed and passed him a mason jar full of clear liquid. Frye took a sip and passed the jar to Purdy. Purdy waved it off but passed it along.

The wind shifted, and Durham could hear a few of the words spoken around the fire.

"Did you…Oz…cabin?" Frye said, some of the words lost in the rustling of the remaining leaves in the trees. He seemed to be informing them about Oz's murder. Durham watched the men's reactions carefully through the binoculars.

Stan Purdy excused himself abruptly and walked away from the circle.

"Nothing suspicious there," Durham said to himself. He attempted to read Frye's lips through the lenses, but all he could make out from behind the man's graying beard was *"…Savage."* One of the other men talked for a couple of minutes. Frye listened attentively. Purdy returned and took his seat, and he stared at the fire sullenly.

Frye told another joke, apparently, because several of the men laughed. Then he stood and picked up his shotgun.

"That damn Tom ain't gonna shoot himself," Durham said, putting words in Frye's mouth. *"Reckon I'll mosey on."*

Frye waved and walked back into the trees.

Durham continued watching the fire from his turkey blind and was barely aware of Frye's return until the man lifted the edge of the tarp and scooted underneath. He sat with his back to the boulder.

"You spooked Purdy," Durham said.

"Yeah. Soon as I mentioned Oz, he went pale and walked away."

Durham said, "I still need to know what Purdy's car was doing in Oz's garage. Need to draw him away so I can arrest him on suspicion and question him someplace where I can control the agenda."

"Gonna be tough," Frye said. "I don't know what it was, but the way he acted, he did something he wishes he could take back. He's burrowed in for the duration. Safest place for Purdy right now is The Ridge. The Ridge has always been a safe haven for folks pursued by the law. You'd have to blast him out with TNT at this point."

Durham checked his phone. "They have phone service at The Ridge. It isn't great, but there are bars."

"Why's that important?"

"You don't have cell service at The Shire. The two hills block it out."

"And?"

"Maybe Stan will come off the mountain if his grandparents need him. I can get them to call and ask him to come for a visit. We arrest him when he drives off the mountain and put the thumbscrews to him."

"Kind of cold, man," Frye said. "Using a man's grandparents to entrap him."

"Beats calling in the Marines to level The Ridge. Here's the thing. I need your help to nab him."

"I was afraid of that."

"I don't know where the exit to The Ridge is. Bobbi and I missed it on the way and wound up in The Shire instead. I need you to show me where he'll be."

"And that's it? Just Purdy?"

"No promises, man. The meth is a big part of this story. Because of all the crank we found at Oz's stores, the DEA's gonna show up sooner or later. Once they find out The Ridge is cooking with a vengeance, they'll put 'em out of business."

"I see. Nothing I can do to stop that, is there?"

Durham laid his hand on the butt of his Glock. "Tell me that's not a threat."

"It isn't," Frye said. "I'm thinking out loud. I'm working through my options. Okay. I'll show you where Purdy will be. I only ask you to tell me when you're nabbing him."

"I'll give you credit for the bust if you want."

"No. I don't want that. I want to know he's off The Ridge."

Durham shot several pictures of The Ridge encampment with his phone camera. "The cinderblock huts are the cookhouses?" he asked.

"Yes. Hold on. Someone's coming."

351

"Here?" Durham asked.

"Up the road."

Durham didn't hear anything over the rustling leaves and the wind coursing through the tree canopies. "Where?"

Frye pointed toward the southern end of the camp, and what looked like a four-wheeler path leading off into the trees. Seconds later, Durham heard an engine and snapping of fallen tree limbs as a car wended its way along the hill to The Ridge.

"Good ears," Durham said.

A dark car came into view through the trees, made one last winding turn, and pulled into the clearing.

"Hello," Durham said, watching through the binoculars. "New players."

The car doors opened. Carl Royster and Darrell Tanney stepped out and looked around.

"Nope," Durham said. "Same ol' scumbags. This is a twist I only half-expected."

He dropped the glasses and shot pictures of the camp using his phone's zoom lens. He watched the screen with one eye and the real people with the other. The men around the campfire didn't stand when Royster and Tanney walked up. Durham couldn't tell whether it was due to familiarity or a simple absence of respect. The exception was Stan Purdy, who became highly agitated. Durham switched the camera to video. He wanted to capture the moment.

Purdy stood and got into Darrell Tanney's face. He said some things Durham couldn't hear.

"You catch that?" he asked Frye.

"Somethin' about Oz. Didn't catch the rest."

Purdy held his hands in the air, cocked his head, and backed Royster toward the tree line. Purdy looked as if he was trying to make some point or was protesting something. Royster looked worried. Tanney tried to step between them.

"Shit's going down," Durham said.

Royster pointed at Purdy with his finger and said something that drove Purdy into a rage. He shoved Royster to the ground and stood over him until Tanney wrapped him in a bear hug. Purdy struggled as Royster pushed himself back to his feet and glared at him. Royster said something to Tanney, who put Purdy in a sleeper hold. Purdy struggled for a few seconds before going limp. The men around the fire all stood and moved to help their companion. Tanney dropped Purdy's limp body and pulled his service weapon on them.

Even from a distance, the command voice they taught him at the academy rang clearly through the trees. "Highway Patrol! Touch me and spend the next ten years eating state food!"

Their modest motivation broken by fear of prison or—worse— being ventilated by Darrell Tanney, the men mumbled and bucked up but ultimately scattered. The attraction of the firepit had diminished. One by one, they slunk away to their respective hovels. Within a minute, the clearing was empty save for Royster, Tanney, and Purdy.

Royster opened the trunk of the car. Tanney manhandled Purdy into it and slammed the lid. Royster took the back seat, and Tanney drove.

"How quickly can we get to the tire pile and Bobbi's cruiser?" Durham asked.

"Took us twenty minutes to get here."

"What if we went overland?"

"Maybe ten."

"How long will it take them to get off the Knob?"

"With all the switchbacks, fifteen minutes at least."

"It was Royster and Tanney all along. They're going to kill Purdy to cover their tracks," Durham said. He grabbed his radio. "Choctaw One, Durham. Copy?"

The radio crackled, and Bobbi said, *"Chief Navarro. Durham?"*

"We need a roadblock. Maybe two. Call the Staties or the sheriff's department. Get Pete and Earl out here. We need to cover both the roads off Choctaw Knob."

"You're calling in a lot of resources. I need more, Durham."

"Not on an open frequency. I'm on my way to you. ETA ten. Have the engine running. We need to move. Vehicle of interest is a black Lincoln MKZ." He read off the tag number, which he'd written as soon as the car arrived.

"Durham!" she said, but he had already stowed the radio on his belt and was running along nearly imperceptible footpaths behind Frye. He heard Bobbi make the BOLO and call-out and smiled as he tried to keep pace.

"If they're driving off The Ridge, they'll probably take Wiley Cook Road," Frye said over his shoulder, barely breathing hard. "The exit is hard to see. It's west of mile marker fifteen on the Pike. You'll want to concentrate your people there."

Durham transferred the information to Bobbi and fell back into step behind Frye. Recently bared tree branches lashed at his face as they launched into thick forest and down into a shallow ravine, where Frye made a hard right and ran along the bottom of the hollow. Seconds later, they burst into a clearing and Durham saw

354

the immense pile of tires, with Bobbi's cruiser already turned around and facing downhill. Durham checked his watch and smiled. Eight minutes.

Durham tore open the driver's side door. "I'm driving," he said. "We're way behind and we need to catch them."

Bobbi didn't argue. She slid across the seat and made room for him.

"Frye!" Durham shouted. "Navigate!"

Frye climbed into the back seat and barely closed the door before Durham dropped the car into gear and firewalled it, sending rooster tails of leaves and dirt into the air behind him.

"It was Royster and Tanney," he told Bobbi as he threw the car into a four-wheel drift at the next switchback. "They showed up at The Ridge. Tanney choked Purdy out and stuffed him in the trunk. I'll bet you ten bucks Tanney killed Oz, and he's going to finish covering his tracks by killing Purdy."

"Why?"

"To protect Royster. Royster is Trent McCool's protégé. His political base is Choctaw, and it's dying. Politics runs on raw cash these days, and with dark money PACs all over the place, nobody tracks it all. Royster washes the hands of the meth cooks on the Knob, makes sure the SBI and DEA keep their distance, and they cross his palms with silver using dark money. McCool knows everything about everyone in Choctaw. You think he didn't know Oz was creeping people's houses when they were out of town? Royster got in bed with Stan Purdy at The Ridge. Tanney ran interference for him. Using McCool's intel, they extorted Oz to participate in the distribution using his stores, threatening to expose his midnight skulkery if he didn't."

"But why murder Savage and Oz?"

"Oz? Covering their tracks. He talked a good game, but I bet we could have broken him in a minute and a half. His only hope was to roll over on Royster. That's why Trent McCool called in all those favors for the *habeas* writ. They needed to get Oz out of the station. Why they killed Savage, I don't know yet. We'll find out, though. I have phone video of Royster and Tanney abducting Purdy and stuffing him in their trunk, seconds after Tanney announced he was a state trooper. He committed a felony in the line of duty. Tanney's finished. Royster, too, once the word gets out he's funded by a meth dealer. They're both going to prison. He doesn't know we know about that yet, though, so we need to stop them before they get off the mountain."

"There are a dozen holes in your story, Blade," Bobbi said.

"I know. Royster can fill them in, if we can catch him."

"Take the next left," Frye called from the back seat. "It'll intersect with Wiley Cook Road."

Over the car radio, Pete called out, *"Choctaw Two in position. Deputies are covering both exits to the mountain. Troopers in transit. Nobody's getting off this hill, Chief."*

"Next left will take you straight to Wiley Cook Road in about a quarter mile," Frye said from the back.

Durham threw the car into a power slide as he took the corner. A stop sign appeared ahead.

"There," Frye said.

They were seconds from the stop sign when Darrell Tanney's Lincoln blew through the intersection.

"Hold on," Durham said. He flipped on the lights and siren and barely touched the brakes as he ignored the stop sign and drifted the car sideways, smoke boiling off the tires, to fall in behind Tanney. Tanney glanced once in the rearview mirror, then took another long look, and smoke belched from the Lincoln's tailpipe as Tanney firewalled it.

"He's running," Durham said.

"He can't get off the mountain," Bobbi said.

"He doesn't know that." Durham goosed the cruiser to inch closer. "Frye! How far to the main road off the mountain?"

"Another mile. Maybe ten turns."

Durham tailed the Lincoln through the last of the switchbacks on the Knob, and suddenly the road straightened and sloped gently toward the Choctaw Valley. Ahead, Durham saw the road blocked by multiple vehicles, their dome lights flashing a rainbow of colors. Pete and Earl stood in front of one of the vehicles, their shotguns at the ready.

Darrell Tanney saw them at the same instant, and he reacted immediately, twisting the wheel and jerking the parking brake to spin the Lincoln halfway around in a bootleg turn, facing Durham, who was in no mood to play Chicken in two-ton automobiles.

"Look out!" Bobbi shouted as Durham executed his own bootleg turn and Tanney's car blasted by.

"He's going to make a run for the other side of the Knob," Frye said.

"How many exits are there?"

"Three I know of. Maybe he's planning to hide out at The Ridge."

"I'm not letting him get to either place," Durham said. He glanced in the rearview mirrors. Two of the assembled law enforcement cars had broken the roadblock and were in pursuit.

Within seconds, they were back into the switchbacks, climbing the mountain. Durham watched Tanney's taillights carefully as they turned right and left along the eastern face of Choctaw Knob.

"He's trail braking," Durham said. "He won't make the other side of the mountain before he wears out the pads."

"So let him," Bobbi said.

"They're no good to me if they drive off the mountain and die," Durham said. He kept one eye on Tanney's brake lights and the other on the road ahead. The worst thing he could do was try to edge Tanney onto the shoulder just as a motorhome came around the next corner. "I'm putting an end to this."

He punched the throttle again, and the rear end slipped over the center line as the car lurched sideways in the next corner. Tanney's car inched closer.

"He's driving exactly the way they taught him at the academy," Durham said. "And he's pretty good at it. They teach us some different stuff in NASCAR."

"Bump and run?" Bobbi said.

"Bump and run," Durham said.

Bobbi tested her seatbelt. "Shit. Okay. Just don't kill me."

"I'll get out here," Frye said.

"Sorry. You're strapped in for the whole ride," Durham said. "I'll try to make it gentle. I've done this before. First, we let him know we're back here."

"He already knows," Bobbi said.

Durham didn't answer. Instead, at the next short stretch of asphalt, he gunned the engine and drove squarely into the back of Lincoln, which fishtailed but maintained control.

"Careful," Bobbi said. "There's a suspect in there."

"He should have made better life decisions," Durham said. "I don't want to push them over the side, so I have to wait for a right-hand corner with no oncoming traffic."

"Traffic ain't usually a problem on the Knob," Frye said from the backseat.

"But the risk is never zero," Durham said. He checked the rearview mirror again. The freight train of cop cars behind them was impressive. "Bobbi, flip the PA and hold the mic to my mouth." When she had, he called out, *"Carl Royster and Darrell Tanney, you are under arrest. Please pull to the next overlook and exit the car."*

They blew past the next overlook several seconds later, and Tanney never slowed.

"Strap in and hold onto something," Durham said. "I only ask nicely once."

The switchbacks were predictable—left, right, left, right. Durham timed his approach to the rear of the Lincoln so he could ram it square on the straight stretch between corners. Coming out of a left hander, he bumped the Lincoln twice, which set the car fishtailing wildly.

The opportunity came on a long decreasing radius switchback with a solid rock wall a hundred feet high to the outside. As they turned at the sweeper, Durham firewalled the throttle and tapped the Lincoln's right rear taillight hard enough to send it into a long lazy spin. Tanney sawed frantically at the wheel, trying to turn the spin into a full three-sixty, so he could continue on, but he wasn't good enough, and the car bounced into the ditch between the road and the rock wall, crunched against the fallen boulders there, and came to a stop. Durham slammed the brakes, the tires screaming in protest, and skidded to a stop beside the Lincoln, cutting it off from the road and pinning it alongside the sheer rock face of the mountain. He and Bobbi jumped from the cruiser with weapons ready.

Pete and Earl arrived seconds later, followed by the sheriff's deputies and a couple of state patrol cars. By then, Royster and Tanney were in cuffs, and Durham had trotted around to the rear of the Lincoln to temporarily free a shaken Stan Purdy from the trunk, before also clapping cuffs on him.

"I'll have your job for this!" Royster blustered as the officers crowded around.

"You're gonna need one," Durham said. "Carl Royster and Darrell Tanney, you are under arrest for conspiracy to distribute narcotics, for the abduction of Stanley Purdy, and for the murders of Winlock Savage and Oscar Tattersall, for starters. You have the right to remain silent..."

He finished mirandizing them, repeated all but the kidnapping charge for Purdy, and asked Pete and Earl to escort them to the deputies' cruisers for transport to the Choctaw PD.

"Where's Frye?" Bobbi asked, as they headed toward her cruiser.

Durham scanned the area. Frye was nowhere to be found.

THIRTY-FIVE

Trent McCool blew into the police station minutes after Bobbi and Durham booked Tanney, Royster, and Purdy. At Durham's suggestion, Bobbi had placed Purdy in the interview room, chained to a D-ring in the steel table, while slamming Tanney and Royster in separate holding cells, far from one another.

"What's your plan?" Bobbi asked.

"Tanney and Royster stuffed Purdy in a car trunk," he said, as McCool walked through the door. McCool had dressed hastily, and his hair was uncombed. "I'm gonna let him stew about that before I ask any questions. I suspect the phrase *'he who squeals deals'* will be uttered at some point."

"I'm informed that Carl Royster has been arrested," McCool said to Bobbi. He purposefully ignored Durham. "I'm his attorney. I need to talk to him."

"You're welcome to do so, if you don't mind doing it in his holding cell," Bobbi said. "Interview room's busy right now."

"With whom?"

"Another suspect," Durham said. "Aren't you interested in Darrell Tanney? I heard you were his surrogate father."

"More like an uncle," McCool said. "His surrogate father would be Roger Gimball, if we were to employ labels. Of course, I'm concerned with him. He isn't my client though, at least not yet. Royster is. What are the charges?"

Bobbi rattled off the offenses they planned to present to the DA. McCool shook his head as she did.

"Chief Navarro, I don't have to tell you Carl Royster is a powerful man. These are serious allegations. I do hope, for your sake, you have ironclad proof."

"If you come at the king, you best not miss?" Durham quoted. "Sounds threatening to me. Is he threatening a law enforcement officer, Chief Navarro?"

"Naw," Bobbi said. "Mr. McCool is far too smart to make a mistake like that. Especially considering he might be next on the hit parade."

"What do you mean?" McCool said.

"Royster is your sock puppet," Durham said. "He's been under your control ever since you stepped outside the Central Prison walls in Raleigh. Tanney might as well be your godson. I find it difficult to believe they could undertake such a convoluted enterprise as the money-laundering meth scheme on the Knob without your knowledge."

"Tread carefully, Agent Durham," McCool said. "Without evidence, such statements border on slander."

"I have three people in detention. Every one of them is going to prison. One of them *will* cut a deal and roll over on you for less time. Get your affairs in order, Mr. McCool. Maybe they kept your old cell warm for you."

"Your supervisor will hear from me," McCool said, his voice frigid.

"Ask Royster how that worked for him," Durham said. "You want to see him in his cell, or wait for the interview room?"

He fumed as he glared back and forth at Bobbi and Durham. "I'll be back," he said, and he stomped out of the station.

"Bet you won't," Durham said. He phoned Malik Mourning.

"Hear you're wrapping things up," Malik said.

"We're getting there. I'm headed in to tear apart my suspects, see if I can get them to roll over on one another. Their attorney was in on it, too, and I believe he's about to be in the wind. Check private planes flying out of the area. He'll probably be on one."

"Any destination in particular?"

"He'll head south. He has a buttload of money squirreled away in the Caymans. Trent McCool."

"Got it. I'll give our friends at the FAA a call."

"Also, I have a case for the shitheels at the DEA. Meth cooking operation on Choctaw Knob. Have them call Chief Navarro for the details, but it's kind of a major operation, for a mom and pop. Someone's probably going to earn a promotion out of it."

———

"The lab results came back from Purdy's Hyundai," Bobbi said a couple of hours later, after hanging up her office phone. "We have a match. Winlock Savage took his last ride in the trunk."

"You want to do the honors?" he asked.

"You go ahead. You found him. You take him down. I'll watch from observation."

Stan Purdy sat slumped over the table, his head resting in his crossed and shackled arms. He snored slightly, but jerked awake when Durham slammed the steel door shut with a huge bang.

"Da fuck are you?" Purdy asked, his voice slightly slurred.

"North Carolina SBI Special Agent Wade Durham," he said, flashing his brass. "Your name is Stanley John Purdy?"

"Wait," Purdy said. "Wade Durham? Wade the Blade?"

"We share the same body, but today I'm an SBI agent, and you, Mr. Purdy, are in a heap of trouble."

"Whadya mean?"

Durham opened the manila file he'd purposefully overstuffed with papers to make it look more comprehensive than it truly was.

"I have your entire life story in my hands, Mr. Purdy. Your permanent record from school, your juvie history, your employment history, banking records, medical history, and an appreciably voluminous history of interaction with the police."

"So?"

"Your grandparents say hi, by the way," Durham said.

"My grandparents?"

"Clarence and Flossie? They own Clover Hollow Honey, don't they?"

"Sure. What about 'em?"

"Nothing. I visited them. They seem like awful nice people. And what they're doing to save the bees is commendable."

"Fuckin' bees," Purdy said. "Hate the little barb-assed fuckers."

"Tell me about your work with Clarence and Flossie. What do you do for them?"

"I deliver honey," he said. "It ain't hard. I load it, take it to the store, and drop it off."

"Easy as pie," Durham said. "Any idiot could do it."

"Damn right."

"So why do you keep delivering your honey to the wrong address?"

"What?"

"We discovered eleven cases of Clover Hollow Honey at Oz Tattersall's hardware store."

"So?"

"First of all, the hardware doesn't sell honey. Second, you worked part-time for Oz at the hardware, so you should know the hardware doesn't sell honey. Finally, the invoice only accounted for ten cases of honey. The eleventh contained something else entirely."

Purdy started to say something, but Durham held up his hand to silence him. "Don't lie, Stan. Seriously. Your prints are all over the eleventh box. It doesn't matter, anyway. We'll deal with that later. What I want to talk to you about is how you came to be in the trunk of State Senator Carl Royster's car this afternoon."

"When you find out, you let me know. I remember talking to Royster, and next thing I wake up bouncing off the insides of the fenders and the car s like it's about to roll over in ever' corner."

"What were you and Royster talking about?"

"Nothin' important. That bastard Tanney done drugged me or knocked me out or something. For all I know, I might have severe brain damage."

"I wouldn't be a bit surprised," Durham said. He pulled out his telephone and showed Purdy the video he'd shot from his vantage above The Ridge. "Allow me to fill in the blanks."

Purdy watched, and his face screwed up as he saw Tanney put him in the sleeper hold.

"Fuckin' Tanney," he said. "If he weren't a state trooper..."

"What?" Durham said. "What would you do?"

"It'd be bad, for sure."

"Okay," Durham said. "Let's skip the small talk. You're going to prison, Purdy. How long is up to you."

"Prison?" he yelped. "For what?"

"To begin with, the murder of Winlock Savage."

"You ain't got nothin' on me there," Purdy said.

"Except for your car, which we discovered hidden in Oz Tattersall's garage, with Savage's blood in the trunk. Want to explain to me how it got there?"

"Must have been Tanney," he said.

"Why would Tanney be hiding your car?"

"I don't want to talk about this no more," Purdy said.

"Sure," Durham said. "That's your right. Just so you know, the charges you're currently facing carry a possible death sentence. At the very least, you'll die in prison a century or so before your time is fully stacked. But go ahead and be a stand-up guy. I hear they admire that in gen pop. I'm gonna grab a Coke. Want anything?"

"No," he said. He stared at the table.

Durham joined Bobbi in the observation room. "Tenderizing complete," he said. "Now I let him marinate a little. Want to grab a bite over at the Grille?"

"I *am* hungry," she said. "On the SBI tab, right?"

"Of course," he said. "It's one of the major perks of the job."

366

"I heard you arrested Senator Royster," Kylee said as she took their orders.

"Word travels quickly in Choctaw," Durham noted.

"No comment," Bobbi said. "But I imagine there's going to be a hole on the ballot next election."

Without asking, Kylee slid onto the bench next to Bobbi, facing Durham. "Did Royster kill Savage?"

Durham said, "Not clear yet. I don't think he did the killing itself, though. That was someone else, but with any luck we have that person locked up too. I only need to figure out which one it is."

"I've been thinking about it a lot since last night," Kylee said. "It's strange. I went skinny-dipping with a guy who pumped my grandmother. That's creepy, isn't it?"

"Not as creepy as skinny-dipping with a dead guy," Durham said.

"Oh, yeah. Good thing I didn't go to bed him. I'd do a shitload of burn time for that. And I was tempted. It was a close thing. Did Savage kill her?"

"I don't know," Durham said. "The tests aren't back yet on the blood from Patti's clothes. If it was Savage, we already have his DNA on file, so we'll know quickly. Either way, we're a lot closer to knowing now than we were a two days ago."

Kylee turned toward the counter, but stopped and said, "Thanks, both of you. I didn't come here to find out what happened to Patti. Or maybe I did, and I've been in denial about it. But it's been on my mind. It's good to know someone still cares forty-five years later. I'll get your drinks."

"She's a good kid," Durham said. "You and she could be buddies."

"What are you, a fucking yenta?" Bobbi said. "I have enough friends."

"Just saying. I probably wouldn't be as far along on this case without her help. She knows stuff. She has her ears to the ground. She could be an asset down the road."

"I don't see Choctaw becoming the murder capital of North Carolina, Blade. More like a ghost town."

"Move on, then. You're a good cop. I bet we could find a place for you at the SBI."

"Naw. For better or worse, I reckon I'll ride this town straight to the ocean floor."

"You never know. Except for Oz, all the original ski resort investors are still in. If they can locate someone to take his place, it could still happen, especially since Savage's lawsuit is going away."

"I hadn't thought that all through," she said. "I'm exhausted. Haven't slept more than an hour or two at a stretch in days. Haven't looked much past the end of this investigation. One hundred twenty-two hours, huh?"

"What's that?"

"You said the other day you wrap cases up, on average, in one hundred twenty-two hours."

"I say a lot of things."

"Is every case like this?"

"No," he said. "This is not typical. That's why they sent me rather than some coat-and-tie wingtip guy. If you mean is this case typical for *me?* Well, yeah. Sort of. I seem to inherit the problem children."

"Because you're the best."

"With problem children. Some cases I suck at. Malik is a pro at allocating agents according to their strengths. He's a good boss. If he quits, I'll probably retire."

"So, when do you sleep? Seems I haven't had time in days."

Kylee arrived with their drinks. Durham expected her to hang around and pump them for more information, but she retreated immediately to the kitchen.

"I'm not a forty-hour-a-week kind of guy," he said. "And my circadian rhythm is sort of out of whack. When I'm on a case, I build up a sleep debt. I try to pay it back between cases. Malik sees to it I have enough time. Fact is, I'm supposed to be on vacation right now."

"Must be nice, vacations. Haven't taken one since I moved here."

"Once this thing is over, you should go. You've earned it. Grab your guy in Glen Alpine and head to the Bahamas for a week."

"He's moving to Baltimore," she said.

He took a sip of his drink. "Say again?"

"Glen Alpine. He's an EMT, but he's studying to be a physician's assistant. He pulled an internship at Johns Hopkins, lucky bastard. No. I shouldn't say that. It wasn't luck. He's good. He deserves it. And…I'm prattling away."

"Tough deal," Durham said. "Especially for him, being a race fan and all. There's not a decent stock car short track within an hour of Baltimore. Beltsville used to be nice, but they closed it."

She wadded a napkin and tossed it at him.

"Nature abhors a vacuum, Bobbi," Durham said, as Kylee appeared with their plates. "Something will turn up."

———

Through the observation glass, Durham and Bobbi watched Purdy stare at the mirror and fiddle with his cuffs.

"He's marinated long enough. Time to play Pump the Perp," Durham said. "Come stand at the doorway with me and play along."

She followed him into the hallway, and Durham cracked the interview room door before saying, "I say it's horrible and archaic. Why go back to hanging? What's wrong with lethal injection?"

"I'm with you. The needle's fast, for sure," she said. "And humane."

"You think the politicians in Raleigh care about humanity? They want executions cheap and easy. Not much cheaper out there than a stout rope and a scaffold. Reusable, too. Don't need a doctor to pull the lever on the trapdoor. Any ignoramus can do it. Sometimes it seems like we're marching backward. Oh, well, not my neck getting stretched, right?"

"Not this week," she said.

"Gotta have a word with Purdy. You get Royster's and Tanney's signatures on those affidavits, will you?"

"Sure thing, Blade," Bobbi said. She walked into the observation room and closed the door.

Durham found Purdy sitting straight upright in his seat. His eyes were wide, and his forehead was shiny with fear sweat.

"What are you talking about?" Purdy asked.

"Oh. You overheard? Sorry. Nothing. Shop talk. State Senate's considering reinstating hanging as an execution method. I brought you some iced tea. Figured you were getting parched."

"How do I know there ain't no truth serum in this drink?"

"There is no such thing. You watch too much television," Durham said. "It's iced tea from The Grille. Besides, you're going to tell me what I want to know anyway."

"What makes you think that?"

"Because, if you don't, you might get to be the first person to try out the state's new scaffold at Central Prison. I hear they're building it extra high. You aren't afraid of heights, are you? I mean, you wouldn't be up there all that long anyway, but I know phobias can be a bitch."

"You're jerking me off," Purdy said.

"Sorry to disappoint you. Royster and Tanney are rolling over on you. Chief Navarro's typing their affidavits as we speak."

"Whadya mean, rolling over?" Purdy asked. "And what's a fuckin' affidafix?"

"Affidavit. It's a confession. They're laying the murders on you. Makes sense, when you think about it. Here's the way I see it. Winlock Savage was strapped for cash, and Senator Royster gave him a way out. With Royster's district depopulating like crazy, his campaign funds were drying up. He and Tanney found out about the meth operation at The Ridge, and realized they had a little money laundering goldmine opportunity that would keep Royster in stump money for years to come. He set up a couple of dark money PACs and had his cut of the 'donations' from the Ridge directed into them. Untraceable money. The sweetest words any criminal ever spoke. In return for all that sweet, sweet moolah,

Royster—with his pet troglodyte Darrell Tanney—was tasked with keeping The Ridge safe from development. Unfortunately, the Town Council wanted to build a ski resort that would have blown The Ridge off the mountain. Royster couldn't oppose the resort outright, because his constituents wanted it, but endorsing the resort meant butchering his cash cow.

"His solution was to recruit a recognizable face for the resort opposition, and funnel money to him through the same dark PACs he was front-loading with drug money. Win Savage was the perfect patsy. He was vain, kind of dumb, and he liked to be in the public eye. He was also strapped for cash, and he was motivated to keep the ski resort off the Knob as well, because he wanted to protect The Shire."

"The Shire," Purdy snorted. "Buncha hippie pansies."

"Notwithstanding, you were already muling meth for The Ridge through your grandparents' honey company. You'd pick up ten cases of honey from them, slip in an eleventh case full of shatter from The Ridge, and deliver it to Oz at the wrong store. Oz took the ten legit cases to his grocery, and the eleventh headed on to the next node in the distribution channel. Four pounds of shatter each week. That's some major production. You hillbillies up there must be running your labs twenty-four-seven.

"You also worked at the hardware store part-time. You discovered Oz's extracurricular burglaries and reported them to Royster. Royster saw an opportunity to blackmail Oz, maybe to get him to increase his participation in the distribution scheme. In return, Oz demanded the Ridge crank stay out of Choctaw. How am I doing so far?"

Purdy slurped at the bottom of his iced tea and glared at Durham.

"Win Savage took his role as the Savior of Choctaw seriously, and now he had a chance to save it again. He thought he was on the side of the angels, a position with which he was wholly unfamiliar, but he kind of dug it." Durham pulled a sheet of paper from his folder. "Win Savage's cell phone records." He pulled a second sheet out. "Darrell Tanney's cell phone records." A third sheet of paper he named as, "*Your* cell phone records."

"So?" Purdy said.

"Cell phones are little computers. They're always performing operations in the background. One of those is location services. Your phone registers its location wherever it goes. Look at these three sheets. I've circled one particular location, which appears on all three phones at exactly the same date and time—Monday, the week before Savage died. You were there, Tanney was there, and Savage was there. The location was The Ridge."

"So we were all there at the same time? A lot of guys were there."

"According to Tanney's phone, he was there three or four times a week."

"And?"

"Your phone, of course, shows you there a lot."

"I live there. Get to the point," Purdy said, scowling.

"According to his phone, Winlock Savage had never visited The Ridge before. There are lots of Knob entries. He visited The Shire regularly. But his phone never shows him at the location of The Ridge before last Monday."

"Don't mean nothin'."

"Oh, it means a great deal, Stan. In your case, it might mean everything. I told you Tanney was rolling over on you. He said Savage wandered into The Ridge, discovered the meth operations, and saw Tanney. He did the math and came up with Royster. He asked a few questions, and by the time he returned home that evening he knew he'd been played for a patsy. Savage was a proud man, and he didn't like to lose. He contacted Royster and demanded to know why he'd been manipulated. We have that call logged right here. He threatened to withdraw the lawsuit, because he realized it was being manipulated to protect Royster and his drug-related cash flow. According to Tanney, Savage threatened to turn him in for trafficking in illicit substances."

Purdy no longer looked defiant. His head drooped and his eyes fixed on the chain of his cuffs inside the D-ring on the table.

"Savage returned to The Ridge on Friday night," Durham continued. "He left his cellphone at home. Why, I don't know yet. It's not important. He walked in on you talking to Tanney and Royster, and he raised a genuine stink. He attacked Royster, exactly the way you did today, and you stepped in to break them up. Savage got physical, and you knifed him, once, in the chest."

Purdy shook his head.

"It weren't like that," he said.

"Tanney says it was. Swore to it. He's going to sign an affidavit that you knifed Savage, and then Tanney and you tossed him in the back of your Hyundai, grabbed Oz's master padlock key, and drove Savage over to Chuck Hogan's smokehouse to dispose of the body—and presumably any evidence—in the heat."

"Weren't like that," Purdy repeated.

"He who squeals deals," Durham said. "That usually becomes the official story. Sorry, kid. This is going to be tough on your grandparents."

"*It weren't like that!*" Purdy shouted. "You stop lying about what happened. Whatever Tanney told you was a lie!"

"I don't see it," Durham said. "You're trying to save your ass. We have Winlock Savage's blood in *your* car trunk, Stan. Not Tanney's. Not Royster's. You killed him and you transported him to the smokehouse, and you and Tanney hung him on a hook to roast. Don't worry about Tanney. He's looking at some stout time himself, as an accessory. He'll get out someday, though. You won't be so lucky."

"Will you let me tell my side?" Purdy demanded. "Or have you already put the noose around my neck?"

"Your buddy Tanney's tying the knot right now," Durham said. "He says you begged Oz Tattersall to hide your car in his garage until the heat blew over. Oz was no fool. Once he heard about Savage's murder, he figured out pretty quickly how you and Tanney and Royster were involved, and why you needed to hide the Hyundai. He demanded a bigger chunk of the meth money in return for not turning you in. So, you killed him."

"No!" Purdy squealed. "I never shot nobody. That was Tanney! He shot Oz."

"Your word against his."

"I was there! I was in the car. Tanney's car. My prints are probably still on the steering wheel. Tanney walked up on Oz's porch, stood off to one side, and waited for Oz to open the door. When he did, Tanney gave him both barrels. I saw the whole thing."

"Tanney says he was in the car and he sent you onto Oz's porch with the shotgun."

"It ain't true. Not a word of it! I'll sign a paper and swear on a truckload of Bibles."

"Well," Durham slapped a legal pad onto the table. "You'd better hurry. Chief Navarro is a notoriously slow typist. You tell me everything that happened, and I'll take it to the DA, who'll sort out who gets tried for what. Cooperation and telling the truth will go a long way toward him offering you a deal. Oh, and if you can tell me where I can find Tanney's shotgun, I might be even sneak you in a little ice cream."

THIRTY-SIX

"Smooth," Bobbi said, when Durham rejoined her in the observation room.

"Not as smooth as the next move," he said. "We'll interrogate Tanney next. I'll take Purdy into your office. You lead Tanney to the interview room, but make sure he sees me talking to Purdy on the way."

"Got it."

Seconds later, Bobbi unlocked Tanney's cell and cuffed him to take him down the hall. Durham directed Purdy to Bobbi's office, ostensibly to retrieve a pen and some paper. Durham waited until Tanney had a clear line of sight on Purdy, and Durham made a show of shaking the prisoner's hand and giving him a pen.

After depositing Purdy in a holding cell, Durham walked in on Tanney, who was chained to the table in the same fashion as Purdy had been.

"Hell of a thing," Tanney said. "Decorated state trooper on the wrong side of this table."

"The only decoration you ever saw was on the department Christmas tree," Durham said. "Just so you know, Purdy rolled over on you. You're going to prison for at least life. Play your cards wrong and you might get to see what a gurney and a spike in your arm feels like."

"Fuck that hillbilly twat," Tanney said. "He don't know shit."

"I have video of you assaulting and abducting a private citizen under the cover of duty. You identified yourself as a highway patrol officer, drew your service weapon, and you committed two felonies in the course of a minute. I will shortly have the shotgun used to kill Oz Tattersall, which I suspect will belong to you. I have a witness who confirms you stuck the knife in Winlock Savage's chest that stopped his heart, and you and Stan Purdy hung him in the smokehouse. You're both stout lads. You could have managed it between the two of you. At Royster's direction, you forced Oz to hide Purdy's car, using the same leverage you always used—outing him as a serial burglar. Oz became nervous. Muling a little shatter now and then was one thing. Accessory after the fact in a murder— especially a high-profile murder like Win Savage's—would mean a life sentence for a guy Oz's age. He'd also have to face the burglary and larceny charges which would almost certainly be divulged in the process. He demanded to be out. Being out was never part of Royster's master plan, so Royster had you kill Oz to silence him. You and Royster drove to The Ridge today to remove the last loose end, Stan Purdy. If we hadn't stopped you, Purdy would be face-down in a river by now."

"I want my lawyer," Tanney said.

"Great. Right now, I suspect he's somewhere over Georgia, headed for a refueling stop in Key West before continuing on to Georgetown. I can try to call, though. Face it, Tanney. Purdy rolled over on you. Your own attorney, whom I believe to be balls-deep in this conspiracy, is running for the border, leaving you high and dry. What do you think Royster's going to do once I sweat him and he hears his biggest ally is on the lam? Who is the jury going to believe? An honored state senator, or some roughneck failed state trooper assigned to be his butt-wiper? Guess what, Tanney? You're the patsy in this story. You're the fall guy. You're going to ride the bolt for Carl Royster."

"No!" Tanney protested. "They're all lying. You want the real story? I can give you every bit of it, but I want immunity."

"Ain't gonna happen," Durham said. "You dishonored your oath and your badge. You're stacking heavy time the hard way. How much, and whether you get to pull it in segregated pop with all the other dirty cops—well, that's still up for grabs. Squeal and deal, Tanney. I'll let you think about it for a few minutes."

———

"FAA confirms McCool's King Air departed Marion Airport twenty minutes ago," Bobbi said. "You called it."

"Guy's facing a life sentence," Durham said. "Might as well run. Doesn't matter, Tanney rolled on Royster, and Royster rolled on McCool. The federal marshals in Key West will nab McCool when he lands there."

"What a clusterfuck," Bobbi said.

"Lot of charges to go around. Between all the confessions so far, the real story's taking shape. Savage thought his fame would keep him safe at The Ridge. Purdy was cranked, misinterpreted something Savage told him, and shut him up with a knife in the heart. Tanney's done his time in court, and he knows about stuff like DNA, but he also knows DNA is destroyed by heat, among other things. They left Savage in the smokehouse and drove directly over to Oz's house, where Tanney intimidated Oz into hiding the Hyundai. Oz got nervous when he figured out the Hyundai must be the murder vehicle, and he went to Royster to complain. He demanded to be let out of the conspiracy altogether. Royster ordered Tanney to take Oz out after Oz threatened to blow the whistle to the DEA on the entire operation. To limit loose ends, Tanney had Purdy drive the car to Oz's cabin on the Knob, where Tanney delivered the double-barrel kiss off. Royster and Tanney drove to The Ridge today to eliminate the final loose end. Case closed. All we have to do now is stack the charges for the DA."

"And McCool?"

"He pulled Royster's strings. He gave the orders. If he makes it offshore, he can never come back."

"Fine with me," she said. "Trent McCool always gave me the creeps. Got a call a few minutes ago. The DEA raid on The Ridge is a go. They're kind of salivating over it. Gonna put on a big show. Choppers and everything."

Durham dropped a bill on the table. "Ten bucks says the squatters bugged out."

"Why?"

"Andy Frye. The Law on Choctaw Knob. He doesn't like government types any more than he did when he lived on The Ridge. When he disappeared after we crashed Royster's car, I figured he was headed back up the hill to warn his cousins about the inevitable raid. Blood is thicker and all that. I don't care. It serves two purposes for him. First, he saves his kin from prison terms, and second, he resolves the conflict between The Ridge and

The Shire. DEA boys might take out some labs, but the cookers will be long scattered."

"Gonna annoy the fuck out of them."

"Inside every dark cloud," he said.

"Strange," she said. "I've been hearing stories about the squatters on The Ridge ever since I hit this town. Been there for almost three hundred years. Hard to think of them as gone forever."

"Leaving does remove the only barrier to the ski resort," he said. "This town might be on life support, but it ain't dead yet. The Knob's a big place. I figure there's lots of space to carve out some ski runs without disturbing The Shire."

"I'll write the reports for the DA and deliver them later today." She glanced at her watch. "Rough estimate is one hundred eighteen hours."

"What's that?"

"I met you one hundred eighteen hours ago. You beat your average on this one."

"*We* did, Bobbi. Couldn't have done it without you."

"Oh, you *could* have. It might have taken a lot longer."

Her telephone rang. A video call from Dr. Naomi Patel. She put it on speaker and held the phone so Durham could see it. On the tiny screen, Neni looked one inch tall.

"I completed the evaluation of the extraneous blood on Patti Masters' blouse," she said. "Very interesting."

"In what way?" Bobbi asked.

"When I discovered the semen in her underwear came from Winlock Savage, I presumed I'd also discover his blood on her blouse. I mean, the boy got around. So, I bet myself her lover was the murderer."

"It has always been a possibility," Durham said. "What did you find?"

"I can state with the greatest confidence that the blood on Patti Masters' blouse did not belong to Win Savage," she said. "Beyond any possibility of a doubt."

"How so?" Durham asked.

"The blood on her blouse, which presumably came from her murderer during the struggle, belonged to a woman."

THIRTY-SEVEN

Mags McLeod was locking the front door to her Main Street office when Durham and Bobbi found her.

"A minute, Ms. McLeod?" Bobbi asked.

Mags surveyed them both, especially their serious expressions. "Something I can help you with?"

"Can we step inside?" Durham asked. "I need to ask a few questions."

"Sure," she said. "Come on in. We'll use the conference room. It's more comfortable than my office."

She led them through the hallway to a ten-by-twelve-foot room dominated by a whiteboard at one end and a conference table that filled most of the floor space. She directed them to sit. She took the head of the table.

"I have a fucking showing," she said. "But if this is going to take a while, I could call and postpone it."

"Shouldn't take long at all," Durham said. "I want a DNA sample."

"Trade you for it," she said, seductively. Immediately, she stopped smiling. "Sorry. Force of habit. Why?"

"Need to rule you out as a suspect," he said.

"Suspect? For what?"

"The murder of Patti Masters," Bobbi said. "In 1977."

"What?"

"Her murderer was a woman," he explained. "Other information I've received points me in your direction."

"What information?"

"You knew Patti Masters was having an affair with a student. You denied knowing it the other day, but testimony from Patti's daughter makes it clear you were informed about the affair by Beth Rose Clarney."

"That conversation again? I don't remember it, Wade. Honestly."

"A murderer wouldn't claim to know their own motive if they could avoid it. Deborah Masters overheard the entire conversation in which Beth Rose told you Patti Masters was sleeping with a student. The DNA evidence we received the other day confirmed Patti Masters' lover was Winlock Savage."

"No!" Mags said. "I don't believe it."

"Please," Durham said. "Don't say anything. You're already tying yourself in knots with your own words. The other day, you said you discovered Savage was having an affair. You and he fought about it, and he subsequently broke up with you. That was the first week of your senior year, the same time Savage was having sex with the principal. You were jealous and angry when he dumped you. You stalked him and found him having sex with Patti Masters, confirming what Beth Rose Clarney told you. After he left, you confronted Masters in a rage and demanded she stop seeing Savage, or you'd turn her in. The confrontation turned violent, and you smashed in her face, killing her. The detective at the time was convinced her murderer was a man. He looked at the hands of every boy in the school in the next couple of days, but he never checked the girls."

"Total fucking bullshit," she said.

"Prove it," Durham said, and he held up the DNA swab kit.

"Fuck yeah, give it to me," she said. "I'll swab whatever you want, because you are barking up the wrong fucking tree."

"Easy to prove," he said.

She grabbed the kit, tore open the paper cover, and pulled out the cotton swab, which she ran all over the inside of her mouth before handing it back to Durham who secured it in the medium at the bottom of the test tube.

"Now," she said. "You want to hear my side of the story?"

"Whatever you want to tell me," Durham said.

"That swab isn't going to give you shit, because I didn't kill Patti Masters. I didn't even know Win was fucking her until you told me. You got the story ass-backwards, Agent Durham."

"So, enlighten me," he said.

"Maybe Beth Rose told me Principal Masters was screwing a student. Maybe she didn't. To tell you the truth, I had my own problems to worry about. I already knew Win was cheating on me. I didn't know with whom. Things were pretty shitty between us by the end of the summer. Now I know it was because he was sneaking around with Patti Masters, but like I said, I didn't know that at the time. I was probably listening to Beth Rose with half of one ear, and I didn't care what the principal was up to."

"But you said you discovered Savage cheating on you."

"I did, but not with Patti Masters. I caught him fucking Beth Rose Clarney, upstairs at a party one night over Labor Day weekend. He'd disappeared, and I went looking for him. I found him, all right, bruising Beth Rose's cervix with that improbable log splitter of his. I gave him both barrels. Screamed at him what a cheating shit he was. He broke up with me shortly after. Said I didn't trust him. Well, duh. That was at least a month before the murder. Go ahead and test my DNA. It won't lead you anywhere. On the other hand, we already know Beth Rose was having sex with the fucking horndog, and she knew Patti Masters was screwing a student as well. Do I have to write out a fucking primer on who you should test next?"

"It's a stretch."

"Not at all," Mags said. She crossed to a bookcase against one wall of her office, searched for a few seconds, and discovered the volume she was seeking, the 1978 Choctaw High School Yearbook. She opened it on her desk, with Durham and Bobbi looking over her shoulder.

"Beth Rose and I were cheerleaders together," she said. "We were kind of rivals, but we also weren't. I mean, until I discovered she was doin' my guy, I thought we were fuckin' besties." She found the page she was searching for and pointed at a picture of the 1977 Choctaw High School cheerleading squad. Durham picked out Mags McLeod immediately, in the middle of the front row. Her surgeon had seen to it she hadn't changed much.

She pointed to another woman, in the second row. "This was taken a week after Patti Masters was murdered. That's Beth Rose. Notice anything interesting?"

"She's wearing a cast on her right arm," Bobbi said.

"Claimed she slammed her hand in a van door," Mags said. "Broken wrist and lacerations. the kind of injuries you'd see in such an accident. Or maybe if you caved in some woman's face with your fist. Notice she's a healthy young lady as well. Strong. I never bought the car door story, but I also never connected Beth Rose with Patti Masters' murder. You get her DNA and compare it to the blood on Principal Masters' shirt. I bet you get a match."

———

"We know who killed your grandmother," Durham told Kylee at dinner that evening. "We need to get the final test results, but the whole story rings true."

"So? Who was it?"

"A student at the high school. A woman."

"A woman?"

"A woman whose history suggests lifelong emotional instability and occasional aggressive and violent behavior. She had bipolar disorder, the bad kind. Best guess is she murdered your grandmother in a manic jealous fit. She was also sleeping with Savage, and discovered he was having an affair with Patti, and she lost control."

"If the testing pans out, will you charge her?"

"No," Durham said. "I'm sorry. Pressing charges against this woman would serve no purpose except to check some box on a form. She's circling the drain already. End stage dementia."

"I suppose I should say I'm sorry, but I'm not. She deprived me of a grandmom."

"So, I'm done here," he said. "I'll help Chief Navarro pull together all the paperwork, but by midnight tonight I'll be off the clock. Between you and me, I'm looking forward to my own bed in Charlotte. I have a vacation to finish."

THIRTY-EIGHT

It was a razor-sharp Carolina autumn day on Lake Norman. A late-season tropical storm had canceled a king mackerel tournament in Myrtle Beach in which Durham had planned to compete, but the skies over Huntersville, north of Charlotte, were a transparent, deep, almost hypnotic blue. Durham had opted to spend the weekend on his cabin cruiser, *The Blade*.

It was an ostentatious watercraft for a guy on an SBI agent's state salary. Forty-six feet long, with a twelve-foot beam, *The Blade* sported twin Merc diesels, three staterooms, two full heads with a half head off the salon, and a newly installed quartz-topped counter in the galley. The boat had been confiscated five years earlier during an SBI sting, and he'd bought it for pennies at a poorly advertised government auction a year later. Moving it to Lake Norman had cost more than the boat itself. He'd spent two years renovating and updating the instruments, furnishings, and décor. It spent most of its time moored at a marina off I-77 in Huntersville, but Durham enjoyed taking it out on the odd free weekend to anchor in the middle of the enormous man-made lake and allow the waves to rock him to sleep under the stars.

He removed the steaks from a plastic bag in which they had been marinating. He'd bought them from a specialty butcher in uptown

Richard Helms

Charlotte, near his high-rise. It was prime and marbled and delicate to look at. He patted the meat dry with paper towels and seasoned it with garlic salt and pepper. The propane grill at the stern had been heating for several minutes. Hasselback potatoes were five minutes from finishing in the galley air fryer, and the salad was tossed and dressed.

He exited the galley and the salon through automatic sliding doors and slapped the steaks on the grill. They sizzled immediately as they hit the searing cast iron grate, and Durham closed the lid.

"I'm glad I took the weekend off," Bobbi said from the chaise behind him. Five weeks earlier, she might have worn a bikini and a smile, but it was late October, when sweats and jeans were the order of the evening. "With any luck, Choctaw will burn to the ground before I get back."

"Naw. Pete and Earl are in charge. They're good cops."

He chuckled.

"What's so funny?" she asked.

"The raid," he said, which was all that was necessary.

"Still chortling over that clusterfuck?"

"Chortling. Good word. I'm reveling in the mental image of Todd fucking Edwards and his crew of gung-ho DEA SWAT goons descending on an empty shanty town on Choctaw Knob. He burned up the telephone lines to Malik Mourning's office afterward, which is all the satisfaction he's gonna get. Hell, they were cooking when I was there. What can I say? Oh, and you still owe me ten bucks. Told you they'd bug out."

"I never took the bet," she said. "What in hell do you have against the DEA anyway?"

"You ever heard of Shannon Ogilvy?"

390

"Nope."

"Neither had anyone in the SBI. She was the pitcher for the championship team in the College World Series fast-pitch softball tournament four or five years ago. Now she's a lab tech at DEA in Charlotte. Todd fucking Edwards hooked her into pitching at our interagency softball tournament last year. Total ringer. She was underhanding smoke at us all day. Nobody could hit her."

"This is all about *softball?*"

"I had a hundred dollars down on that game."

"How much of the malbec is left?"

"A glass. Maybe a little more. I have another bottle."

She walked, still wobbly on her land legs, to the wet bar at the back of the stern porch and drained the bottle into her glass. "Want some more?"

"I'm good. We'll open the other bottle with dinner. Hope you slept okay last night."

"Are you kidding? It was like being in a cradle. I woke up sucking my thumb once."

He opened the grill, and a cloud of smoke and steam rose over the stern of the boat. As he flipped the steaks, he said, "Yeah, the forward cabin's pretty comfortable. It was a bit busier at the stern, especially when the wind kicked up around one. No biggie. I'm used to it. Like it, in fact. I think you're right. Like a cradle. Guess we never forget that feeling."

"Thanks for inviting me."

"Figured you could use some time to decompress now that the Savage case is in the DA's hands. Sure you want yours medium well? I hear there's a statute against that in this state."

"You might have to arrest me. Got your cuffs on you?" She giggled.

"No rush. We're anchored in the middle of the lake. Where are you gonna run?"

"It's also illegal to anchor overnight in the middle of the lake, right?"

"The Lake Norman marine police and I have an understanding. They don't hassle me, and I don't keep them waiting when they need me."

"Cozy," she said.

"Just another example of positive interagency cooperation."

"Like that softball game."

He served the steaks with a chimichurri he'd made earlier in the afternoon and a garlic butter sauce for the potatoes. He held his glass aloft.

"To Choctaw," he said.

She clinked and they drank, and she made the same yummy face she had the first time he'd poured her a glass. "This is so smooth."

"The Argentines know how to make wine," he said.

"What'll happen to them?" she asked.

"The Argentines?"

"No. The guys. You know."

"Purdy's gonna go down for voluntary manslaughter on Savage. He has mitigating factors. He was high. They were fighting. He'll do time, but not a lot, because he squealed first. Tanney's going to ride the bolt for Oz. He drove to Oz's cabin with the express intent of blowing him into the next life cycle."

"And Royster?"

"You know how it goes, Bobbi. He's got pull. He knows people. He'll take a hit. Probably lose his senate seat, get disbarred. Might stack some nominal time in a Club Fed and waltz out in a suit that's still in style."

He removed the steaks from the grill and turned off the gas. He placed the meat on a side table to rest while he put the salad in bowls.

"A thousand years ago, four barons burst into Canterbury Cathedral and butchered Thomas a' Becket because the king made an offhand comment wishing to be rid of an insolent prelate."

She raised an eyebrow.

"You aren't the only one who paid attention in history," he continued. "Becket lost everything. The king had to flagellate himself in front of his people in penance, but that was all. It's an old story. Royster was being attacked when Purdy killed Savage, and he wasn't even on the mountain when Tanney shot Oz. The DA's smart, though. She'll figure out a way to ensure Royster and Trent McCool pull some time, probably for conspiracy. McCool's in the worst shape. Even on a conspiracy beef, it's his second ride. He'll probably die gasping at concrete block walls."

"The good news is the ski resort is back on track," she said. "Tim McCool told me yesterday before I hauled ass out of town. They found an investor in Asheville to take Oz's place. Maybe the town won't die after all."

He plated the dinner and slipped her plate and salad bowl in front of her. After he was seated, they launched into dinner.

"Oh. My. God!" she said. "This steak!"

"I have a guy," he said. "Cops have a guy for everything. This guy has the best beef in town. It's like butter."

"So fucking tender! Let me ask you something, Blade."

"You know how I feel about—"

"Tough shit. I think the name's cool. I wish I had a nickname that tight. No. I'm serious. When you invited me on this weekend cruise—and don't get me wrong; I'm appreciative, and I'm having a great time—but did you have some sort of expectations if I accepted?"

Durham savored a bite of the succulent ribeye, and swallowed before saying, "Of course I did."

"Oh," she said. "I see."

"What do you see, Bobbi?" he asked, before sampling the potatoes.

"I mean, I'm not saying it's a *no*, right? Let's get that off the table right away."

"A *no?*"

She paused for a second. "Sleeping with you. I'm not saying it's out of the question."

"That's nice to hear," he said. "But that's not why I invited you, Bobbi."

"Why, then?"

"I've been a cop twice as long as you. Hell, I've been a cop twice as long as anyone I know, and I know burnout when I smell it. You haven't been out of Choctaw for more than two hours since you landed there. In a high-stress job like ours, you can't keep it firewalled for months on end without blowing a gasket. I wanted you to see it's okay to get away once in a while. Cut loose a little. Choctaw will still be there when you get back, and after the last several weeks, I have a feeling it's full up on crime for a while."

"And that's it?" she said. "Your entire expectation?"

"Cross my heart," he said. "My intentions are purely altruistic."

"*Purely* altruistic?"

"Okay," he said. "*Mostly* altruistic."

She placed her napkin on the table and stood next to him. "Stand up," she said.

"Yes ma'am." Durham stood, facing Bobbi.

"Bend down," she said. "You're so fucking tall."

He bent down, and she took his face in her hands and planted her lips on his. Their lips parted, and for a moment their tongues danced across one another. And then, as quickly as it started, it was over, with a sweet peck and a brush of cheeks.

"All right then." She patted his cheek and took her seat again, picking up her napkin.

"All right, then," he echoed, taking his own seat.

She said, "Just wanted to get it out of the way."

"I appreciate your initiative," he said. "I liked it."

"Me, too." She attacked her steak with renewed vigor. "We should try it again sometime. Maybe after that second bottle of malbec."

"Also nice to hear," he said. "I'll grab the corkscrew."

ABOUT THE AUTHOR

Retired clinical/forensic psychologist and college professor Richard Helms is the author of twenty-six published novels. He is the recipient of the Killer Nashville Silver Falchion Award (twice); the Mystery Readers International Macavity Award; the Short Mystery Fiction Society Derringer Award (twice); the International Thriller Writers Thriller Award; and the Private Eye Writers of America Shamus Award (twice). His story "See Humble and Die" was featured in Houghton-Mifflin-Harcourt's **Best American Mystery Stories of 2020**, edited by Otto Penzler and C.J. Box. His short stories have appeared frequently in *Ellery Queen Mystery Magazine*, *Alfred Hitchcock Mystery Magazine*, *Black Cat Mystery Magazine*, *Mystery Weekly*, and various anthologies and collections. A former member of the Mystery Writers of America Board of Directors and president of MWA's Southeast Region, Richard Helms was presented with the SEMWA Magnolia Award in 2017 for his service to the chapter. Richard Helms and his wife Elaine live in Charlotte, North Carolina.